Couch
World

CATHY YARDLEY

needs to get out more. When not writing, she is probably either cruising the Internet, sleeping, or watching D-list movies and adding to her unnatural mental store of character-actor trivia. She can hum along with all the theme songs on Cartoon Network's "Adult Swim" and is learning Japanese from anime. She considers Daria a positive role model. Her family is considering performing an intervention for her addiction to pop culture.

For those similarly addicted, drop her a line at cathy@cathyyardley.com.

cathy yardley

Couch World

RED
DRESS
INK
™

First edition January 2005

COUCH WORLD

A Red Dress Ink novel

ISBN 0-373-89509-7

www.RedDressInk.com

Printed in U.S.A.

To Kathryn Lye, my editor, for believing in me and understanding where I'm coming from.
(Even when I don't!)

And to Chris Becker. He knows why.

ACKNOWLEDGMENTS

I would like to thank DJ Atum, DJ Ariel and most especially San Francisco's DJ Amber for answering all of my voluminous questions on being a DJ and the San Francisco club scene. I'd like to thank Mike Johnson, for being my connection to the world of San Francisco's club bouncers (and for getting me into 550, back in the day) and for basically having more personality than one person should be blessed (cursed?) with.

Also, I'd like to acknowledge Sister SF, the female DJ collective in San Francisco, whose Web site was too helpful for words. If you have any interest in being a DJ at all, check out http://www.sistersf.com.

Finally, I'd like to thank Millie Org for fielding my questions about being a reporter (and just being a good friend in general).

chapter 1

I wake up and have no idea where I am. That's not a bad thing. If I did know where I was, I think I'd be worried.

I roll over to get my bearings. Late-afternoon light is coming in through a window. The room is a mess which I notice immediately. There's a bra on the coffee table that looks out of place amongst the mess of women's magazines. A *Cosmo* babe scowls at me ferally from an electric-pink cover. My pertinent stuff is piled carefully on a copy of *People:* cell phone, iPod and the latest book I'm reading. I remember drifting off to sleep with it last night, barely remembering to shut off the light…which is behind my head, isn't it? It is.

Ah, yes. It's coming back now.

I check the time—2:00 p.m.—according to my cell-phone display. And it's Wednesday. I've got things to do, I think while lying back and stretching. The sheet I've got wrapped around me smells like spring-lemon detergent with a hint of musty linen closet. The rest of the room smells like baby powder and girl. Good night's sleep last night, I find myself recalling. That's always a nice way to start.

I hear someone stirring around, using the bathroom. Like I

said, it's two o'clock in the afternoon, and someone else here isn't working a day job.

I'm in the apartment of the Strippas, I remember with a click. In fact, I can see Candy's picture, her face pouting and proud, up on one wall. She's framed the ad they took of her, and that time when she was on the cover of the *Spectator*, wearing a tiny swathe of panties and crossed black Band-Aids over her nipples. It's not a bad picture. Barely airbrushed at all, or so she says.

Liza comes stumbling into the living room wearing a T-shirt and thong. The T-shirt could be a wee bit longer I notice, uncomfortably, when she bends over and surveys the contents of her fridge.

"Morning, PJ. You sleep okay?"

"Great. Thanks," I say, and I mean it. "Your couch is really comfortable."

"Thanks." I can tell she's proud. Like a good hostess.

"You coming to the club tonight? I'm punting."

She claps her hands, does a little happy dance. "Which club?"

I have to think about it. Wednesday, Wednesday... "Technique. I'm subbing for DJ Nightshade."

"Cool. I'm off at two, I'll drag the others. You know we love seeing you spin."

I smile. They really are nice.

"Oh, that reminds me, though," she said, leaning on the refrigerator door, a can of Diet Coke in one hand. "You can't stay here tonight. We're having company later."

I've learned not to ask what the Strippas mean when they say this. At twenty-nine, I still hang on to what naiveté I have left. "No problem. I'll have Sticky hook me up."

She walks over, taking a long sip of her soda, and then rumples my hair. "You are too cute."

The Strippas tend to think of me as a stray cat they can occasionally pet-sit for. I don't disabuse them of this notion. They really do have a comfortable couch.

"Did you want to grab some lunch later?"

"Would love to, but I need to do some laundry." I think about it. The Strippas live in the Tenderloin, or thereabouts. "Nearest bus line is where?"

"There's one two blocks down. By the BART station."

"Thanks." It's easier to be in the city. The club, Technique, is actually sort of a pain to get to, over by the Warehouse District…sort of. It's hard to explain San Francisco geography. "I really do appreciate…"

"Oh, knock it off. You know you're welcome anytime."

Another hair-rumple and a small cheek pinch. Those, I could do without.

"I'm gonna go back to bed a bit, okay?"

"I'll be quiet," I assure her.

"I won't." She winks at me. "Freddy's over."

Yikes. That pretty much propels me out of bed and into the shower. By the time I'm dressed, she's not kidding about not being quiet. She sounds like an opera singer practicing scales. I leave a note that thanks all of the Strippas, and I hastily pack my blue duffel bag, stuffing my sweats/pajamas to the side of my laptop. I also fold up my bedding, leaving it in a neat pile at the end of their couch. One of the key rules to the way I live is: leave the place you stay the way you found it. Don't mess up bathrooms, don't eat their food, don't leave your crap all over the place. Most of this is general knowledge. Common courtesy stuff. You're always going to need a couch, and you want people to be okay with letting you be a repeat visitor. There aren't a lot of A-list couches. There's also the slim possibility that you will need to relocate in a hurry. I sleep in pajamas that I can, if necessary, run outside in. Most of my stuff is always in my bag or close to it, and my shoes are forever next to my bag.

Honestly, the Strippas hover just above B-list, because they tend to have a lot of "company." Not that I judge their lifestyle. They're sweet, and whatever they do, to whomever they do it, is all right in my book. But when they bring strangers over…well, let's just say sometimes I haven't *always* trusted their judgment. I sleep light when they've got guys over. That contingency I mentioned? Only time I've had to run was when one of my couch owner's overnight guests, besides myself, woke up drunk and unruly and spoiling for a fight. It wasn't pleasant. I had to buy a new pair of jeans and duffel bag after that one. Luckily, I hadn't gotten my laptop yet…it was still with a friend.

Digressing. Anyway, I haven't made the same mistake twice.

I'm dressed, duffel bag slung over my shoulder. It looks warm out for September, but in the city, the wind tends to make everything cold. I'm wearing a beat-up leather bomber jacket, big sweats, my hair is in wet braids that leave water trails on my T-shirt. I go to the Laundromat… Just a little load, my towel's got some funky smell I want to get rid of. I listen to beats on my iPod while the washer's running, and go over my playlist. I ignore a few people looking at me oddly, especially one woman with her small child, and a guy who looks as if he's doing his laundry on lunch break from some office. By the time everything's dry, my stomach is kicking up a fuss. I only eat two meals a day, and I figure it's time for meal number one. I hit a little dive on the way, grab two steaming tamales wrapped in corn husks. They're heavenly. The sure giveaway to finding the best Mexican restaurant is to look for where approximately eighty percent of the patrons don't speak English, and where there's always a line. This meal is pretty cheap, pretty filling and just about perfect. I won't be going on until eleven, maybe closer to twelve. I figure by then, I won't have any food left in my stomach.

It's a valid concern. Getting up on the decks still makes me a little nervous. Even after two years or so of spinning.

Still, I've got a more pressing concern right at the moment, above and beyond losing my tamales on Nightshade's gear.

I need to find a place to sleep tonight.

Samantha Regales walked up the street toward Technique, the club where her agency, Whitford Modeling, was holding one of their parties. Her thigh-high black patent boots clicked menacingly on the sidewalk. There was a line to get in the club, which for a Wednesday midnight, was a good sign. She bypassed the line, ignoring both the threatening looks from pissed-off people waiting, and the covetous looks from packs of club boys who didn't tear their eyes from her. Considering she was wearing a short burgundy minidress from Miu Miu, she would be offended if they weren't staring. She had her shoulder-length dark walnut hair up in a twist that looked casual and only took forty minutes to get right. She walked up to Sticky, her favorite bouncer.

He stared at her. His eyes were practically bugging out of his head as she did a slow turn. One of her runway specials. "You like?" The question came out as a purr, but was still audible over the hum of the crowd.

"Too sexy," he said, and she allowed him to hug her. Not too close nor too long, but enough that he could smell her perfume. Sensi, by Armani. She was just trying it out. Seemed to trigger the right response, she thought when she finally had to tug away. Of course, she could be wearing motor oil and Sticky would have the same reaction.

As it should be, she decided with a smile.

"I'm here for the party," she stated.

He nodded. "I thought so. A lot of youngsters tonight. I'd better escort you."

"I know the way to the VIP room," she reproved, putting a little distance between them. "Thanks, though!"

With a quick wave and a killer smile to the bouncer, she walked inside. She headed right for the party.

There was already a solid crowd from the agency there, she noticed with a frown. The agency wasn't A-list, like Stars or something, but it was trying to position itself as young, hip, a little more diverse. The agents and models were clustered in knots, with each orbiting a different client. The clients were old, Samantha noticed, and a good deal of them were male, but there were females as well—magazine people, a few designers.

"Samantha!"

Samantha was quickly converged on by Jenna and Andrea, her two modeling friends. They were sisters, younger than she was—seventeen to her nineteen. She wondered what their parents thought, letting them go to a party at midnight on a school night. Then she grinned. Probably the same thing her parents would if they realized where their only daughter was.

"There's a couple of big names here," Jenna reported, scanning the crowd and sipping what looked like a Diet Coke. "A couple of really big photographers. Like Amos Salvador."

"Oh, *him,*" Andrea said, rolling her eyes. "He's such a letch."

"Shut up," Jenna said. She was the more dominant of the two. "You wouldn't be saying that if he came up and said he wanted to photograph you. Your career would jump if you had some shots by him."

"Yeah, well," Andrea replied weakly, then turned her attention quickly back to Samantha. "How are you doing? Go on any calls this week?"

"Five," Samantha said, feeling a little smug when the two of them stared at her with envy.

"Any callbacks?" Jenna said, looking at her manicure instead of at Samantha.

Samantha frowned. "I haven't heard yet."

"Well. I'm sure that you will," Andrea reassured.

Samantha was sure that she'd meant to be comforting, but thought the comment was sort of insulting. Samantha had not been having a lot of luck lately and it worried her. She'd signed with Whitford three years ago, when she was still in high school. She'd basically hounded and hammered away until she got in. It had taken her a year, but she remembered the high school cheerleaders' faces. It had made dieting and exercising worthwhile.

Then, she'd been a hot new face at Whitford. Now, she was having trouble getting her agent, Stan, to return her calls. This week was the first busy call week she'd had since she started college, and she was a sophomore even. She figured that her hounding him again had contributed to that. She'd track him down later and talk face-to-face.

Straightening her shoulders, she asked, "Who have you talked to?"

Jenna and Andrea looked at each other, startled. "Um…Stan told us to talk to that man," Jenna said, pointing to a paunchy guy with obvious transplants. "He's a scout. He's looking for faces for *Seventeen*."

Samantha rolled her eyes. "They're usually looking for four-teen-year-olds. Anybody else?"

They both shook their heads.

"Do you recognize anybody from—hey!"

Someone had covered her eyes with his hands. "Hey, beau-tiful," she heard, and spun around.

"Aaron," she said with a smile. "I didn't know you were going to be here."

"When I heard there was a models party? Where else would I be?" He winked at her.

Jenna and Andrea crowded around, smiling. "Samantha, who's your friend?" This, from Jenna.

"Aaron, also known as DJ Dizzy-Spin," she said. They were so high school sometimes, she thought. Aaron was cute, but he was also low level—good for an ego boost, but he knew ab-solutely no one. He was eye candy. "Aaron, these are my friends, Jenna and Andrea."

The two of them giggled. Samantha felt embarrassed for them.

"Nice to meet you," Aaron offered, but he kept his atten-tion focused on Samantha. "So…want to dance?"

She glanced around. Few of the models were dancing. "Um…"

"You'd stand out," he said, his voice persuasive.

Samantha smiled. Those were the magic words. She was a good dancer, she had to admit.

There was a DJ playing some generic sort of hip-hop with a good beat. Samantha let Aaron lead her, smiling a little as Jenna and Andrea watched but didn't follow. And then she began to dance.

Most models don't have curves. Despite losing weight at her agent's insistence, she still had breasts and hips. It might be a drawback in her profession—she felt sure it had cost her sev-eral runway gigs. But she also knew, that when it came to men, the curves helped. After a cursory scan of the room, she knew a couple of the older men were watching her.

Aaron tried to move closer, and she teasingly moved away, finally nudging him so that there was space between them. She didn't want to look as if she was unavailable. That wouldn't help her at all.

Then, subtly, the music changed. It was funky, sexy. A beat that would really let her show off.

She got into the music, dancing with Aaron but making sure to display herself to the crowd. She saw her agent looking toward her as she moved in front of the DJ booth. The DJ himself was someone she didn't recognize…he looked old for a DJ, although he also looked cute. She smiled at him. He was too focused on the turntables, so he didn't smile back. She kept on dancing.

She felt as if she could've gone on forever. The music crescendo was thundering, and she saw Aaron smiling at her, saw others whispering to each other. It was working. She didn't know why she hadn't thought of it before.

When the song ended people were actually applauding. She smiled and wondered if she should bow, or what.

Then she saw Aaron clapping…*and looking at the DJ booth.*

What the hell?

She looked around. They weren't clapping for her. They were clapping for the DJ. Jenna and Andrea came up to her.

"That guy stepped in and took over as DJ while you were on the floor," Andrea explained. "And suddenly, everybody in the crowd started whispering. We were hanging out by Amos, and the designer he was talking to said that the guy had been a DJ at all the major fashion shows in New York. He'd even done work in Paris and Milan…"

Yeah, but he was stealing *her* spotlight, Samantha thought sourly. "Did I look like a complete idiot out there?"

"Of course not," Andrea said.

"You were doing really well," Jenna added, although there was a gleam in her eye. "You definitely stood out."

Samantha felt sick.

"Don't worry, nobody was paying attention to you," Andrea said comfortingly. "They all wanted to talk about the guy."

"Does this guy have a *name?*"

Aaron put an arm around Samantha, and she shrugged it off. "That's Jonathan Hadeis," he said. "As far as house and trance, he's huge…he's one of the originals. He knows people in the music industry *and* the fashion industry. If you're famous, odds are good he knows you."

Now Samantha went from irritated to intrigued. "Really."

Aaron laughed. "Don't even try. You're sexy as hell, but Jonathan Hadeis? So out of your league."

She frowned, yet watched as Jonathan descended from the booth and was immediately embraced by people, smiling at him, laughing with him, shaking his hand.

People had said Samantha wouldn't make it as a model, either. Or she wouldn't be able to balance being a model and being a student. She'd had a good time proving them all wrong.

Her agent stood on the fringes of the crowd, trying to talk to Jonathan. And failing miserably she noticed with a smile.

She dismissed Jenna and Andrea attempting to flirt with Aaron, ignored the rest of the crowd, and focused like a sniper scope on her quarry. Proving that Jonathan Hadeis wasn't out of her league might be just the challenge she was looking for.

Leslie Anderson leaned back against the cool vinyl of the booth. The music was something loud, grinding…something Rick's friend Sticky called drum-and-bass. He'd even asked her, "Do you like drum-and-bass, or maybe tribal? They're playing jungle in the other room."

She'd made some noncommittal sounds, even while wondering what the difference was exactly. She got the feeling that Rick would know.

"Having a good time?"

She smiled. Rick was looking at her with a mixture of worry and interest, under a veneer of booze-tinged euphoria. "I'm doing fine, honey."

"Is it too loud?"

It was deafening. The smile didn't waver a millimeter. "No. It's pretty good. Drum-and-bass, right?"

He grinned, leaning over to give her a warm semihug in the crowded confines of the booth. She felt comforted when he left his arm around her shoulders. "You keep this up, you're going to sound like a regular club kid."

She grinned back at him. That was the point. Not to be a club kid—at thirty-five, she'd missed her window on that one—but to show him that she could fit in quite well, thanks very much.

His friends crowded into the booth, jostling her closer to Rick, which wasn't a problem...*and* squeezing her up against the rather impressive girth of Sticky, which was a little problematic.

"Rick! Happy birthday, man!"

Rick was suddenly engaged in a roaring conversation with somebody across the table. Another round of shots was ordered. She'd already stopped drinking hours ago, and even then, she'd only had two beers. So far, all of Rick's old friends had stopped by to buy him a "birthday shot." He was doing pretty well, considering he'd already had about five, but who was counting?

She'd be driving them back to his apartment. She'd figured as much when she agreed to go out.

"So," his friend, a guy with a pencil-thin goatee and several tattoos, said engagingly, winking at her. "Is this her?"

She couldn't help it. She held her breath.

Rick's smile widened to the point of goofiness. "Yup. This is her. Leslie."

"Man." The guy leaned over and shook her hand, as well. She just kept smiling. "You guys have been going out how long?"

"Four years," she said with a little tinge of pride when Rick gave her shoulders a squeeze.

"Four years," the guy echoed. "So why are we only meeting you now?"

She winced. She was wondering when that was going to come up.

Rick wasn't so far gone that he hadn't anticipated the question. "This isn't really Leslie's scene," he said, and his tone was conciliatory. "She doesn't go out to clubs a whole lot, Andre."

Andre's look was…well, maybe she was reading into it, but it seemed a little judgmental. Or wary. "So what is your scene…Leslie, huh?"

Definitely a challenge. "Oh, you know…"

"She's a stay-in-and-watch-videos," said a girl on the opposite side of the table—what was her name? Kendra, she thought. "She's not into going out."

Kendra had been sulky all evening. And she'd been staring at Rick most of the night, as well, and had purchased two of his birthday shots.

"Really? Huh." Andre made a little nod, like *so that's how it is.* "And that's why you're not coming out as much, Rick?"

"It's my birthday," Rick sang out, surprising everyone into a laugh and taking a little of the edge off. "I can do whatever the hell I want."

Sticky's laughter was like a low sonic boom. "Yes, you can," he said, patting Rick's arm and consequently almost launching Leslie forward, as well. "I have to go check on PJ, but I'll be right back, okay?"

Leslie nodded as the shift of bodies continued to accommodate Sticky's leaving. Three more people took up the space that Sticky's absence had created.

"Who's PJ?" Leslie asked, trying to change the subject.

"She's a DJ," Kendra replied. "She's sort of Sticky's pet."

The rest of the table laughed. Leslie joined in with a low chuckle, more to keep company than because she could see what was so funny.

Next thing she knew, Kendra and Andre were swapping stories about Rick's earlier, hell-raising rave days. Rick quickly joined in. Leslie looked down at her glass of Sprite.

I should have gone out with them more. But Rick was right…this wasn't really her kind of scene. She was a stay-at-home-and-watch-videos kind of girl. She'd never really felt that was something to be ashamed of.

"Coming through," Sticky said, and the crowd made way to give him back his seat. She'd met Sticky a few times—he was one of Rick's best friends, and she liked him a lot. "Sorry."

"How's PJ?"

"Doing okay," he said, although something in his voice made her wonder what was possibly going on. He had a sort of tentative voice—and from what she knew about Sticky, the man was *never* tentative. "How are you doing?"

The beginnings of her answer were drowned out by the burst of laughter from Andre, Kendra and Rick. "Doing all right," she said, leaning a little closer to Sticky so he could hear her.

"You look a little tired."

Leslie wasn't tired. She was exhausted. She hated to say it, but she felt all thirty-five of her years. She'd remembered going out sometimes in college…coming back in at four in the morning, getting up the next day at nine or so. Now, she snuck a glance at her watch. One-thirty, and she felt as if she could just crawl into a grave and pull the dirt over her head.

"I'm fine," she repeated. "I guess I haven't been out much lately."

Sticky leaned a little closer…he was wearing cologne. It was nothing overpowering or tacky. He was dressed to the nines, and he looked every inch ghetto-fabulous in a gray suit. The club was pretty upscale, all things considered—this was Rick's crowd.

"Don't let Kendra get to you," he said. "Or the others. They miss Rick, is all. It's not just you, though. Now that Rick's got a real job…I guess he doesn't have time for his old friends so much anymore."

She figured the same thing. Still, it didn't make her feel better.

"Don't worry about it," Sticky reiterated.

She nodded.

"I'm going to need to talk to your boy for a minute. Is that okay?"

She nodded, tapping Rick on the shoulder. He tried to maneuver out of the booth, but got caught up in Kendra (who refused to budge an inch, which forced him to crawl over her. *Going to have an issue with you, missy,* was all Leslie could think).

"Rick turns thirty," Kendra announced, poking at the remains of the small cake that somebody had brought. "Wow. He's practically *old.*"

Definitely going to have an issue with you.

Kendra's smile turned catlike. "How old are you, again?"

Bitch.

But before Leslie could answer, Rick was back at the booth…motioning Leslie to get out. She left eagerly, avoiding the side of the booth Kendra and Andre were camped out in.

"What's up?"

"Sticky told me you're tired," he said, and he stroked the side of her cheek. In that moment, she would have done anything for him—stayed until five in the morning, if need be. His eyes were warm with concern. "How do you feel about going home?"

Home. Sleep. She felt as if he was offering her heaven. "But…it's your birthday," she forced herself to say. "Are *you* okay with that? I mean, I don't want to take you away from your friends."

He sighed. "You're not. They're just…well. We'll talk about it later," he said with a little look at the knot of friends staring at them nearby. "Why don't we just go home."

She smiled. "Sure. No problem."

She turned to give Sticky a hug. "Thanks," she said.

"Um…" Sticky held her a little longer. "There's this thing though."

She stopped and looked at Rick…who was suddenly looking a little guilty. "What?" she asked gingerly.

"I have to do this favor for Sticky."

"Sure," she said, still wondering at their expressions. "Do you need a ride?"

"No, I'll be closing the place down," Sticky said with an easy chuckle. "The thing is…PJ needs a couch."

Leslie blinked. "You want us to move a couch? Now?"

But Sticky just bellowed with laughter. "No, no. PJ just needs a place to stay tonight."

"Oh…okay."

Rick still had a sheepish look on his face. "I said she could stay on my couch. We'll need to give her a ride."

Leslie felt a little pit of tension tighten in her stomach. She'd been looking forward to taking Rick back to her place…maybe making him breakfast in the morning. Her place, with her pillow-top mattress and down comforter—it was still chilly in San Francisco. Her home, where every square inch didn't have some kind of electronic device on it, where there wasn't a big-screen TV and three different kinds of video-game console strewn on the living-room rug.

Sticky stared longingly at her, coming very close to giving her Bambi eyes…a daunting prospect.

She'd be a bitch herself if she didn't give in. "It's your birthday," she said brightly, giving Rick a little kiss on the jawline. "You can do whatever the hell you want."

Rick's goofy grin reappeared. "I love you," he whispered, enveloping her in a bear hug.

She looked at Sticky, imploring.

"I'll go get her," he said. "I'll hurry her right along."

"Great," Leslie said.

She waited until Sticky disappeared into the crowd, heading toward the DJ booth. She turned to Rick. "Is PJ a friend of yours?"

The birthday shots were kicking in now, and he was having a little trouble focusing. "What?"

"This PJ…do you know her?"

"Huh? Oh. No. She's a friend of Sticky's, pretty much. I've heard lots about her, though," he offered.

"You mean she's a stranger?"

"Any friend of Sticky's…" he said, and then paused. "Is more than likely to be nice. I think. And he wouldn't let one of his dangerous friends stay at my house," he added.

Fabulous, she thought, gripping her car keys like a vise. Just fabulous.

chapter 2

I'm just finishing up my set, but they're keeping the club open until five. It's two o'clock now. The bar's shut down, and people are going to be looking for more relaxing music…ambient, trance, stuff to take them off their dancing-induced high. (Or whatever other high they've been cultivating tonight.) It's been a good night, a good crowd. Lots of beautiful people wandering in, some kind of big-deal party. The promoter, Chuck, has been a nervous wreck. I need to talk to him about paying me.

I nod to DJ Nightshade, who's taking over for me. We've already traded demo CDs, and I talked to him a bit about my setup, friendly. But other than getting paid, I had more pressing problems. With the Strippas off the list, I needed to see what couch I could sleep on tonight.

I see Sticky in the crowd, wave to him, and he gestures at his watch. I guess he has somebody. I rub my fingers together— *cash first.* He gets the message.

Chuck's deep in conversation with somebody, a tall guy in expensive clothes. Not club-flashy like a lot of the guys here. Tasteful. Chuck always responded well to money. Chuck also liked guys like this one. I didn't want to salt him, but I really needed the money. My cell-phone bill was coming up—and I still had this stupid eating habit I needed to support.

I walk up to him, smiling. "Chuck. I don't mean to interrupt, but I finished my set." *So pay me, you cheap bastard.*

Normally, he scowls at this point. Because of my setup, and because of my negotiating skills, he pays me about seventy-five a night. Most DJs get fifty, and that's if they're lucky—it helps their careers to get the exposure, or at least that's Chuck's argument, and he's generally right. I had some arguments of my own.

But Chuck's not upset. Instead, he's smiling at me like a benevolent godfather. "PJ! Just who I wanted to see."

Immediately, my guard goes up. If I had a wallet, I'd grab it.

"I want you to meet somebody," he says, and then, I swear to God, he puts an arm around me. He *never* does that. "PJ, this is Jonathan Hadeis. He's from NYC."

"Nice to meet you," I mutter. I look at Chuck. "Um, Chuck…I need to get going."

"Jonathan *Hadeis,*" he says with emphasis, and the beginning of a warning scowl. "From *New York.*"

I look at Jonathan. Nice-looking guy, and obviously somebody Chuck wants to impress. I hold out my hand and he shakes it. Guy's got big hands, I think, and smile.

He smiles back. Very nice.

I still don't see the point in this.

My cell phone vibrates, and I say, "Excuse me," and look at the screen. Text message from Sticky—*Got couch. Leaving now.*

"I have to go," I say to Chuck. "I'm sorry, I just need to get paid."

He winces as if he can't believe I'd even bring up something so gauche as payment, while his important friend looks on. He's funny that way.

"Now," I add. I'm tacky, and I'm also hungry. I'm funny that way.

He grumbles and pulls out his wallet, giving me four twenties. "You did really, really well tonight," he repeats with a cheesy smile.

"Thanks," I reply, although I know he doesn't really mean it. He doesn't have an ear for music, what he has is a lot of connections. Whatever works, I guess. "It was nice meeting you," I repeat to Jonathan Hadeis of the nice smile.

I walk toward where I saw Sticky, and I feel a hand on my shoulder. I whirl around, immediately defensive, clutching my duffel bag.

It's the Jonathan guy. I'm now belatedly wondering if Chuck was trying to pimp me, or what.

"Listen, you really were incredible tonight," he says, and I roll my eyes and try not to look at my watch. "I mean that."

"Thank you," I say. I mean, if he means it, it's always nice to hear.

"Did you make that mash mix yourself? What the hell *was* that?"

I laugh, relaxing. If he's wondering about the mix, he's not interested in jumping me. He sounds like he's a music guy. "That was Ice Cube…mixed with the Teletubbies."

He bursts into laughter. Nice smile, and nice laugh. Seems cute enough. Not that I'm interested—my life is way too simple to warrant a complication like a boyfriend—but if Chuck was trying to fix me up, at least he's got good taste.

"You've got talent. Has anybody ever told you that?"

I shrug. This sort of thing—I mean, I like to get my name out, same as any DJ who's trying to make it. But what do you answer?

"Yes, people tell me that constantly?"

"No, most people either ignore me or tell me I suck?"

It's not exactly win-win.

He's staring at my face as if he's trying to read Dostoyevsky. "You don't know who I am, do you?"

"No," I answer honestly. "But I get the feeling I'm supposed to."

He pulls out his wallet and gives me a card. "I've worked at MotherClub in NYC, I've been a DJ for radio and for clubs for years. I work with a lot of designers. I've done some production work for various artists. And," he says with peculiar emphasis, "I've managed some other DJs, on and off, over the years."

I blink at him. "Boy. I'm feeling stupid."

He laughs. "I like you, PJ. And I really think you could make it. I think you could be a success."

My stomach clenches up, and it's not just the fact that I haven't eaten in hours. "You really think so?"

"In fact…"

My cell phone vibrates wildly. I glance down. It's Sticky. *"Outside. NOW."*

I sigh. "I have to go. I'm really sorry," I add, meaning it. "Thank you. It's a real compliment when it comes from someone who knows the business."

"I want to represent you."

"I'm sorry?"

"I want to manage your career," he says. He crosses his arms. "Unless you want to be spinning for seventy-five a night for the rest of your life."

I think about it. The clench has turned into a Gordian knot.

Then I think about the cell phone. If I don't go now, my couch is going to evaporate. And as much as I want to talk to this guy, a night on the streets is not going to be conducive to my career or my health. It's about fifty-five degrees out there. Bad for the equipment.

"I really have to go, but I'd love to talk about it," I offer. "Could I maybe meet you later? Some other time?"

"What's so important?" He glances at his watch. "It's only two."

"It's a long story," I say. "I can't miss this ride."

"I can take you," he says. "I'd think, if you were serious about being a success, you'd want to make time for it."

Okay, that I don't like. I don't like being pressured…and I don't even know this guy.

"I'd think if you really think I'm worth it," I say instead, "you'd reschedule. I've got someone waiting for me. I have to leave."

I grab a pen, write my cell-phone number on the back of

his business card. "If you're still interested," I say, handing him the card back, "you can call *me.*"

With that, I turn, muscling my way past some tall, skinny women and head for the door. My temper's burning. I don't care if the guy was cute and was from NY and could hand me a record label and a European tour on a silver platter. I don't like getting pushed around.

I see Sticky and a couple… I seem to recognize the guy, but the woman's a stranger. She has bags under her eyes and looks exhausted and kind of peeved. Fantastic. Just frickin' great.

"Where were you?" Sticky looks at me, concerned.

"Talking to some guy Chuck introduced me to," I say. "Sorry," I add to peeved-woman.

"What guy?"

"We have to go," the woman interjects.

I hope she's got a comfortable couch. She's looking at me as if I'm either a thief or a bug.

If this were any more fun, it'd be a funeral.

"Some guy named Jonathan Hadeis," I reply, shaking my head. "Says he wants to be my manager."

Sticky's eyes literally bulge out of his head. *"Jonathan Hadeis wants to be your manager?"*

I nod. "I'm sorry," I repeat to the woman. "My name's PJ. And you are…?"

"Leslie," she says, and she reluctantly shakes my hand. Her boyfriend just smiles, the goofy smile of the drunken. I smile back.

Sticky grabs my shoulder. "What did you say?"

"He wanted me to hang around. Said if I was really serious about my career, I'd hang. I was already keeping you waiting," I point out. "You blew me up twice."

"If I'd known *that,* I'd try to find you another damn couch! Are you crazy? Did you get his card or something, at least?"

I wince. "Sort of. Kind of." I sigh. "Not exactly."

Sticky makes a gurgling noise.

"Listen, I gave him my number. If he's really serious about repping me, he'll call." At least, I hope to God he will. Sticky's reaction has me several more notches above nervous. "And Leslie here is being kind enough to put me up. So I'll just go with that, okay?"

Sticky shakes his head. "You are crazy. And stubborn."

"You love me," I say, giving him a hug. "Besides, you knew I was crazy, right?"

Sticky looks aghast. "That wasn't what I meant."

I shrug. It's been a long time, and I knew what he meant. "Well, I am stubborn. Listen, I'm playing at Grotto tomorrow. Or rather tonight." It's two in the morning, after all. "Line me up?"

He nods, understanding. He'll get me another couch. I can't imagine Leslie being the type to let me stay for more than one night.

I follow Leslie and her boyfriend (Rick, I find out) to their car. It's nice, an Acura coupé something-or-other. I remember it's not cheap. My husband leased one similar…but lower-end. We couldn't afford more. Hell, we couldn't afford *that*.

I close my eyes. I'm suddenly exhausted. I just want to put tonight behind me and get some sleep.

I think about holding Jonathan's card in my hand and then handing it back.

I'll probably regret that.

"Rick lives over by San Mateo," Leslie informs me. "We'll get you all set up."

"Thanks," I say absently.

Damn it. Just… Damn it.

Leslie was beyond exhausted. It didn't help that sleeping on Rick's bed wasn't as comfortable as her bed at home, and the fact that he was snoring heavily in her ear was an added challenge. But if you got right down to it, she realized that neither the bed nor the noise were what were preventing her sleep-heavy eyes from shutting.

Miraculously, over the sawing of Rick's snores, she could hear the shuffle of someone in the living room. Maybe…was that the sound of someone opening a drawer?

She thought she heard these sounds. She thought she'd heard

them since they settled into bed for the night, leaving that stranger out there, with all of Rick's stuff.

Granted, it'd probably be difficult for a small woman like "DJ PJ" to walk off with several thousand dollars' of electrical equipment and a big-screen TV—Rick's most valued possessions. But…maybe she was going through his paperwork. Maybe she'd get a charge card in Rick's name and run it up. The whole thing was ripe with awful possibilities.

Maybe she's just going through the kitchen to eat something.

Or maybe…to get a knife.

How could Rick sleep when stuff like this could be happening in his own living room? How could he expect *her* to sleep?

She'd been tossing and turning enough that Rick, a cuddler by nature, finally gave up and was now curled up on his own side of the bed. She tentatively got up, shivering at the cold in the room. Rick never used his heater. The other reason she loved it when they stayed at her apartment. She pulled on a set of his sweats and walked over to the door, listening.

The sounds were minute. It was tough to tell what the woman might or might not be doing out there in the living room.

Leslie decided to get a glass of water. Sure, she could get it from the bathroom, but the kitchen had the glasses, didn't it?

She stepped out, wincing a little against the light.

PJ was sitting up on the couch, still wearing the jeans and sweatshirt that she had been wearing that night. She was wrapped in a blanket, too, her only concession to the cold of Rick's apartment. She was also wearing headphones connected to her laptop, and she was nodding her head in syncopated rhythm with whatever was playing. She quickly removed one of the earphones.

"I'm sorry," she said. "Was the light keeping you up?"

Leslie thought about saying—*Yes, it was, do you mind?* But then PJ would be doing whatever it was she was doing in the dark, and Leslie wouldn't even be able to peek…

"Uh, no," Leslie said. "I was just…getting a glass of water."

PJ's smirk said as clearly as words: *Sure you were. Getting a glass of water at four in the morning.*

"I'll be asleep soon," PJ assured her, and Leslie felt like an idiot. "I just...tonight worked me up." She paused. "Thanks again for letting me stay here."

She sounded sincere—and polite. Leslie sighed.

"It's Rick's place," she said, gesturing around...and then realized that might've sounded ungracious. "It's really no problem. We both took today off, anyway."

"Oh." PJ looked temporarily confused. Then awareness dawned on her. "Right. Wednesday. Workday."

"Yeah." Leslie went to the kitchen, got a glass of water that she didn't really want and sipped at it. "I guess you don't have a day job, then."

PJ grinned. "No." She took her headphones off, shut down her laptop. She placed the two back carefully in her duffel bag. Leslie had to credit her with neatness—she had spread no belongings around, and only took up half the couch as it was. She barely made a noticeable change in her surroundings. "I don't have a day job."

Leslie looked at her. "Where do you normally live? If you don't mind my asking."

PJ shrugged. "I don't normally live anywhere."

"You're homeless?" Leslie didn't mean for that to sound so horrified.

"No," PJ said. "I don't have an apartment or house of my own, but believe me, I know some homeless people. I'm definitely not homeless. I stay at other people's houses, that's all."

She spoke with conviction, Leslie noticed...not that PJ was trying to show that she was better than homeless people, but to point out that she certainly had it easier.

Curiosity. One of Leslie's worse faults. She sat down gingerly on the arm of Rick's La-Z-Boy, reasoning that sitting on the arm of it wasn't the same as actually sitting down and settling in for a conversation.

"So...you just stay on your friends' couches?"

PJ shrugged again. "Generally. I don't stay on anybody's

couch for too long. Don't want to wear out my welcome, or anything." She stretched, looking very like a cat. She looked tired…and a little amped up. Leslie belatedly wondered if she was on something. Still, she sounded articulate, and she didn't seem as potentially frightening as she had when Leslie was staring in the dark in Rick's bedroom, wondering what PJ was up to.

You are such a judgmental prig, Leslie chastised herself.

"How did you get this way?"

PJ stared at her. "'This way?' What way is that?"

Leslie felt herself warm with a blush. "I mean, how did you come to stay on other people's couches?"

PJ smiled, a little aloof. "It's a long story."

Leslie waited. And waited. And realized that there was a silent *and it's a story I don't feel like telling you* at the end of it.

"Oh," Leslie said awkwardly. "Sorry. I'm a reporter, so I guess I'm just naturally curious."

"Really?" The chilly, closed-off sensation that PJ had projected melted away into genuine interest. "Who do you write for? And what sort of stories do you write?"

Leslie's blush didn't disappear. *Why did I say that?*

"Well, I work for the *Bay Area Citizen,*" she said. "Do you know that paper?"

"If you know the club scene at all in San Francisco," PJ said, "then you know the *Citizen.*"

Leslie smiled. "Well, I work for them."

"Have I read any of your articles?"

"I doubt it. I do features from time to time, but haven't done anything big yet."

Actually, she'd only written one feature piece that the editor had accepted…and that was sort of a favor. As a general rule, she worked in the personals section, proofreading the pleas for male-seeking-female, male-seeking-male, female-seeking-male…desperate-seeking-anyone. But PJ didn't have to know that.

Leslie didn't know why she felt the need to impress someone who had bummed spending a night on the couch of a stranger, but it did make a difference, somehow.

"So, how long have you been a DJ?"

"Professionally? About two years," PJ answered, smothering a yawn with the back of her hand. "I was spinning just for fun for about three years before that."

"And…"

"What's going on?" It was Rick, his hair sticking out of his head at crazy angles, looking very much like a blinking, annoyed cockatoo. "Why's everybody up?"

Leslie immediately felt guilty. Shooting to her feet, she walked over to him. "I'm sorry, honey. Did our talking wake you up?"

He blinked. "You weren't in bed," he said, sounding confused.

"I'm coming to bed now," she soothed.

"'Kay." Then he blinked at PJ. "Who are you?"

"That's PJ," Leslie answered instead, nudging him toward the bedroom. "She's a friend. She's sleeping on the couch, remember?"

"Oh." His voice sounded as if he didn't, but he was drifting back to sleep even as he took steps toward the bed, so he probably didn't care, either.

She looked back at PJ. "Sorry, thanks for answering my questions. Good night."

"'Night," PJ answered.

Leslie closed the door behind her. Rick had already tumbled back into bed, and she wound up stripping in the dark and climbing in next to him. He was wonderfully warm. His arm went around her, and she snuggled in. She did notice when the light went out and PJ was silent. Seconds later, Leslie herself was asleep.

I finally got some sleep. I was too torqued last night, especially after the great Jonathan Hadeis fiasco. I kept playing that scene over and over in my head. I've been wanting to "make it" as a DJ for the past two years, and I've worked damn hard to get where I am.

Of course, some people would argue that where I am is homeless, but that's not the point.

I stayed at Leslie and Rick's place until about eleven. The two of them started getting up around 10:00 a.m.... I could hear them futzing around, talking in low voices. I sleep light. And, I hate to say, the couch wasn't all that comfortable. It was a dorm special, with the center sagging badly where the springs were shot. The whole apartment was decorated in early Ikea, with a couple of cinder-block-and-plank "bookshelves" that housed hundreds of video games. It was obviously his place. And it was equally obvious that she didn't have much of a mark on it. No frills or femininity anywhere...not even in the bathroom, which is the room most women stake out when they start to mark their territory.

I'll bet that she'd rather be at her house. And I got the feeling she was trying hard to convince him of that, as well.

I got out of there around eleven. Cal Trains from San Mateo's a pain in the butt, but I finally got where I needed to go. Chang's Laundry, over in the Mission. Not the greatest neighborhood, but not bad, either. And most importantly, Chang's Laundry was cheap, and it was warm.

Wednesdays and Saturdays are my laundry days. When you only carry one duffel bag's worth of clothes, you've got to do it regularly.

It's early enough in the afternoon that most people are at work. There's a Hispanic woman with two small kids, doing laundry, and a bachelor. He keeps shooting me looks, but I ignore him. I'm wearing a pair of boxer briefs and a tank top, and a pair of very thin flip-flops. The thing is, I do pretty much *all* my laundry on Wednesdays and Saturdays. Chang knows me well enough not to care that I do laundry in my underwear. Generally, I listen to my beats and ignore anything else going on, or anybody who might be staring. And generally, the people there really don't care.

Tonight I'm DJ-ing at a small sub-lounge called Grotto...a new place, relatively trendy. I need to call Sticky, see where my couch is for after. And I need to get a demo together.

I want to represent you. Unless you want to be spinning for seventy-five a night for the rest of your life.

I close my eyes. That guy's voice was going to haunt me for a week, I could just tell.

I had to be stupid enough to hand the card back.

I look at my laptop. I'd been working on a kick-ass new demo anyway…the one I gave DJ Nightshade last night was passable, pretty good, but I was always trying to improve. This one was going to rock. It was going to blow minds. This one was going to get me to the next level.

Next time, I told myself, I was going to be ready. He was in the Bay Area, right? He would be at the clubs I worked at. I'd spin, I'd work the crowd into a frenzy…and then I'd drop my demo on him. He'd understand where I was coming from. I'd have the upper hand. And then, maybe, just maybe, I'd sign with him. After I'd done a lot of research, and after we'd had a strong conversation about what it was I wanted and what I would and would not do.

"Excuse me…PJ?"

I turn around. And immediately feel cold all over.

It was him. Jonathan Hadeis. Speak of the devil.

I feel an immediate desire to run, and then I remember what I'm wearing. It makes the desire to flee even stronger.

I go for casual. "Um… Hi?"

He was staring at me, not surprisingly. He looked—amused, I think, and also in a little bit of shock. "Sticky said that you do laundry on Wednesdays," he explains with a laugh in his voice. As if he couldn't believe it the first time he heard it, and now that he was here, he *really* couldn't believe what he was seeing.

I'd be having words with Sticky later, that much was fucking obvious.

I decide the best way to go about this is to not act embarrassed…just tough it out. "I guess you really wanted to see me," I say, trying not to focus on just how much of me he was seeing.

It's hard to sound cool when you're sporting a pair of SpongeBob undies and a tank top that says Porn Star.

"I feel like our conversation ended on the wrong foot last

night. I thought maybe we could discuss it a little more, without you having to rush off…"

"You could have just called me," I point out. "I gave you my number."

"Yeah," he said, and he pulled out the card I'd handed back. "But… Well, I prefer to deal face-to-face when I can."

My demo's not ready, I keep thinking, staring at my laptop. I haven't shown him what I can really do. I'm standing here in underwear.

There are several ways this could be worse, I remind myself. The fact that I can't seem to come up with any ways doesn't really help.

"So. You think I'm pushy," he says, and he doesn't sound pissed off about it…just uses it as a jumping-off point.

I cross my arms. "Yeah," I agree. "You are."

Sticky would be appalled.

He laughs. "At least you're honest," he mutters, not perturbed in the least. "Listen, I've been called pushy by other people. When I decide I want something…I can be really single-minded about it."

I remember people used to say the same thing about me. Driven, they used to call me. Among other things. I tended to prefer that to "bitchy" or "psychotic."

"Well, ambition's not a failing," I say, trying to be at least a little conciliatory.

"No. I don't think so. I think if you don't want something badly enough, if you aren't willing to work hard and sacrifice, then you might as well pack it up and go home," he replies. "God. That sounds like a bad motivational tape, doesn't it? Did you want to sit down?"

I sit down next to him on a hard Formica bench in a really hideous orange. This is feeling more like a business meeting, I think, trying to ignore how cold the damn bench is through the thin fabric of the boxer briefs. "I want to be a successful DJ," I state. "I'm just careful about how I'm doing it, that's all. I'm very clear on what I want."

"Mmm…so, what's up with the homeless thing?"

I really wish people would stop focusing on that. Fortunately, I've fielded this particular question before. "I gave up absolutely everything to be a DJ," I say by rote. "I don't have any overhead. I'm sort of a guerilla DJ. I focus everything on the music."

"Really."

Some people buy this—some promoters have even included it in their flyers. I got a blurb in a tiny newspaper once. Jonathan, I notice, doesn't actually look impressed.

"Well, if it works for you."

He obviously has his doubts.

"How many gigs a week do you do?"

"I work pretty steady," I say. "Couple times a week. And I get paid for all of them."

He nods. "Mostly small stuff?"

I shrug. "Differing sizes."

"What kind of music?"

Now we're on familiar ground. "Mostly break beat and bass-and-drum. Some trance, nothing too light. Some house and hip-hop. A very little jungle."

He's frowning, and he's taking out a small, expensive-looking PDA. "No specialty?" He's taking notes.

I suddenly feel nervous.

"Break beat's my favorite," I say. "But it depends on the work I get. I can't afford to specialize too much. And I have eclectic tastes."

He nods, and I actually perk up at his approval. When I realize this, the fact that I do bothers me ever so slightly.

"Do you—"

We're interrupted by the loud buzz of a dryer. "Excuse me," I say, get up, and unload the clothes in my dryer into a rolling cart. I self-consciously wheel it over to a folding table. "You don't mind, do you?"

"Not at all."

I can feel his eyes on me, watching me fold. I don't have the upper hand in this. It's not going as well as I'd hoped.

I turn, and he's staring. He doesn't look disapproving. He looks...I can't actually describe what he looks like. Puzzled, maybe. Like he can't get a bead on me.

I'm kind of used to that. It would make sense.

He walks over to me, and I can't help it. I stiffen. Uncomfortable.

"Listen, I like you. And I still think you're talented."

Here it comes, I think. The offer. Is this something I really want to do? Is this something I'm ready for? Yeah, I want to be a top DJ...but, do I trust this guy?

"But I'm rethinking the whole management thing."

It stings like a slap. "What?"

"I just don't like to rush into things," he says, and his voice is lazy, almost a drawl.

I blink at him. "So what was all this about?"

He smiles at me. It's still a nice smile, I think, annoyed. "Getting to know you. Not rushing."

"I see." I don't mean to sound bitter. Though, wasn't I just wondering if I should do anything with him? It did make sense.

But I really am that good, damn it!

"So," I begin, "maybe you should come to Grotto tonight. Hear me play?"

He looks...fuck. Amused. That's going to get old quickly.

"You want me there? Really?"

"I asked, didn't I?"

Now I sound like the pushy one. Argh.

"All right," he says, and now he looks satisfied. I'm wondering if maybe I got set up here. "I'll see you tonight."

"Okay," I say, offhand. "I'll just...finish up here."

"Right. Good luck with that."

I nod.

"Oh, and PJ?"

"Yes?"

He smiles, and it's a wicked one now. "Nice undies."

Damn it. I'm completely annoyed, but somehow I find myself laughing anyway.

★ ★ ★

Ever since the modeling-agency party, Samantha had been…well, confused. She was still a little annoyed that her big entrance had been ruined, but shot through that was interest. Specifically, in Jonathan Hadeis.

She'd quickly asked questions and was even more intrigued by the varying opinions she got.

"He's weird," stated Cassie, a model who was a little higher on the food chain than she was. "I've heard about him, from one of the designers. He's DJ'd at almost all the big New York and Italian shows. Not so much Paris. He's a darling of the design world."

"I heard it's because he's a dealer," Kylee broke in. Samantha had been hanging on the fringes of the conversation. There were important people around, people who she didn't know. People who she wanted to know.

"He worked at MotherClub," one of the guys in a three-piece suit said. "He was part owner of Sapphire for a while, too, I think."

"So how'd he get the money? I'm still saying drugs," Kylee said in a fascinated tone of voice. She reminded Samantha of a gossipy neighbor.

The guy ignored her. "He has some kind of past, and there were rumors that he got his money in some unusual way, but it never got cleared up. The important part is, he's got money, and more importantly, he's got contacts. In the music industry, in fashion, even in movies to a certain extent. If you want to be anybody, then you ought to know him."

Jonathan Hadeis. Samantha made a mental note of his name. And his face.

She thought about him all day. Jonathan Hadeis was doodled on her statistics notes…his face was more on her mind than the sociology professor's lecture. So when she went home, she decided to take some action.

She threw herself across her bed, picking up her phone. Jonathan Hadeis wasn't the only one with contacts.

"Hey there," a deep voice answered. "This is Sticky."

"Sticky," she purred.

"Baby girl," he answered. "What's going on?"

"You don't even know who this is," she said with her sexiest laugh.

"Are you kidding? Voice like that? Only the sexiest woman I know."

"It's Samantha," she said, still laughing, although she felt a little insulted. She'd have to work on the sexy voice.

"I would've guessed that in a minute," Sticky said. "What can I do for you?"

"I was wondering what you know about somebody named Jonathan Hadeis."

Sticky went reticent. "Why do you want to know?"

Well, that was odd. "He was at the agency party last night, at Technique," she explained. "He was causing a stir. People were saying he was huge with record-exec and fashion people, that he knew anybody who was anybody."

"Sounds like you know plenty about him," Sticky answered. "I don't know…don't think I can add to that."

"They said he might be a drug dealer, too," Samantha said, deciding to see if that caused as much of a reaction with him as it had with everyone else Kylee had been speaking with last night.

Sticky's pause was noticeable. "Drug dealer, you say?"

"Because he's got so much money. You know what it takes to make money as a DJ," she ventured. "Still, I don't think it's true."

"Really." He still sounded worried. "Why not?"

"Because of the way he dresses. He just didn't *seem* like a drug dealer."

"They never do," Sticky said. "I might need to look into this. Thanks."

"Why are you sweating it?" she finally said. "I thought you'd know of the guy, but I didn't think he had anything to do with you."

"Because I know about people, but people don't *know* me, right?"

Samantha felt her cheeks heat. "That wasn't what I meant." Well, it probably was what she meant. But it wasn't what she would've said to him.

"As it happens, I spoke with Jonathan Hadeis this morning."

She squealed, she couldn't help it. "You know him? Personally?"

"You could say we've got a working relationship." Sticky's voice was tight. "He seems like a good guy. I didn't know about this drug stuff, though."

"So, he's buying a club?" Sticky knew every bouncer and doorman in the city. If you wanted security for a new club, Sticky would be one of the first people you'd call.

"I don't know. He mentioned he was thinking about it, but this was more personal," Sticky said. "I called him because of PJ, actually."

"PJ?" Samantha went through her mental Rolodex. "Sort of scruffy-looking DJ? Dark reddish brown hair, looks like she cuts it herself?"

Sticky's booming laugh almost deafened her. "I'll be sure *not* to tell her that the next time I see her," he said. "She's one of my best friends—but you're right, the girl does not know how to dress herself. Anyway, he heard her DJ last night at Technique. You did, too, you know," he mentioned.

She shrugged. Like the music was something she paid attention to. "So? What does he want with her? I mean, if he's opening his own club, I imagine he's got plenty of contacts, big names from New York that he could bring out." Maybe he'd have parties there, with tons of famous people—designers, people who might see her and want her to work for them.

She was getting more fascinated by this Jonathan Hadeis by the minute.

"He's interested in repping her," Sticky corrected. "He wants to be her manager, maybe."

Samantha's fantasy of being discovered quickly imploded. "Oh."

"Don't sound so disappointed."

"I'm not. I just…wondered."

"Got some interest in the guy, huh?"

Samantha turned over, leaned back against her pillows. "Maybe."

"Well, watch yourself," Sticky said, and he sounded more big brotherly than his usual sweet-lecherous self. "The guy's got to be late thirties. And since I keep sneaking your ass into my club, I know you're nowhere near."

"I can take care of myself," Samantha said. She'd been doing it for long enough, hadn't she?

"I'm going to be picking PJ up at Grotto tonight," Sticky said, reverting to his usual come-on voice. "Maybe you could stop by, have a drink with me."

Sticky was a good guy…and he did know every doorman in the city, as she'd said. He had a lot of pull if you wanted to get into cool clubs. However, he was out of shape, and his face, while cute, wasn't model handsome. And let's face it…he was a bouncer. You might hire a guy like this if you were Christina Aguilera and you wanted a bodyguard. But date a guy like Sticky?

Samantha didn't think so.

"I've got a lot of studying to do tonight, sweetie," she said, deliberately trying for a kind tone. Ordinarily, she'd have shut a guy down without even blinking—but Sticky did get her into his club, and since she was only nineteen, it was a risk. She didn't want to burn that bridge.

He paused. "You know, Jonathan might be there."

The simple sentence was electrifying. She knew where Jonathan was going to be. She'd have a shot at actually talking to him this time…and giving him a chance to check her out.

"I'm guessing you're changing your mind."

She blushed again. Damn it. "Well, I'll try to make it out there."

"I'll have a diet ginger ale waiting for you," Sticky said. "Later."

When she hung up, she thought about just how guilty she needed to feel. She decided not to bother. The important thing was, she'd found out that Jonathan was focused on music, that he was interested in PJ's career. And that he'd be at Grotto tonight.

She could take it from there.

chapter 3

"If I just get through tonight alive, I'll be happy," Rick muttered. "Thanks for doing this. I'll owe you one."

Leslie smiled at the thought. "I like your grandparents," she said. "It's not really a hardship, or anything."

He snorted. "I like their house," he said. They lived in a multimillion-dollar home in the Berkeley Hills. Rick's family was what could be called "filthy rich" in more crass circles.

"They do have a beautiful view," Leslie agreed. "We'll just be able to see the sun setting behind the Golden Gate Bridge."

"Half an hour of my grandmother asking me what I'm doing with my life," Rick said darkly, "and I'll be ready to jump off the damn bridge."

"I thought they were happy about your new job?"

"I've only been at it for a couple of months. Guess it doesn't count until it's longer than a year."

The two of them settled into uncomfortable silence. Rick's fluctuating job record was a sore point with the grandparents. If anything, Leslie's own spotty job record was something that had been common ground for both of them.

"They'll go easy on you," Leslie finally said. "Besides, most of your cousins will be there. You know how the great-grand-kids distract them. And Simone's new baby will be there. Your grandmother will be way too focused on him to rip into you."

"From your mouth to God's ear." But Rick seemed cheered by the thought.

By the time they pulled into the long, curving driveway, al-ready crammed with various Lexus and Mercedes-Benzes, she could feel Rick wavering on the edge of a bad mood. But the mood inside the house was much more lively.

Now it was Leslie's turn to tighten up.

She really did love his grandparents, and for the most part, liked the rest of his family. It was a little intimidating to be among so many people who, in her estimation, had "made it."

She was the one who rang the doorbell, while Rick jammed his hands in the pockets of his Dockers. His grandfather opened the door.

"Leslie!" He had a booming voice, and he looked like Rick probably would in about forty years. He was spry, and at sev-enty-six, he looked surprisingly mischievous. "There's our girl." He gave her a bone-crunching hug, and she laughed.

"Oh, and you brought him," he said with a wink, and then gave Rick a man-hug, one of those paltry affairs. "Your grand-mother's cooking, and the great-grandkids are turning the liv-ing room into a fort. It's mass hysteria."

"As usual," Rick said with what looked like a reluctant smile.

"Feel like a drink?"

Rick's sigh of relief spoke volumes. "If you're making one for yourself."

Leslie watched as Rick followed his grandfather into the family room, where there was already heightened conversation going on…a chorus of male voices, and what sounded like a basketball game.

"Leslie, dear. There you are."

She turned. Rick's grandmother didn't appear as if she be-longed in the palatial home that she and her husband inhab-ited. She was wearing a thick white sweater over a pink shirt with a curved Peter Pan collar, and a pair of tan slacks that could have come from someplace like Ross rather than Neiman Marcus. And as for the tiny strand of pearls she was wearing, she might've received them for first communion. "Hi, Grandma," Leslie said, giving the tiny woman a hug. The hug Grandma gave back seemed delicate, especially compared to her husband's almost painful strength.

"I'm so glad to see you, dear." Rick's grandmother lingered over the hug, making Leslie feel that much more awkward. "How is Rick?"

And this was why she felt awkward. Rick's grandmother always made a point of pulling her aside…finding out how he was doing in this surreptitious fashion. It always made Leslie feel complicit, but after a few hemmings and hawings, she found talking to the older woman about her concerns and dreams for Rick almost comforting. Most of Leslie's friends were her age, and either married with kids, or divorced with kids. Neither group really listened to her woes about Rick's prolonged adolescence with much patience. Rick's grandmother, however, never tired of the subject.

Which is how Leslie got shuttled off to the kitchen, which smelled really good. She was cooking turkey and was stirring homemade gravy in the pan. It wasn't even Thanksgiving. There were mashed potatoes and green beans, in plain-looking china, staying warm on the stovetop as Grandma mixed. "How's he doing? Does he still have that job? Where is he working, again?"

Grandma forgot those kinds of things. Of course, considering Rick hadn't held a job for longer than maybe seven months in most of his adult life, a lot of the family forgot, as well.

"He's working as a project manager," Leslie answered. "For a company that sells comic books. He seems to like it."

"Comic books." Grandma shook her head. "Well. As long as he's happy. How are you two doing, dear?"

"Fine," Leslie said, although the words felt funny in her mouth.

Grandma turned from the stove, her eyes beady like a blackbird's. "Seriously. What's going on?"

"Nothing. You know he celebrated his birthday?"

"Thirty years old," Grandma sniffed. "Not that you'd know it, from how he acts."

Leslie didn't know how to answer that.

"Now, now, dear, I didn't mean to upset you," Grandma hastily added, and Leslie was surprised to find that she was sort of upset, around the edges. Stress she could deal with, but Rick was already going to be stretched tight as piano wire tonight…the last thing she needed to do was add to it and maybe wind up in a fight driving home. "He'll come to his senses," Grandma added. "You know, you're the best thing that's ever happened to him. I was telling Grandpa just the other day…she's the best thing that ever happened to Rick. What is he trying to do, screw up his life?"

"Thank you," Leslie said with as much dignity as she could scrape together.

"Well, we love you," his grandmother said, as if that settled everything. "And I'm not going to wait for what's left of my life for that boy to come to his senses. Dear, could you put the mashed potatoes out on the table?"

Leslie did as she was asked, trying hard to ignore the ominous tone of her statement.

They had managed through the carving of the turkey, and all the way through clearing off the table, and Leslie thought she was safe. It wasn't until the dessert course, when Leslie held Rick's cousin Simone's baby and cooed over it, that Grandma dropped her bomb.

"So, Rick…thirty years old."

Leslie stiffened, and saw Rick go straight as an ironing board in his chair. "Yup. Must make you feel pretty old, huh, Grandpa?"

Grandpa guffawed, as did several of the male cousins and an uncle or two. "I'm still young enough to—"

Grandma cut across Grandpa's statement of bravado. "So when are you going to finally settle down?"

Rick's family was never quiet, but it was amazing how fast everyone became absorbed in their slices of chocolate-cream pie. Leslie felt humiliation hit her in a wave.

She watched the muscles on Rick's jaw ripple, and he stared down at his slice of pie, systematically destroying it with his small dessert fork. "Grandma," he said, his tone of voice a warning.

Grandma looked sublimely unconcerned. And she didn't back down an inch. She looked like a four-foot-eleven samurai.

"Grandma," Leslie said. "Really. It's—"

"Sweetie, you can't look at that baby in your arms and tell me it isn't something you've thought about."

Leslie felt that like a razor cut on her heart. She shut up.

"Leslie's got a career," Rick ground out. "You're always telling me that I need to figure out what I want to do. What about her? She's still trying to make it as a journalist. That's what she really wants to do. Why wouldn't that be important to her?"

"That's an excuse," his grandmother countered. "She doesn't need a career, she needs a family."

"Wait a second," Leslie said. She loved holding Simone's baby…and sure, she'd entertained some fantasies that had grown even stronger since she'd turned thirty-five. It would be even harder now to conceive, but she still wanted a career. She still had those aspirations. It wasn't as if she *had* to pick one or the other, right?

And she wasn't going to let feminism retreat fifty years just because a tiny birdlike elderly woman was trying to help her get married.

"I do want to make it as a journalist," Leslie said, her voice just tentative enough to convince…well, no one. The cousins didn't look convinced, anyway.

"See?" Rick's voice rang triumphant.

His grandmother didn't look convinced by that, either.

People were still engrossed in their desserts.

"So why can't you marry her?" His grandfather now, sounding clueless. Perhaps deliberately so. "What's her having a career got to do with the price of bread, huh?"

"This sounds so fucking—"

"Rick!" His grandmother snapped, scandalized. "Language! There are children present."

Rick looked ready to bite through his fork. "Look. I just believe that if you're going to be in a relationship on that level...that level of *commitment,* I mean...you've both got to be whole people. I'm still getting my life together, and I feel like it's almost there. But I don't want Leslie to feel like this is all she has. I want her to have something of her own...something she's proud of." He took a deep breath. "I just don't think you can have a marriage that works if you're not both equal. If you're not going to be okay without the marriage part, you know?"

Leslie stared at him. It was more than they'd said in all four years that they'd been together. Maybe his grandmother was onto something.

She was still thinking about it later as they drove back to her apartment. He was still brooding, still unhappy. "I'm sorry that your grandmother ambushed you," she whispered.

He sighed. "It's not your fault."

She bit her lip, wishing that were true.

"And I'm sorry they put you in that position. Used the whole biological clock as an argument. I was so pissed. That was low," he said darkly, "even for her."

"Did you mean what you said?"

She could feel him tense without even touching him. "Which part?"

"About being equal and whole." She took a deep breath. "About...getting married."

He was quiet for a long, painful minute. "Leslie, I know you're not happy. And I get the feeling you're still looking to do something...prove something. Make it." He sighed again, drawn out and edged in frustration. "Until you do that...I don't see how you could be happy. You'd get married, and you'd just feel like you settled. You'd be happy for a while, but...I don't know. Maybe I'm talking out of my ass here."

She gave a perfunctory snicker. "No. Maybe you're right."

The bottom line was, he thought he was right. Which meant that he wasn't going to marry her until he thought that she'd proven all she needed to prove.

Which meant, de facto, that until she hit some kind of career success, she wasn't going to get what she really wanted...which was to marry him and have kids.

She looked out into the darkness of the San Mateo Bridge, across the waves, cresting, tipped with the reflection of the moon.

Now she just had to succeed at her job, prove she didn't need the marriage and the kids to show that she could handle them.

She laughed, bitterly, silently. And after eighteen years and at least eight different careers, how hard could that be, right?

Samantha sipped on a diet ginger ale at the dark-wood bar of Grotto, a new restaurant/lounge that was boasting a DJ, just like the restaurants in Europe. These places were new enough to be on the radar screens of people dying to be seen; however, odds were also good that they weren't going to last the year. She considered using them as an example for the statistics quiz she was expecting to have tomorrow morning at eight.

She really should be home, studying. Of course, she wasn't worried—it was just a quiz, and she hadn't screwed up a test yet.

Still, if she wasn't studying, she should probably be sleeping. Sure, it was only ten o'clock. But she had a call tomorrow afternoon, after her statistics class. This was for camera work, so she ought to be drinking a gallon of water and getting as much sleep as possible—God knew that the lens was unforgiving and those auditions were beyond relentless. But she wasn't. She was here, listening to fairly decent break beat and getting ogled by older men in suits who looked as if they were at a convention.

She saw Jonathan Hadeis walk in the door, and smiled.

He was the reason she wasn't being reasonable. And she wasn't going to go home until she found out more about him...and he knew more about her.

She straightened the hem of her dress—Max Mara, on sale from eBay, new with tags. She hated having to go garage sale for couture, but loved the effect. She waited for him to notice her. He was walking toward the bar, a small smile on his face. He looked...damn. Wickedly sexy. Sort of like a somber Colin

Farrell. She noticed that other women noticed, and felt strangely territorial.

She leaned back slightly, making sure the push-up bra did its work. The guys at the end of the bar stopped talking, too intent on the picture in front of them.

Jonathan walked up to her, nodded to the bartender...and proceeded to walk right past her.

She blinked, falling out of her deliberately sexy pose. He had only given her the barest of looks, but damn it, he had looked. And then his eyes had slid past her and moved forward, like a man on a mission.

Okay, she wasn't a top model yet. She understood that, as much as it still frosted her. Designers ripped her to shreds.

"Your nose is too straight."

"You need to lose fifteen pounds."

"You don't have the right look."

"You don't have *any* look."

Stuff like that, pulling no punches. She'd done what she could to fix what they'd commented on, and resigned herself when it came to the rest.

But when it came to men—since high school, she hadn't had a problem in that department. A quick smile, some dance moves. She was a nineteen-year-old Cleopatra, was what Sticky called her. Getting men to pay attention was not a problem.

Until tonight, apparently.

Samantha felt her temper simmering...and yet she still felt that same feeling of resignation, just like at the auditions. Jonathan knew people, he was admired. If she wasn't right for him, if he chose not to take her up on...

She'd just have to be patient. She hadn't made the cheerleading squad until senior year, and she hadn't gotten into a modeling agency until she'd hassled them to death. She might not be picked right off the bat. But she was patient, persistent. She played to win.

Jonathan was talking to the hostess, she noticed, before he got settled at a front table by the DJ booth. And then she remembered—Sticky had said that Jonathan was here to maybe sign the scruffy little DJ. DJ PJ, if you could believe that one. He was here on business—and from the sounds of it, business was something he was good at.

She wasn't going to distract him. But she was going to find out what was going on.

Heading over to the table, she straightened, getting into "game" mode. She set her face. Walked up to him. Took a deep breath.

"You're Jonathan Hadeis."

He looked at her again…that same sliding one, the one where he checks you out, then sort of discounts you. She didn't flinch, although she dearly wanted to.

"Yup, I'm him." Jonathan sounded diffident. "And you're…?"

"Samantha. Regales," she said, shaking his hand.

"You're familiar," he said, his eyes finally narrowing as he gave her a thorough look-over. "How do I know you?"

"Last night. At the Cooper Modeling Agency party. Over at DV8." She smiled, one that she knew was winning and kind of innocent. She got the feeling that that might work. "You gave me a hug when I asked."

"Oh, right," he said with a broad grin. "I remember. You all looked great. Nobody paid any attention to the DJs with the models wandering around."

Had she ever met anybody in this business this self-deprecating? It must be because he was so well-known, she reasoned. He didn't have anything to prove. Most of the guys that she knew, the ones that bragged about their connections, were barely more influential than she was. Which meant not at all, in the modeling world. But here was this guy, laid-back, willing to help.

"May I sit down?"

He looked as if he had to think about it, which offended her a little. Then he motioned to the chair, and she sat down, putting her glass on the tabletop. "I'm waiting for someone, though," he said.

She nodded, wondering if she should mention that she knew what he was there for. But that might make what she was doing seem too much like stalking. And she wasn't stalking. She was just…interested.

It sounded stupid, but stalking was for unattractive people. Why else would they need to?

"So. Been a model long?"

"Not very," she said. "But I'm working really hard. I've done a couple of covers, some camera work. Some ramp work, although I'd love to do more." Of course, the covers were in the Philippines, not Milan or anything. And her camera work consisted of posters at Mervyn's, where she was sitting on a beach ball, wearing baggy overalls. Not that he needed to know that.

"Mmm." He made a noise of acknowledgment. She noticed him look at his watch, a quick, supposed-to-be-sneaky glance.

"You were really incredible last night. On the turntables, I mean," she said, deciding to put the focus back on him. Most guys liked that. Although she was getting the distinct impression that he wasn't "most guys."

"Don't mention it." He winked at her, and she felt her pulse race a little. He looked sleepy and almost sly. "I mean, spinning records for pretty girls isn't exactly a hardship."

She loved the sound of his voice. She wondered what he was like when he DJ'd for all those designer fashion shows. Probably held his own, she thought, feeling a shivery warmth in the pit of her stomach. Probably looked down on all those sneering runway models, ignoring them as he mixed his music.

She was still in the middle of a music video-type daydream where she walked out on the catwalk and he finally perked up and took notice…until she realized that he had finally perked up and taken notice.

PJ was "in the house." More to the point, PJ was on the decks. She looked, not to put too fine a point on it, like a homeless person. Which, according to Sticky, she was. She was wearing cargo pants in a dark charcoal gray, that was probably originally black but had faded from too many washings. It looked a little frayed. She wore a sweater that was too big for her. Her chestnut hair was cut in shaggy, uneven layers that looked more unkempt than deliberate. She was a mess, in short. Samantha couldn't believe she actually did business and presented herself in such a manner. She didn't know how the woman kept getting jobs.

She pulled out her records and exchanged a few short words with the dreadlock DJ who was finishing out his set. Then, with the easy blended rhythm of a perfectly smooth transition, PJ took up the stage and started playing her own mixes.

She was good, Samantha thought grudgingly. She'd heard her mix before. PJ was usually in the same club that Sticky bounced for because they were such good friends. And Samantha usually went to the clubs that Sticky bounced for because he'd sneak her in as long as she didn't drink. Which she wouldn't do anyway…too many calories, not to mention she wasn't about to risk a DUI and her scholarship.

PJ's eyes were low-lidded, and she had her headphones half on and half off her head. She scanned the crowd even as she mixed the music. It was funky, just this side of sexy. It sounded new, too. The wanna-be hip crowd ate it up.

Samantha was about to make a pithy comment about the whole scene—the best way to blend into a hip crowd is to pretend you're way too hip for it—when she noticed that Jonathan had effectively forgotten that she was sitting next to him. He was staring at PJ with rapt attention, his own eyes half-closed, as if he was taking in the scene and trying to absorb the music through his skin.

Whatever Samantha was about to say stalled in her throat. She took a sip of her ginger ale to try to wash it away, give herself time to regroup.

"She's good, isn't she?" She decided it was best to pay some attention to his interests. High-School Boyfriend Hunting 101…more about him than about you, she always said.

Jonathan was only half listening. "Hmm," he agreed. At least, she thought he agreed.

"She's got a weird story behind her," Samantha said, deciding to show that she was plugged in to the scene, at least. "She—"

Jonathan held up a hand. "I'm sorry. I really need to hear this."

Samantha felt awkward…painfully so. She stayed silent until one song bled into the next, and then another circled through it.

He finally turned back to her, looking almost dazed. "I'm sorry. I just…she's brilliant, isn't she? Just fucking awesome."

Samantha blinked. "Yeah," she said tentatively. She thought she was good, but apparently he was taking it a few steps further.

"She could be playing big rooms. European tours. She could rock Madrid, play the clubs in Amsterdam," he said. He was half muttering to himself and he certainly wasn't focused on Samantha. She got the feeling he'd be talking to the people at the next table if she weren't sitting there. "She just needs to be managed properly."

And that was where he came in, Samantha thought. And looked at PJ, who probably had no idea just how lucky she was to get his attention. For the moment, PJ was the only woman on Jonathan's radar.

That same sick, sliding resignation. Samantha couldn't spin and had no interest in it even if she could learn how to. And even if she somehow did get enough interest to learn, she wasn't going to be brilliant. Not like PJ…and now, unless it involved PJ somehow, there was no way she was going to get his attention.

Suddenly, a flash of insight hit her.

"Would you excuse me?" Samantha got up, and Jonathan only halfheartedly paid attention, still mesmerized by the music. "I know you've got business to attend to. I'm sure I'll see you around."

"Sure," he said with a wave. "Nice seeing you again."

Samantha walked outside, whipping out her cell phone, and called Sticky. It was the only way.

Grotto is new, and I'm playing ambient to please the audience. Populated with avant-garde hipsters, too rich and too old to be club kids, they're looking for music that's on the bleeding edge of new. White-label records that barely have the song title written on in Sharpie, stuff that maybe has a thousand pressings if they're lucky. Or MP3s lifted from obscure music Web sites, mixed by DJs from Moscow or Africa or whatever. They're listening to say they were the first to hear the mix. It's not necessarily my favorite route. Personally, I like to work a crowd. I've seen DJs playing the very, very new as people walked off the dance floor in disgust…and at hip-hop places, you ought to know better, frankly. If you don't play hits they know, they'll leave you practically before you drop the needle to vinyl. My favorite experience was watching an older guy play "Erotic City" by P-funk, and watching a crowd of teen-pluses go out of their minds. That's what I like to do.

This crowd wouldn't go out of their minds if you put LSD in their tap water. It takes a lot of effort to be that cruelly bored by the insignificance of it all. Whatever blows their hair back, is generally my philosophy.

The problem is, my underwear conference with Jonathan is acid-etched on my memory. I am going to impress Mr. MotherClub NYC DJ, or die trying.

I've been dipping into my stores, playing stuff that I know is solid, even if it's wasted here. Very minimum scratching and some complicated transitions…stuff that an amateur would fuck up if they tried to beat match. Beat matching means slowing down something or speeding up something to match your next song. Done improperly, it sounds jarring…as bad as a needle drop that scratches unintentionally. I'm sweating a little. But the songs stand up, and the whole thing blends. I'm mixing my ass off.

I work like that for two hours, a full set. DJ Angelo comes up on the decks about twenty minutes before he's supposed to, and he watches me, quietly and without interrupting. I barely notice him until he's tapping my shoulder, holding up a record. He's tagging in. He's got a dolly full of his stuff…his headphones and three large silver-toned locked boxes full of records. He's got one out of its sleeve now, and he gestures to the turntable.

I feel as if I've just gone running around the block. With my full duffel bag, no less. I nod in acknowledgment and pull my record off.

He looks at it, then looks at my laptop. "Is that a Final Scratch record?"

I nod again.

"That is so cool." He sounds reverent.

I smile a little. I get that reaction every time from other DJs. And, honestly, it is cool.

I pack up my stuff, and Angelo and I trade demos. He also hands me his card, so he can ask about Final Scratch, see if maybe he can digitize some of his vinyl. I get a lot of requests like this also. I've done it for a few people, but it's time-consuming. I figure if it gets bad, I'll be able to trade digitizing music for couch time. Always planning, as Sticky would say. Although he's usually kidding when he says it.

I finally walk off the decks. Jonathan is sitting up front. I've been trying not to look at him all night. He's dressed up. He looks very New York club scene...not ostentatious or anything. Just sophisticated. You can tell the difference.

I feel my stomach start to flip-flop, and I tell it to knock the hell off.

Before I can get over to his table, I hear squealing, and I'm instantly assaulted.

"PJ!"

The Strippas have arrived in a burst of color and skin. Liza's wearing a baby-doll-pink angora sweater that shows off her midriff and a pair of white Daisy Dukes, her blond hair in two minuscule curly pigtails. She looks like a porn Cindy Brady. Candy's got on her black bustier top and a pair of black spandex hot pants that look very Olivia Newton-John from *Grease*. Meghan's wearing a vampy red dress...an off-the-rack version of what Sticky's friend Samantha usually wears.

The crowd, I notice, looks scandalized at the latest addition to their trendy scene. However, I also notice that most of the men look intrigued.

"Did we miss your set?" Liza asks, a little breathless, as if she'd just run inside the restaurant looking for me. Of course, she usually sounds a little breathy.

"Yup." I shrug.

They are the picture of group disappointment.

"Well," Liza says, and she tugs at her sweater. "That sucks. I shouldn't have even bothered to dress up." She looks around, rolls her eyes. "And you know the only reason I'd show up someplace like *here* would be to see you, sweetie."

I love Liza sometimes. Even if she pinches my cheeks.

I finally get away from them—they have to go to work— and I feel a little bolstered for my meeting with Jonathan. It doesn't hurt to have your own fan club, show that you're recognized.

My palms are sweating a little. I wipe them on the strap of my bag.

"Hi," I say, then wince. Jesus. I sound like Liza.

"Hi back at you," he says, gesturing to the seat across from him.

I sit down, putting my bag carefully under the table. My laptop and my two Final Scratch records cost over five grand. I'm not about to lose them to a grabby hipster in a cheap suit.

He's drinking something, dark golden in color in a square glass…very manly, expensive and on the rocks. He studies me. He has that tendency.

If he's impressed, he's certainly not letting on.

Finally, I can't stand it. "So. What'd you think of the set?" I ask with forced casualness. As if what he said meant absolutely nothing to me.

"Hmm." He takes a sip of his drink.

Hmm?

What the hell?

I'd already broken the ice, made the first move. Damned if I was going to play it needy and ask him *could you please clarify your monosyllabic grunt?*

I waited. I wished I had a glass of something, even water. It's a good prop, gives you something to do.

"Not bad," he says finally, as if he's been hunting for something nice to say and this is the best he can come up with.

I'm about to tell him exactly what he can do with his offer to manage me, but of course, that's assuming that said offer is still on the table…which, with a ringing endorsement like "not bad," is probably not even an issue. I flirt with the idea of punching him or pouring his drink over his head. Cliché? Sure. But probably satisfying.

Then I see something…it's like reading the crowd when you're up on a high platform, when you can't hear what anyone's chanting but you can see it in their eyes, in their motions, in the way they sway and smile and grind.

"Not bad," my ass. You liked it. You really, really liked it.

I lean back, feeling relief flood through me. I shrug, cool as a Frigidaire. "I could've been better," I say. "This isn't really where I feel most at home, but for ambient, it's not bad. I'm still working on some stuff."

He looks at me. "Don't milk it."

I grin, and he grins back at me. We both know what's up here.

"I want to represent you," he says, and I feel it…a rush of adrenaline, like I'd just downed about twenty Twinkies. "I think that, properly managed, you could be the biggest DJ period. You'd make Paul Oakenfold look like a wedding DJ."

The grin I'm wearing spreads. I feel like the Joker. "No shit?"

"No shit." He looks somber, though. I don't know that I've ever met a DJ as damn serious as this man. "But I need you to think really, really carefully about whether you want to go through with this or not."

Well, yeah, there was that. "What, do I need to sign in blood or something?"

He doesn't even crack a smile. He's got that serious-as-an-IRS-audit look about him, so I feel some of my buzz at his compliments wear off, and I buckle down. "This isn't going to be fun," he says. "Remember before, when I told you people called me pushy? Think driven."

I nod.

"You're going to have to be, too. I'm not going to take you on if I think you're going to be half-assed about the whole thing."

Offended, I feel my back straighten, my fists clench a little.

"I work damn hard," I say. "You don't honestly think what I just did was easy."

"This isn't about your DJ skills," he says with a dismissive wave of his hand. He almost knocks into his square glass. I motion to a waitress. I'm going to need a drink if this keeps up. "I need you to get focused on what happens when you're *not* on the decks. Haven't you ever heard of promotion?"

"I network," I say, even though the word *network,* used as a verb, makes me feel like taking a bath in Lysol to get rid of the ick factor. "I told you, I work a couple of nights a week…three to four, as a general rule. I wouldn't do that if people didn't know who the hell I was."

"You're getting paid peanuts. Under the table," he counters. "You're the blue-label DJ. You want to position yourself as a premium. And that means getting your name out there as something other than the cheap, homeless work-for-hire."

Now I'm bristling. "I see."

"And you're going to have to be a whole helluva a lot less touchy," he adds with a gentleness that hides what he's saying.

He's right on that count, I suppose, but it's hard not to feel offended when you're told you're the blue-light special of the music world. "What, exactly, am I going to have to do?"

"Whatever I tell you to, basically."

Now I'm more than bristling. I'm looking at him as if he's insane.

"Not like that," he says. "But I know what I'm doing. You're going to have to trust me."

That doesn't sound much better, honestly.

"I know about promotion. I know people. I can get the right people to hear you, to see you, to meet you. They'll want to know more about you, and once they hear you spin, they're going to want to sign you," he says, and the confidence in his voice is mesmerizing. "But I can't get them to do any of that until we build up more of a name for you here in the Bay Area. And we can't do that until we line you up some more publicity, some more promotion and some more high-profile gigs."

"Okay. I'm with you so far," I say, although my voice is a little hesitant.

He stares at me. "Really?"

"I'm not stupid," I say, although I feel a little weary at the conversation. "I know what you're saying."

"I want you to sleep on it," he says. "Think about if this is what you really want. And if it is…I want you to call me."

His eyes are a light blue-gray, almost eerie looking. He looks as if he could actually stab me with his gaze. He's got some intensity issues, I'm thinking.

"The minute you call me," he pronounces, "we'll get started."

"All right," I say.

He holds out a hand for me to shake. I reach over and shake it.

It feels very final. Just this side of binding.

I'm still holding his hand—he's got big hands, or I'm just on the small side—when I hear Sticky's booming laugh. I look over, and he's walking toward us…and Samantha is on his arm.

Sticky has a really bad habit of falling head over heels for beautiful, cruel women. I feel like his aunt most of the time, always wondering when he'll meet a "nice girl." He keeps asking me to point one out.

"We meet again," Samantha says to Jonathan, immediately releasing Sticky's arm. Sticky looks disappointed, then resigned, as the two of them sit down, she to Jonathan's left, Sticky to his right.

Jonathan nods. "I take it you know PJ."

"Sure," she says, then looks at me. "Of course," she blurts, and she shoots me a smile…the one she usually reserves for people who matter. "Great set."

Samantha has just acknowledged me, I think. Said "great set."

Man. I'm important enough to get a kiss-up remark in front of a honcho like Jonathan. Although, I suspect, it was more to impress him than compliment me.

"Are you two friends?" he asks.

Jonathan looks mildly curious, especially when he compares the two of us visually. She's wearing something slinky and expensive, her long black hair doesn't have any of those flyaway wispy things, and she's wearing enough makeup to lacquer a table. I'm wearing my usual…black pants and a sweater and a long-sleeved shirt that says "Grab a straw…'cuz you SUCK." My hair is finger-combed from my shower this morning. I'm wearing Chap Stick.

To add to my surprise, she nods at his question.

We are? I mean, she's a tangential part of my social circle, but we're hardly party pals.

"We've known each other for a while," she assures him.

He looks at me for confirmation, something I find hysterical, especially when she frowns at his reaction. "Yeah," I finally agree. I'm unable to resist. "We're tight."

I hear Sticky snicker. She frowns more.

"In fact," Sticky chimes in, "Samantha…PJ needs a couch for tonight. Didn't you say that you wanted to hook her up?"

I try to discreetly motion to him that a slumber party at Stickbug Samantha's is *not* what I need tonight. I was thinking comfy couch somewhere, even the Strippas if they were available. I can't imagine Samantha offering to put me up. Considering she's on Jonathan like dryer lint, however, I think Sticky's looking for a little payback. He gets that way, sometimes.

But she's nodding, all smiles. "Sure. Whenever you're ready, PJ."

I blink at her.

"Just remember to think about what I said," Jonathan adds.

I have officially entered the twilight zone.

chapter 4

Samantha wasn't pleased. She shifted gears hard, causing her ancient Honda Accord to squeal in protest. PJ was in the passenger seat, looking dazed, clutching her blue duffel bag like it was a baby. Samantha was going to have to put her up on her couch, deal with making sure she felt at home. Samantha didn't like anybody else in her place. She rarely had overnight guests anyway, but she generally saw her apartment as her sanctum. There were clothes strewn around her living room, and her desk was out there, with her accounting and statistics and marketing books. She didn't want this little person sneaking peeks through her shit, basically. Or eating her food.

Not that PJ would probably have a burning desire for canned tuna in water or barley and celery, the main contents of Samantha's fridge. But it was the principle of the thing. She didn't like her privacy invaded.

Still, there was a bigger picture here.

"So…" Samantha said slowly. "How long have you known Jonathan, anyway?"

And this was why she was putting up with all of this. PJ was, from the looks of it, one of the most important people in

Jonathan's life. So PJ would have to know something about Jonathan. Any weaknesses. What he was like. *Who* he might like. Things of that nature.

Samantha was nothing if not persistent.

PJ shrugged. "Not long."

And then fell silent.

Samantha's grip on the steering wheel tightened. "And he's going to be your manager, huh?"

"Apparently."

Samantha remembered why she didn't like Sticky's friend. Sticky himself was a doll—unfailingly sweet, and while he flirted outrageously, he never ever put the moves on her (unlike other grabby club people that she knew). But whenever PJ was around, Samantha got the distinct idea that PJ was sizing her up, and finding her wanting.

"Don't talk much, do you?" Samantha finally said, with a little bite in her voice.

"Guess not."

Now, that was just bitchy. Samantha gritted her teeth. "You know, I met Jonathan at one of the client parties for my modeling agency," she said in a conversational tone. "They say he was one of the biggest DJs in New York. He knows all the fashion designers there. He even performs at their shows."

"Really?"

Samantha didn't know if PJ sounded surprised because she was trying to be ironic, or because she really didn't know about the fashion thing. She kind of doubted PJ followed the fashion world at all, not if her clothes were any indication.

"If he's taken an interest in you, you must be really good." Samantha let her doubts shade the statement, and was pleased when she caught a glimpse of PJ's scowl.

"Well, I imagine he's got really good connections, and if he's as good as everybody says…" PJ let the statement trail off.

"I'll bet he's that good," Samantha said, remembering him sitting there, tall, lanky, completely indifferent to everything but the music. "I'll bet he's better."

"If you've taken an interest in him," PJ said, and now the

sarcasm was more than apparent, "then he must be extraordinary."

"Are you really going to sit there and tell me that you're going to have a man manage your career that you know absolutely nothing about?" Samantha said with exasperation.

PJ was silent for a minute. Then she said, "Of course I didn't. I did a ton of research, e-mailed everybody I knew that knows that scene."

Now she was getting somewhere, Samantha thought smugly. "And what did they say?"

PJ was now silent for more than a minute.

"Well?" Samantha prompted.

PJ turned to her, her eyes low-lidded, even if her gaze was fiery. "What, exactly, makes you think that I owe you an explanation for what I do and don't do?"

Samantha felt her blood boil. "Considering I'm giving you a place to sleep tonight, the least you could do is be polite!"

"I was being polite," PJ said, and her voice was low and dangerously soft. Not drama, like a Clint Eastwood thing. Just very clearly pissed. "At least, I was until the grilling because you want to find out more about the guy you'd like to bone. So spare me, okay?"

Samantha couldn't even form words. She spluttered instead, sounding like an idiot.

"And if this is the price for putting me up for one night," PJ added, "then you can fucking drop me off anywhere. I don't need this kind of shit."

For a split second, Samantha actually thought about it. They were close to her apartment, in Berkeley…

She could drop PJ off anywhere, there were plenty of places still open. It was only…

Well, maybe not plenty of places, she amended, looking at the darkened storefronts, already haunted by homeless people in their sleeping bags, crowded into doorways. At midnight, there wasn't a whole lot open. But she had a cell phone, didn't she? And she had plenty of friends. Friends that didn't have class in the morning or an audition in the afternoon.

PJ crossed her arms. "Just let me out."

Sticky would be pissed, Samantha thought, and felt guilt seep into her. "Never mind," she said. She didn't want Sticky mad at her. After all, he might think Samantha was hot, but he saw PJ as some sort of pet. Samantha wasn't about to abandon his pet to the Berkeley streets. She might never get into a club again. Sticky had that kind of pull in San Francisco. "You can stay on my couch tonight. But I've got an early class in the morning, and I don't want you letting yourself out."

"Forget it," PJ said in that same pissed tone of voice. "I'll figure something out."

"Don't be stubborn," Samantha snapped, impatient.

"You can let me off anywhere." PJ's arms were crossed. "By the BART."

"It's too late for the BART to run now. It's after midnight." Samantha answered. She sighed. "Fine. I'm sorry I pried, okay?"

"Whatever."

"I mean it. I shouldn't have asked you about Jonathan." Samantha felt humiliation roiling through her now. That it would have to come to this. "I just…I'm interested in him."

"Yeah, well, I'm not. Not that way," PJ said, her words clipped and sharp. "He's going to be my damn manager. Possibly. I still have to think about it. And if this is the kind of attention I'm going to get working with him, it might not be worth it."

Samantha gaped at her. "Are you kidding? He's going to skyrocket your career!" Surely the woman wasn't stupid enough to turn her back on an opportunity like this, just because she was working with someone famous?

"I can do fine on my own."

She might, Samantha thought. She might just be that stubborn.

Of course, if PJ signed on with Jonathan, and Samantha could somehow work that to her favor…

"Well, you do whatever you feel like doing," Samantha said, her voice supremely indifferent. "I'm sure you're right. I mean, it's not like he even knows this scene, right?"

"There's that," PJ said, but to Samantha's satisfaction, she sounded less sure of herself.

"Besides, he'll probably find someone else that he likes even better."

She pulled into her driveway, glad for once that PJ wasn't responding to her statements. "I've got a Hide-A-Bed," she said, knowing it was horribly uncomfortable. "And my class is at eight. Is that okay?"

PJ made a noncommittal noise. She was thinking....

From the way she was frowning, that much was obvious.

Samantha let her into her apartment, noticing just what kind of a state it was in. She really ought to put those clothes away—they were dry-clean only, and they were gathering dust on the hardwood floor. The whole thing was about as big as a linen closet. "This is you," she said to PJ.

PJ sat down on the Hide-A-Bed couch and winced. Probably felt the bar. It was pretty old, a hand-me-down from her grandparents. She barely sat on it at all, herself.

"Thank you very much," PJ said, and her voice held no trace of sarcasm. She really did sound polite.

"No problem. I'll go get you some bedding." She had some threadbare quilts around. It took a minute to dig them out...she used about a ton of blankets, including one electric blanket and a down comforter. The Bay Area just kept getting colder, it seemed. She was finding it harder and harder to get warm.

PJ was still sitting in the same place when Samantha dumped two blankets and a quilt, and one very thin pillow, on the couch next to her. "I'm going to bed now," Samantha said.

PJ nodded. "Good night."

Samantha wondered why PJ looked so distraught. She couldn't really be considering whether or not she should sign with Jonathan. He was handsome, he was rich, he knew all the right people. He even made models envious, a ridiculously tricky pursuit.

She didn't understand people like PJ, she thought as she climbed into bed. But then, she didn't really know people like PJ, and hoped that she didn't have to. She'd already met Jonathan twice. Now she'd really wage a campaign to get his attention.

★ ★ ★

Leslie sat at her desk in the outer office of the *Bay Area Citizen,* one of the city's oldest newsweeklies. And, she thought as she looked at her surroundings, one of the grungiest. Started in the sixties, during the whole "free love" hippie culture, it still had pretensions of being hot, hip and happening. Their club section was the bulk of the paper—if you didn't count the personals, which frankly, Leslie didn't, even though that was her job. Probably *because* it was her job.

She'd gotten a job here on a whim, after the dot-com that she'd been a project manager on imploded with a whimper. Unemployed, and unfortunately living at home, she'd snagged this job out of the want ads. She'd actually been hired as a secretary, but the personals editor had quit shortly thereafter, and nobody else had wanted the job. Nature abhorred a vacuum, and Leslie abhorred living at home, so she moved naturally into the vacant position and into her quaint, doll-size apartment by the Haight. Sure, a large part of her neighborhood looked like a crack convention, but they were slowly and surely renovating, and the nicer it was, the higher the rents would be. Besides, her stuff was nice, and her locks were numerous. She was managing.

But today was different. She fidgeted in her chair, looking over the personals that had come in via e-mail request. She had left a voice mail for Sydney, the head of features. She was asking to be transferred…promoted, basically, to features writer.

She couldn't remember being this nervous at any of her other jobs. But then, she hadn't had a marriage offer hinging on employment before, either.

Her eyes skimmed the male-seeking-female requests.

SWM, 48, seeks female, aged 18 to 32, for friendship, companionship and anything else that comes our way. Open-minded women preferred…

She smirked. Translation: Do you have hot friends? That maybe you're attracted to? And would you mind if I videotaped you?

She glanced through the rest.

SWM, 30, looking for someone for private adventures. I won't tell your boyfriend if you don't tell my girlfriend.

SWM, 22, looking to be someone's slave…

DHM, 52, good-looking, hot lover, wants someone to she-bang…

SBM, 88. Looking for someone who's patient and who lives in a one-story house.

There were reams of this stuff, she thought. She had to make it over the wall into actual journalism. She was getting too old to start a whole new career.

"Leslie? Leslie Anderson?"

She blinked. It was Sydney, the features editor. He had a gruff voice, but not a very loud one. She wondered how long he'd been yelling.

"I swear to God, is there a Leslie Anderson here?"

"I'm here!" She bounced up like a jack-in-the-box.

He scowled at her. "Did you want to come to my office, or should I just continue shouting…"

She got up before he finished his diatribe, beelining for his office and letting him shut the door behind her. "…for the entertainment and amusement of everyone in the outer office?" he finished, between the two of them.

"Sorry about that," she muttered.

"I hate yelling," he grumped. "Don't make me do that again."

"Noted." Not an auspicious start, but hey, at least she never made the same mistake twice. Then she thought of her last seven jobs and past two boyfriends.

Well, not the exact same mistakes, anyway.

"So. You've been with us, what, two months?"

She frowned. "A year and a half."

"No kidding." Leslie would have thought it was a bad joke if he hadn't sounded so surprised. "You're the personals editor, huh? And now you want to work on my team full-time."

"That's right," she said, trying to gauge him. "Everybody knows that the *Citizen*'s features section is—"

"What have you written lately?"

"Uh, a few small things." When she was a secretary, she'd tried to break in that way, writing stuff on spec, for free. It hadn't really gone anywhere. "Mostly music listings, a couple of book reviews." She saw him make a face. "And I tried a restaurant piece when the regular guy got hit with food poisoning."

"Ah, yes. The Thai place," Sydney said with a malicious grin. "I think he got that joint shut down. Good investigative piece."

"Um, yeah. So I e-mailed you a couple of story ideas..."

"I deleted the e-mail," Sydney said dismissively. "I hate getting pitched by e-mail. What were they?"

This was going to be stressful, Leslie thought. She growled low in her throat, then shut her eyes and tried some deep breathing. When she opened her eyes, he was still looking at her, only this time with a smirk on his face. "I wanted to do a piece on that graphic artist from San Francisco who does floral murals on bridges, or the old couple that runs that immense cat shelter."

At least she got rid of his smirk. "You're kidding me, right?"

"I take it you don't like the ideas."

"Oh no, they'd work...if we were the *Bumfuck Gazette*." He rolled his eyes. "Cat shelters. You've got to be fucking kidding me."

Leslie flinched, both at the comment and the tone.

"I don't know if you realize this—" and his small voice started to crescendo as much as his lung capacity would allow it "—but we're the third alternative newsweekly in San Francisco now. We have maybe a fifteenth of the circulation that papers like the *SF Weekly* get, for Christ's sake. Advertisers seem to think we're just turning into one big joke. I'm doing everything I can to prove to them that we're not. And how do we do that?"

"By writing stories people want to read," she said. "I'm not a complete idiot."

He scowled back at her. "If you're not a complete idiot, then could you please explain to me how a story on an *old couple that shelters cats* is of any interest to a twentysomething raver that lives in the city? Or maybe a thirty-year-old woman shopping for BCBG over in Union Square? Could you please tell me how that makes you anything *other* than a complete idiot?"

Leslie should have kept her mouth shut, listened to his advice. Not brought up the old-couple story, obviously.

Today was not her day, she thought. And as the T-shirt said, tomorrow wasn't looking good either.

"I was looking for more of a local-story feel," she said, trying to retrench, to reposition herself. "I can submit more contemporary stories…"

"More contemporary. Oh, that's a good one," he said, raising a bushy eyebrow. "Come on, Leslie. For Christ's sake, I need something that's going to sell papers. Unless somebody sinks a sub off the Golden Gate Bridge, I need to come up with something *juicy*."

"Maybe if you defined 'juicy,' pal."

Leslie gasped. Ordinarily, those kinds of quips stayed safely in her head. Apparently, the internal censor was sleeping in this morning.

His eyes widened, and to her relief, he laughed. "Well, at least you've got some feistiness. That'll help." He leaned back thoughtfully, looking for all the world like a shorter version of Mr. Jamison from that paper Spider-Man worked for. "Juicy. As in sexy. Something with a bit of scandal, something racy. Drug use. Adultery. Famous people…or beautiful people. Lots of money. Things that happen at midnight. Things that don't happen to normal people. Things that boring people are terrified of." He raised an eyebrow at her. "Get it?"

She nodded. "So. You want me to do a piece on the hookers in the Mission District or something?"

She'd meant it to be a joke, the kind of witty remark that dry, urbane people tossed off left and right at cocktail parties. Until she realized that Mr. Jamison might take her up on it. Might even press for the investigative-reporter angle. Ask her to go undercover, say.

She felt herself start to sweat.

"No, no, no," he said, waving his hand impatiently, and she felt a cool tickle of relief. "Haven't you even *read* the paper lately? We opened with the strip clubs last month, we've done a piece on the massage parlors, the hundred-dollar-tip places. Hmm. Maybe transsexuals," he mused.

"So, juicy, but not hookers," she quickly clarified.

He looked a little disappointed, but nodded. "Something original. We might want to try something that might appeal to the rich. Something freaky, funky. Something *urban,* with a hint of an edge."

Blah, blah, bullshit, bullshit. Leslie had heard the words so often, from the reporters and from Sydney, that she wondered if he even knew what he was talking about when he bandied them around. Urban? They were in a city. What was she going to do, crack the story of the city's previously undiscovered cult of butter churners?

"You listening to me?"

She didn't miss a beat. "Every word."

"So that's why I don't think you can be on my team, kid."

Now she did a double take, startled. "Huh?"

"Every word, huh?" He grinned unpleasantly. "If you could give me something like I've just described, maybe we could talk. Maybe something more on the night beat. Or give me a char-acter...someone special. Somebody I'd want to read about."

Leslie's mind shuffled through possible story ideas that she had, categorically rejecting most of them. "The aftermath of dot-com..." She saw his frown. "Er...the cult of Xbox play-ers?..."

His scowl deepened.

"No," she corrected herself. "How about former ravers hav-ing babies?"

"Ice-cold," he said, and started to head for the door.

"I got it!" And she prayed that she did. "How about a story about a homeless DJ?"

His hand paused on the doorknob. "Huh?"

"I know this woman," Leslie said, her words tumbling out like clothes from a dryer. "She's homeless...she spends every night on somebody else's couch. She just has a blue duffel bag, with her records and her laptop and that's it. And she DJs at some of the hottest clubs in the city."

His face was completely impassive. Leslie wondered if she should make up something… *How about a story about a woman desperately trying to get a promotion just so she can frickin' get married?*

Who'd believe it?

"Homeless DJ," he said, and released the doorknob, walking back and sitting down behind his desk.

"That's right," she said.

"Why don't you tell me some more?"

"Um…"

That's when it occurred to her. She didn't know much more.

"I'd have to go deep undercover," she said, wincing at how cliché the phrase sounded. "Really get to be a part of her world, get under her skin."

"Right," he said, sounding enthused. "Fine. How long is it going to take you?"

She had no idea. "A month?"

He frowned, then shrugged. "Why not. You're not a real reporter anyway, it's not like I don't have stories in the pipeline," he said, and she grimaced. "You realize you're going to have to keep manning the personals desk, right?"

Grrr. "Of course."

She got up, shook his hand. "You won't regret this."

"No, but you might," Sydney said, holding her hand and forcing her to look into his eyes. "Because you realize if you fuck this up, it's the only chance you're getting at breaking into features here, right?"

She blinked. "Um…"

"So good luck." He winked at her, then sat back down. "I'll talk to you again when you're done."

Samantha walked into Technique, breathing deeply, something that she knew did wonders for the skimpy little dress she was wearing. It was just an outfit she'd pulled together at Bébé, nothing couture, but considering the crowd at Technique, it was just trashy enough to be considered stylish. It emphasized her strong suits: breasts and legs.

If it was obvious…well, that was the idea.

She saw Sticky's eyes bug out and knew that she had taken a step in the right direction. "Where is he?" she asked.

"Damn," Sticky breathed, ignoring her question. He gave her a hug, a lingering one, and she tolerated it. "You look hot."

"Jonathan?" she reminded him.

Sticky's eyebrow went up. "Ah. Hence the dress."

She wasn't going to feel guilty about this. "I want him," she said, shrugging.

"And apparently, you get what you want," Sticky said, and she wasn't sure if he was complimenting her or not. "Hell, you could get whatever you wanted from *me* in that dress." He wiggled his eyebrows. "I don't suppose…"

"Just tell me where he is, Sticky," she said, smiling to take the sting out of her impatient remark. She didn't want to waste time flirting here at the door when there was big game inside.

Sticky sighed. "If I must. Last time I saw him, he was in the VIP room, talking to some promoters. You might want to try there."

She pretty much had free access to Technique's VIP room, something that Sticky had set up, which the other models had largely envied. It was one of the reasons she gave him a kiss on the cheek. "Thanks," she whispered in his ear, enjoying the way his whole body tensed.

"New perfume?" he asked blandly.

She nodded. "Sensi."

"Works for you." He took a step back, and she could see he was breathing just a little bit harder. "Go on, I've got to watch the door."

As she started to turn and walk away, she heard him say, "Good luck."

She smiled. In this dress? Like she'd need it.

She wove her way through the crowd, heading up the stairs to the VIP room. She could vaguely see people through the darkened glass. In the VIP room, you could watch the crowd below—although odds were good the show going on in the

VIP room surpassed anything going on down on the main floor. She smiled at the door security, Tommy.

"Lookin' good," he said, never meeting her eyes once.

She took another deep breath and watched his eyes widen. "Thanks," she said with a sassy grin.

Having boobs might cost her a couple of runway jobs, she thought as she walked through the door, but they sure did help when it came to dealing with men.

She searched the crowd. It wasn't a big room, and it wasn't really packed, so she picked him out immediately. He stood at the bar, wearing a black suit with a midnight-blue shirt. He looked dark, serious. Handsome as hell.

He was talking to a few promoters. The promoters looked enthused, their gestures broad, their voices raised over the steady thrum of the beat pumping out of the speakers. Jonathan looked as composed as always...like a seasoned warrior or something. She grinned at the thought, waiting for the right moment.

It seemed to take forever, but finally the promoters moved on while Jonathan got a drink. She walked up, steeling herself.

"I'll buy that for you," she said in the husky voice she'd been working on for a week or so.

He turned, looked at her. "Samantha, right?"

"Right." She put a twenty down on the bar after the bartender set Jonathan's drink down. It looked like scotch, or something similar, just like what he'd been drinking at Grotto.

"Anything for you?" the bartender asked.

She paused. Besides Sticky's conditions of letting her into his club, she didn't really react well to alcohol and she'd driven here tonight. But if she ordered her usual—diet ginger ale—she was afraid she'd look childish in front of Jonathan. The last thing she wanted was to remind him that she was younger. A lot younger.

"I'll just have a Diet Coke," she said. The bartender nodded, got her her drink, even though Jonathan's expression turned amused.

"Take it easy on the hard stuff," he commented, taking a sip of his own drink.

"Do you know how many calories are in those things?" she said, already figuring out how to work it to her advantage. "I have too many, and I'll never fit in a dress like this again."

As she'd hoped, it made him look at her dress, and just exactly what kind of body filled it. He stared for a long moment.

"Well, I'd hate to have you do anything to ruin that," he finally said in a low, thoughtful voice.

Finally! She smiled, leaning against the bar just so, causing her legs to seem even longer and her chest to stick out. She noticed several other men sitting up and looking at her, but the only one she really needed to was standing next to her. "Do you like it? It's new."

"It's cute," he said.

And turned back to his drink.

She gritted her teeth. That was unprecedented. Normally, if she got a guy to look at her body, the offer for drinks–dinner–back to his place was a foregone conclusion. Still, he'd ignored her at Grotto…he had paid more attention to the music.

He needed more convincing.

"So, how are you enjoying San Francisco?" Small talk, while she figured out a new plan of attack.

"It's great," he said. "A real change of pace from New York. Mellower," he said. "Like moving from tribal to ambient."

"I've been to most of the clubs in the city," she said. "If you ever need somebody to show you around, I'm your girl."

If you ever need somebody to do anything for you, I'm your girl. Jesus, could she sound a little more obvious?

"I'll keep that in mind," he said.

What did a girl have to do? Strip naked?

"Listen," he said, before she could try something even more humiliating. "I appreciate your…help. You're very sweet…"

She couldn't help it. Sweet? *Sticky* was sweet! People that you blew off were sweet!

Like hell she was sweet. And no *way* was she getting blown off by Mr. Important Jonathan Hadeis!

"Let me just get straight to the point," she said. "There's just one thing I want from you."

His eyes widened.

She took a deep breath. "A job."

Now she paused, surprised at herself. She couldn't quite bring herself to say "fuck me till morning," as she'd originally planned...but this was completely unexpected.

"A...job." He sounded as surprised as she felt.

"I was talking to PJ," Samantha said slowly, trying to plan what she'd say next. And damn if it didn't rankle that she was bringing up PJ again! "She mentioned that you wanted her to change her image."

Now she had his rapt attention. "Yes. If I'm going to be presenting her to record executives, I need her to have the complete package."

"Well, you know I'm a model," she said, wondering if he'd give her body another once-over. He did, but it was more cursory than admiring, she thought, disgruntled. "I could help her. I know what looks good, what would work on her."

He looked intrigued. "All right. How much would I have to pay you?"

Considering she'd come up with this on the spur of the moment, she had no idea. "You're a man with a lot of connections," she said. "Maybe...how about you just owe me a favor? And if I need it, sometime, I could collect."

He laughed, and she was surprised. She had never seen him laugh before. She liked it.

"What, are you in the Model Mafia?"

She grinned, laughing a little with him. "Just a favor," she said, holding out her hand. "Deal?"

"All right," he said, and he shook her hand. His hand felt warm and firm in hers. She lingered, ever so slightly, until he pulled away. "So. How do you plan to start?"

Her smile never wavered, even as she thought:

Well, the first step will be to convince PJ that I'm not a bitch.

chapter 5

It's now a Friday night…and I'm not spinning. I'm at a club, sure, because I'm going to meet Jonathan. It seemed like neutral ground—and it's not as if I have an office, or anything. Besides, Sticky's going to hook me up with another couch. No way in hell am I staying at Samantha's again. For one thing, it's in Berkeley…not quite the pain in the ass San Mateo was, but still. And I thought that sofa bed was going to give me permanent spinal damage. Jeez.

Once Samantha figured out I didn't know all that much about Jonathan, she finally stopped pumping me for information and rather ungraciously left me to my own devices in her living room. I tried spinning for a while, but I was distracted by the whole scene. For one thing, she didn't have a single picture of her family or friends anywhere, that I could tell. That's not as unusual as you'd think, actually… I've been in a lot of houses that don't have any pictures of people. But the weird thing here was, she had tons of pictures. Of *her*. And I don't mean like Candy's picture at the Strippas…that was a memorabilia thing, a badge of honor, sort of like putting your diploma up when you graduate from college. Sure, Samantha had clippings, stuff from runway work she'd done. But she also had pictures that her photographer had done, pictures of herself from high school. Test sheets from the photographer, for God's sake, framed elaborately. It was like sleeping in a Samantha shrine.

Needless to say, I'm running on about two hours of sleep. Not all that unusual…but at around 6:00 a.m., I swear to God the woman was up and jogging in her room. She managed to open and slam shut every cabinet and drawer in her kitchen, and I woke to the unbelievably unpleasant aroma of cooking barley and celery. Ugh. I already have trouble facing food before noon, but this was enough to make me stick to a liquid diet for the rest of the day.

I glance at my watch. I told Jonathan to meet me at a small bar at the Karmic Club, which is pretty cheesy and easy to get into. Consequently, it's usually not packed, not even on a Friday, despite their best intentions. I figure it's the quietest place we could talk without being conspicuous.

"PJ?"

I look up, and there he is…Jonathan. I gesture to the seat next to me. I've had about six hours to get ready for this meeting, so I don't even crack a smile. I've got my game face on. I've got my game *everything* on.

"Thanks for meeting me," I say, dredging up some meeting protocol from back in the day, when I worked the eight-to-five.

"I take it you've thought about what we discussed," he says, jumping straight to the point.

"That's why I'm here," I agree.

He motions to a waitress, who hurries over, looking at him with longing. He's wearing a black suit with a black shirt…he looks like death, but in the sexy way, not the creepy way. The waitress has read the fact that he's rich, and she's hanging on his every word. He orders a G&T.

I order a diet soda. I've got too much to discuss tonight, and I'm not going to get sloppy when it comes to salient points.

His eyebrows go up when I order. Something imperceptible shifts in his attitude…like he suddenly realizes that I mean business.

"First of all, if you think that I'm not serious about being a success, you're wrong."

I bring that up because his suggestion rankles me, it has since he first made it, the very first time we met. Better to get that out of the way before it festers longer.

He shrugs. "We'll see."

Take a deep breath. "We're seeing that now. You're right. I need a good manager, somebody with connections, if I'm going to take my work to the next level. So I did some research on you. Internet research. Talked with some friends, people who have heard you. I even got some downloads off your CD."

He starts, looks disconcerted. "I don't have downloads on my Web site."

I look at him, wait for him to make the connection. When he doesn't, I finally say, "I didn't necessarily get them from *your* Web site."

"Somebody pirated my songs?"

I sigh. "Apparently."

He starts to whip out a PDA, one of those expensive Tungsten models, the kind that expands the screen out. Looks like a *Star Trek* communicator. "Who," he says, and he sounds raw. "Tell me the Web site."

"I don't have it on me. I'll look it up for you later. Hell, if you did a search, you could find it yourself." Although I doubt it. I found it on one of the more obscure music-swapping sites, ones that only digital DJs use—and at the moment, there are precious few of us. I don't want to necessarily narc on them. I put the call out, and somebody hooked me up, that's all.

I'm getting off topic. The waitress brings our drinks, is not disappointed by the tip Jonathan leaves her. I get the feeling that our service is going to be stellar for the rest of the night. "The bottom line is, I've decided to sign with you."

He still looks pissed. He also doesn't look surprised by this announcement at all. "And…?"

"And, what?"

"You didn't just ask me to meet with you to accept my offer

of management," he says with a touch of impatience. "What else did you want to talk about?"

I blink at him. "You don't have a whole lot of bedside manner, do you?"

"I don't coddle my clients," he says. "And I don't know if you're my client yet or not. I get the feeling you've got a condition or two, and that's why you called me tonight."

He's good. I'll give him that. "Was it my voice? That gave it away?"

"What are the conditions?"

I straighten my spine. "I'm not trying to be a diva," I say, forcing my voice to stay steady, "but I still feel like I know what's best for my career. And if you're going to be my manager, you've got to understand that I'm not going to do anything that I don't believe in."

His eyes glitter a little at this one. "That's sort of wide open," he says, and leans forward a little, like a poker player pushing his chips in. "Want to narrow that a little bit?"

"I'm not going to DJ for a strip club, for example," I answer, although I think about it. "Unless somebody I know works there."

He seems a little startled by this. "Uh...okay."

"And I'm not going to dye my hair and change my name and start playing Top 40 at under-eighteen clubs."

He scoffs at this one. "Do you honestly thing I'd make you? I'm trying to help your career, not retire you."

"I'm not going to sell out," I say, a little more impassioned as I work up to the subject. "I don't want to become some publicity-whore wanna-be that's only doing the work to see their name on a review. I'm serious about what I do. The music." I tap my finger on the cold tabletop, punctuating each word. "That's what I'm in this for. Not all the other stuff."

He narrows his eyes. "And this is your definition of being serious about success?"

I start to bristle.

"Maybe you should define what success is for me." His voice downshifts, as does his whole demeanor, and I'm thrown a little off balance. "I want to be sure we're on the same page here. What, exactly, do you think my management would get for you?"

I pause. I'd made a mental list of exactly this point, and I'd all but written it down earlier. I typed it out on my laptop, but didn't think I was going to need a crib sheet tonight. "Um…"

Embarrassment, or getting screwed over? I choose embarrassment. This is too important. I power up my laptop. "Sorry," I say, as it takes a few minutes to warm up. "I actually have a list of what I'm looking for."

I'm pleased that he looks both surprised and impressed when I pull up the Word document with my demands…such as they are. "May I see that?"

I show him the screen. He takes a second to skim through my list, nodding slightly, fixated. "You want to work four or five nights a week, and be well paid. Check. Work at the large clubs. All right. Get paid a couple hundred a night, at least. Work your way up to being a producer, in digital media." He lets out a low whistle at that. "And eventually do a world tour, working the big clubs in the big cities…L.A., Chicago, New York, Miami, then Amsterdam, Madrid, London and Paris."

He looks at me, nudging the laptop back at me. I take it back, relieved. My whole life is on this one slim computer.

"Is that all?"

I look at him, not sure I heard him right. "It's a start," I say carefully.

He smiles. "I can get this for you," he says, and from the tone of his voice, something resonates. I believe him. At least, I know he's completely confident in his assertion.

"But we need to get a few things clear," he adds, and I brace myself. "First of all…if you're going to do all these things, then people need to hear your work. People need to know you by sight, and know your name. You're going to have to raise your profile."

That sounds daunting, but I don't say anything.

"Do you know what I mean? By raise your profile?"

I shrug.

"That means that you can't keep wearing ratty old sweats and printed T-shirts," he says, and his voice isn't mean or dictatorial. It's logical, and just this side of warm…like he's concerned that I haven't noticed this.

I glance down. I'm dressed down, granted. And the doorman had given me a look, like he didn't want to let me in, but he knew he couldn't turn down the drink money. "What sort of clothes are we talking about?"

"It's a complete-package thing, PJ. But we'll get to that." He frowns. "You've got a lot of friends. You need to leverage that a little more."

"Leverage…my friends." Any way you put it, that sounds shitty.

He sighs, obviously not liking my spin on his statement. "Think about it. Doesn't Sticky do favors for you? He gets you into clubs when you obviously don't meet the dress code. People let you sleep on their couches, for God's sake…and we'll be getting into that in a minute, too."

I am definitely starting to feel uncomfortable.

"I'm not saying use your friends in a cold-blooded manner. I'm just saying, if you've got friends who are willing to help you out, like letting you stay at their houses or buy you drinks or whatever…why don't you let them help you with your career?"

I sigh. "If I knew anybody at the big clubs, I would."

"I'm not necessarily talking about that. What did I say you needed to make it big? More exposure. Promotion. Getting your name out. Being recognized."

I nod. I'm still not quite sure where he's going with this.

"I'm talking about *publicity,*" he finally spells out. "You need to leverage on that. Get some buzz going."

"I'm not—"

He reaches out and takes my hand. The gesture is so unexpected that I actually shut up.

"You're serious about being a success," he says, and he's pretty passionate about it himself, so I just nod. "You want this to work. You just need to trust me. I'll help you. We'll change your appearance—nothing you wouldn't approve of. We'll get your

name out. I know promoters, I know lots of influential people. Including record people."

I'm betting I have suddenly glazed over. *Record people.*
The idea of a "DJ PJ" white-label vinyl pressing…or maybe
even a CD. It's enough to give me chills. *Big time,* I think to
myself.

"But we've got to build you up, justify my calling them," he
says when I touch back to earth from my wild daydreaming.
"So you've got to trust me. Okay?"

I nod. "All right."

"So the first thing is publicity. We're going to leverage off
of a friend of yours, and get your name out to thousands in
the city."

"All right," I say. His enthusiasm is contagious. "What's the
first step?"

"Hi, PJ."

I look up. It's Leslie. Of Rick-and-Leslie. Of the pissed-off-
at-lending-me-a-couch Leslie.

Reporter Leslie.

"Leslie," Jonathan says, shaking her hand. "I'm glad you could
make it."

Oh, no. I glance at her, staring at me, and Jonathan, who's
grinning.

Oh, *hell* no.

"This isn't starting out as well as I'd hoped," Leslie said to
Jonathan, her voice concerned.

She wasn't reassured when he shrugged. "She's stubborn.
She's *beyond* stubborn," he said, swirling his drink around in its
squat, square glass.

The "she" in question was currently in the ladies' room. And
since Leslie had walked into the shabby little bar, "she"—PJ—
had been shooting poisonous glares at Leslie for most of the
evening.

"This is going to be helpful to her career, though," Leslie argued. "I don't see why—"

"She's still scared," Jonathan answered. "She's got tremendous talent, and once I can get her past her own insecurities, we'll finally have a stellar DJ. But not until I can get her to grow the hell up."

Leslie blinked. He was certainly being candid. Still…

He looked at her, and his lips, which had been drawn taut, curved into a smile. Leslie wasn't attracted, but she could see how someone else, who didn't have a rock-solid relationship, might be. "You're not going to put that in your article, I trust?"

"No, no. Of course not," she assured him. "I'm going to be focusing on PJ." She paused. "Although…why do you think she's this way?"

His eyes darkened, but he only shrugged again, feigning in-difference. "Any number of things. The important part is, she loves the music, and she'd do anything for it. Once we position the article as helping her career, which ultimately helps her music, she'll go along with it." He lifted his glass to Leslie. "I appreciate this, and I'm glad you looked me up."

"Not a problem." And with Sticky's help, it hadn't been. That man seemed to know everybody in the city.

PJ came back to the table, suspicion clear on her face. She could tell they'd been talking about her. She sat down next to Jonathan. "So what, exactly, do I need to do?"

Jonathan smiled. "Just answer some of Leslie's questions. Show her the ropes. Tell her about yourself. That's all." He looked at Leslie for corroboration. "Isn't that right?"

"Sure," Leslie said, although she wasn't sure. She hadn't writ-ten a features story like this before. She'd need to make sure it was hip, edgy, stuff like that.

"So I'm supposed to show Leslie the dark, gritty, 'other side' of DJ-ing, huh?"

Leslie sighed to herself. She doubted she was going to have trouble with the edgy portion of the program, at least. At this point, PJ seemed to be one big edge…a human razor.

Jonathan glanced at his watch. "Listen, I've got to go. I'm meeting some friends from New York later tonight, and I want to tell them all about you."

Leslie perked up. New York people. That could add something to the article. "Should PJ go with you?" *And, as reporter, naturally I should go along, just to get the story…*

He looked at PJ, and Leslie could swear he looked protective, which seemed a little weird, but what did she know?

"Not this time. We need to work on some things first."

PJ nodded, and she actually seemed relieved. "I've got enough to think about tonight," she agreed. "And besides…I'd rather work on my demo before I meet anybody important."

PJ obviously didn't lump Leslie into the "important" category. Leslie felt hard-pressed to blame her, but it still rankled.

"Okay. Listen, work on your demo. Are you working tomorrow?"

Jonathan was completely focused on PJ.

"Yes," PJ said. "I'm working the Naughty Schoolgirls night at X-scape."

Leslie goggled a little. That one would be a good one to cover. She'd just have to make sure that Rick was out with friends, not volunteering to go with her.

"Okay. Next Friday, you meet with a stylist, okay? Somebody to work on the overall packaging."

PJ made a face, and Leslie giggled.

"PJ," Jonathan said, warning and amusement in his voice.

"Yes, boss."

"I'm not your boss, I'm your manager. This is all about you, and you know it." He leaned over, and, well, if Leslie saw that right, he stroked PJ's shoulder, one of those comforting things. You usually saw gestures like that at family gatherings or funerals. It was sort of a "buck up" with a little more feeling in it. "You talk with Leslie here. And are you going to be okay for a couch tonight?"

PJ looked startled, then fumbled with her cell phone. "Sticky hasn't called yet," she said, and Leslie realized PJ sounded a little worried. Then she smiled. "But he will. He always comes through."

"You know my number?" He waited until PJ nodded in response, and he grew very serious. "Then you know if you ever, *ever* need a couch, you give me a call. Okay?"

Leslie saw a complex tumble of emotions cross PJ's face. She finally shrugged. "Yeah, okay."

Jonathan nudged PJ's face up, until it was staring into his. "I mean it. I don't want to worry about you."

Leslie wondered absently how many agents actually did this with their clients. Of course, that also begged the question of how many agents had homeless people for clients. She guessed this was new territory for everyone involved.

"All right, I'm out. Leslie...it was nice to meet you." He shook her hand. Then he looked at PJ, and ruffled his hand over her head, as if she were twelve instead of in her late twenties. At least, Leslie guessed PJ was in her twenties. "You...I'll call you tomorrow."

"Right."

PJ watched as Jonathan walked out of the room, Leslie noticed. "He's protective of you," Leslie said. "That's got to be great."

PJ didn't answer. She didn't even look back at Leslie until Jonathan had left the room. "I'm sorry. What?"

"Nothing." She wasn't sure what their relationship was, but she suddenly got the feeling that PJ wasn't, either, and probably wouldn't want to be cornered about it. "So. About this article..."

PJ sighed. "Listen, I know Jonathan thinks this whole article thing is a good idea. But Jonathan doesn't know the local club scene like I do. And frankly, while I value him as a manager, I don't think this is a good idea."

Leslie felt as if she'd been doused in ice water. "Why not?"

"Because...it's not me. It just feels so...so..." She made a vague motion with her hands.

"Tacky?" Leslie supplied, feeling a little offended.

"Whorish."

Leslie flinched. Make that *really* offended. "I'm offering to write an article on you," she said sharply. "I'm not suggesting a centerfold."

"It's not that." PJ waved away the comment. "It's just, oh, I don't know. It just seems like overkill. My whole appeal has been underground. I don't want to look like a sellout."

Leslie leaned back. "Did I mention that this is going to be in the *Bay Area Citizen?*" She shook her head. "They're as underground as they come. If they were any more underground, they'd be bankrupt. You get my point?"

"So how is that going to help my career?" PJ smiled, as if Leslie had just proven her point.

Leslie suppressed the desire to shake PJ until she saw sense. "You're sort of attention-phobic, aren't you? Isn't that a weird thing for a DJ? I thought you guys fed on the attention of the crowd."

Wrong answer. PJ's eyes shuttered closed, her expression flat in that smoothed-out, bland way that people who suppress their feelings get when they're really pissed off.

Leslie wasn't going to get her article this way. That much was obvious.

"Sorry. Forget I asked." She sighed. "Well, can you look at it this way? This could be a really big boost for me."

PJ's expression opened up, just a fraction. "What do you mean?"

Leslie thought about it. She could salvage her pride, or she could get her article. The article was going to have to win out. "Remember when I told you I was a reporter?"

PJ's eyes widened. "You're not a reporter?"

"Not exactly," she said, feeling a little humiliated at PJ's look of amused shock. "I mean, I work for the *Citizen*. But I've been trying to break into features writing, and a story about you, a homeless DJ, was just the thing that my editor—"

"What do you do there, again?"

Leslie frowned, thrown off track. "What?"

"Are you a secretary? Receptionist? What, do you clean up or something?"

Leslie gritted her teeth. "I actually work there. I'm something of an editor, myself," she said.

"So, wouldn't this be a step down? What are you editor of?"

Leslie had really, *really* hoped that it wouldn't get to this. "I'm editor of the personals," she muttered.

"The *personals?*" PJ whooped. "No shit?"

"Oh, shut up," Leslie said in a low voice, but PJ was too intent on her crowing to notice.

"So, if you wrote a story about me, you'd get out of the personals and into real stories."

Leslie nodded. Of course, there was the bonus of showing she had a successful career, or the start of one. And possibly getting married. Maybe having kids. Things that she'd wanted before she had turned thirty-five this year, and things she definitely wanted before she turned forty. But frankly, PJ had enough to laugh about right now, and Leslie wasn't about to pour gas on that fire.

PJ sighed. "Well. I can see where you're coming from," she said. "But…well. I don't know. I don't know that I'd be that interesting a subject, honestly. I mean, I'm not as interesting as you'd think. My life's an open book. My days are pretty routine. I mean, downright boring."

Leslie grimaced. Of all the DJs in the world, she had to get one with a sense of humility? Most DJs with any business savvy whatsoever would be jumping on her offer. She needed to come up with something else, some better angle to get PJ to agree to the story.

PJ's cell phone rang, and she held up an apologetic hand to Leslie as she answered it. "Hello? Sticky! I knew you would come through for me," she said. She turned slightly away from Leslie, into the corner of the booth they were sitting in. "What?"

Leslie watched with interest. She would definitely want to talk about Sticky's "couch-pimping" role in the article, she decided. That had to be stressful. Leslie didn't think she could do it…go through life not knowing where she was going to sleep that night, staying at some stranger's home. Trusting someone else to "hook her up." She didn't know if it was courage or stupidity, but whatever it was, Leslie didn't have enough of it in her system to want that kind of life.

PJ frowned as she covered her opposite ear so she could hear better. "Samantha? Ugh. I don't care, I'm not going to stay at her house again. I thought I was going to have a hunchback when I woke up," she said. "Nobody else? Not the Strippas? Maybe Cecil?" She made a humming sound. "Well, let me know if you hear back from anybody." Another pause. "No, I'm not so desperate that I'm going to shack out at the Weed Kids'. Thanks, as usual, for everything, Sticky. Talk to you later."

She hung up, then looked at Leslie.

"No luck, huh?"

"Not yet." PJ tried to sound confident, Leslie could tell, but there was a little waver of doubt in her voice.

Leslie got a flash of intuition. "You could stay at my place tonight if you want."

"Thanks, but I'll wait to see what Sticky comes up with," she replied, but she was polite, much as Leslie remembered from when PJ was at Rick's house. "San Mateo is a little out of the way."

"I don't live in San Mateo. That's Rick's place. I live in a little apartment over on the Haight." She shrugged. "It's tiny, but it's mine."

PJ's eyes looked speculative. "Right by the bus line?"

"MUNI, bus line, you name it." Leslie waited. "You mentioned you wanted to work on a demo, right?"

"Yeah. But what does—"

"I'll bet that'll take some time. Time you don't want to spend moving around, going from club to club," Leslie said as the idea began to form in her mind. "New look, new music, working with your manager. And it sounds like Sticky's run a little ragged, as well."

PJ looked guilty. Leslie actually felt a little guilty because she was manipulating PJ into feeling guilty. But there was a point here.

"You could stay at my place for a few weeks," Leslie offered. "Be settled, give Sticky a breather, take the time you needed to work on your demo. Have a sort of 'base camp,' if you get my meaning."

PJ nodded slowly, obviously considering the possibility. "What would you want from me?"

Leslie stared at her. "What do you think?"

PJ stayed quiet.

"It's just an article," Leslie said. "It can't hurt you. I promise."

Finally, PJ sighed. "I guess. But I won't answer any questions I don't feel comfortable with, okay?"

Leslie felt relief bathe over her. "Sure. Whatever."

"And…" PJ looked more than wary. She looked scared. "I don't know. Just don't crucify me, okay?"

Leslie felt…she wasn't sure how to describe it. Responsible, for lack of a better term.

"Don't worry," Leslie said with more confidence than she felt. "Everything will work out perfectly."

Now, if only she could be sure she was telling the truth. For both their sakes.

I'm at Leslie's house. It's a marked contrast from Rick's. It's in a worse neighborhood, for one thing. Nothing demilitarized (and I've spent a few nights in some real hellholes, so I'm not complaining). And what it lacks in location, it more than makes up for in interior decor. I feel as if I've stepped into a Pottery Barn ad.

Leslie comes out of the hallway with an armful of linens— mauve-colored comforter, two pillows with pink pillowcases, a twin set of pink-tinted ivory sheets. She dumps them unceremoniously on her purplish gray overstuffed couch. It's a visual Symphony in Girl.

"I hope you're comfortable," she says, and her tone of voice really does sound as if she's worried I might not be.

"This is great. Thanks."

"Did you want to unpack some of your things, get settled?" She gestures around, and before I can stop her, she's taking the decorative candles and chtotchkes off the coffee table, sweeping up magazines and little knickknacks with one arm. "I mean, you're going to be here for two weeks. No sense in you living out of your bag."

"Really, I don't want you to go to any trouble," I say, watching, aghast, as she dumps everything on her kitchen table. Already, I look as though I've invaded her living room, which is not supposed to be the point at all. I feel that I'm imposing, and I hate that. It doesn't help that I'm already a "one-of-these-things-is-not-like-the-others" skit in her frilly and feminine environment.

"So, are you tired? Should I let you get some sleep?"

I glance at my watch: 2:00 a.m. "I'll probably be up for a few hours," I say. "I've got a book light, though, and I'll keep my headphones low. If anything I do bothers you, just let me know." I get the feeling her walls are paper thin, which means I'll hold off on mixing some of my own tracks until I figure out just how sensitive she is to noise. This could really put a crimp in the whole demo-building portion of this plan, I suddenly realize.

"I have tons of bookcases in my room, I won't hear a thing," she says, although I get the feeling from the look on her face that she's simply being polite. "I'm pretty wired, too, actually. Do you mind if I ask you some questions? Just prelim stuff, nothing you'll have to concentrate too hard on."

She thinks I'm tired. For me, this is early evening. I probably won't be falling asleep until four or five, if I'm lucky, but I humor her. "Sure. Shoot."

"Why do you sleep on other people's couches?"

And this is her idea of a softball. I shake my head, sit on the couch and sink about two inches into the plushness of the cushions. "What you mean is, why would anyone choose to sleep on other people's couches, right?"

She looks a little embarrassed, and laughs. "Yeah."

"It's more common than you'd think, actually. Haven't you ever watched *Behind the Music?* Early days, starving artists…they're always crashing on other people's couches."

"Yeah, but how long have you been doing it?"

Ouch. "Two years."

"So…?"

I could've sworn reporters were supposed to be more diplomatic than this, but I've never really been interviewed, so what the hell do I know?

"I guess I haven't gotten to the 'wildly successful' portion of the program yet," I say. "But when I do, and I buy my pimped-out mansion with my bling-safes and whatnot, I'll have a roomful of couches and let any starving DJ I know crash for a few nights."

She laughs at this. I hope to God that Jonathan realizes how painful this whole thing is for me. I feel like such an asshole.

"So, you're basically homeless," she says.

"Not really. I have touchstones—a cell phone, e-mail, stuff like that. Truly homeless people don't. Refrigerator-box homeless people."

"Why don't you just get an apartment?"

Wouldn't she and, say, my mother love to know the answer to that one?

"I hit a certain point in my life where I just didn't want the hassle. Besides, this way, I get to meet a lot of different people, see what they're like. What their lives are like. You'd be amazed what I've learned about people just by looking at their living rooms."

"Really?" She's digging for a piece of paper and a pen. At some point, she's going to want to start taping me, and that will feel really weird. "So, tell me. You stayed on my boyfriend's couch. What did that tell you about him?"

Ugh. I want to stay on this woman's good side, and telling her that I felt as if I was sleeping in the Land of Perpetual Bachelor would do nothing to further that cause.

"He's very…"

…*childish immature commitment-phobic*

"…fun-loving."

She grins at me. "Don't tell me. The video games, right?"

"He's got a good job, he's got a big family that he loves very much but that also makes him a little nuts, he's a reformed club kid, and he's a terrible cook. He probably has his guy friends over every weekend."

She bursts into startled laughter. "How the hell did you get all of that?"

I close my eyes, picturing the place. "He's got a family picture with loads of people, and everybody else in the picture is smiling. He's frowning a little and looking off to one side. You can tell he used to be a club kid because of his CD collection. Besides that, he had about four boxes of empty Corona bottles in the living room, so either he's got friends or he's got a serious drinking problem. I assumed friends because most of his games are big multiplayer deals, and he had two Xboxes, so he's playing linked games. If he can afford two Xboxes and a sweet big-screen, he's got some kind of good job."

"But his furniture's so crappy!" she protests, then realizes what she said and blushes a little. "I mean, well, you know."

"He's a guy. The only guys I know with good furniture are married ones," I reply.

She's chewing on that one. Then I see the gleam in her eye.

"No," I say before I can think about it.

She looks surprised. "No, what?"

"No, I'm not going to tell you what your living room says about you."

Now she looks surprised and offended. I might've chosen a better way to put that. "Why not? What, does it say something bad?"

"No," I tell her, and realize that no matter what I say, that's what she's going to believe. This isn't going well, not at all. "It doesn't say anything bad. It just…it goes against the code of couch ethics."

"Couch…ethics." Now she looks intrigued, and skeptical. "You've got to be pulling my chain, here."

"Okay. Maybe it's not a code," I allow. "But there are definitely rules if you're going to live this way for any extended period of time."

She looks at me expectantly.

I wrack my brain. They're just rules you *know*, instinctively. It's not like I've considered compiling a manual. "You don't want to stay on any couch for more than a couple of days at a time, or for more than a couple of days in a month's period. Preferably two months."

Now her eyes widen. "Jesus. You must need to line up a ton of couches."

"Yes, but at least you've always got a potential couch to fall back on. Wear out your welcome, and that couch goes off-limits," I explain. "If I'm going to be on a couch for more than one night, I do what I can to help out. If they have dirty dishes, I wash them. I volunteer to vacuum. I don't touch their food. I don't use their phone. I don't watch their television unless they're watching it, as well. And as a general rule—" I gesture to the newly cleared coffee table "—I don't unpack. It's already an imposition, and it's impossible to stay out of someone's way when you're in their living room. So you do what you can to make yourself invisible."

She's scribbling furiously on her pad of paper. "What else?"

"That's about it."

"Where do you get couches? Or, I guess, where does Sticky line them up?"

"Sticky knows everybody." This isn't an understatement, either. "If, by some weird force of nature, Sticky can't score me a couch, every now and then I go online and find one. Couch-surfing.com is one of the better ones—those people are open-minded, and when I say that I'm a DJ, they're all over it."

She peppers me with questions for the next hour and a half. After a while, I force a yawn, look at the face of my cell phone pointedly. "Aren't you going to work?"

"Oh! Oh, jeez," she says, and stands up in a rush. "Shit, I've got deadlines tomorrow, too. I'll let you get some rest," she says graciously.

"Thanks." I begin constructing my couch bed with her mountain of linens.

"PJ?"

I look over. "Yup?"

"Seriously. Off the record." She crosses her arms. "What does my living room tell you?"

I sigh. "That you've got a romantic side, you find your home a comfort, and that you've got a great sense of design."

She smiles hesitantly.

I don't add *you're using Crate & Barrel as a substitute for Prozac*. Would go against my code of couch ethics. You understand.

chapter 6

Leslie and Rick were out at a chic restaurant in North Beach. Her parents loved Italian food, and they loved the city, even though they were currently nowhere near it. Not up in the hills, like Rick's parents. Not Marin, or Palo Alto. They lived in suburbia…even farther, actually. Fairfield, the midpoint between San Francisco and Sacramento. Hotter than hell in the summer and relatively cold in the winter, with affordable housing.

They always met Leslie and her brother in the city, if at all possible. Which was why, thankfully, family gatherings were few and far between.

Tonight, Rick sat at her right side, occasionally holding her hand under the table. In the four years they'd been together, she hadn't really subjected him to one of their "dinners." She'd introduced him to her parents a couple of times, nothing official. She preferred to spend time with his family, and so did he. It worked out better that way.

"So, how's that family of yours?" Her father sat next to Rick. Her mother sat next to her.

"Doing well. Thanks," Rick said.

"Still have that gorgeous house up in the hills?"

Rick nodded, looking at me. Ever since her father found out about the mansion, he'd asked about it, as if it was a celebrity Rick was related to.

"I'll bet the view's incredible," her father said, as always.

His shamelessness embarrassed the hell out of her.

Her mother, on the other hand, was focused on her brother and his beautiful, vivacious date, Aimee. Aimee weighed maybe twenty pounds, and all of it was tits. Still, she wore what looked like a real Caroline Herrera suit and carried what looked like a real Louis Vuitton handbag. She screamed "class."

Leslie looked over at her younger brother, Mark, who was frowning over the menu like it was a cryptonomicon. His hair, blond like hers, stuck up in unruly tufts. He wore a button-down Oxford (his girlfriend's doing, Leslie felt quite sure) that already sported a spot from the olive oil that went with the bread. He pushed his glasses up on his nose.

Her brother was the classic Silicon Valley nerd. Unlike most of the rest of the world, including herself, he had gotten out rich. And now he was just getting richer.

She sometimes was thankful that he hadn't offered her a job. She didn't know if she could deal with the humiliation. She also didn't know why he *hadn't* offered her a job.

Yet another facet of the ring of hell that was family dinners.

"So, Aimee," her mother all but purred. "Mark tells me you're a clothing buyer at Neiman Marcus."

Aimee smiled demurely. It went with the suit, Leslie noted. "Yes. I purchase all the formal wear. I also arrange for trunk shows from some of the top designers."

"I wish you could do something with Mark's clothing," Leslie's mother said, and Leslie could see that Aimee was thrown. "You've got such taste, obviously. That's such a beautiful outfit."

"Thank you," Aimee said.

"And you're so young! That seems like a lot of responsibility for someone so young. Do you enjoy your job?"

Aimee's smile was like the sun. "Oh, I *love* my job. I love working with clothing, and I love the store."

Mark finally put the menu down and nudged her. "Tell them."

Aimee blushed, just the palest shade of rose. "I don't think…"

"Come on," Mark prompted, then saved her the trouble by stating, "She's getting promoted. She's going to be in charge of the entire women's section. She'll have people reporting to her, she'll chart sales trends. Isn't that awesome?"

There was crowing. Leslie's father had their faux-Italian waiter order champagne, though he was quick to amend quietly "not the most expensive one, though." She watched as Mark grabbed the waiter, changed it to the most expensive choice, and tipped him handsomely for the trouble.

She looked at Rick, who sported an expression of amused horror.

Unfortunately, her mother chose *that* moment to turn to her daughter. "Did you hear that? Promoted to the head of her department. And she's younger than you."

Leslie winced. "I can see that, Mom," she said in a quiet tone of voice.

Her mother didn't get the hint. Instead, she turned back to Aimee. "Leslie's had five jobs in the past, what, eight years?"

Fortunately, at that point, Rick cleared his throat. "Still, Leslie's doing well in her job," he said. "She's going for a promotion of her own."

Both Leslie's parents looked surprised—both that Leslie was going for a promotion, and that Rick was the one who was telling them.

"That's great, Leslie," her father said, sounding puzzled. She felt herself sit up a little straighter under their attention. "What are you going for? I mean, what is it a promotion from…what is it you do, again? You're an editor?"

"I didn't know you were an editor," Aimee says. "For which newspaper?"

Leslie sighed. "I'm an editor at the *Bay Area Citizen*."

"No kidding!" The colloquialism sounded weird coming out of Aimee, but Leslie let it slide.

"I'm trying to switch over to being a features reporter," she said for her father's sake.

Her mother frowned. "From editor to reporter. Isn't that more like a demotion?"

Trust her mother to look at the downside. "Not really. The features department is the heart of the *Citizen*." Even if the personals were its major source of revenue. "And once I'm writing stories for them, the whole journalistic world will open up. I really enjoy writing."

Her father looked at her, puzzled. "I didn't know that. Have you ever written at any of your other jobs?"

"No," she said.

"Then how do you know?"

"I've written little things now and then," she answered, feeling more and more defensive. "I think, given the opportunity, it's something I'll love."

Her father sounded skeptical. "Well. You'll let us know when you have a story running, then, right?"

"Definitely," Leslie said.

It was a turning point…the first time her parents had shown an interest in her job in a long time. She beamed at Rick, who winked at her.

Then the champagne came, and to her surprise, her brother stood up. "I'd like to make a toast."

Leslie blushed. Mark had never been a guy for big gestures, but the fact that he was going to toast his girlfriend's promotion was sweet—and the fact that he'd now have to toast Leslie's attempts at a career change was satisfying. For years, he'd always tried to one-up her. She thought it was because he was the baby of the family. Still, she held her glass expectantly.

To her surprise, he toasted her first. "To my sister, the next Pulitzer Prize winner for local features," he said. She smiled, even though she wished he hadn't added the "for local-features" bit.

"And to Aimee, for her promotion…and for *agreeing to be my wife*."

Aimee blushed and smiled, one of those demure, Madonna-like smiles. My parents were floored.

"What? You two are getting married? This is wonderful!"

Suddenly, there was a burst of activity. Her mother was hugging Aimee, her father was clapping her brother on the back. Even Rick shook Mark's hand, congratulating him.

"So, when's the happy day?"

"We were thinking September," Mark said, holding Aimee's hand. She smiled back at him, and Leslie couldn't help but feel a pang of envy. They looked so happy, so in love.

She looked at Rick, who was pouring himself another glass of champagne, assiduously avoiding looking at her.

"You'll let me help you plan your wedding, won't you, dear?" Her mother was almost begging, and Leslie stared at her. Aimee looked surprised, as well...and reluctant. "Please, Aimee. I've always wanted to help one of my children with a wedding, and I don't know how many chances I'm going to get."

"Mother," Leslie protested, horribly embarrassed.

Her mother turned her stare to her, and to Rick. "Well? It's true, isn't it?"

She was challenging Rick, in particular. Leslie turned to Rick, hopefully...wondering, herself.

She watched as Rick turned to her father. "Did you know my grandparents recently had the house appraised...it's worth close to four million now?"

"No," her father said, effectively sidetracked.

As they talked, Leslie saw her mother's face fall, and then her attention turned solely and completely on Aimee.

Leslie looked at Mark, who shook his head. Then she toasted him, and drank the champagne in her glass. Finest champagne at the restaurant, she marveled, and it still tasted bitter.

"So. This is a rave."

I looked at Leslie. At least she didn't have that "woe is me" expression that she was wearing when she got back from dinner with her parents. She'd come home, depressed, and asked me if I wanted to go out. To someplace where she could, and I quote, "party her ass off" and "put the whole fucking night behind her." And she did put this whole emphasis on wanting a story that was hip and edgy. As soon as she mentioned a rave, I figured there was no way I could explain one to her. I'd really need to show her.

"Yup. This is it."

She leans over, whispering. "Am I just square," she says, "or is this basically just a party in a warehouse?"

I can't help it. I burst into chuckles. "What the hell did you think a rave was?"

"I don't know. You always read about it in *Newsweek,* or see it on…hey, stop laughing at me!"

I try. I swear to God, I really do try.

When I regain composure, I take her over to the bar. They really shouldn't have one here (I can't imagine they got a liquor license), but Leslie looks as if she needs a drink to wash down the disappointment that her "rave" scene was not much wilder than a backyard barbecue. The music's better, though. The music is off the hinges, actually. Not that she'd realize that.

"I'm going to check out the DJ, see who's spinning," I say. "Are you going to be okay?"

She takes a long pull off of a multicolored drink. I'm suddenly praying it's just Bacardi and nothing too weird. "Yeah, sure," she mutters, looking around. Then she sees a couple of kids wearing strategically painted liquid latex and mesh. They look like poster children for Heatherette. "Holy shit."

"Just people watch. I'll be back in a minute."

I head for the decks—a relatively crude turntable setup, with a sound system that reverbs all wrong. Somebody needs to check the levels. I step up, introduce myself.

I'm well known enough that most DJs have heard of me. Unfortunately, I'm not so well known that people are, you know, impressed.

"That's a nice beat," I say to the DJ. Kid's name is Sammy.

He grins back at me. "Thanks. I just started spinning."

"Mind if I ask how old you are."

The grin widens. "Fourteen."

Fourteen. I feel suddenly and overpoweringly old. "Sounds good, Sammy. Got a demo?"

He shakes his head, looks at me like I'm nuts.

"Want mine?"

His eyes widen. "Really?"

"Why not?" I know, he's only fourteen. But he may be playing a main room by the time he's seventeen. Weirder things have happened. Besides, he's got talent. "Just e-mail me when you've got a demo, or if you're playing. You're good."

He couldn't be more proud if he'd gotten the Nobel Prize and a platinum record on the same day. "Thanks," he says, trying to sound cool and failing utterly.

I'm walking off the decks when I see Samantha, and my mood plummets a bit. "Hey there. Is there somebody important that I didn't see come in? What the hell are you doing at a rave?"

She sniffs. "I've been thinking about your problem."

"Which problem would that be?"

"Your image." She doesn't even crack a smile. She's like the Terminator poured into a stick-figure body. "You said that you needed a different look. More to the point, you actually need a look, period."

Ouch. Eyebrow waxing is less painful than her version of the truth. "So where do you fit in?"

"I'm signing on as your stylist."

Oh, like hell. "And what's in it for you?"

She smiles tightly. "I asked Jonathan if I could work with you."

Aha. And the truth emerges. "Well…I'd hate to waste your time, and I don't want to waste Jonathan's money, so why don't we just wrap this up right now."

"And how exactly were you planning on doing this yourself?" She crosses her arms and stands in my way. "I can help you."

"Funny how altruistic you get when a powerful, well-connected and, frankly, hot-looking guy comes into the picture."

"Listen, you don't have to like my motives. You don't even have to like me," she says, as if this is the easiest thing in the world. "You just have to wear what I buy for you, land your deal and leave Jonathan to me. How tough is that, right?"

"Um, leave Jonathan to you?"

"You know what I mean," she says. Although I'm serious, it sounds weird. I have no idea what the hell she's talking about. Finally, seeing how incredibly obtuse I am, she spells it out: "Whatever I do with Jonathan, you just let me do. Okay?"

"Had no intention of stopping you whatsoever." This little person is psycho. No wonder Sticky fancies himself in love with the girl. He's the patron saint of the useless (me) and the psychotic (Samantha, and his last six girlfriends.). "So, what's next? And is it going to take long?"

She purses her lips, and I realize—she's got no game plan. Whatsoever. I think she figured I'd be a tougher sell than this. Still, it's my career. I don't like this girl, but this whole thing is just transactional anyway. She'll just, I don't know, go somewhere, get me some clothes. How hard can that be, really?

"How about I meet you at Ross? You can point me to a few outfits, ta-da, all finished, then you can jump Jonathan at your own discretion and I'll discreetly cheer you on from the comfort of my own couch. Or Leslie's couch. Whatever."

"Ross? As in Dress For Less? Are you high?" She shakes her head, and I suddenly feel a headache coming on. "We'll definitely need to get you some clothes, but high end, dear. If you're going to sell to a record label, we need you to look your best."

As if she knows what the hell she's talking about. "I'm sorry. You've been a stylist before?"

"No," she says sourly. "But look at me…and then look at you."

Okay. Girl's got a point there.

"So. We go to someplace that's expensive…"

"First, I think we need to figure out what your look's going to be," she says reflectively. Jeez, she's warming up to it. I'm not liking this at all. "It could take a while."

"Define a while."

She makes a nebulous motion with her hand. "And of course, we're going to need to work in makeup…and you can't leave your hair that way."

Oh, for God's sake.

"Fine," I say ungraciously. "When do we start this grand experiment?"

Samantha's eyes narrow speculatively. "When were you planning on seeing Jonathan next?"

"You are eventually going to help me, right? I mean, this isn't some big scheme to try to weasel your way into the sack with Jonathan?" I know I sound spiteful, but I don't have time for this. "I haven't got anything against it, but if I have to go through with it, I don't want you wiggling and strutting in front of my manager when you're supposed to be working with me. I just want it over with. Suck up to him on your own time."

"Oh, this is going to be a joy," she states.

"I'm so with you on that one."

Suddenly, I hear catcalling and crowing. Samantha and I both look over.

"Whoo-hoo!"

It's Leslie. She's standing on top of a box that's sort of acting as a stage, with a couple of other girls. I grin. She looks as if she's having a good time, at least.

Suddenly, the other girls whisper to each other, and then they all yell, "One… Two… Three!" and yank off their tank tops.

Leslie goggles for a minute. Then she does the drunken smile, gets a "what the hell" look on her face.

By the time she's got the last button undone, I've sprinted over there. "What the hell are you doing?" I yell, climbing up and tugging at her to get down before she hurts herself.

"Yay!" She flashes her white lace bra at the crowd. They're yelling like it's Mardi Gras.

"This isn't *Girls Gone Wild*," I scold her. "What the hell?"

"I was thirsty," she says. "And the fruity drinks were good."

She's a lightweight, that much is obvious. "I was gone maybe half an hour," I say slowly, so she'll track. "How many drinks did you have?"

"Two," she says, then frowns. "Maybe three."

Maybe more. Jesus. She's going to be sick as a dog.

Samantha is standing behind me. "I'll be seeing you soon," I say. She nods at me. I turn back to Leslie.

"Well, you'll have something to write about tomorrow. Welcome to a rave, Leslie."

Every time the phone rang, Leslie felt it like a bullet in her head. No, not like a bullet in her head…at least that would be quick, and painless, and end the endless misery of her hangover. She would unplug the phone if the cord weren't buried behind a really heavy bookshelf.

"Anderson!"

She winced. Sydney didn't have a loud voice, but somehow, at all the wrong moments, it always seemed piercing. "Yo," she answered in a strangled whisper.

"How's the article coming?" He sounded smug.

"Dandy," she answered.

"Came in a little late, did you?"

"I was researching the article." *I was dancing topless at a rave.* She had no idea being hip, urban and edgy would have quite so hefty a price tag.

"When did you say you'd turn that in?" His smirk spoke volumes. "Or maybe you should just stick to the personals desk? Nobody's complaining about the job you're doing there."

Goddamn, the man could annoy her. If he was going to become her boss, that could pose a problem, she thought with a little note of despair.

"I don't suppose you're just hazing me," she said.

"This is the big leagues. We don't haze people." His grin almost split his face. "Not until they're officially a part of the department, anyway. So as long as you stay in personals, I'd say you're safe."

"Fine. Well, I think you're going to like this article," she said, trying not to sound as disgruntled as she felt. "In fact, I think this article is going to blow you away."

"Well. I stand here, ready to be blown."

Nice. And he had a sense of humor. She just couldn't wait to work for this guy.

"Trust me, you'll like it," she said, then realized, in the context of what he'd just said, that she was just fueling the fire. "The article."

His eyes narrowed. "I know I'm going to be sorry I asked this, but how many sources are you using?"

She blinked. "Um…"

"Because I know you're not just talking to the interview subject, right? You're not just doing some minibiography of this person?"

She hadn't realized that she shouldn't, but she decided to play it off. "Of course not."

"So who else are you talking to?"

"I was planning on talking to her manager, and a good friend of hers. The guy she calls her couch-pimp."

"That'll read well, at least." He frowned. "Were you planning on talking to anybody who *doesn't* have a vested interest in her looking good?"

There it was again, that silent *you idiot* that seemed to be tagged to the end of all his sentences.

She sighed. "I will see what I can do. Her arch-nemesis is in Gstaad right now, but maybe I can make a phone call."

"Cute, Anderson." He rolled his eyes. "I'm giving out valuable journalism tips, and you're making jokes."

"I'd rather be making deadlines," she said, gesturing to the inch-high stack of personals that had been faxed and e-mailed in.

"Yes ma'am, you are feisty," he said as an afterthought. "You pull this off, and I think you'll be a nice addition to the team."

He walked out. She didn't know if she felt better at his back-handed compliment, or worse, knowing that might be the best that she could get if she went over there to work.

Her phone rang, and she picked it up just to stop the sound from stabbing into her head. "Yes?"

"Leslie?" It was Rick. "Whoa. What's up?"

"Just having a bad night. Day, I mean," she said, rubbing her eye with one hand. "What's going on?"

"I just wanted to let you know that I don't think I can see

you tonight," he said. "Kendra...you remember, Kendra from my birthday?"

Oh, yes, she thought with a sneer. She remembered Kendra.

"Anyway, tonight's *her* birthday, and she's having a party. At her house."

Wonderful. Leslie would just bet that Kendra would love to have Rick over there, without his shrewish, uncool, older girl-friend. "I see."

"Come on. Kendra's a friend, just a friend. Besides, she bought me a gift and everything on my birthday."

"They're your friends, Rick," she said, hoping that didn't sound too bitchy. It certainly felt that way. "Have I ever given you a hard time? You've got your own life."

"I know," he said. "But sometimes...I don't know. You just seem sort of sad. Left out."

She'd never liked feeling like the outsider in his social life, sure. But she understood, and sort of bought into, the whole "separate worlds" theory. If she had more friends, she'd certainly...

Well, no. She probably wouldn't. Rick was, at the moment, her entire social life.

Not including last night's rave.

She grinned. "Whatever." Then she had a brain flash. "Say, is Sticky going to be there?"

"He doesn't have to work tonight," Rick said, his voice sounding curious. "Why?"

"Would you mind if I tagged along? I wanted to talk to Sticky about PJ."

"Is she still staying at your house?"

"Yes."

"How's that going?"

"Going okay. It's barely like she's there," Leslie said, leaning back and wishing she kept aspirin at her desk. "She doesn't touch anything, doesn't even use my towels. I had to make her take a spare key."

"Are you sure you want to do that? I mean, you barely know her."

Leslie thought about the way PJ had made sure she got home last night…how she'd done everything but tuck her in. She'd even suggested she drink water and take a few vitamins. "She seems nice enough," Leslie said.

"Well, she's a friend of Sticky's," Rick agreed.

"So, can I come?"

She heard as well as felt Rick's hesitation. "Um, well, sure. Why not, right?"

They'd been together for four years, and yet he still didn't really…she gritted her teeth. "If you want, I can come in a separate car. Then, when I'm done talking to Sticky, I can leave. If it would make you more comfortable."

He let out a sigh. "I'm not saying that, Leslie. Don't twist my words."

"Well, I just think it's a little strange that, after all this time, you're feeling weird about me going with you to a party."

"It's not like you've ever volunteered before," Rick responded with a little heat. "So forgive me for being surprised."

She thought of a retort and bit her tongue at the last minute. "Sorry," she said instead, even though she didn't really feel it. "Listen, I'm just pissy and hungover. I'm sure I'll be fine tonight."

"Wait a sec. Hungover?"

"Long story," she said. "So…friends?"

He laughed. "Friends."

She wanted more than that, she thought, but she'd settle. For now. "Okay, then."

"I'll pick you up around eight," he said. "I want to meet the girl who's taking my girlfriend out drinking on a school night."

She hadn't really thought of it that way, she reflected as she hung up the phone. But her life had definitely changed since PJ entered it.

chapter 7

"Samantha Regales?"

Samantha's head bounced up like a bobblehead doll. "Yes? I'm here. I'm over here."

The woman, a frazzled, dumpy-looking woman in black jeans and a black T-shirt, looked her over. "You're going to be next."

Samantha nodded, a little more slowly, and tried to calm her racing heart. She sat very still, tried to focus.

"Wow. This is one of the weirder places I've ever seen."

She turned…and then blanched. It was PJ, and her friend, the amateur stripper, Leslie.

"I'm assuming all these women are models?" Leslie said, staring in wonder.

"You'd be assuming correctly," Samantha answered.

She was going to have to show PJ her clothes today anyway. She wanted to teach PJ the art of presentation. When she realized she was going to be at a cattle-call audition, she had quickly rung PJ up, telling her to get over here. She wanted PJ to see, firsthand, some of the most beautiful women on earth, and how they worked it. If anything, maybe being in the same room with fifty towering models might give her a little style by osmosis.

And if maybe, just maybe, PJ learned to have a little respect for Samantha and what she did, all the better.

Leslie was looking around, and Samantha could see behind the facade of amusement. She was intimidated. Some of these women had faces that were so heartbreakingly beautiful, you wondered how you had the temerity to vie for the same catwalk as them. Samantha had learned to get over that—attitude mattered, just as much as beauty. Sometimes, more so.

She looked, to see PJ's reaction. It wouldn't hurt PJ to feel a little intimidation, Samantha thought. In fact, it might do her a world of good. She might be the best DJ on the West Coast, for all Samantha knew, but this was Samantha's world, and PJ ought to respect that, and her.

PJ was looking around, craning her neck to get a glimpse at everyone.

"Guess my lack of tits isn't going to be as serious a factor as you thought, huh?"

Samantha winced, and Leslie let out a bark of surprised laughter before quickly covering her mouth.

"Could you say that a little louder?" Samantha hissed. "I'm not sure the designer heard you."

PJ shrugged. "Okay." She cleared her throat. "GUESS MY LACK OF—"

Samantha jumped up and grabbed PJ's arm. Hard.

"Ouch," PJ said, laughing and pulling away. "Sorry."

"If I lose this gig because you were fucking around," Samantha said, feeling the urge to strangle PJ pump through her veins, "you will be. *Very* sorry."

PJ's expression was unapologetic. "Listen, you wanted me here, not the other way around." She still didn't look intimidated, either by her surroundings, or Samantha's threat. "I'll try to behave, though."

Samantha had trouble believing that. "Come here. I want you to see this."

She took them off to the side. There was a little gap in some high curtains that partitioned the room, a large, gymnasium-size affair. They had a catwalk set up, and were taking models in, one by one, and having them strut, to see how they moved, to see their carriage and bearing and general presence. "You see that?"

PJ squinted. Leslie looked over PJ's shoulder, curious. "What am I looking at?" PJ whispered back.

"The way she looks. Sometimes, they walk, and they have no expression. She's swinging her hips more, moving like she's walking into a bar and wants people to notice her. Look!" Samantha nudged PJ. "See that? That wink, that little sexy smile before she turned?"

PJ looked at Samantha as if she was insane. Samantha huffed.

"Listen, I don't have the most beautiful face in here," she said in a low voice. "That much is obvious. But believe me…when I get out on a catwalk, I *own* it."

"Um, okay," Leslie said with that same nervous little giggle.

But PJ finally looked as though she got it. At least, sort of. "Sometimes I feel that way a little. When I'm spinning, and everybody's grooving, and going out of their minds."

"Exactly." Samantha was amazed at how relieved she felt.

"Tourists?"

Samantha turned, to find several models behind them, one from her own agency, if she remembered correctly. "Excuse me?"

"This is for models only," one of the women said. "I think the designer would be pissed off if they found out you had brought your little friends here to watch you."

Samantha grimaced. She hadn't counted on that.

"Samantha Regales! You're up!"

No time to think about that, to worry about that. "Stay here," she told PJ and Leslie. "I'll be right back, so *don't go anywhere.*"

She didn't wait for their response. Instead, she followed Ms. All-In-Black behind the curtain. "Okay. The designer's at the end of the ramp." She threw a long piece of material around Samantha's waist, pinning it, catching a little of Samantha's skin in the process. Samantha didn't even flinch. "She's going to want to know how you move. One time down, one turn, and back."

Samantha had been watching some of the other women, prepping, seeing what the reaction was. It might seem amateur to the others, who were trying so hard to look as if they didn't care, even though the perfume of despair hung heavy in the air. Samantha nodded, getting into performance mode. She got this way before football games and cheerleading competitions, before the SATs, and before her big finals.

I own this.

She walked slowly, less jaunty than the previous one, but more animated than the ones before. She did a slow, regal walk, enjoying the way the material swished around her legs. There were a legion of assistants in black, and one woman in a sixties-inspired A-line and dark glasses, watching her.

Love me, she thought. *Don't take your eyes off of me.*

She got to the end of the catwalk after interminable seconds, did a slow turn, pause, looked over her shoulder. No wink—she was too courtly for that—but a sideways glance. If she gave a guy at a bar a glance like that, she'd have his phone number in less than two minutes. She'd clocked it once.

Then a more sexy strut. She looked better from the back, she found out. Besides, it again made the material move. She enjoyed that.

Her heart was pounding by the time she got back to the opening. She turned, trying not to be hesitant, as if she was asking *was it good for you?* with the insistent insecurity of a virgin.

She looked at the designer and her entourage, daring them to reject her. Daring them to *try*.

The assistant looked at the designer.

"*No.*"

Startled, Samantha missed a step, bobbling a little. "I'm sorry?"

"No. You won't do. Not at all." The woman who curtly denounced her was wearing what looked like a purple caftan over black skinny pants, with some kind of hat that looked like the successful mating of a beret and a hunting cap. "Not in my show."

The designer crossed her arms. Samantha smiled hopefully. "Maybe if you just—"

"I said no." She gave Samantha a withering look. "And, just for further notice, you might consider losing another ten pounds. Thank you."

Samantha accepted the verbal slap. It wasn't the first time she'd heard that or something similar. "Thanks for your time," she said, holding her head up and forcing her eyes to stay clear until she exited the building. She allowed a few tears to mist up as she walked back to her car.

Persistence, she told herself. That's what had gotten her this far. She wasn't going to let some ugly caftan woman stop her. She wasn't going to let anything stop her.

Then suddenly, she remembered. Brought PJ. Who brought Leslie.

Oh, shit.

She rushed back again, through the curtain, and looked, aghast, at the scene in front of her.

Leslie and PJ were sitting in the middle of the room, on some folding chairs. The models were fanned out around them, trying assiduously to ignore them, but it was impossible not to notice that every set of eyes was riveted on the pair.

PJ had a pink pastry box propped up on her lap, and she was devouring a custard-filled éclair with an almost erotic single-mindedness. One of the models was staring at her with a mixture of fascination…and an equally powerful sense of lust.

PJ took a big, gaping-mouth bite. Some of the cream spilled onto her finger, and she licked it off, making little yummy noises.

The collective eyes of the models widened. Samantha thought a few of them were hyperventilating.

"That is *so* disgusting," a woman to Samantha's right said, her tone horrified. "Can you imagine how many *calories* are in that thing?"

"Yeah," her friend answered, but her tone held more longing.

"And that chocolate mousse–filled cream puff she ate before…" The woman's horror edged on the border of obsession.

Samantha walked up to PJ, who had traces of chocolate around her mouth, which grinned widely. "So! How'd you do?"

"We're leaving," Samantha said, her buzz at signing for the show waning quickly. She was about to be in the middle of a riot.

"But I haven't finished," PJ replied, pulling out one of the most sinful-looking fruit tarts Samantha had ever seen.

"Now," Samantha said. "We're leaving *now!"*

"Jeez," PJ said as she allowed Samantha to drag her out of the room. Leslie trailed, chuckling.

"No matter what else you say, Samantha," Leslie said when she finally caught her breath. "You've got to admit PJ's got *presence.*"

I am standing in fluorescent light, wearing what looks like a minikilt and a shirt that shows my stomach because it's cut ragged and too high and sports the brand FCUK, which Samantha thinks is really edgy and I think is somewhere above high school. I mean, it was funny the first time I saw it. That was, what, five years ago? And she's supposed to be the model here.

What Jonathan sees in her, I have no idea.

"Did you try the pants?"

The pants are worse. Think Uma Thurman in *Kill Bill, Pt 1.* Good God, tracksuit hell. And paired with, I swear to God, some kind of frilly shirt like the kind they parodied on *Seinfeld*—I never saw the episode, but I saw the trailer on *USA Late Night.*

I belatedly wonder if she's smoking crack. If it made her thinner...

That was uncharitable. Sticky would be very disappointed in me.

I step outside the dressing-room door, feeling naked in full clothes. Well, semifull clothes, I guess, covering my stomach.

"Stop hiding," she says, playing Katinka, the fashion-Nazi from the movie *Zoolander.* She crosses her arms and scopes me derisively. "Come on. Walk toward me. Turn around."

I start to take a few steps and she gives me such a look of distaste that I freeze.

"We've got to teach you how to strut," she says.

"Like hell," I reply. "No strutting. Nobody said anything about strutting. Getting the clothes are bad enough."

"Yeah, well, Jonathan said you looked like shit and needed fashion resuscitation. So he called me in." She sounded as if she'd just drunk sour milk. "You want to blow this off, be my guest. I've got better things to do. And, frankly, better people to do them with."

She makes a career out of being a bitch, I swear to God.

"Well, is this going to work or not?"

I nod, curt. This whole thing is stupid, it's not working. She's stepped right off the pages of "The Devil Wears Prada," and I'm acting like a Goddamn milk cow, but so be it. Call it the equivalent of lying back and thinking on my music. People have died for lesser causes.

I fake a strut, as best I can.

"Now you're just mocking me."

"Stop being such a girl," I snap.

She finally does, doing that head-tilt-finger-on-cheek maneuver perfected by Serge in *Beverly Hills Cop.* I half expect her to say, "Well, this is a very important piece."

"It works. I think it finally does something for you."

"Get the fuck out," I say.

Leslie is in a chair, obediently taking notes, and she chuckles, quoting right back at me, *"No! I cannot."*

We both laugh. Samantha doesn't get it. She's probably too young—probably hasn't seen *Beverly Hills Cop,* except maybe edited on cable. Leslie's older, but more importantly, Leslie's got a better sense of humor.

Of course, turtles probably have a better sense of humor.

Samantha glares at me, as if she'd just read my mind. I feel a fraction of guilt, and stare at my socks, which are beginning to fray about the toes. I'll have to pick up new ones. At the flea market, probably. I could put a down payment on a house for the price of a six-pack of socks at this chichi boutique.

"Try on the pants," she barks.

I throw Leslie a look, wondering if she could do something to help me out. Say, set fire to the lingerie section as a diversion so I can make a break for it. She sends a look of commiseration—she's been on this three-hour extravaganza with me, even if she has gotten to sit down—but then she turns back to her notes when Samantha turns the evil eye on her.

I sigh, march back to my little fluorescent cubicle, and strip. I put on the hip huggers and realize that my big-ass granny undies are sticking out of the top of them. While the revealed underwear-band thing worked for people like Marky Mark or any wanna-be-gangsta kid riding a BART train with his waistband hovering around his knees, I get the feeling my personal stylist will be displeased, so I do what I can to stuff the underwear out of sight.

If she insists on one of those G-string thingys, I am going to be out of here so quickly, there'll be a sonic boom. To prevent that actuality, I grab a French-cuffed oxford shirt that actually covers my waist. I walk out, hunching a little by the time I get to my "coach."

Samantha shakes her head. "No, no. That shirt's just a jacket."

"No, it's not. It's a shirt."

"You'll wear it as a jacket. Over that BabyGap tank."

"I thought you were kidding with that."

She looks at Leslie. "Everybody knows that BabyGap is worn by adults," she said, and points. "You knew that, didn't you?"

"I'm just a reporter," Leslie mutters.

"Hopeless," Samantha says, rubbing her temple. "The two of you. Hopeless."

I look at Leslie, who's laughing but manfully keeping it contained. She's shaking on the seat in the corner as if she's having a seizure. I giggle, hiding it less successfully as it comes out in a snort.

Samantha shakes her head. "Okay. We'll just go with two outfits to start. The mini, the midriff shirt, the college-colors sweater and the kelly green Chloe dress."

I hated—no, I *loathed*—the dress. "Couldn't we get something in—"

"Don't say black," she says, beating me to the punch. "Don't even think black."

Her eyes added an unstated *or I will go model-ninja and wreck your ass.*

I keep my mouth shut. Three hours. God knows how long she could pull out the torture if she really put her mind to it.

Leslie nursed a glass of water. She was at Kendra's loft, somewhere in the city, just above Mission, in a relatively nicer neighborhood. Kendra had friends scattered everywhere around the posh but sparsely furnished apartment. There were large photographs on every wall…Kendra worked at her father's shipping company, but fancied herself a photographer. There was even a large picture of Rick and company at Rick's birthday party.

Leslie noticed that she wasn't in that one. She gripped her glass of water tighter.

Rick was right there in the middle of it, laughing with his friends. She didn't know why it was so difficult for her to get along with the people he was close to. She figured a lot of the blame lay on her for not trying harder in the beginning of their relationship to get to know the people he did. It just wasn't something she was used to, though. With her past relationships, they had a little more in common.

Not that she didn't have a lot in common with Rick, she thought hastily. It was just their diverging social lives. And why was she dwelling on that, anyway? She was here on a mission. She was going to talk to Sticky about PJ. The article, that was the important thing. Even Rick thought so.

When Sticky entered the apartment, there were approving cries of "Sticky!" and he seemed to shake hands with everyone, hugging men and women alike, a broad smile on his face. Leslie didn't think she'd ever seen him unhappy—unless you counted when he was actually working. Then, he looked like a football player, all game face and don't-fuck-with-me. Apparently, there was a legend going around that he'd pretended not to know one of his friends from high school, simply because he was working a particularly rough club with a rough bunch of owners, and he didn't want anybody he knew mixed up in it.

If she had the chance, she might write a story about Sticky, as well. She still needed to figure out how to frame it for Sydney.

She walked up to him, and he smiled at her with just as much warmth as everybody else. "Leslie! I wasn't expecting to see you here."

She hugged him. The guy was a great hugger. "I came here especially to see you, actually," she said. "Got a minute?"

"Sure," he said easily, still waving to someone across the room. "What's on your mind?"

"I thought we could talk about PJ. I need some more sources, some background on her, for the article."

Sticky sighed and immediately crossed his arms...not a good sign.

"What? Is there a problem there?"

"I can tell you what I think of PJ—which, incidentally, is that she's amazing on the turntables and one of the best friends a guy could have," he said, and he had none of his usual joviality. "But when it comes to her background, I think you're really going to need to go to PJ herself, you know?"

"I've tried," Leslie said with a little asperity. "But she gets closemouthed...just like you're getting now. What, was she in prison or something?"

She'd meant it as a joke, but Sticky's face was dark as a thundercloud. "Why don't you just leave her alone?"

Leslie's eyes widened. "*Was* she in prison?"

"No, she wasn't in prison," Sticky said with an impatient huff. "She just had a rough time before she started DJ-ing, that's all."

"What did she do before she was a DJ?"

"She worked in computers," Sticky said. "Listen, I don't feel comfortable talking about this. If she didn't tell you, then maybe you should, you know, let it drop?"

"If I don't cover this, my editor won't think I have a story. Which means PJ won't get any publicity," she argued. She remembered the night that Jonathan Hadeis had offered to represent PJ…how Sticky had been shocked, and had taken the initiative to contact Jonathan himself. "You know how she is. She's not going to do what's best for her own career. A little background. That's all I'm asking for." She paused. "When her career takes off, she'll thank you later."

"That's what you'd think," Sticky said. "PJ's really touchy about her past, though, and I totally respect that. I don't want to hurt her."

Leslie couldn't help but be intrigued. What the hell was PJ hiding, anyway? "Fine. We'll stick with stuff that's more related to you. How did *you* meet PJ, anyway?"

His expression, which had been defensive, softened, and he leaned against the wall behind him. "That's a funny story, actually."

Leslie smiled encouragingly.

"We met…God, I think it's five years ago, now," he said with a tone of surprise. "I was a lot younger then. I was doing some construction work…was a bouncer at night at a couple of clubs, but still needed a day job, you know?"

No, she didn't know that. Still, she nodded.

"Well, I was a little smaller then," he said, gesturing to the girth of his stomach, "and I had a tendency of taking a little afternoon nap when the foreman wasn't looking. We were working at this huge hospital building, and it was all hurry up and wait anyway." He started laughing at what was coming up, Leslie could tell. "So, there's PJ, working away in her office, when suddenly she hears this weird noise. She can't figure it out, and it starts scaring the hell out of her. She thinks it's coming from her ceiling, so she gets a broom and *pokes* at a ceiling tile."

Soon, he was laughing so hard that Leslie had trouble making out what he was saying. "I damn near fell through the roof," he explained. "I was sleeping up in a crawl space. Guess I was tired enough to start snoring. She thought the damn place was haunted or something."

"So you introduced yourself, and the rest was history?"

"I worked on that building for almost a month," he said. "I

bought her lunch for scaring the hell out of her, and then I found out she liked dance music. Invited her out to the club I was working at. Took her a while to get there, of course, but once she did, she was hooked. Even introduced her to Dylan…that's the guy who taught her what she knows about spinning."

"Really?" *Dylan,* she wrote down. Maybe she could talk to him.

"Yeah. She wasn't great to begin with, but she learns quick, you know?"

"I'll bet." She wanted to talk more about PJ's job, but got the feeling that Sticky would object, so she just skirted it. "So, was it your idea for PJ to spin full-time? And how did you become her couch pimp?"

He chuckled at the appellation. "I'm just a simple bouncer, blessed with many friends," he said, in what she presumed was a *Godfather*-inspired accent. "Seriously, I know a lot of people, and when PJ needed a place to crash, I hooked her up. She became one of my best friends, of course I'm going to help her. But after a while, it turned into kind of a game. A challenge. And since she could get a lot of people into clubs with her the next night, she turned into a sort of pet that had side benefits. She doesn't stay with anybody that long."

"Haven't you ever worried about her?" Leslie wished she was jotting down notes on this. "I mean, have any of the couches ever turned into bad situations?"

Sticky's expression clouded. "Just one, that I know of," he said. "I didn't hook her up with that person. I'm very careful about who I let PJ go home with."

Now he really did sound like a pimp, albeit a protective one. "What happened? With the bad couch?"

"She won't tell me. She just ran out of there with her bag. She called me from her cell in an alley. She didn't have her shoes. Got glass in her foot, and it's not like she has health insurance," he said darkly. "I reamed her good after that. That's why she wears slip-ons and doesn't ever unpack."

Leslie's eyes widened. "I thought she didn't unpack because of her code of ethics, or whatever. Because it was rude."

Sticky looked at her with dismissive surprise. "Sure she does," he said, and she felt like an idiot. "Well, I'm sure that's an element of it. She knows how to make herself invisible at a couch's house. But there're a lot of reasons for anything she does."

Leslie was beginning to get that sensation. "So…when you met her at…where was that, again?"

"Saint…" he started to say, then frowned. "At a hospital where she was working." He looked at her with faint accusation.

"Okay. The hospital. You encouraged her to DJ. What were her biggest reservations?"

Sticky thought about it. "Confidence, I guess," he said. "It's a rough business. If you don't have the confidence, then you're going to get mangled."

"Sounds like journalism," Leslie said, and smiled when Sticky laughed. "Why didn't she have confidence?"

"She wasn't exactly surrounded by supportive people," he said, and she could tell he was thinking of someone specifically.

"Oh?" Leslie tried to sound casual. "That's tough. Following your dream, without people who back you up…" She thought of her own parents. "I know what that's like."

"It was a little more extreme in PJ's case," Sticky said darkly.

"Oh?"

Sticky seemed to catch himself, stopping abruptly. "And you could talk about that with PJ, but I wouldn't suggest it. She doesn't like thinking about it, much less talking about it."

"So, she's always worked in the city, then? And lived here…such as she does?"

"You're definitely going to have to ask her," Sticky said. "Listen, I have to say hi to some people. Is that enough?"

Leslie nodded. "That'll be fine for now. I may call you with more questions, if that's okay."

"That's fine," he said. "Just…you're not going to hurt her with this, are you?"

"I'm just writing a little story here," she assured him. "What harm could come from that, right?"

He looked mollified, but as he was walking away, all she could think was…PJ had worked at a hospital, starting with a Saint's name. There weren't that many of them.

chapter 8

Samantha sat in one of the cavernous classrooms in Dwinelle Hall, one of the largest and oldest buildings on campus. She was sitting toward the back, and nodding off. It was a low-level sociology class. The professor, a short, bug-eyed man with a gray goatee, was going off at length about "Lost Illusions" by Honoré de Balzac. She'd already read the assignment and thought the guy was a screaming whiner. She respected that he wanted something better for himself. She hated the fact that he cried when he couldn't get it.

She didn't have time for losers.

She glanced at her watch. Almost noon. Jenna and Andrea were ditching school, and the three of them were going shopping in Union Square. Samantha was pretty sure she'd be seeing Jonathan soon…she was helping PJ buy clothes for some kind of big event, obviously, and if PJ were performing, then Jonathan would be there. And Samantha would be waiting. She might work with PJ, but there was only so much you could do with someone who didn't care how they looked. Jonathan would notice the difference. She felt confident of that.

She shivered a little. It was freezing in the classroom. Probably the only thing that kept students awake, she supposed. She was wearing a turtleneck and her leather jacket, and she still felt like an icicle.

She heard the bells of the Campanile tolling the hour, and playing the noontime concert. Even before her professor could say, "All right, next week's reading…" most of the students were up, jostling their way out the door.

She felt a hand on her elbow, and turned.

"Samantha. Hi." It was Pham, her T.A.…teacher's assistant, or some such, for those who don't go to college. "You missed section this week."

She hated section. She loved that her classes held two hundred students or so, where she could sit anywhere, or even miss class, and no one would really give a damn. Section was ten people or so and the T.A., who meant well. This was where most of the homework was involved, since Berkeley professors obviously didn't have time to do stupid, menial tasks like grading. Or, some would argue, teaching.

"I'm sorry, Pham," she said in her best "I've been naughty" voice. "Something came up." Something being a call from her agent telling her to get over to the city for an audition.

"Well, I wouldn't mind so much, normally. I mean, I know you're one of the smartest people in the group."

He was buttering her up, she thought with a smile. Although she was one of the smarter ones in the group, she had to admit.

"But the problem was, the professor's insisted that we give pop quizzes. So you missed one." He looked nervous, as if he couldn't look her in the eye. "And you, uh, didn't turn in your homework, either."

It sucked that you couldn't just get graded on midterms and finals. The section grade weighed in at about a third of the total, and she needed to keep her grades up. Her grant depended on it.

"I'm sorry," she said again. "I can turn the homework in to you. And I'll be happy to take a makeup pop quiz."

"But I'm not supposed to give makeups for pop quizzes," he

said. "And I'll have to grade down for the homework, since you're turning it in late."

Little pencil-pushing feeb, she thought derisively, then realized that she was starting to think like her father. Instead, she pulled Pham to one side, away from the stream of students flooding out into the hall. "This was a special circumstance," she said, her voice deliberately pathetic.

His eyes widened. "Really?"

"I've been going through a lot of…personal problems," she said. "I just need a little time to sort things out. Can't you make an exception?"

He started to shake his head. She could tell he was a letter-of-the-law kind of guy.

She took a deep breath, putting a hand on his shoulder. Let her eyes well up with tears. "*Please,* Pham. This is important."

He let out a long sigh then looked around. "Okay. You can turn your homework in to my box. And I'll e-mail you the pop quiz."

"Thank you so much, Pham," she enthused.

"And…" He looked around again. "Don't tell anybody, okay?"

"Of course not." She hugged him, then watched his face light up. She figured she owed him at least that much.

She put her sunglasses on and headed outside. She'd get the stupid homework and pop quiz done tonight, no problem. And she'd have to start buckling down. It wouldn't do for her to lose her grant. Her parents helped as best they could, but they'd had kids a little later in life, and really, her father was as good as retired.

She saw Jenna and Andrea, and waved to them. "Hey! You guys ready to go?"

She didn't bother to ask them if they wanted lunch first. To the best of her knowledge, neither of them really ate.

Andrea looked at Jenna. "I can shop for a few hours," she said, "but I've got a call at three."

"Me, too," Jenna said. "It's in the city though, so it's on the way."

"Really?" Samantha felt a stab of jealousy. "What call?"

"Oh, just some shoot. You know Stan," Andrea said with a nervous laugh.

Which meant it was a pretty big deal, indeed.

Why didn't he call me?

Andrea must've read her thoughts because she laced her arm in Samantha's. "It's no big deal," she assured her. "We probably won't even make it, anyway."

Jenna's expression said *speak for yourself.*

"He's just throwing something at us because we can't make it to tonight's model party," Andrea added, giving Samantha a squeeze.

"I think he's just desperate," Jenna said with a derisive snort. "I mean, this is the second party this month for the agency. Doesn't that strike either of you as desperate? They're trying to build up their clientele base, but I think they're just—"

"Wait a minute," Samantha interrupted. "There's another party tonight?"

Samantha watched as both sets of eyes widened, and the two girls exchanged a worried look.

"Didn't you know?" Jenna asked.

Now Samantha was feeling very, very nervous.

"Where is it going to be?" She kept her voice low, modulated, even though fury was starting to simmer in her stomach.

"Um, over at some club. I forget where," Andrea muttered.

"They're having a dinner at Ruby Skye," Jenna said, then yelped when Andrea pinched her. "Owwww…*bitch!* What was that for?"

Andrea sent a pointed look to Jenna, then nodded her head at Samantha.

"Well, she's the one who asked. And she should be pissed at Stan, anyway."

"Ruby Skye, huh?" One of the richest clubs in the city. They only had top talent there. Prince had done an impromptu gig there when he wasn't even touring. Sean Paul had played there, too…they'd shown it on MTV.

It was beyond insulting.

"It's not that big a deal. I didn't hear about any girls getting anywhere from the last party," Andrea said.

"I'm going anyway," Samantha said, glowering. "If only to show Stan that he can't keep fucking around with my career."

The three of them walked down the hill toward the BART station in an uncomfortable silence.

"So. How is it going with Jonathan?" This from Jenna.

Samantha growled. "It's going."

"You're working with him, at least, right?" Andrea chirped. "I'm sure he'll come around. And then you'll have a boyfriend with tons of money *and* tons of contacts."

"Or something," Jenna muttered.

Samantha turned on Jenna. "Why don't you just go ahead to your call, Jenna? I'll just go shopping with Andrea."

Jenna's eyes widened. "What?"

"I don't need attitude," Samantha said. Jenna and Andrea had come to *her,* not the other way around. "If you're going to make catty little comments, I just don't need this shit in my life right now. Okay?"

"Okay. Sorry," Jenna said, looking at Andrea questioningly. "I didn't realize…"

"I don't need high-school bullshit," Samantha reiterated.

They fell back into silence.

"So you're going to call Stan tonight, huh?" Andrea tried desperately to change the subject.

"Oh, yeah," Samantha said, ignoring the fact that Jenna was sulking next to her, and focusing on Andrea's statement. "I'll be calling Stan tonight, all right."

I wake up sobbing.

I know what I dreamed, and it's the sort of thing where you think you'll never be able to forget. Then you open your eyes and you just feel like shit, but the dream's gone. All the emotions are still churning, and now there's not even a way to logic it out. It's animal instinct. Just this side of terrified, and I'm not sure why. The fact that I'm in Leslie's house doesn't help. I glance at my watch. It's four o'clock in the morning.

I go to the bathroom, look at myself in the mirror. I look like somebody punched me. I throw up what little dinner I had. It doesn't help. I brush my teeth, wary, jumpy, staring at the mirror as if somebody else is going to pop in the room.

I am, officially, freaking out.

I walk back to the living room, and pace a little, wondering if it will wake Leslie or her neighbors. Of course, me in my socks is hardly elephant tramping…but I'm not in my right mind right now.

I pick up my cell phone, look in my recent calls until I recognize Sticky's number and hit the send button. I know it's late, he's probably finished a shift. But it's…fuck. I don't remember what day it is. I'll just hope this is one of his late-and-out-to-breakfast days, instead of a day when he actually gets to sleep at an early hour, like three-thirty.

"Hello?"

"Sticky," I whisper.

"PJ? That you?" He whistles. "Calm down. What happened? What's wrong?"

"Nightmare," I say. "Pretty bad."

"It's okay," he says. His voice is like a sonic cuddle, and I grip the phone as if it's his hand. "It's okay, baby girl. Do you remember what it was?"

"Do I ever?" I hiccup a little sob, get a grip. "No. I don't remember. I've got to figure it was the accident."

"Okay. You're still at Leslie's, right?"

I look around. Shades of pink and mauve, as far as I can tell from the thin ribbon of light from the bathroom door. "Yup."

"Just talk it off. How's that going?"

"What, staying here?" I shrug. "It's fine. Weird to feel so settled, you know?"

"I bet," he says. "Are you sure you want to stay there?"

"You know me," I say with a little laugh. "I stay wherever. And it is sort of nice, not moving around so much."

"Because if you want, you say the word, and I'll find you another couch. No problem."

"Sticky," I whisper, "don't you get sick of taking care of strays and fuckups like me? Don't you have your own problems to take care of?"

"PJ, you are, like, my best friend," he says with enough deliberate Valley Girl accent to take any hint of sentimentality off what he's saying. "If I don't take care of you, who the hell will?"

"I could give it a shot, for starters."

"Baby girl, you took plenty of care, of yourself and other people who I will leave out of this conversation for the sake of my blood pressure. So don't worry about it. I don't."

"I do," I say. "I mean, at some point, I can't keep going on like this."

I hear the alarm in his voice immediately. "What are you talking about?"

"Nothing dramatic," I quickly clarify. "Just…I mean, I'm twenty-nine. I can't couch hop forever."

"Well, no. But when you're ready, don't you think you'll know?"

"Yeah. I suppose."

"There you go." He sounds as if he's solved the secret to staying thin without exercising. "It's just that easy."

"I love you, you know that?"

"Who doesn't?" But he knows. I can tell. It's just that we're not like that…if he can help it, he doesn't do mush.

"All right. I'm going to read, maybe play some solitaire, until I can get some sleep."

"Love you, too, baby girl," he says. "Sleep tight."

I hang up the phone, and I start to go turn out the light in the bathroom.

"Is everything all right?"

I let out a little scream, jump and whirl. Then I hold the arm of the couch as I catch my breath. "Jesus, Leslie."

"Sorry," she says. Her hair's sticking out, and she's wearing some silky-looking pajamas. Sort of like people in the forties used to wear, sort of classy. I never believed people actually slept in stuff like that. "I didn't mean to startle you. I just heard something, thought I'd check."

I'm suddenly wondering… "Did you hear my conversation?" Then I remember—I'm in her house. I'm in her living room. I can't exactly play the privacy card here. "I mean, did I wake you? I'm sorry."

She shakes her head. "No problem. I just wanted to make sure everything was all right," she reiterates. She looks at me with a curious and slightly suspicious stare. "Everything *is* all right, isn't it?"

"Well…yes. And no." I sigh. "I had a little nightmare, that's all."

"You were talking in your sleep?"

"No. I was talking to Sticky," I explain. "I just gave him a call. He's, well, he's sort of my support network."

"Really."

"And I don't know that you need to put any of that into the article," I say. Hospitality be damned.

She stands up a little straighter. I've offended her, I can tell, but I can't bring myself to apologize. That one, I meant.

"Well, I was just…you know." She stretches. "I'll just go to the bathroom, then go to bed. I can't do too many more of these four-hours-of-sleep nights. I'm not a young woman any-more."

She shuffles past me and shuts the bathroom door, plunging the room into darkness. She brings that up, every now and then…her age, I mean. I get the feeling that she only says it when she's pissed off.

That means I'll have to apologize. I probably should have Sticky look for a new couch. Hell. I should probably find one myself—poor Sticky shouldn't have to do all my dirty work.

She steps out, and I'm tucked on the couch. "Leslie…I'm sorry. About the article remark."

"No problem," she says, but I don't believe her. One woman knows when another woman's pissed.

"I trust you," I say, although even as I say it, I sort of won-der. "I mean, whatever you think will work in the article…I'm sure will be fine."

"Thanks."

Still pissed.

I take a deep breath. "Really. I know you won't do a hatchet job on me."

"I'm really tired," she says instead.

"Right. Right. Sorry," I say quietly. "Good night."

She starts to head for her room. The whole place is quiet—I'll just bring out my book light and read once her door's closed. If she could hear me whispering into my phone, then mixing beats is definitely out.

She pauses at her bedroom door. "Good night, PJ. Sorry you had a nightmare."

I don't feel better, necessarily. But I'm glad she's not pissed at me anymore.

Still, I definitely need to find a new couch.

"How are those personals coming?"

"Doing fine," Leslie said automatically to her boss, Miranda. "I'm catching up."

"Good," Miranda said with a skeptical look on her face. "It just seems like you've been on the phone a lot lately."

Leslie could feel embarrassment color her cheeks. "I'm just…following up on something."

"Well, make sure it's on your own time, okay?"

Leslie nodded, and made a great show of typing in personals into her layout sheet. That is, until Miranda walked down the hall and back to her office. Then she looked surreptitiously at her list. She had every hospital in the San Francisco Bay Area with a "Saint" in the name written down. There were nine of them, and she'd called seven. She was going to have to extend her search down to San Jose, at this rate.

She typed in a couple more personal ads (*Cinderella type seeking Prince Charming who's got more than a glass slipper* was particularly memorable) and then, when she saw Miranda's door close for a meeting, she picked up the phone again, this time calling Saint Genevieve's, in Belmont, just south of San Francisco and San Mateo. After several interchanges with operators, she finally got to the H.R. department.

"How can I help you?" the pleasant-sounding woman asked.

"Hi, yes, my name's Leslie Anderson. I'm checking the references of one of our job applicants," she said in the tone she'd perfected over the last four or so phone calls she'd placed. As a general rule, she was a lousy liar. Now she'd done it enough to almost believe she really *was* checking PJ's references.

"All right. What name, and what period of time?"

That was trickier. She had no idea when PJ had started the job, only a vague idea of when she'd left. "Her name is PJ Sherman, and she would have worked there…now, where is that résumé?" She made a big show of shuffling papers on her desk. "I can't remember the start date, but she would have left your company in early 2002."

"Let me see what I can pull up. The name sounds familiar."

Leslie wondered if she were laying it on too thick with the "I misplaced the résumé" ploy, but at least the woman was trying.

"PJ…that's a nickname, right? What's her full name?"

"She has it down as PJ," Leslie said, trying as best she could to sound disapproving.

"Do you think…it isn't Persephone Jane, is it? Persephone Jane Sherman?"

Persephone? "It certainly could be. And if it is, I can understand why she's going by PJ."

"It *is* sort of unusual," the woman agreed. "Let's see. Yes, she left in—"

Sudden, abrupt silence on the opposite end of the line. "Is there a problem?" Leslie asked, curious.

"No. Ah…er, yes. She did work here. From 1999 to 2002."

Something was wrong. "I see. In what capacity? I mean, what exactly was her job title?"

"Systems analyst. At least, when she left, that's what she was doing. She started as a programmer."

Programmer? Systems analyst? "Is there a supervisor that I could speak to about her job performance?"

"I'm sorry…what company did you say you were with, again?"

Leslie was taken aback. None of the other hospitals had asked these questions. Of course, "Persephone Jane" had never worked at any of the other hospitals, either.

"I'm with a small start-up. Citizen Systems," she said with a burst of inspiration. "She's applying to be our CIO. It could be that there was a slight misrepresentation of her qualifications." She made it sound as suspicious and ugly as possible, and immediately felt guilty doing it, but she got the feeling if she was going to get anywhere, it would be as a person trying to prevent someone from lying. There was almost a sort of altruism in that.

"Well, you might want to learn that, by law, all we're really allowed to do is confirm that she worked here."

Leslie could feel the frost in the woman's voice. "I'm just trying to protect our interests, miss."

"I can respect that. But you've got to respect our position. We don't want a lawsuit. Therefore, all we can tell you is…yes, Persephone Jane Sherman worked here from 1999 to 2002."

Leslie clenched her jaw. "A question. If there was something positive, a supervisor could tell me that, without legal repercussions, right?"

"I really can't say. I can say that if she had good performance evaluations, she would have copies." A pause. "Which she would have given to you."

The woman was suspicious—and she must've guessed that there was something not kosher about Leslie. Leslie felt the grip of panic, of being caught in a lie. "Well, I'd like to thank you for your time. You've been very…helpful."

Leslie hung up, then wiped the sweat off her palms with a tissue. She'd never make it as one of those undercover investigative reporters, she realized. She felt too guilty.

Still, it told her that PJ had worked at St. Genevieve's, and the time period, and what her job was. She might be able to go over there, say she was a reporter…see if anybody working there knew her, knew about her aspirations toward being a DJ.

But why?

It didn't really have a relevance to the story. She got the feeling Sydney would tell her that it wasn't edgy. Who was going to give a shit about the fact that she used to be a computer geek, right?

But there was something else there. She got the feeling that the H.R. department only trotted out that line, not because they thought Leslie was someone that shouldn't have been asking, but because something bad had happened. Maybe she'd quit because she had to, or else she would've been fired. Maybe she had flamed out. Whatever it was, Leslie got the strong impression that there was more to the story. Sticky had gotten closemouthed, and the H.R. woman had gone from Ms. Helpful to Ice Queen in under five seconds...*as soon as she'd seen PJ's file.*

So what was going on here?

"Having a nice break?"

Leslie jumped, startled. "Sorry?"

"Well, at least you're not on the phone," her boss said with a sarcastic smirk. "Now you're just sitting there, staring off into space."

Leslie looked down. "Sorry. I've had a lot on my mind lately."

"Why don't you come over to my office for a second," Miranda said.

Oh, shit.

Leslie followed the tall Miranda over to her office, feeling the watchful gazes of everybody else in the makeshift clusters of desks and cube farms staring at her. Miranda closed the door on their curiosity and surveyed Leslie with an impatient sigh. Leslie sat down and waited for the hammer to fall.

"What is going on with you, Leslie?" Miranda paced, an impressive sight considering she was five foot ten even before she strapped her stacked heels on. "You've been coming in late, you've been behind in processing personals. We've been getting complaints. I know you've only been working here for a year and a half, but you've always been one of the most competent people on the staff. This isn't like you."

Leslie felt guilt flush through her in a hot wave. "I know," Leslie said. "It's just...I feel like I've hit a dead end. In my job."

She took a deep breath, swallowed hard. "I've been thinking of a change."

Miranda's eyes widened, and she perched on the edge of her desk, crossing her arms. "Meaning, you've been thinking of quitting?"

"No," Leslie said quickly. "Just…I was thinking of maybe…trying to write. For features."

"Features? You mean, you'd work for Sydney?"

Leslie nodded.

"Does he know about this?" A trace of amusement crossed Miranda's face.

Leslie nodded, and then, judging by Miranda's response, immediately realized she shouldn't have.

"You mean, you talked to him *before* you talked to me." Miranda was an imposing sight when she wasn't angry. Leslie wished she had that kind of presence. She also wished she were anywhere but in this office. "So you're trying to worm your way out of your job."

Shit. Shit, shit, shit.

"I just want something with some career advancement," Leslie said. "I'm thirty-five years old, Miranda. I just don't want to be typing in personal ads for the rest of my life!"

"How, exactly, is that my problem?" Miranda's green eyes bore into Leslie, and Leslie was proud of herself for not flinching in response to it. "Fine. So, has Sydney given you any assignments yet?"

"He's letting me work on a story," Leslie admitted.

"Fine. Work on your story." Miranda stood and opened the door. "But if you get behind in your work again, or if I catch you using your time here to do his work…you'd better hope you fit into his department. Because you're going to find yourself booted out of mine. Do you understand?"

Leslie's eyes widened. She nodded, refusing to look scared.

"Consider this your verbal warning," Miranda said, and now Leslie felt a chill in the pit of her stomach. "I'll have a confirmation of verbal warning sheet on your desk in the next five minutes. You sign it, and I'll give it to H.R."

Leslie nodded again, and walked to her desk slowly, as if she'd just been given an execution date. Now her only hope of reprieve was writing this story and having Sydney hire her. There wasn't any other way out.

chapter 9

Samantha had been roiling since she'd watched Jenna and Andrea get into taxis to go to their call. She hadn't even picked up anything cute to wear, she was still so aggravated.

Which explained why she was here at Technique, at nine o'clock, instead of at home, studying and doing the homework and pop quiz that Pham had generously given her leeway on.

She hit her cell phone. She had her agent's cell-phone number, and she'd already left three messages. She motioned to the bartender for another diet ginger ale. The bartender, an androgynous-looking Chinese woman with a shaved head that sported a massive tattoo, gave her an impatient look before sliding over the glass.

"Stan, I can't believe you didn't include me in that call. A photo shoot? For who?"

Stan was at someplace equally loud, but she could still make out the irritation in his voice. Like he had reason to complain! "Samantha, honey, you've got a really distinctive look. Jenna and Andrea are more corn-fed, more generic…"

"More white, you mean," Samantha said sourly. "And younger."

"They can pass for younger, is the important part," Stan said sharply. "I can say that Jenna's fifteen, maybe even fourteen, and they'll believe her. You've got too much up front to be able to say that, sweetie."

God, she hated it when he pulled that "sweetie" crap. "I'm getting tired of this, Stan. I went on five calls last week, and nothing! What the hell is going on over there?"

"I only line up the auditions, sweetheart. The rest is up to you."

Samantha grimaced, then realized what she was doing and forced her face to smooth out into impassivity. "So you're saying it's me, is that it?"

"I'm saying it's *them,*" Stan said impatiently. "Listen, I'm doing what I can. And here's some good news—I'm putting you up for the Danielle Ichiba spring show. How's that for some pull?" He waited. She didn't make any encouraging noises. Eventually, he continued, "I can't promise anything there..."

"Yeah, well, no shit," Samantha said, taking a sip of her ginger ale.

Stan paused. "Listen, sweetie," and the nickname now sounded more like an epithet than an endearment. "Let me tell you something. In this business, everybody's pretty. Everybody's thin. And sometimes it's not just what you look like, it's who you know. Okay?"

"So who does Andrea and Jenna know?"

"Their father's rich. Big guy in computers," he explained. "That opens doors."

Samantha knew she was pouting, but couldn't help it. "I know people."

"Club kids and college students don't blow my skirt up."

Samantha winced.

"The Danielle Ichiba call is in three weeks," Stan said. "I've done what I can. I suggest you do what I tell you—lose five pounds, and lose the goddamn attitude. Or lose my cell-phone number. Clear?"

Before she could answer, he'd hung up the phone. She stared

at her phone, then clicked it off viciously, throwing it in her tiny purse. Then she drank the ginger ale in a few big gulps.

"Whoa. You might want to go easy on that stuff."

She turned. It was Aaron, staring at her as if she was in the *Sports Illustrated* swimsuit edition. "What's going on?"

"A whole lot of nothing," she said, her voice bitter.

"I don't get to see you much during the week," he said, and he stroked her shoulder. He didn't even notice that she was upset. "Want to dance?"

She sighed. He wasn't a big DJ or anything, but she could use a little pick-me-up. She nodded. "I just have to pay for my drinks."

"Let me." He put a twenty on the bar, nodding and winking to the bartender. The bartender lifted one eyebrow.

Obviously, he didn't realize she was just drinking diet soda. Samantha wasn't about to educate him.

He tugged her to the main room, smiling at other people who recognized him, then he pulled her close. The music was Latin-influenced house, with an infectious, happy beat. Samantha started dancing. "You playing tonight?" she asked, wondering if he worked much or if he just hung out at clubs all the time, paid or not.

"Yeah. I was punting…standing in for a DJ who got sick," he said with a shrug. "His loss. I'm just on a break."

Punting. The term made her think of PJ. "I'm surprised PJ didn't pick up the gig," she said speculatively.

"That one? She's playing for kiddies tonight," he said, rolling his eyes. "I forget where. I didn't know you knew her."

"Oh, yeah. We're tight," Samantha said, echoing PJ's ironic tone.

"Really?"

He wasn't listening to her. It occurred to her that he never really listened to her. He wasn't even looking at her at the moment. He was more intent on looking around, seeing who was looking at them. Who was going to notice that DJ Dizzy-Spin was dancing with a hot model, who might or might not be his girlfriend or something.

She suddenly felt sickened. "I have to go."

"Hey," he said, stroking her arms. "What's going on?"

"I just have to leave. I shouldn't even be here tonight."

He followed her, to her annoyance. "What's wrong?"

"I just need to leave." She shrugged off his hand. Why did guys have to get so grabby, anyway? "I'm not feeling well. And I've got class in the morning. I've got a ton of homework to do."

"Um, right." He smirked. "Okay. Well…call me?"

"Sure," she said, more to be rid of him than anything.

He let her go to the door, and then he went back to the dance floor. Once she was out, she looked for Sticky's familiar hulking figure.

He turned, wearing a fierce scowl, until he recognized her. Then he smiled at her. "Hey, sexy."

"Hi," she said. "Where's PJ playing tonight?"

He blinked. "She's over at…wait a second." He whipped out his cell phone, typed in a text message. "Let her answer, and I'll let you know. What's up?"

"I just want to see if she's taking my advice or not."

"I can't believe that you're coaching her on how to look," he said, shaking his head. "She showed me those outfits you made her buy. I mean…*damn.*"

"She looks better, then?"

"She looks different," Sticky said with a laugh.

Samantha scowled at him. "I know what I'm doing."

He held up his hands defensively. "Nobody's saying you don't."

She saw the way he looked at her, then she let out an exasperated breath. "Sorry. I'm having a shitty day."

"Want to talk about it?" He tilted his head. "Two shoulders, no waiting."

For a second, she thought about it. He was a good listener, she had to give him that.

"Here she is," Sticky said when his cell phone chirped. "X-scape. That eighteen-and-over place." He gave her the address. "I'll bet she's hating life. But she's there early. That place doesn't get going until eleven or so, and it's only Thursday. And, you know, school's still in."

"Don't I know," Samantha said with feeling. She looked around for a cab.

Sticky put a hand on her shoulder. She was getting sick of guys grabbing her, and spun. "What?"

His eyes were hound-dog sad. "Listen, I meant it. If you want to talk later…I'll be up."

She shrugged negligently. "Yeah, okay. Whatever."

She didn't want to look at his unhappy response, so she didn't glance back as she got into the cab. She'd head over, check on PJ.

With any luck, Jonathan would be there. She'd had enough strikeouts for one day. She figured she was due.

I didn't used to have an entourage. And when I thought about one, I never realized an entourage would be so bloody annoying.

I'm here at Club X-Scape…admittedly, not an A-list venue, an eighteen-and-over bop club that plays a lot of Top 40. Still, it's seventy-five bucks I would not have had ordinarily, and they let me come early to practice. Staying at Leslie's the way I have been, getting into creating music, I'm getting away from the actual turntable, and that's never good. The important part of DJ-ing isn't just lining up the music. Any idiot with a couple of CDs or a media player can set up a playlist at a party. The real art of being a DJ is tactile: putting the needle down, manipulating the speed. That's why iPods and MP3 players, and straight laptops, aren't given a lot of credence by DJs, but Final Scratch is not only accepted but admired. You get all the hands-on qualities of a record…that's all it is, really, a record. The thing is, the record reads directly off your laptop. Whatever you've got loaded in your computer is sent to the Final Scratch record, and then, when you drop your needle, it acts just like you've got the song pressed into vinyl. You can skip, scratch, the whole nine yards. It's actually really cool. Besides, there's absolutely no way I could live the way I do if I didn't have this setup. Getting jobs with it has helped, too.

"So, what are you doing now?"

That'd be Leslie. "I'm practicing."

"Practicing what?"

"Scratching." It's not a skill I'm really good at, so I've been working on it. "What I really need to do is find somebody who's really good at it, somebody who can work with me."

"Sort of like continuing education?"

I smirk. "Something like that."

"So…just computer skills aren't enough, huh?"

"Something like that," I repeat. "Actually, for most DJs, computer skills aren't important at all."

"Huh," she says. And then, with an elaborate casualness that I can see coming a mile away, she adds, "I guess you've got a background in computers, though, which makes it different for you."

I scratch unintentionally, and I step back. The Final Scratch records are expensive. I don't want to fuck them up just because a reporter has caught me flat-footed. "I guess," I say, not sure how to respond. What the hell is she trying to say?

"What sort of computer work did you used to do?"

Son of a bitch. "Something unrelated to being a DJ," I say flatly. "Trust me. I like this much better."

"I understand you were working at a hospital—"

"PJ!"

I have never been so happy to be interrupted in my life, even when I figure out it's Samantha, standing at the bottom of the stairs. "Yeah?"

"You're not wearing any of the clothes I bought," she says, sounding more like my aunt Ethel than a gorgeous nineteen-year-old club bunny. "What happened?"

"Didn't want to waste them on this venue," I call down, wincing when she, too, comes up on the decks. There ought to be some sort of policy—DJs only. In fact, I ought to tell the two of them to step off so I can get some work done. "I think there's a two-person weight limit on this platform," I lie, looking at them both pointedly.

"I don't weigh that much," Samantha says airily, and she really isn't kidding. She's been looking a bit bonier than when

I first met her. I have no idea how people find that attractive. Sticky especially.

"What, is there a party going on here?"

"Apparently," I call back down…and then notice it's my wayward manager. I have my full, crack-marketing, packaging and publicity team present. I feel like I should be reading off an agenda. "Could you ladies excuse us?"

Samantha is already off and running, heading down the stairs like a heat-seeking missile with boobs. "Jonathan!" She gives him a half hug. That's sort of unprofessional, but then, I don't think she took the job to advance her career.

Leslie looks ticked that she got thrown off track. "We'll talk later," she says. "This is an early night, right?"

"My set's up at midnight," I assure her. She's going to be my ride back to her house. I consider, again, looking for another couch, especially if she's going to be asking me questions about St. Gen's.

She nods, and then heads down the stairs. Jonathan is trying to pry himself from Samantha's grasp—apparently she can't have a conversation with him without touching one or both of his arms, or his shoulder. It's been a long time since I've been attracted to a guy, to the point where I might consider doing something it. Like I've said, it doesn't really fit my lifestyle. But when I do get to that point, I hope I'm never that obvious.

Of course, I'm not nineteen anymore, either. Samantha might act sophisticated, but she's probably got enough estrogen pumping through her system to turn a wrestling team gay. She might not see it, but she's got just as much *Tiger Beat* as *Vogue* in her makeup.

"How's it going?" Jonathan asks when he gets to the top of the steps.

"It'd go better if my helpful reporter and stylist would let me focus," I complain, and then feel bitchy. "Sorry. I'm just a little on edge."

"How's the demo coming?"

I grin. Finally, someone who wants to talk about something

important—not clothes or old jobs. "Funny you should mention," I say, handing him a CD.

His eyes light up. "All your new stuff?"

"Stuff I've been tinkering with." I'm proud. "And I really think it's good."

"I know it will be." He tucks it away in his coat pocket. "So. What are you doing two weeks Saturday?"

I think about it. "Don't know that I'm booked. I have some stuff during the week instead," I justify, feeling like a slacker for not spinning on one of the busiest club nights of the week.

"You're booked now," he says. "You're playing at Technique."

As I've played Technique tons of times, I'm not terribly impressed. "Thanks," I say, still not wanting to sound ungrateful.

He can tell, and his eyes are still twinkling with humor. "The main room, PJ. You're going to be playing the main room. I've got postcards made up, and they're going to be distributed at all the clubs in the city tonight." He hands me one.

I go into a sort of trance. "I'm headlining?" I've never played the main room of anywhere. For bigger clubs, like Ten-Fifteen, the main room is for big name, visiting DJs...people from Chicago or New York or L.A. Nobody local gets a crack at those things unless they're huge. This is a big step. An important step.

"I've also invited some of the biggest promoters in the city there. Rented the VIP room, with an open bar. I'll start lining up some more regular gigs. And none of this seventy-five-dollars-a-night crap, either. From now, you're getting paid higher scale, and you'll get more promotion."

I'm shocked. I mean, I knew that he was going to be my manager, and technically, this is what managers do, right? But it's been a long, long time since anybody else looked out for me, or believed in what I was doing. In fact, it's been a long time since anybody but Sticky gave a damn, it feels like.

Next thing I know, I'm hugging the guy. Once the initial surprise is over, he hugs back. I feel a little teary, and I don't mean to grip hard. I'm not trying to pull a Samantha here. It just feels nice.

He pulls away a little, but he doesn't let go. He strokes my cheek and smiles, a really nice smile. I'm starting to see what Samantha sees in the guy.

Probably not the wisest thing to see in my manager.

"Thank you," I say, pulling away. To my embarrassment, I feel a tear creep down my cheek, and I turn and wipe it away. "Man. I feel like an idiot."

"Why?" He's still smiling. He pulls out his wallet. "Here."

I blink at him, at the hundred-dollar bills in his hand. "What's that for?"

"Expenses," he says. "I want you to pick up a kick-ass outfit. Two, actually. After your big night at Technique, there's going to be one more hurdle. We'll see how well Technique goes first, though."

I feel nervous flutters in my stomach. He's talking record execs. I can tell. My excitement is warring with sheer clawing fear.

"You'll be fine," he says sagely. Then, to my surprise, he kisses my cheek. "Knock 'em dead tonight, and I'll talk to you more tomorrow, okay?"

I nod, dumb, and watch him make his way down the stairs. Below, Samantha is torn between staring at him with cow eyes, and glaring at me like murder. Leslie is busy jotting something into that little notebook of hers.

Since Leslie's busy and Samantha's otherwise occupied, I've got the perfect chance to practice before the upcoming set.

I don't mind that he kissed me on the cheek. I think it's been three years since anyone, including my ex-husband, kissed me anywhere.

Too bad I can't focus anymore.

chapter 10

Samantha stared at the statistics textbook like it was the Rosetta stone. Ordinarily, this stuff came like second nature to her. She was good with numbers, people had always said so. But tonight was Saturday. Tonight was PJ's big night, at Sticky's club Technique. Tonight was the practice run for Jonathan's record deal. She knew, because she'd hassled PJ into telling her.

Tonight, Jonathan was going to be schmoozing. He invited important friends who would spread the buzz about his new, unusual protégé.

Tonight would be a perfect night to see him.

She glanced at the clock. Nine-fifteen. She still had plenty of time to knock off this chapter, throw on something cute, get Sticky to let her in the club. And then she'd just "happen" to bump into Jonathan in the VIP room. He'd see her, say she looked incredible, ask to buy her a drink. And then they'd have a real conversation.

If she were really mean, and she let the fantasy play out, PJ would screw up beyond royally. Jonathan would be utterly disappointed and in need of cheering up. Samantha would then suggest that they go out to a late dinner, forget the whole thing. He'd take her back to his house, they'd order some twenty-four-hour gourmet (which she felt sure he'd know how to procure) and then they'd make lazy, luxurious love till dawn. At which point, she'd be his, and vice versa. As it damn well should be.

The phone rang. She was still in a delicious delirium of day-dreaming when she answered it. "Hello?"

"Are you studying hard?"

Her sexual engine went from revving into the red zone to stone-cold neutral in two seconds flat. "Hi, Dad."

"We hadn't heard from you, so I thought maybe we should check in. See how classes were going."

At nine o'clock on a Saturday night? He was calling to check up on her…make sure she wasn't out partying. It was annoying. "Dad…"

"What? A father can't worry about his only daughter?"

Samantha grimaced, then quickly stopped it. Wrinkles, she warned herself. And stress didn't help her complexion, either, and she might be going on a call Monday. But still, she was amazed how much her father could torque her system after all these years. "I'm fine, Dad. In fact, I'm supposed to be study-ing for a big test on Tuesday," she said, knowing that school-work was one thing that he always took a back seat to.

"That's my girl," he said, and she could hear the pride in his voice. And hated the fact that she still wanted to hear it.

"So, why are you calling?"

Now she could hear the pride erasing beneath anger. "Don't take that tone with me, young lady," he warned. "I'm helping pay for you to live on your own to go to that goddamn school, don't you forget it…"

She heard Tagalog. Her parents didn't revert to their native language unless they were angry and didn't want her to know what they were talking about. She closed her eyes, her world centered on the shuffling on the other end of the phone line. Her mother was now on the phone, with a choice, curt word to her father.

"Samantha, honey?"

"Everything all right, Mom?"

Her mother sighed. "Listen, Samantha, we just got a note from your school. Reminding us of the conditions of your scholarship. You've got to get good grades in order to keep it. At least a three-point-seven grade-point average. I mean, from what the letter said..."

Samantha screwed her eyes shut even tighter against the pounding in her head. "Yes, I know, Mom." She'd gotten a copy of that same letter.

"And, well, you know, your last report card wasn't quite as good as it has been. Your father's worried that you've been distracted lately."

"Tell Dad that I'm working hard and that I'll do fine."

Another quick exchange in Tagalog. Her father didn't sound convinced, that much was obvious. He got back on the phone.

"I know what college is like. I'm not that old," he said. "You meet boys, you go to some parties. You forget what's really important."

"I haven't met any boys, Dad," she protested. Jonathan was in his late thirties, or even early forties. Hardly a boy.

"And you were starting to talk about other stuff. Modeling? I don't want you hanging out with that sort of crowd. Don't want you going to parties. You lose your priorities, and you'll lose everything. And then you know what will happen to you?"

No, I can't remember, Dad. I've only heard your speech every week for my entire life. Why don't you tell me again? Maybe this time it will stick.

She would have rather swallowed her tongue than admit what she was thinking...so she did sit through the speech, yet again.

"You don't get a good education, you wind up like me...working the best years of your life, getting screwed over by pencil pushers, go out on disability and are then of absolutely no use to anyone. You'll never make anything of yourself if you don't get a degree, Samantha. And then you'll be like me. Spent, bitter...your whole life wasted. You don't want that. I don't want that for you."

"I know that, Dad."

"I could have made something of myself," he said. "I didn't want to end up this way."

"I know that, too."

He sighed. "Well, okay, then. I'll let you go ahead and study. Just…make me proud, okay?"

"Yes, Dad."

"Here's your mother. She wants to tell you something."

Another quick shuffle. Samantha felt her eyes welling up. The last thing she wanted was puffy eyes, so she thought of the catwalk, pictured herself walking down the ramp, wearing a Vera Wang original in one of her fashion shows. The tears held themselves at bay.

"Samantha, I just wanted to say I hope you're taking care of yourself."

"I am." She would turn at the end of the runway, she thought, and give just a little hint of attitude…keep the side-long glance, that sort of invitation. That seemed to go over well.

"You're not eating too much, are you?" Her mother worried. "I mean, I know that you used to eat when you got stressed, sweetie. So no candies, okay? Just stick to vegetables. And take your vitamins."

Samantha's grin was humorless. "I'm definitely watching what I eat."

"All right." Her mother paused. "Your father just has been a little stressed out lately. He's been meeting with the social worker. You know how he is about that sort of thing. The more we can do to keep him steady, the better."

Samantha saw why her mother had brought the subject up. That meant that her "perfect daughter" had to stay perfect, for at least a little while longer.

"Okay, Mom. I have to go. I have to study."

"That's my girl," her mother said. "I'll call you next week. I love you."

"I love you, too, Mom." And she did. She loved them both.

She hung up the phone in its cradle, as if it weighed fifty pounds. She stared at her book. Tired or not, she had to keep pushing at this. She didn't really have a choice. And there was no way she was going out to Technique. She really was behind in this class. She needed to bite the bullet. It wasn't as if Jonathan was going to pay attention to her, anyway. That was a stupid, childish dream. She wanted things, sure. And the modeling was starting to turn around for her. But Jonathan…well, she might have to finally realize that there was something she couldn't work hard enough for. There were things out of her reach.

Her phone rang again. She figured it was her mother, calling to remind her of yet one more thing that she couldn't fuck up. "Yes?"

"Samantha?"

Samantha almost knocked the chair over. "Jonathan?"

"Yeah, it's me. Listen…I'm just taking PJ over to the club. She's setting up."

Samantha forced herself to calm down. He was talking about PJ again. Why didn't she just get the hell over it? "Yeah. Tell PJ to break a leg tonight." *Among other things.* But that was mean even for her.

"You're not going to be here?"

Did he sound disappointed? Or was she just deluding herself? "I have to study tonight," she said, with every ounce of regret in her body.

"On a Saturday night?" He laughed. "You're kidding, right?"

She thought about explaining it to him—her grades, her scholarship. Her boatload of guilt. Then she realized it was way more trouble than it was worth. "I'm getting a little behind," she said. "This is the only time I can catch up."

"You're a model and a student, huh? And a stylist."

Now he sounded impressed. She felt herself puff up a little. "It keeps me busy," she said with what she felt was just the right combination of humility and cockiness.

"Well, I haven't seen you model and I don't know what your grades are, but I can say that you did an incredible job with PJ. I don't know how to thank you."

Samantha felt her heart start pounding frantically. *Oh, I can think of a couple thousand.* "It wasn't anything."

"I really appreciate it." And his voice sounded warm, almost creamily comforting. "Too bad you won't see it for yourself. If you change your mind, I'll be in the VIP room."

Samantha paused. "Are you...I could see you tonight?"

"I really want to thank you. But if you have to study..."

Samantha took a long look at her books. Then at her closet. "Maybe I'll see you tonight."

"I'll keep an eye out for you," he said. "Good night, Samantha."

"See you later," she replied, and hung up the phone. Now it felt weightless, and so did she. She floated over to her closet.

At that moment, she didn't give a damn about her scholarship. Didn't care about disappointing her parents. She only had one shot at this.

And Jonathan just asked me to meet him.

She found her sexiest outfit, and tamping her guilt down, she went in the bathroom to get ready.

Leslie stood with Rick on the main dance floor of Technique, taking in all the sights and sounds. It was a Saturday, so all the "tourists" flocked to the clubs. It was a meat market. She'd heard PJ describe the scene, but she'd become so used to going with PJ to less crowded venues during the week, and spending time with Rick on the weekends, that she hadn't seen the phenomenon up close. "Damn. This place is jumping," she said, turning to Rick and wiggling a little in front of him, her smile suggestive. "Wanna dance with me?"

He looked around, a skeptical look on his face. "I don't think there's even enough room. The floor's packed," he said. "When does PJ come on?"

"Pretty soon," she replied. "I think her set starts at eleven. Come on. Dance with me."

He laughed. "Didn't you know? Straight guys don't dance if they don't absolutely have to."

She pretended to pout. "And when, exactly, are straight guys forced to dance?"

"When they're trying to get a girl in bed, of course," he answered, winking at her.

"Well, maybe I'm putting new standards in place." She pulled him close, put her arms around him. He swayed with her—pretty much all they could do in the crowd—and nuzzled her neck.

She felt as if she'd been neglecting him. After all, in a roundabout sort of way, the only reason she was working this hard on the article was for him. For *them*. She hoped, on some level, that he understood that.

"So, you're almost done with the article, then?" he said in her ear, to be heard over the pulsing music.

She nodded, leaning closer to his ear. "This is the last thing I have to cover. This is the capper," she explained. "In a way, it's PJ's triumphant start to a new phase of her career."

"You really like her, don't you?"

"Yeah. I think she's nice." She paused, thinking about it. "I also think she's got some things to hide."

"Really?" Rick sounded surprised. "Like what?"

"Who she used to be. I get the feeling that something happened at her job, or something…I mean, I can't prove it. But I just have this hinky feeling that she didn't just decide to be a DJ and quit her day job. I also don't think that she just started sleeping on couches. Who would just do that?"

"So did you find out why she did?"

"Sticky's being closemouthed…"

"And for Sticky, that's saying something," Rick agreed.

"And PJ? For all she's concerned, you'd think she was born in 2002. She doesn't admit to any kind of life before she became a DJ. She's like a born-again disc jockey."

Rick laughed at that, and Leslie smiled.

"What are you putting in your article?"

"I'm sort of positioning it like that—woman with no past and no future, living in the eternal present of music."

Rick looked at her askance. "Um…okay."

"Trust me. It reads better." Or at least, she hoped so. "Besides, this is more about how she lives and the music…and I think a lot of people will like it."

"Why?"

"Because I think a lot of people like the idea of changing their lives completely," Leslie said. She was clinging to him now, the pounding bass and the press of bodies practically ignored. She hardly got to speak to Rick like this anymore, since he got his new job, since she was trying to get ahead in hers. "I mean, she's basically running away to join the circus—except nobody does that anymore. Anybody can run away to join this."

"That's a good way of putting it," Rick murmured. "You should put that in your article."

"Will you read it?" She felt vulnerable asking.

"I don't know anything about writing," he protested.

"I trust your opinion." She smiled, kissing his jawline. "That's one of the things I value about you. I know that you'll tell me the truth."

If anything, their relationship had been him being truthful.

"Okay." He hugged her close. "What, exactly, do you need from this, again?"

"I just thought I'd write about her standing on decks, you know, working the crowd."

"Have you seen her do that?"

She nodded, wondering what he was getting at.

"I'm tired," he said. "I can't believe I'm saying this, but I had a really hard week at work. And I was wondering if you wouldn't mind cutting out early with me."

"I kind of need to cover this," she protested weakly, feeling her knees give a little when he got a bit more insistent in his nuzzling. They were in public, and she wasn't a teenager anymore. Still, every woman buckled with a well-placed, well-executed nuzzle.

"But won't you pretty much know what happened?"

She gasped…and gasped again when his hands grazed a little lower than her back. "Rick…honey, I can't just lie!"

"You wouldn't be. You could just ask how it went. You know what she'll look like up there. It's just a little creative license."

"I really need to do this," she said, regretting it.

He sighed. "Okay. If you really feel you need to." He pulled away, to her infinite disappointment. "Listen, I'm going to go get a drink, okay?"

She stood, feeling bereft as he made his way to the bar. She looked up at the DJ that was currently working the floor.

She really did like writing. For her, it was more about finding out things. Seeing why things worked. She liked the whole investigation portion of it. The writing was tough, but even that was pretty worthwhile.

If she kept going with it, she thought she'd feel fulfilled. But what was the point, if Rick wasn't there, backing her up?

She saw PJ making her way up to the decks. She was dressed up in one of Samantha's selected outfits. She looked good. She looked nervous, and she didn't strut with Samantha's brand of self-confidence, but Leslie knew all that would change once she put her record down and started working her magic with the crowd.

She looked over to Rick, who now had a bottle of beer by the neck and was slowly drawing off of it. Despite being thirty, he had always been a partyer… Somebody who would love to close the place down. He and his friends were the same in that, which was probably why Leslie had never really fit in with that crowd.

Now he was saying he was tired. That he'd had a tough week at work. That he wanted to go spend some time with her, to feel better. That wasn't like him. That showed that maybe, just maybe, he was mellowing.

And here she was, being hard-core career woman, staying in a club when he wanted to go. The complete opposite of what they'd ordinarily be doing.

She walked up to him. "I had this idea."

He smiled at her. "Yes?"

"I think I'll leave the article hanging," she said. "I've seen it before. It ends with a sort of question—just before the biggest night of her life. She's nervous, but she's ready."

He raised an eyebrow. "Do you really think that'll work?"

She shrugged. "If not…like you said. I can use a little creative license." That felt shitty saying, but she let it go.

He smiled even more widely. "Let's go home."

She thrilled at the phrase.

chapter 11

I've played Technique before, but never the main room...always one of the side rooms, as an "alternate" while somebody who was making their name worked the main. Now, I'm the one that's moving up a rung.

I would never have thought of it as nerve-racking, but strangely, it sort of is. It would help if I were wearing my own clothes, I guess. This miniskirt-and-boots number, coupled with the midriff top, make me feel like a Volvo-driving soccer mom trying to be Britney Spears. Very day-old Pop Tart, very tacky. Thankfully, it's still dark and...

The spotlight turns on the booth, alternating magenta and ice-blue and yellow light. Fabulous. Just frickin' swell.

I need to nail this one. Show Jonathan that I can work a crowd, especially since he's promoted the hell out of this. I saw flyers for myself at the last club I worked, and it was a trip—looking at this little black and red glossy postcard with:

DJ PJ

TRIBAL PSY-FUNK HARD HOUSE DRUM-N-BASS
Playing the Main Room at Technique

And then the date, and the time, and the address. I mean, I've seen thousands of these postcards. If you haven't, you haven't been to a club. But I've never made them up myself, and when promoters print them and I'm on working for them, I'm usually billed in a list of five different DJs and some kind of theme. Like "Naughty Schoolgirls Night" or "Pimps'-n-Hos' Night" or "Drag Queen Races." And I'm usually second from the bottom on the list of performing DJs.

I want to live up to the graphic design on these postcards. Lame, yes, I know.

It helps that Dylan, my old mentor, is playing before me. I'm matching up to his rhythms, and after all this practice, it's not hard. It's like wading into perfect-temperature bathwater, comfortable and...

Scratch.

I blink in shock, staring at my Final Scratch record. Dylan is staring at me in horrified disbelief. This is totally amateur hour. I haven't scratched on the transfer in two years.

This does not bode well.

I'm onto my first song, but I can see the glares from the floor...hootchie-mama club-bunnies staring at me derisively, well-dressed dandy-boys giving a visual question: "Who's mixing this? My kid brother?"

Really, really does not bode well.

I don't see Jonathan, and that's a blessing, although he probably heard that, up in the VIP room with the promoters he invited. Right now, he's probably wishing he'd never heard of me, never offered me anything.

I take a few deep breaths. The fact is, I'm a great DJ. That sounds stupid, just saying it out loud, but I know I'm good. If I'm going to get scrubbed out of this business, it's not going to be because of my skills. I might not be able to dress well, and schmoozing may be outside my repertoire, but damn it, I can play.

I switch over (smoothly this time, thank God) to something more tribal, a little group I found on an MP3 legal swap, and trowel on the bass with a shovel.

The crowd isn't starting to move, I notice. They're not feeling it.

I'm sweating now, I can tell. It's not just the heat of the tri-color spotlight or the crush of bodies letting off steam from the dance floor below. The cool air of the fog machine makes the condensation on my too-exposed skin go clammy. I don't feel sexy. I feel desperate, and as any club denizen will tell you, desperation isn't sexy.

I want it too much. The crowd is starting to head for the bar, for the lounge, anyplace from the dance floor that is starting to die of beat stagnation, and I am scared shitless.

I think I see Samantha, just watching, arms crossed. And Leslie is around here somewhere, I can tell. I wish I could see Sticky, my human security blanket, but he'd be working the door. I don't need this.

Dylan is still standing there. And he strokes the back of my head, and smiles, leaning toward me. I take off one of my headphones, look at him beseechingly, tilt my head to listen.

"What's the absolute worst thing that could happen if you fuck up right now?"

I feel my stomach clench, feel the water I drank earlier. "I'm trying really hard not to think about it right now, Dyl. If you don't mind."

I am having enough trouble spinning without somebody trying to fuck with my head in an attempt to make me feel better.

He smirks and shrugs, an almost girlish gesture of disregard. But his eyes are serious. I feel as if he's going to call me *grasshoppa* at any second. As in *"focus on the music, grasshoppa"* or some such.

"Any accident you can walk away from isn't that serious."

Sigh.

He winks at me. "My other helpful piece of advice—if you're going to fuck up, might as well be memorable and fuck up big."

I look at the dance floor and people are starting to dwindle. This one's a wash, I think.

My stomach eases up, slowly, like a fist stretching out, finger by finger.

"What the fuck, huh?" I say with more confidence than I feel.

"Yeah," he says. "You still working on that P-funk mix?"

I nod. I wasn't planning on playing it…it's not quite ready.

"Throw it down," he orders.

I start to shake my head, and he just cocks one eyebrow and crosses his arms.

"What? You afraid you're going to scare away the crowd?"

I am surprised into a snort. "What crowd, you mean?"

Why not? It's a freeing feeling. If I've fucked up this far…screw it. Might as well make it spectacular. Sticky would probably approve.

I mix it over, gradually, almost tentatively until Dylan gooses me under my miniskirt, right through the underwear. As he's gay, I'm more surprised than offended, but it's the distraction I needed. I throw the switch and suddenly it's my music, flooding the half-full dance floor.

It's a sexy groove, I have to admit. It's a mix of tribal, a little Arabesque and some smoky hip-hop bass. Too mellow to be really drum-and-bass, and too funky to be house. I consider it aural foreplay.

Try saying that one out loud. You'll make new friends, no question.

The change of game plan is working. At least, it's stemmed the tide of vacating dancers, and they're starting to grind and groove appreciably. Dylan smiles, gives me a quick hug (and one more goose because he can't get over the fact that I'm in a micromini) and then leaves the decks to me. Looks like it's *grasshoppa*'s turn to prove herself.

I up the bass and switch over to something a little more traditional, a Top 40 hip-hop mixed over some house of my own. The crowd, sensing something familiar, comes back with a vengeance.

I'm still sweating, but I've got a handle on it. The needle slides over to where I want it to, the beats flow over each other like cream and honey and I'm okay. I'm starting to get to the crowd.

By the end of the first hour, I've got the dance floor back to where it started, and they're starting to jam for real.

By the end of the second hour, you couldn't get to an inch of floor space with a crowbar, and they're yelling, they're hooting, they're doing everything but tearing the speakers apart.

DJ Speedy is after me, I notice. He's Filipino, dark skin and short-cropped hair. He's looking at the crowd with a mix of awe and nervousness.

"Damn. You always this good?"

I shrug, play the humble card, but I feel like a goddess. I could part seas right now. I'm ready to supernova, I have so much energy running through my veins.

We make the switch over, swap demos. I hug him, which surprises him—I'm not usually a hugger. But I have to hug someone. I have to *do* something.

After packing up my gear, I descend the steps on shaky legs, and not just because of the stacked heels of my new boots. I need a drink, or a grounding cord, or *something*.

When I get to the bottom of the stairs, there's a small crowd. I'm going to find Sticky, Jonathan, and a couple of other friends and fellow clubbers. Party my ass off…I've earned it.

It occurs to me at some point in my celebratory haze that the man who is standing next to me is familiar. I think I didn't want to notice it until he steps in front of me, puts his hand on my shoulder.

"Persephone," he says. "I didn't think I'd see you."

At which point, my mind pulls a complete disconnect. The club, as far as I'm concerned suddenly goes silent as if someone's hit the mute button.

"Um… Hi. Lucas."

He grins, the half grin that I remember thinking was so shy and cute, his big bluish green eyes looking like…

Well, the romantic answer would be the Mediterranean, but the color always reminded me more of the reflective side of recordable CDs, the blue ones. For me, that was sexy.

"I'm here on business," he said, which I very much doubt, but remind myself I no longer care.

I nod, wracking my useless brain for some easy out. "I have to…"

"Can we talk?"

I look around. I should just say no. Quick, clean, over with.

Then he gives me the Lucas Special. A little, well, not lip quiver. But a sort of psychic wince, prepping himself for the shutdown he's expecting. His look of prepared pain is instinctual, and that makes it worse.

"All right," I say instead, because I hate the hurt that's forming in his eyes. I never could take that hurt, knowing that I was the cause of it. Damn it. Damn *him*.

"Great," he says.

I walk and my heart feels as if I'd stripped gears somehow. From sixty to zero, in fifteen seconds. Or, I should say, from career high to ex-husband, in under thirty.

Samantha had gotten ready at light speed, but she had lingered over her makeup…tasteful, making her look just older enough to seem mature. If she was going to make the next move, she'd need to leverage off his "good job" comments, make it seem that she was older than nineteen. She prayed no one else from the agency would be there—it wouldn't do to have *that* image of her stick in their minds. But the key here was Jonathan.

He had sounded so enthusiastic. So encouraging. So genuinely disappointed if she wasn't going to be there.

There wouldn't be a more perfect opportunity in the near future. And she was all about timing, especially when combined with persistence.

Sticky let her into the VIP room, and she scanned it like the Terminator. It was a fairly upscale crowd. Thankfully, she didn't recognize anyone. She got several approving looks, but not from any guy who mattered.

She spotted Jonathan in the corner, and, after taking a deep breath and a quick visual inventory in one of the mirrors, threaded her way through the crowd, smoothly stopping at his side. He was deep in conversation with several men. She wondered if they were important, record people or producers, or maybe club owners.

"She's incredible," Jonathan was saying.

"She got off to a rough start," one of the men, a guy in a black silk shirt, said with a note of skepticism.

"You mean that one scratch in the beginning?" Jonathan's derision spoke volumes. "The slow start? That can be smoothed out. You've got to admit...for the rest of the session, she ripped it off the hinges."

There was a look of reluctant admiration in the faces of the people surrounding him.

"But the prices you're asking," black-shirt-guy said.

"Wait until she gets her first record deal," Jonathan countered. "And then see how much it's going to cost to book her. Get the deal in now and it'll be a lock. You'll see. But you don't have to..." And Jonathan's smile was calculated...it looked as if he was almost encouraging them to hold off. "I don't mind making more money."

They grumbled. Then they all started juggling their calendars, little leather notebooks or Palm Pilots.

Jonathan spent a few minutes scheduling, and Samantha waited, feeling a glow of warmth and reflected pride. He was so obviously a prime businessman, so good at what he did. He was well respected.

He looked fantastic, too. A cut above. He looked like the most luxurious man there. She wanted to just wrap herself up in him.

"And who are you?"

One of the other men finally noticed her hovering, and was staring at her with an avaricious leer. "I just wanted to speak with Jonathan," she said.

"Damn," the guy replied, looking at Jonathan with envy and bitterness. "Anything you *don't* get?"

Jonathan just grinned and winked at her. "Business, guys," he said, and there was more grumbling and remarks like, "I'll be calling you tomorrow" or "I'll e-mail." "We'll nail down the schedule."

Jonathan put an arm around her shoulders, and she trilled. It was less than a hug, but his side was pressing hard against hers. He was more animated than she'd ever seen him.

"I think I love the entire world tonight," he said expansively.

She held her breath and smiled back at him, giving him a tentative half squeeze that he returned with a full hug. He seemed to be almost drunk, although she couldn't smell any alcohol on him, could smell nothing on him but his obviously expensive cologne. He smelled delicious, actually.

He released her, much to her regret. "Come walk with me," he said, taking her by the hand. "I want you to see your handiwork. She looks amazing. Just fucking *amazing*."

Samantha felt pride, as well as lust, at that comment. "Thanks," she said. "I worked really hard. And believe me, with PJ, it was not exactly easy."

She wondered, belatedly, if that sounded too bitter. It *was* his client, his star pupil, she was bitching about.

He just laughed, and she felt relieved. "She's stubborn. How many times do I have to tell people that?" He looked looser, like a live wire. If she didn't know better, she'd think he was high. But she got the feeling a guy like Jonathan didn't lose control over anything, much less give it over to mindless stuff like heroin or coke.

It was just one more reason she thought she could fall in love with him.

He guided her through the crowd. She saw eyes follow the two of them, imagined people thinking they looked like a gorgeous couple.

He laughed, and she felt his hand tighten on hers.

"I want you to do something really special. I just got her booked into the side room at 550. Not main room—but it'll be a special night and a special crowd. I'll give you two thousand dollars. I want her to look unforgettable."

Two thousand dollars. Spoken so casually, he made it sound like pocket change. "Uh…"

"The record execs will be there," he explained as his eyes looked up to the decks. He was staring at PJ, as best he could...he could probably only see her legs, and the kick-ass boots Samantha had made her buy. "I need her to make an impression on them. Her music will make impression enough, but it's a whole package. I need you to make sure she's her absolute best."

Samantha's shoulders tensed. "I don't know, Jonathan. I mean, main room at Technique is no biggie. But something like that...I mean, she's more than stubborn. It would mean more makeup. I'd...I don't know. We'd have to do something with her hair. It would take a *ton* of work." Samantha crossed her arms. PJ was no model, that much was obvious. If she fucked up this record deal, Samantha did not want to be haunted by the failure. She'd come too far with Jonathan.

She got the feeling that this could be it—the deal closer. If she tricked out PJ into looking like an elite hottie, if PJ got the record deal, Jonathan's bliss would make tonight seem like a funeral.

And Samantha would be there, as the recipient of his good mood. And that's when she'd hit.

Jonathan turned to her. "She doesn't need a ton of work."

Something about his tone of voice struck her as funny. But then, he'd always been protective of PJ. "I mean..."

"She's beautiful," he persisted.

The feeling intensified. "I wasn't trying to pick on her. She's just..." She searched for a more diplomatic way of putting it. "That sort of thing doesn't interest her. She's too into her music."

He nodded. She figured that comment would resonate.

Then he smiled at her, a smile that made her feel sugary in the pit of her stomach. He stroked the side of her face, almost cupping her jawline, and leaned in.

She pursed her lips, her eyes going soft and dreamy.

"I have faith in you," he whispered, and she shivered....

And then nothing happened.

She focused, and noticed that he'd blinked out—he was now focused on the music.

"She's finished," he announced. "That's the other DJ. She'll be down in a minute."

Samantha could have ripped out her own hair—or PJ's. Of all the guys she could have been in love with, this one had to have an obsession with music that bordered on insanity. Still, it was what made him the businessman he was. And nobody could fault him for that.

He took Samantha to the base of the stairs. "I want to see her, celebrate, talk about the big night. Maybe we could all brainstorm together," he said absently, but anything that might've been between them had vanished. His focus was entirely on PJ now, she could tell.

She'd just have to work on that. She could get Sticky to grab PJ. He would do anything if Samantha asked him to.

She was at the top of the stairs, and suddenly Samantha felt it again—that funny twinge. Jonathan was staring at PJ as if she was a gold magnum of Cristal, a four-million-dollar diamond. A miracle with a blue duffel bag.

It was one thing to respect your client, Samantha thought with a sniff. But this could definitely get in the way of their relationship.

She was staring at him, thinking of work-arounds to "the PJ problem," so she noticed the exact moment when his expression of rapture went black as a tornado funnel. Samantha looked over, and saw PJ reaching the back of the stairs…and a good-looking guy with reddish brown hair stopped her. He was talking with her. She obviously looked shocked.

And then the guy took her arm, and she followed him to one of the quiet side rooms without a bit of struggle. She looked…tolerant.

There was obviously something between the two of them, Samantha thought. An idiot could tell that.

"Who the hell is that?"

Samantha got the feeling that Jonathan wasn't really asking her. Which was a good thing, since one, she didn't know who the guy was; two, she didn't really *care* who the guy was; and three, she suddenly had a bigger issue.

Jonathan wasn't obsessed with his client, she thought, feeling fury bubble up through her like lava.

He was in love with her.

He was in love with a scrawny, old, scruffy little DJ who lived her life on other people's couches. It was inconceivable.

"I'm sure he's just a friend of hers," Samantha said with a bitchy little hook that guaranteed he wouldn't think that of PJ.

Now he looked as if he was in a killing rage, but compressed, in that cold, somber way that she had first noticed about him.

"If she comes looking for me," he said with a sub-zero voice, "you can tell her I had shit I had to deal with. And I had to go back to my house."

She nodded, not wanting to touch him or deal with him. She was perversely pleased.

Then he shook his head. "No. That's stupid. Just tell her…tell her I'm going to be in the VIP room."

Now Samantha was beyond shocked. He had been pissed, but he was caving. Because of PJ.

This was beyond inconceivable. This was intolerable.

"I will," she said with a hollow voice.

He nodded, not even paying attention, and headed back to the VIP room, with none of the vibrancy and spirit she'd seen before he witnessed PJ going off with some guy.

She had a rival. A punk-ass rival who had the one thing Samantha didn't…music. It just happened to be the one thing Jonathan valued above everything else.

Samantha straightened her shoulders. This meant changing her strategy. Taking out an obstacle. In a big way.

Apparently, she had to change her second statement. Now she cared about who exactly PJ had left the room with. She cared very, very much.

chapter 12

I just wanted him out. Out of my life, honestly, but out of my club would be a damn good start.

I take him to a relatively quiet corner of the club. It used to be the smoking room, before smoking got outlawed. It also used to be a make-out room. Now it's just storage. Broken bar stools, a few speakers, some various promoter crap. Tarps and cleaning supplies.

"You look good," he says, and I don't know what offends me more…the slight sexual edge in the comment, or the fact that he sounds so damn surprised.

"Yeah, well." I put my duffel bag down on a crate. "You're here on business, huh? Clubbing with clients?"

He looks down and to the left. Any detective would tell you he was lying. I didn't have a detective's license, but I had four years with this guy. It was training ground enough.

"No. I just really wanted to see you."

"I don't know why." I'm not trying to be a bitch here. I honestly have no idea what the hell he wants. "I waived alimony."

"The judge wouldn't really let you waive it," he said, shuffling his weight.

Now I know it's serious.

"Is this what this is about? You're worried that I'm going to suddenly start suing you?"

The idea has a perverse sort of merit. Other than the fact that I'd rather eat pincer-bearing millipedes than take a check from Lucas, an alimony payment would definitely take the edge off of paying my cell-phone and wi-fi bills.

"I think maybe we should get something in writing that says you won't."

I tap my toe, as sort of a nervous habit. With these new boots, the taps reverberate through my whole body. "Did you get a new job?"

He shakes his head. "No. I'm still with Maritime Communications...you remember? I got that job with them as a product manager..."

"Then you're getting married," I guess.

His face reddens.

I don't... Let me put it this way. It's not that I'm surprised. I mean, I *am* surprised. But not shocked. Lucas wasn't really the sort to stay alone. He started dating again before I'd unpacked my suitcase at my mother's house, and his new girlfriend answered the door when I dropped off the signed divorce papers. It wasn't that he was some kind of hottie that cruised bars, either. He was a serial monogamist. He needed relationships like Prozac, a way to keep the edge off. A way to function.

"So...when's the lucky day?" I don't really care. I'm just buying time.

He puffs up a little. "April," he says, and there's a ring of pride. "It has to be."

He wants me to ask why. He's *dying* for me to ask why.

So, naturally, I don't. "And your wife wants to make sure I don't hit you up for alimony, huh? That's sound financial planning, especially considering the way I live. I imagine she knows about your homeless ex-wife."

He grimaces. I mean, he honestly looks pained. It's sort of amazing to see. "She's got a point, Persephone. We've got a lot on our plates. With my budget... An alimony payment would ruin all our plans." He shifts his weight, puts his hands in his pockets. He looks like a stereotypical guilty schoolboy. It's how I've often thought about him. Probably because we met when we were so young, and only twenty-two when we got married.

There ought to be a law.

"Our escrow just closed," he says, and he's pleading with me. He actually takes my hand. I let him, because I'm floored.

"You bought a house?"

We'd meant to buy one. Never got to that point, couldn't get the money situation together, it was never the right time.

"It's a three-bedroom, out in Contra Costa, good school district, a new suburb. I just paid off my car. We're going to need every penny we can get…"

And here it comes. You know how you get that eerie sense of premonition, right before someone says something you can almost guess, but your subconscious is trying to protect you, so the actual words still hit you like a brick?

"…because the baby's due in June. That's why the April wedding. I'm going to be a father."

English no longer makes sense to me.

"Cynthia—that's my fiancée's name—she just wants to make sure that everything's in order. It's everything that's best for the baby. You have to understand that."

I don't understand anything at the moment. "You closed escrow?"

He smiles weakly. "Yup. It's a great house. You'd like it."

He was always a pro at having the absolute worst thing to say. To me, anyway.

A marriage. A house. A paid-off car.

"Well," I say, and my stomach is more queasy than it was before the needle-drop on my set, "I hope you're happy?"

It sounds tentative. I mean, I don't want the guy to be *unhappy*. I really don't. But this is all hitting me hard. It's like finding out the kid you baby-sat for is retiring.

That's probably a bad analogy for an ex-husband. Not an incorrect one, though.

"So...you'll sign the paper?"

"See if your lawyer can e-mail it to me," I say. "I'll sign it, fax it back to him. Okay?"

"I'll need it by March," he warns.

Ten bucks says Cynthia keeps him on a real short leash. Wish I'd thought of that.

"By March," I agree.

He smiles, nudges me on the shoulder. "You really do look good."

I smile back, but I don't mean it. I just think, *Schmuck, you didn't even notice the music.* A schmuck with a house. A new wife. A baby on the way.

"You don't own an SUV, do you?"

He blinks at me. "What?"

"Nothing. Never mind."

I don't know if I feel young or old. I do know that I feel really, really strange.

"You are...better, now, aren't you?"

I glare at him. "Would depend on how you defined 'better.'"

He takes the hint. "I just...worried. That's all."

"It's been years," I assure him. "I'm fine."

"You know...you could come to the wedding. If you wanted." He voice is warm, encouraging. Sympathetic. Possibly pitying. "Cynthia's hired a killer wedding planner. It's supposed to be gorgeous."

And the award for most clueless goes to...Lucas! For his performance in Schmuck Ex-Husband!

I sigh. "I think I'm going to be busy. My career's sort of taking off right now."

"Well. That's great." He doesn't believe me. I'm neither surprised nor concerned.

"I have to go," I add.

He nods, then gives me a warm hug. It's not quite like a hug from Sticky. It's warm, and sensual, and at the same time giving...like he'd rather be torn apart by horses than torn from your side.

I remember, however obliquely, why I loved this man...

schmuck or not, clueless or not. Despite his neediness and the fact that, beyond hugs and sex, his idea of support was spending your money on stuff to try to make you feel better.

Good luck, Cynthia.

I pull away from the hug, amazed to find I'm a little teary. "Gotta go," I say.

I turn, and start to bolt, running smack into Samantha. "Hey there," she says.

I don't want to talk to her. "I…have to go to the bathroom," I blurt out, the only thing I can think of.

I notice that she's walking into the storage room as I make a break for the ladies' room. It doesn't bother me—she's so wrapped up in Jonathan, I don't think she's going to be hitting on my ex-husband. But some part of me feels as if I should stop her. The last thing I want is for anyone to find out about him.

Or, more to the point, about me.

"Samantha? Honey, you've hardly touched a bite of dinner."

At her mother's gentle rebuke, Samantha tried to concentrate. "Hmm?"

She was sitting at her parents' house, in their small eating area next to the kitchen. Her mother had curried chicken and rice, along with some very depressing broccoli that she'd microwaved. Samantha had pushed her chicken around her plate after cutting it up into minuscule bites. She wasn't hungry, hadn't been hungry.

"What? Are you in love or something?"

Samantha looked up. "Huh?"

Her mother smiled at her, encouraging. "You're so preoccupied…"

"How are things going in school?" Her father was steadily shoveling away the dinner, and he paused only for this question.

Samantha shrugged. "School's fine."

Her father looked at her mother, and her father made that slight frown and head shake…the one that said *don't push her.*

Her father sighed. "What's fine mean? Do you like your classes?"

Had she ever? That always seemed like such a stupid question, however well-meaning. School was just a turnkey, something she needed to get her where she wanted to go. A means to an end, to put it in Machiavellian terms.

"Classes are okay."

Her mother glanced at her father with an amused, indulgent grin. "High school, all over again."

"I like college better than high school," Samantha quickly interjected. She hated any sort of comparison between the two. In high school, before she'd gotten the modeling contract, her life was hell. With the contract, she'd been able to ignore the catty girls with their superior attitudes and bitchy comments about her being Filipina, too tall…too poor, in a nutshell. Her parents had wanted her in a good school district, but hadn't realized exactly how good school districts were populated.

"At Berkeley, there's a lot more diversity, for one thing. And the classes are harder."

Her father puffed up with pride. "I bet my daughter was the only kid smarter than most of the teachers at her high school."

Samantha just smiled, and moved the rice to cover some of the chicken, forcing herself to take a bite. It tasted good, and her stomach made a little convulsion of hunger. It was all she could do not to devour the whole thing.

She forced herself to put the next bite down, and took a long drink of water.

Then her mother nudged her with her foot. "How's the modeling going?"

Thank God her mom asked. It made pushing her plate away easier. "I'm talking with my agent. I've been on a bunch of calls, but the work…" She grimaced. "I don't seem to be getting the callbacks."

"You're a pretty girl," her mother said staunchly. "I have a hard time believing that!"

"Maybe it's time you gave up that whole modeling thing, anyway, Samantha." Her father cleared his plate, got up and walked to the stove for seconds. He had a paunch in his stomach, hanging out over the waistband of his beat-up blue jeans. She felt some of her own hunger wane.

"Pedro," her mother reproached.

"Well, if she's not getting jobs, then why keep hanging on?" He piled more rice on his plate. Samantha watched, in horrified fascination, as he added another spoonful of chicken, ladeling on extra gravy. "You should keep your focus on school, anyway."

Her mother ignored him. After thirty years of marriage, she was used to his broken-record lectures, just as Samantha was learning to be.

"So…is there anybody special?" Her mother looked more like a mischievous girlfriend than a mother. "Any boys?"

Samantha's father groaned. "I don't have to hear this, do I?"

"So eat the rest in front of the TV," her mother said with a wave of the hand.

Samantha's father stood up, immediately complying. However, he gave Samantha a kiss on the forehead before lumbering over to the living room.

"So? Is there?"

Samantha closed her eyes. Jonathan's face immediately popped into her mind. She had been thinking of him ever since that night in the VIP room at Technique.

"There's someone I'm interested in," Samantha said hesitantly.

"Is he a friend of yours from college?"

Samantha got up, covering her plate with clear plastic wrap. She always told her mother that she got hungry later, when she was studying…and when her parents went to bed, she'd systematically throw the food out in the outdoor garbage, so there was no evidence. "He's not from the college," she said, wondering how much she should actually say about him. "But he is a friend of mine."

"Oh?" Samantha saw the faint crinkling of worry lines around her mother's eyes. "And what does he do?"

"He's…" Samantha thought about it. "Well, he's rich. He was a businessman on the East Coast, and he just moved to the city not too long ago. I'm helping him with a fashion project."

The worry lines creased and deepened. Her mother started clearing off the table, shooting a concerned look at the living room. Samantha could hear the sounds of ESPN coming from the TV.

Her father wouldn't be pleased. Then again, her father was so protective, he wouldn't have liked Jonathan if he were a straight-A dean's list Berkeleyite, either.

"I don't like this," her mother whispered, taking the dirty dishes to the sink. "I don't like this at all. Helping him on a fashion project? And he's a businessman? How old is he?"

"I don't know," Samantha admitted. "Older than me."

"Honey, I know you don't believe it, but *everyone* is older than you. You're only nineteen!"

"I know that, Mom," she said, wiping down the table, then getting out plastic containers for the leftover food. "But he's…nice."

And that was what made all the difference, Samantha thought. He was popular, and powerful enough to make models swoon. He had money and connections.

And he was still nice enough to talk to her when he didn't have to, to make her feel…like a person.

It was the first time someone who mattered had shown that he cared.

Maybe she *was* falling in love.

"Of course he's nice," her mother said with a trace of scorn. "You're young and beautiful…even if you are a little too skinny. Men are nice when they want something, Samantha."

Her mother's tone was unmistakable.

"That's not what he wants from me."

"How do you know?"

Because I've been throwing myself at him since I met him, and he hasn't done a thing. "I just know."

Her mother paused in her cleanup ritual, and turned Samantha to face her. "Samantha, sometimes I think that you want too much to be…too old, you know? You want to be a grown-up."

A grown-up? What was this, an after-school special? "I'm

nineteen," she reminded her mother. "I'm a student, and a model. I'm basically holding down two jobs." She glanced at the living room, much the same way her mother had. "And I'm keeping up enough grades to qualify for some grants. I've got a lot of responsibilities."

"I'm just saying," her mother said. "I know how hard you work here. And I know what you do to keep us happy. It's just…you're changing. You seem so unhappy lately. I hate to see you looking like that."

Samantha sighed. "I'll be fine."

"And…I know it's the look, but you've lost so much weight, and you're not eating anything."

"I'm fine," Samantha reiterated.

Her mother, knowing that Samantha had said the final word on the subject, relented, turning back to the soapy hot water in the sink. "So. This rich guy. Is he your boyfriend, then?"

"No," Samantha said, then grinned. "Not yet."

Her mother finally laughed, although she still looked worried. "Just remember what I said. Sometimes, boys and men both…they only want one thing from a girl."

Samantha thought of Jonathan. Of his kindness. Of the way he hadn't taken what she had offered.

When she got together with Jonathan, and she had no doubt that she would…when they were together, it wouldn't be brief. It wasn't going to be someone using another someone for either of them.

"So…what do you think?"

Leslie hoped that her question sounded confident, casual. Maybe just this side of cocky. She'd gotten half-naked at a rave, been in the VIP room of a slammin' party, and lost countless hours of sleep to get Sydney his "hip, edgy" story. This thing was so urban, it practically had graffiti tags on it. She dared him to complain about it.

"Hmmph." The monosyllabic reply was her only indicator. It didn't tell her a hell of a lot.

She sat in his uncomfortable office chair, a rickety, metal folding deal that he'd probably scrounged from the supply room. The more he read, she noticed, the more he frowned. The more he frowned, the harder the chair seemed to become. When he finally looked up, she thought she was going to break her back, she snapped to attention so quickly.

"Yes?" She was sounding too eager, but after the little Metal Chair Inquisition she'd just been through, she excused herself.

"How much is this PJ kid paying you?"

Leslie gaped. "I'm sorry?"

"Turn something like this in to me, you ought to be." With a flick of his wrist, he tossed her small sheaf of papers across the desk. "I haven't read a puff piece this blatant in years. Didn't you go to college?"

She was still too dazed by his criticism to know what to say. She focused on gathering the scattered papers, carefully, like some kind of paper shepherd.

"I don't understand," she said finally. "I got several sources. I thought the piece was, you know, balanced."

"I'm not interested in balance," he growled. "What did I tell you? I need juicy. You've got this thing so glossed up, shit wouldn't stick to it. What about the dark side? Drug use, drinking? This kid sounds like some kind of hooker-with-a-heart-of-gold... *but without the hooker part.* How the hell am I supposed to sell that?"

"Didn't the DJ part interest you at all?" Leslie felt a little of her composure come back, inch by struggling inch. "I mean, the statistic I put in, that more turntables were sold than electric guitars, starting in 1998..."

"Fabulous. I'm sure your *statistics* will get you tenure somewhere." He rolled his eyes, as if he couldn't believe that she'd kicked out her research as a selling point. "What I need is personal stuff. I don't care what your statistics say, most people might like to go to clubs, but not a whole lot of them either know about or care about what it takes to be a DJ. So you're going to have to do better than this if you expect to get published."

Leslie felt her heart almost imploding in her rib cage. She

just wanted to collapse into herself. "So you're saying I have a lot of work to do."

"No," he countered. "I'm saying that you've done enough, and that's it. You're finished. You're not going to make it over to the features section."

Leslie stared at him in shock. "Just like that?" Her voice cracked. "But I've worked so *hard*…"

He shrugged. "Not my problem. My problem is finding stories that sell this paper. If you'd addressed that, we wouldn't be having this conversation."

She couldn't help it. She burst into tears, literally…one of those embarrassing sobs that shotgun out of your mouth without warning.

His eyes widened, and he rolled his chair about half a foot farther from his desk, as if the beat-up piece of furniture wasn't enough to protect him from this crying madwoman. "Hey, now."

Leslie tried to rein it in. She'd had a spotty job record before, sure, but she'd never actually gotten to this point of a complete lack of professionalism. "I'm…sorry…" She hiccupped. "I just…I really wanted this…"

He let out a long, labored breath, like a heavy guy does walking up a flight of stairs. He sounded weary. "I'm not trying to be an asshole, here," he said, his tone gruff. "But if you think you're going to go anywhere in the newspaper business, honey, you're going to have to toughen up."

She nodded quickly. "I know. I don't know why I'm reacting this way."

Other than maybe this makes career eight that I've screwed up. And it makes Rick right—maybe I'm not ready to be married. Maybe I'm using marriage as a consolation prize. And maybe, just maybe, I'd screw that up even worse.

Wrong train of thought to jump on in Sydney's office. The tears started sprinting down her face in a torrent. Now he actually stood up, retreating to the corner of his office that housed his gray metal file cabinets. "Leslie, I'm serious. The article would need a lot of work. And you know, your job needs looking after, too. The personals have been suffering. I didn't mean to bring it up—" and now he sounded alarmed, since her bawling only increased, to the embarrassment of both of them "—but your boss did mention it to me. Well, she *did*."

"I know," she admitted. She was blowing off a lot of personals, and she'd started getting some annoyed calls from people, asking why they were running late. "I don't care. I want to write features."

Another deep breath. He looked completely at a loss as to how to handle her, which Leslie would have found amusing if she wasn't so busy making an ass of herself.

"You'd need more training," he said. "I don't have time for that. None of the other writers have time for that."

"Could you just tell me what was wrong with the piece? In detail? It'd just take a few minutes," she asked. Pride be damned.

"You make it sound like the fact that she's living on other people's couches is the coolest thing in the world," he said.

"I thought that was the point."

"It's an aspect of it, but you're going to have to look at the other side. Don't people think she's a mooch? Does she get tired of sponging off people? And what the hell happened to her, that she'd think this was actually a good life choice?" He shrugged. "I'm just shooting this stuff off the top of my head, but you get the idea."

"So, you want me to be harder on her, in other words." Leslie toyed with the idea. She'd felt a certain loyalty to PJ, and a sort of fascination. Still, she'd also resented her—especially when she left PJ to sleep until noon while she herself went off to work at seven o'clock, catching a crowded bus in the pouring rain. "I could do that. No problem."

"You'd need to do more research, too," he said. "Talk with people who know her."

"I talked to Sticky, and her manager," Leslie protested.

"Let me rephrase this. Talk to people who aren't just interested in promoting her career, huh?" Like he was instructing a two-year-old.

Leslie bit back her original, and considerably uncharitable, reply...especially since she knew he was right. "Okay. I can do that."

"No, actually, you can't," he said, shaking his head. "You've already got a job, remember? You keep losing sleep doing this legwork, and you're not going to do either this *or* the job we pay you for."

"I'm not dropping this," Leslie said stubbornly. "I can dig deeper. I can make this a more balanced article." She took a deep breath. "Especially if you let me bring in a temp. Just to catch up," she assured him quickly when his eyes widened as if he'd been slapped. By a wrench, say, on the back of the head.

"You actually want me to ask your boss to take in a temp so I can work on poaching one of her employees? Are you high?"

She closed her eyes. "I'll ask for some time off," she said. "Then she'll have to hire a temp. And I'll get you the article."

He studied her. "You really want it that badly, huh?"

She nodded vehemently.

"Okay. I'll give you two weeks," he said. "If you can shape the article up to my satisfaction, I'll print it. But no more screwups. And for God's sake, no more crying in my office. My heart can't take things like this."

"Definitely. I'll go ask about time off right now."

He cleared his throat, stopping her before she bolted out his office door. "Leslie, you realize your boss isn't going to be thrilled with this request."

"I know." But she'd deal with it. Otherwise, she'd be calling in with two weeks of stomach flu.

"She's already unhappy with your performance. If we get a particularly good temp in, well, are you willing to risk the job you have to get this article done?"

Leslie felt a queasy burst of surprise, like an ice-cold hand on the back of her neck. "Yes," she said, but not with her previous vehemence.

"Just saying," he said. "And remember...toughen up."

She walked back to her desk, feeling dazed. How good could a temp be, right? And it would take more than just that to fire her, although her boss would probably be reprimanding her when she asked for time off.

She straightened her back and her resolve. She'd worry about the other stuff later. Too much was at stake for her to worry about the consequences, right?

She knocked on her boss's door. *Damn right.*

chapter 13

"Can you believe how many models are here?" Jenna whispered.

Samantha was focusing on keeping her breathing calm, so she just nodded.

"I don't know," Andrea said, twisting her purse strap nervously in her hands. "I don't think I'll be able to make it. I'm only five foot eleven, you know?" She patted her stomach. "And I gained two pounds a few weeks ago."

"Told you that you shouldn't've had those beers at the kegger," Jenna said.

Andrea shrugged. "I puked afterward. I didn't think it would matter."

Sometimes, Samantha felt ages older than these two.

"And how are my ladies doing?"

Samantha turned, glared. Stan. The agent in absentia.

Before she'd signed with Whitford Modeling, she'd met plenty of agents. Of course, none of them had been interested in signing her, but they'd all seemed either like smooth, polished people, or else little, nerdly people. Stan looked more like, well, her first impression of him had been of a wrestler. He was yoked with muscles, and had a smile that looked more carnivorous than friendly.

Samantha wanted to pout, to sulk. To show just how unhappy she was about not being invited properly. However, she was too nervous to throw a fit at her agent. Instead, just like Jenna and Andrea, she crowded around him, looking for any hint of comfort in this convention of competition.

"Samantha, you look good," he said.

Was it just her imagination, or did he sound curt? "Thanks," she said. "I lost those five pounds you wanted me to."

He simply nodded, no further encouragement, and shifted his focus to Jenna and Andrea. "And you two look stunning."

Jenna preened. Andrea just made her wobbly half smile, too nervous to beam.

Samantha was torn between envying them and hating Stan.

"You ready to wow them today?"

Jenna and Andrea nodded. Samantha didn't even respond. She'd had these sort of prep talks before…not in the recent past, granted. But she knew that all that they served to do was keep models from showing their nerves on the ramp. She had too much practice hiding what she was feeling to do that.

"Stan, are your girls ready?" A woman coordinator, headset on and walkie-talkie in hand, said with no inflection.

"We're all going on at once?" Samantha asked, suddenly aghast.

"Apparently," Stan agreed. "Okay. One at a time, and don't compete against each other. There's a good chance she'll pick all three of you…no reason for her not to. Just do your best, all right?"

Again, Andrea nodded. She looked as if she desperately needed a hug. Jenna, on the other hand, sent a sly look to Samantha.

Samantha and Jenna both knew that Stan was lying. This was a competition, against every woman in the room. And most definitely against each other.

Well, a sixteen-year-old wasn't about to get the drop on her. That much was damn certain.

She walked onto the runway with Jenna and Andrea. This was definitely unusual. Normally they wanted to see girls one at a time, like her last audition, to see how each looked, to imagine how each would look in the clothes. Then again, she noticed that the ramp itself was unusual. It looked almost like a tree limb, with crooked, organic-shaped "branches" out to the left and right of the main runway.

Samantha hadn't heard of an audition like this, but didn't immediately discount it.

Andrea fidgeted. Samantha saw the designer woman study Andrea for a second, then write something down. Jenna must've noticed it too because her smile increased a notch.

Danielle Ichiba sat like a queen at the foot of the runway. She was wearing her long white hair in an elaborate bun, and she wore one of her own creations, a Chinese-style dress in a soft slate blue. She had a notebook on her lap, and her legs crossed. She seemed like an unblinking statue, or someone meditating in spite of the activity going on in front of her.

"All right," the coordinator said. "I want you to start walking down the runway," she said, pointing to Andrea. "You'll go to the first point, there, on the left. Then you'll stop, pose. Walk back to the main runway, and then walk down the right ramp. Stop, pose. Then you'll go back to the main runway, go to the front, stop, pose, turn, and walk back to the back. All right?"

Andrea nodded nervously.

The coordinator looked at Jenna. "When she gets to the first stop, you'll start your walk. By the time she gets to the second pose, you'll be starting your first one." Then she turned to Samantha. "You'll follow up. When the first girl is at the main-runway stop and the next girl is on the right one, you'll be on the left. You'll all stop and pose at the same time."

It occurred to her why, exactly, they were auditioning this way. It would be complicated not to bump into each other. Timing was going to be important. If you couldn't handle that, or paused a little too long to make sure that a *W* photographer snapped a picture of you, for example, you'd shift the emphasis from the clothes to the coordination. That wouldn't sell couture. Therefore, you wouldn't work for the collection at all. The key would be working together.

It suddenly also occurred to her that she should've talked to Jenna and Andrea about this. Her reputation was going to hinge on these two youngsters.

Samantha felt her shoulders pinch with stress.

"All right...*go!*"

Andrea started walking. She had a good gait, and considering she wasn't going to be best at coordination, it was preferable that she was going first. She walked to the first stop, posed, smiled. Then headed on to the second.

Jenna started walking.

Samantha watched the whole thing as if it was...what would PJ call it? An *Amtrak.* A complete train wreck.

Jenna's stride was too exaggerated, too unlike Andrea's. She lingered, and she didn't pay attention to where Andrea was, so they both made it back to the main runway together. Jenna had to pause so Andrea could walk around her.

Samantha thought she saw Stan wince visibly before she started her own walk. She was slow, deliberate, trying to be somewhere between Andrea's tentative strut and Jenna's near burlesque. She paid attention to Jenna's position, stopping and posing at the same time as the other two. She tried desperately to remain professional, even as some part of her wanted to hiss at Jenna, *You're screwing this up for all of us!*

There was one hairy moment... Andrea was walking back as the rest of them were making the switch. It wasn't an intuitive switch over. Samantha smiled at Andrea, just to try to relax her, as she moved past her gracefully toward the second position. Jenna was mugging it up at the main position. Andrea retreated toward the back.

Samantha started heading toward the main position, feeling the nerves that having the show's designer in front of the ramp induced. Jenna wasn't moving quickly, was trying to milk every second in front of Danielle Ichiba as possible, making them even more out of sync.

Samantha couldn't help it. She glared at Jenna ever so slightly before smiling broadly for Danielle. Jenna, she noticed, glared right back.

She stood, held her pose, spun slowly, and headed deliberately toward the back.

Jenna and Andrea were already bickering. "You were too slow!" Jenna whispered sharply.

"Yeah? Well, *you* were acting like it was a strip club!"

Samantha grinned at that one. She didn't think Andrea had it in her.

"I thought you ladies looked great."

Samantha turned, stunned. "Jonathan?" She couldn't help it…she rushed forward and hugged him. "What are *you* doing here?"

"Danielle's a friend of mine. I wanted to invite her to a house party I'm having," he said. To Samantha's delight, he ignored Jenna and Andrea and just smiled at her. She basked in it, like a cat in the sun. "You're invited, too, by the way. I want to make sure PJ looks her best," he added in a low whisper.

She didn't care that, technically, it was "business." "I'll be there," she breathed.

"You really did look good," he said with a quick shoulder rub. She wanted to just eat him with a spoon. "I've got to go. I'll call you later with the details, okay?"

"Okay," she said, and watched him as he went back to the main room.

She turned, to find Stan had joined Andrea and Jenna. All three were staring at her.

"Who is that hottie? I've seen him before." Jenna practically demanded.

"Is that your boyfriend?" Andrea asked.

"You know Jonathan Hadeis?" Stan added.

Samantha drew herself to her full height. "He's a friend," she said demurely, her inflection making damn sure that all three of them thought there was more going on than she was admitting to. Just the way she wanted it.

"That's funny," Stan said, and he crossed his arms. "Does Danielle know that you're Jonathan's, er, friend?"

"I don't know," Samantha said, doubting it.

"Because…well. I hate to say this, but she isn't going to take any of you for her show."

Samantha felt her bliss at seeing Jonathan evaporate. "What?"

"Why?" Jenna's voice was now turning puling. She was turning into a seriously annoying young woman. "What the hell did she want? I did everything but turn cartwheels out there!"

That could've been part of the problem, Samantha speculated.

"You just weren't what she had in mind," Stan said, trying to placate. But he looked at Samantha. Once he'd calmed the other two down, he moved on to her.

"You're a friend of Jonathan Hadeis, huh?"

She nodded. "He just wanted to invite me to his house for a party," she said. "Danielle's going to be there. That's why he's here."

Her eyes challenged him. *I'm better connected than you think.*

Stan looked at her speculatively. "Well. Maybe this boyfriend of yours can put in a good word. If you made the Danielle Ichiba show, all kinds of doors could open to you."

She swallowed hard. "I don't want to put that kind of pressure on Jonathan," she said, both to play it cool and because she didn't know what Jonathan was going to do. "Maybe I just can't make it into the show, that's all."

"You might want to reconsider it," Stan said in a low voice.

And that's when it hit her. This was one of her last chances.

Leslie met Samantha on the Berkeley campus, waiting outside of Dwinelle Hall. Leslie, herself, had gone to Stanford…she still had some lingering debt to prove it. Stanford had always been the sworn enemy of Berkeley…at least, according to Berkeley students and alumni. It reminded her in some ways of the supposed rivalry between Southern California and Northern California, as a state. Northern Californians thought that Southern Californians were rude, obnoxious, brain-dead when it came to socially and morally responsible issues, and just general assholes. Southern Californians, on the other hand, rarely thought of Northern California at all.

She wasn't looking forward to this particular interview. She'd done what she could to corner PJ, to get "deeper" and more balanced in her interview. She'd found out about the job, about the stress and why she'd quit. But the article still didn't pop. So she thought a few choice and bitchy quotes from PJ's "stylist" might add at least some flavor, a bit more of a "juicy" aspect.

It didn't help that Leslie really, really disliked Samantha. And again, there was the Northern Cal/ Southern Cal correlation. She doubted Samantha even gave Leslie a second thought, even when they were in the same room together. Which only made Leslie dislike her all the more.

"Leslie?"

She looked up. Samantha was wearing a deep burgundy quilted jacket, trimmed in what she supposed was faux fur, a turtleneck and a miniskirt, stockings and knee-high boots. With her sunglasses, she looked like a young starlet on her way to Sundance or Aspen or the Swiss Alps. She flipped her dark brown hair carelessly over one shoulder as she spoke. Her face was porcelain perfect.

That, Leslie reasoned, would be the other reason why she disliked Samantha. Yes, it was petty, she knew.

"Hi," Leslie said, tamping down those negative emotions for the time being. She was a professional journalist. And she just needed a couple of quotes, besides. "Thanks for taking the time to speak with me."

Samantha simply nodded, as if to acknowledge that, indeed, she ought to be thanked for sparing a few minutes of her precious time.

"I just wanted to talk to you a little bit about PJ," Leslie said, trying as best she could not to let her annoyance color her voice.

"You're still working on that article?" Samantha's voice was cool, amused, way too old for her supposed nineteen years. "Don't they have deadlines over at the *Citizen?*"

Bitch. Leslie smiled. "I'm doing this on spec. So anyway, how did you meet PJ?"

"I knew of her from the club scene, and because she's a friend of Sticky's," Samantha said with a casual shrug that made her hair shift, cascading around her shoulders. She looked like a damn Prell commercial. Not that she'd know what the hell Prell was. She was too young.

Leslie realized she was beginning to get depressed. *Focus, you ninny.*

"And how did you come to be her stylist?"

"She didn't tell you?"

Technically, Leslie hadn't asked. "No. Should she have?"

"I was letting her sleep on my couch one night, and she asked me to help her with her look. I thought about it, and I said yes."

Leslie studied her. *And what, exactly, was in it for you?*

Samantha smiled. "It also put me in contact with Jonathan Hadeis, who I admire and with whom I wanted to work."

"I see. And have you enjoyed working with Jonathan?"

"Yes…and no."

Leslie could almost see the agenda scrolling behind this girl's eyes. She was about as warm as an adding machine. Not that she was old enough to know what a…*oh, give it a rest, Leslie. She's nineteen, you're not. Let it go!* "Really? Care to elaborate on that?"

Samantha paused, tapping her lips lightly. Her lipstick stayed put, Leslie noticed.

"I need to say that I can only talk to you on condition of anonymity."

Now Leslie's ears perked up. This wasn't what she was expecting. She was expecting a petty princess with an ax to grind. And Samantha was no shrinking violet…she wanted attention. No, more than that. For her career, she needed it.

"What's so dangerous that you can't be named as a source?"

"Just promise me," Samantha said, shortly.

Leslie thought about it. Sydney would probably get off on an anonymous source talking trash, as long as it wasn't actionable trash. "Okay, you're anonymous. Dish."

She noticed that Samantha didn't like the tone of her questioning. Of course, Leslie didn't care much, either.

"I would enjoy working with Jonathan more if he didn't disagree so much with having the truth pointed out to him."

Now she was getting somewhere. Leslie scribbled notes. "What truth, exactly, would that be?"

"Well, there are a couple," Samantha said, crossing her legs primly even as she leaned forward, as if she were spreading prime gossip at the beauty parlor. "The first being that PJ isn't a model, or even glamorous, in the broadest sense of the term. You saw how much trouble I had with her. She never respected anything I had to say. She saw it all as one big joke."

Leslie remembered. Of course, she'd been snickering right along with PJ, so she guessed she couldn't really say anything to that point.

So far, this gossip was highly overrated.

"The second point," Samantha said, "was that PJ probably shouldn't get involved with her manager."

Paydirt.

"PJ's involved with Jonathan?" Leslie's eyes bugged out. "Since when?"

"She's not involved with him yet," Samantha said sourly. "But honestly, haven't you seen the way he watches her? He's always around, doting on her."

"He's her manager," Leslie said. "What else would he be doing?"

Samantha shot her a cool, you-don't-understand-anything sort of look. Impatiently, she said, "And he doesn't seem to understand that PJ's still hung up on her ex-husband."

Now, that had Leslie floored. "Her ex-husband? Where do you get this?"

"If you hadn't left early that night at the main room in Technique," Samantha said smugly, "you might have seen her go off with her ex-husband…and come back crying."

"You're kidding. What was she crying about?"

"Well…" And Samantha actually looked around—as if any of the thousands of students milling by the main thoroughfare gave a damn about PJ or what was being said. "Apparently he's getting remarried, and he wants her to sign a waiver saying she won't seek alimony. Ever."

Leslie felt a cold shiver. Alimony. PJ was one step away from the streets, and the guy wanted to make sure she didn't ask for a dime. "That doesn't seem fair."

"You don't understand," Samantha sniffed. "It wasn't the alimony. She was upset at the fact that he's got a new fiancée and a kid on the way. She just can't deal with it."

Leslie's eyebrow rose. Samantha might not be her most reliable source. If anything, she seemed a little too Joan Crawford—high drama, big on the revenge factor. And if there really was something between Jonathan and PJ…well, it wasn't out of the realm of possibility that little miss *Vogue* was looking for some payback. She couldn't go to her editor with this sort of unsupportable stuff, anyway. "Really."

Samantha's smile was small, just a quirk of the lips. "You don't believe me."

"Well, your story seems plausible," Leslie said.

Her disbelief must have been clear in her voice, because Samantha took out her PDA, clicking on it. "Wait a minute, I've got something for you."

Leslie watched as Samantha grabbed a small notebook, wrote down a number, and tore off the sheet, handing it to her. "Here."

"What's this?" She saw "Lucas" scrawled on it, with a local number.

"That's his number."

"Whose?"

Samantha rolled her eyes. "Her ex-husband. Lucas. Lucas Sherman."

"You know him?"

"I met him," Samantha said, with a small shrug. "How did you think I got all this? From PJ?"

"Does she know that you spoke with her ex-husband?"

Samantha glared. "I don't really have a close relationship with PJ, Leslie, if you hadn't noticed. What do you think?"

I think you're looking to screw PJ over, Leslie thought.

"You're the one who's been trying to figure out what PJ's past is. Sticky mentioned it," Samantha said, her voice low, wheedling. "Don't take my word for it. Why don't you just call him?"

Leslie finally verbalized what she'd wanted to say since the beginning of the interview. "What's in it for you?"

Samantha closed off like a camera shutter.

"Nothing," Samantha said. "You're the one who called me, remember? I'm just giving you information. You don't want to print it—you just want to give her side of the story…" She trailed off, letting the pause speak for itself. "Good luck with your article."

"Thanks," Leslie said absently, staring at the number in her hand.

Samantha shot her a look over her shoulder, looking for all the world like a Glamour cover girl.

"If the article ever, you know, runs."

She walked away before Leslie could reply. Leslie closed her eyes, fighting temper, thinking of the article as it stood. Sydney wanted balance. And sure, Samantha might be working an angle here. But damn it all, she might have a point.

She took one more look at the number.

It wouldn't kill me to call.

Dreaming again. Rather, nightmare again. I wake up still feeling as if I'm reeling out of control. I figure out where the bathroom is, flick the light on. It temporarily blinds me. Head for the toilet. Throw up the burrito I had for dinner…urgh.

I brush my teeth about four times and gargle with mouthwash. There is nothing worse than getting sick at three-thirty in the morning. Here's hoping I didn't wake up Leslie—she'll be pretty pissed.

I've still got the shakes. It doesn't surprise me. The big night with the record execs is coming up. With all this additional stress, I'm a basket case.

Need Sticky to talk me down, and I pray that he's still awake.

"Hello?"

"Sticky," I whisper, trying to enunciate the words and not the desperation. "It's PJ. I am freaking out. You gotta help me."

There's a long pause. Shit. This had to be one of his sleeping days.

"PJ?"

And that's when I realize that something's not quite right.

"What's wrong? Where are you…are you at Leslie's? What's happening?"

It's not Sticky. "Uh…"

"You're at Leslie's. I think I have her card here somewhere. Where are you? I'll be right over."

I hang up, then look at the "recent calls" screen. The number is close to Sticky's…but not quite.

I seem to have just phoned my manager to tell him I was freaking out.

Before I can shut off my phone it starts ringing. It's Jonathan. I ignore it, let it ring through. Voice mail shows a message. I ignore it, and dial the number right this time.

"'Lo?"

I did get it right this time, and I cry spontaneously, both in relief and fear. "Sticky," I whimper. "I am having a shitful time here."

He sighs. "Calm down. Calm down. I'm here. What happened?"

"Nightmare." It's all I need to say.

"Bad one?"

"Yeah."

I hear him pause, hear the drag of breath that signifies he's taking a pull off a cigarette. Even though I hate that he smokes, the sound is comforting. Reminds me of my dad, for some weird reason. I mean, weird beyond the fact that my dad smoked…I never particularly found the man comforting.

"Okay. Where are you, Leslie's?"

The phone chimes. "Wait a second. I've got a call coming in." I know who it is…I just want him to stop. I didn't mean to call him. I figure tomorrow I'll tell him that I was drunk or something, or playing a joke on Sticky. Whatever. Something I won't have to explain.

It's a text message.

I KNOW WHERE LESLIE LIVES. BE RIGHT OVER. DON'T GO ANY-WHERE.

"Oh, shit," I breathe.

"What? Are you okay…?"

"I screwed up when I dialed you," I tell him, my breath all in a rush, and I'm feeling nauseated again and I know it'll be one of those really painful dry heaves if I give in so I don't. "I called Jonathan. He just text messaged me…he's on his way over."

"What, now?" Sticky's voice pitches up an octave in surprise.

Leslie's house phone rings. I wince. "Apparently."

I dive for the phone, answering it. "Hello?"

"It's Jonathan." He sounds reedy—he's obviously on the speakerphone at the door buzzer. "Let me up."

"Jonathan, it's r-really nothing," I stammer, wishing like hell that he'd just go away.

Leslie comes out, her hair sticking up, her eyes squinting. For her, this is a school night. She looks pissy, in her long T-shirt and plaid boxer shorts. "Who is it?"

"I'm sorry," I mouth to her.

"PJ, you can either let me up or I can start yelling in the street." He lets me chew on that for a grand total of a second, then says, "And you'd better believe I'll do it, too."

I believe him. I hit the button to open the door, then hang up the phone.

"Who is that?"

"It's Jonathan," I say, feeling more apologetic than she'll probably ever realize.

She frowns. "You're not sleeping with him, are you?"

I goggle at her. "What the hell?"

"Because I'm sorry, but I draw the line at people having sex in my living room." With that, she turns and walks back into her room, the door shutting with a particularly snippy click.

I sigh, pick up my cell phone.

"Sticky, I have to go."

"What's going on? Are you all right?"

"Jonathan's just checking on me."

I can almost hear Sticky pulling his lips into a straight, thin line. "You call me when he leaves," Sticky says, and it's his no-nonsense tone, the one that usually stops guys from starting shit. The one that's right before he cracks some skulls.

"I will." I love him. Nothing funny, or anything. But I feel better.

There's a soft knock on the door. I hang up the cell phone, and take a deep breath. I open the door.

Jonathan looks at me with concern and trepidation, I can tell. He takes me by the shoulders, gazes deeply into my eyes. Not a Romeo-and-Juliet soulful gaze, though. More like a cop checking my pupils.

"What happened?" He looks over the rest of me now that he knows I'm not strung out. I don't know whether to feel relieved or offended, actually. Too many emotions, all in about a fifteen-minute span.

"Where the hell do you live?" It was like the man beamed over here.

"As it turns out, I don't live too far. And it's easy to drive fast at four in the morning."

"How'd you find parking?"

He shrugs. "I'm double-parked out front."

"You shouldn't be here." I'm whispering, looking at Leslie's door.

"Screw that. You sounded scared out of your mind." He strokes my arm, tilts my chin up with his other hand. "What happened?"

"I really don't want to talk about it."

He nods. "Bad acid trip?" he says. He actually sounds sympathetic.

I can't help it. I goggle a little. *"No."*

"I'm not judging here," he says in that carefully neutral voice that people who disapprove like hell always use to make you think they're somehow sympathetic. "I just…if I'm going to be your manager, I need to know this sort of thing."

"I don't use drugs," I tell him, and it's true. Nothing Nancy Reagan, or anything… I just said yes plenty of times when I was younger and much more miserable. But I discovered that couch living and drugs are a bad combination. It's like an extreme sport, my lifestyle… If you want to live, better that you've got all your cylinders running.

He nods, and gestures toward my makeshift bed, sitting on one end of the couch while I crouch protectively on the other. I tuck my knees up against my chest, hug them to me. "I'm fine," I lie.

He looks at me, smiles as if he's relieved. "You're full of shit, is what you are."

"Thanks much," I snap. Anger. It feels like manna from the skies, I swear to God. Nothing beats fear like a nice little boost of adrenaline. "Anytime you want to get the hell out, that'll be just great."

He doesn't cross his arms, or grit his teeth, or even huff out a deep, irritated breath. He just stares at me, with those sort of piercing blue-gray eyes of his. Like he's a priest, or at the very least an interrogator. It's intense. "Talk to me, PJ. I need to know what's going on."

"Your investment's fine. I just had a nightmare, that's all. Just a stupid nightmare." Better to downplay it. He doesn't need to know.

"About what?"

"I don't remember." Which is true, as far as it goes. I mean, I've got some vague idea. It's always variations on a theme…wouldn't take a psychic to divine what I get freaked out about.

"But you have it enough that you call Sticky?"

Now I bristle protectively. "I call Sticky about everything."

Now he crosses his arms. I find that interesting. "I need you to call *me*."

A little weird, I can't help thinking. "You're my manager. Not my shrink."

"I'd like to think I'm your friend," he says, and his voice is mink-soft, shiver-inducing, but in a nice way.

"How have I known you long enough to be your friend?" What, is he kidding me with this?

I have enough trouble without dealing with his friendship.

He looks at me, and then lets out that weird laugh of his…like a rusty hinge. "You know, most people would be flattered or at least think it's nice that their manager, generally a bloodsucking bunch, wants to be friends and has a personal interest in his client's well-being."

"I guess you don't get anything out of me if I'm dead," I say. Yes, it's uncharitable. It's also four o'clock in the morning. You have a nightmare at 4:00 a.m. and tell me how charitable you feel when your boss comes in *your* room to offer his friendship.

He looks at me. And yes, I feel guilty. Damn it.

"I know you're not a sleaze," I offer finally. "I think I can trust you."

"And the friendship thing…?"

I sigh. "Is not really a great area for me. So why don't we just stick with business? I seem to be having enough trouble with that."

He settles in against the couch. "I'm forty years old."

"Um…congratulations?"

"I was born in Minnesota, in a small town…so small, I can't bring myself to remember the name of it," he says, still contemplating the ceiling fan and ignoring me completely. "My father was a pharmacist. My mom worked at the post office. They had me later in life…they were both thirty, which was sort of late in life for the time, considering. My mom took care of her parents, my father went off to Vietnam. He met her when he came back, after her parents had died. Cancer and…something else. I don't remember what her father died of."

I don't interrupt him, but I am puzzled as all hell.

"My mom loved Motown music and sang with the radio every day of her life. She died when I was thirty-two." He pauses, and there's grief there, real as the Ikea special couch I'm sitting on. "I wore my best D&G suit to her funeral, and my father wore the same suit he'd worn to funerals for the past fifteen years. And he threatened to kick my ass, just like he did when I was eighteen and had told him I was moving to New York."

I really, really don't know how to answer this.

He looks as if he's lounging. I've never felt so much tension coming off of someone who looked so relaxed. "I've been a DJ since I was sixteen. I've made money at it since I was twenty. And there is absolutely nothing on earth I love more than music. When I hear you spin, I feel like you're talking to me, as clearly as I'm talking to you now. I would represent you even if you didn't pay me for it."

I clear my throat, syllables fighting over the lump of emotion lodged in my windpipe. "Wish I'd known that before I signed the contract."

He finally turns to me, and his face is so serious it hurts. My little attempt at a half laugh dies stillborn in my chest.

"Now you know more about me than anybody in this city," he says. "If you want to take me up on that offer of friendship, it's open."

I nod. I feel…odd. Like a refugee who's just been given the keys to a mansion. I feel amazed, pleased. Guilty. Not sure what to do with this lavish gift from a relative stranger.

He strokes my face. He does that a lot. It doesn't feel icky, thankfully. It just feels…also odd, I guess.

"Are you feeling better?"

I was feeling better after I spoke with Sticky. Now I was not only feeling better, I was feeling confused.

"Yes," I whisper.

He nods, satisfied. "Then I will see you tomorrow."

He stands up, so I stand up, to lock the dead bolt behind him. I follow him to the door. Then I'm surprised when he turns around and gives me a hug. One of those awkward, wooden hugs, where neither person is quite certain or comfortable with what's going on.

"Good night, Jonathan," I say. "And…thanks."

He smiles, and I have to say…some of my confusion goes away. I just feel warm and comforted, when I lock the door.

chapter 14

I am not entirely sure what I am doing at the Top of the Mark, the swank restaurant above the famous Mark Hopkins Hotel in San Francisco. I do know this, though—as out of place as I feel, it's nothing next to Leslie's out-of-water phobia. She practically begged me to come. I still feel awkward, after her interviewing me and everything. But since she let Jonathan's late-night visit slide, I felt as if I couldn't say no. And a woman only turns thirty-six once, anyway.

Her parents are throwing this shindig, and Leslie wouldn't be more excited if she were getting root canal work done. They pressured her big-time, so she couldn't duck this. I notice that Rick, her erstwhile boyfriend, isn't putting in an appearance. Something I find shitty.

Of course, I've since learned to say fuck all of that, but apparently Leslie hasn't. Still, I'm aiming for maybe one drink, and then figuring out some way to get her out of here. It's not as if she has a lot of friends at this party, if she's begging me to come.

Anything longer than fifteen minutes, and I'm seriously afraid that Leslie is going to hit critical mass.

So the elevator doors open up to the restaurant, a symphony

in dark wood furniture and light, Oriental-white starkness. There are well-dressed people laughing. Correction—there are some well-dressed people, and then there's a *Star Trek* convention hanging out in the corner. I blink, resist the urge to rub my eyes.

"That's Mark," Leslie says with a long-suffering sigh. "My younger brother. He brought some of his friends."

"So, you weren't kidding about the whole Silicon Valley–nerd thing, huh?"

She giggles, and I can tell she's glad she brought someone. I really wish Rick could have made it. I get the impression that the last family gathering was a little traumatic for him. I also get the feeling his traumatization and subsequent flaking is not sitting too well with Leslie.

A guy in a suit approaches us. To his credit, he only gives my graying black jeans and sweatshirt a cursory look and a fleeting expression of disdain, but if there's a dress code in here, at least he's not enforcing it. Since the dot-com bust, I've noticed that nobody can afford to be that picky these days. "Table for two?" he asks.

"I'm looking for the Anderson party," Leslie replies, sounding for all the world as if she ordered people around all the time, a side of her I hadn't seen before. It's actually sort of interesting. "I see them over…hello, Mother."

Leslie's mom is what they now call well preserved. Or Botoxed, depending on who you talk to. She's got ash-blond hair that's meant to give the suggestion of slowly graying maturity without, you know, actually being gray. She's wearing a dark green cashmere sweater that Samantha would probably approve of, and a pencil-slim charcoal skirt in some kind of tweedy material. She's got good legs for a "do-you-really-think-I'm-sixty"-year-old. She gives Leslie the two-cheek-kisses, very European, very out of place. She doesn't hug Leslie, either.

Then she notices me standing behind Leslie. I feel a little naked without my blue duffel bag (although that would *really* brand me as out of place here). I stuff my hands in my pockets and see if I can get away with a guy-styled "hullo" nod.

She's staring at me, and I can tell she's just about to tell me it's a private party when Leslie steps in. "Mom, this is my... friend PJ."

Boy. That's not awkward. "Nice to meet you," I mutter. Well, I don't know that I'd introduce the homeless DJ who was sleeping on my couch as a "friend," either, but I'm the one who agreed to come. It's not like I begged or anything.

"PJ, was it?" She doesn't go in for a kiss, and for that I'm happy. I just shake her hand. "I see. Well, come join the party."

Leslie sends me an imploring look as soon as her mother's back is turned, and since we took the trolley over, I instantly search to see what the bar situation is like. I am definitely going to need some recreational anesthetic if I'm going to fun it up with the Anderson clan.

"Leslie!" That'd be the brother, I guess...he's got the same reddish blond hair as Leslie, and he's a sort of older, goofier, pudgier male version of Leslie's face. He'd be about thirty, I'm guessing. "About time you got here. We've been waiting for you."

"Of course. How often do I get to celebrate turning thirty-six, huh?"

There's a general laugh amongst the pocket-protector set. "At least she's honest enough to admit it!" one jokester quips. I let out one pity chuckle.

Mark holds his girlfriend, one arm around her shoulders and a broad, almost stunned look of joy on his face. He doesn't know how he got her, either, from the looks of it, but he's not complaining. The girl looks as though she owns the place. I take in her perfectly tailored dress-suit, her proud, beaming smile... then the diamond the size of Calcutta, which is weighing down her left hand. Leslie had mentioned that her brother "did pretty well." Unless he'd taken out a second mortgage, that rock said that he was filthy rich. And this girl was no dummy. He might look like a goofball, but he knew how to spend.

I wouldn't want to sleep with the guy, but then, I don't wear jewelry.

A guy comes up...reddish hair going to gray in a hairline

that's already receding. Leslie's dad, I wager. He's wearing a suit that is groomed impeccably, but looks a little old…a little worn.

"I'd like to make a toast," Leslie's dad says expansively.

I swear, I can hear all of Leslie's muscles suddenly bunch up with tension. She holds her glass of champagne so tight that I can see the tendons in her wrist strain.

"To our wonderful daughter," he says, putting an arm around his own perfectly coiffed and expressionless wife. "For being so unique in her life view. Happy birthday, darling."

It's one of the less inspiring birthday toasts I've heard, but I'm no expert. Everybody else sips their champagne, the tinkle of laughter mixing with the clink of crystal. Leslie downs the whole thing in one long, slow swallow.

She's probably got the right idea. I down it, too, and feel a nice, expensive-bubbly buzz start to tickle my bloodstream. Ooh, yeah. Jay-Z's right about the curative benefits of Cristal.

For the next hour, I act as if it's a drinking game…when Leslie takes a drink, I take a drink. I get the feeling Leslie is playing a drinking game of some sort, also. Whenever her father gets up to give a speech, or her future sister-in-law tells a story about vacationing in Greece with Mark on the yacht he rented, Leslie searches for a waiter and grabs another glass. I think we've each had about six by now. They tell a lot of stories at these parties, I notice.

It occurs to me, as I hunt down a waiter to make sure I'm ready for the next round, that Leslie has gotten away from me. I figure she's gone to the ladies' room, and after six flutes of champagne, I see the wisdom in that plan, so I head for the ladies' room, too. As I head into a stall, I hear the click of heels on tile. And I hear Leslie's mom.

"Leslie Anderson, what in the world were you thinking? What's *wrong* with you?"

I freeze. As I'm sitting on a toilet, it's not like it's a hardship, but her mom sounds pissed. No pun intended.

"Who is that woman you brought with you? And…Leslie, are you *drunk?*"

"I just had some champagne," Leslie replies with the carefully enunciated indignity of someone who is trying to deny that they've had too much. "I'm not drunk."

"And who is that woman? Is she one of those people from the *Citizen?*" Her mother sounds scandalized, and I realize I'm just drunk enough to laugh and give myself away, so I cover my mouth with my hands. "God, didn't you tell her where you were going? She looks disgraceful!"

"That's how she always looks," Leslie says, but there's a sulk in her voice. "And...I just wanted to bring a friend."

"What happened to Rick?" Her mother's voice is like an interrogation light. "God, Leslie, you didn't mess that one up, as well?"

Daaaamn, I think. Sticky would be having some words with the woman at this point.

"No, and thanks for your vote of confidence," Leslie says.

"Don't take that tone with me," her mother spat. "Why can't you just be happy for your brother? It's not his fault you are where you are, and he's doing well. Just...be happy. Don't make this some kind of a scene."

"Mother, when have I ever, *ever* made a scene at a family gathering?" Tears now, I can hear them.

"Well, I don't want you to start with this one. This is too important."

I get the feeling this woman would eat her own young if it weren't so damn unseemly. Yikes.

Tell her off, Leslie! I mentally cheer. Leslie was thirty-five years old, oops, thirty-six, had a job and an apartment, and really didn't need this shit.

I don't hear anything. Then I hear Leslie say, "I'm sorry, I don't think I'm feeling well. Tell Mark that I...I think I'm coming down with something."

I'm sitting there, jaw dropped. Oh, no. Oh, *hell* no.

She was just going to *take* that crap?

"Yes, I think that's best," her mother says with the closest thing I've heard to approval in the woman's voice. "Go home. We'll talk tomorrow."

Boy, and if that didn't generate a ton of enthusiasm. I imagine another air kiss, maybe only one side this time because she's ticked off. Then I hear the door close and the snuffling sounds from Leslie.

I go about my business, and then wash up. Leslie is ceremoniously dousing her face with cold water. "You okay?" I ask.

She doesn't say anything for a minute, just stares at the fading cry-splotches on her fair face. She addresses her reflection. "Am I overreacting? I mean…am I just being dramatic?"

I blink. "Are you kidding? Leslie, I hate to be the one to break it to you, but your mom's…"

I wonder if I know her well enough to say a *bitch*.

I shrug. "Your mom's a bitch." Life's too short.

Leslie's eyes flash, and she stares at me. Then she smiles a ragged half smile. "Yeah."

I huff impatiently. "You should've told her off."

"I'm a little old to be rebelling, don't you think?" And Leslie sounds just like her mother in that second…her words clipped, her tone almost too cultured.

"You're never too old," I respond. I'm living proof of that. "Do you like what you do?"

She looks at me. "Personals editor at the *Citizen?*"

"Writing."

She looks down, then smiles, slowly. "Yeah."

"Well then, what fucking difference does it make what you wear, who you marry…any of it?"

She blinks at me, as if this hasn't occurred to her. "Easy for you to say."

"Just try it." I wink at her. "If it doesn't work, you can sue me."

She smiles a little stronger now.

"Look at it this way. Say—God forbid—your parents get deported to Zimbabwe and Rick winds up going to jail for murder or something. You're completely on your own. What would you do if you didn't have anybody to answer to, huh? What would you do if you only had your own expectations?"

She stares at me, and for a split second I think, no, I *fear* that she's going to start bawling again.

"What would I do if I didn't owe anything to anybody?"

I nod slowly.

She grins. "I dunno. Get drunk, I guess."

I laugh, relieved. I let things get a little too deep, there. Still, she's looking thoughtful. I wonder what she's thinking about.

Leslie sat in her cubicle. She didn't know which she hated worse—her job in the personals department, or the article that could free her from that job. Her request for two weeks' leave of absence had translated into two days. Two days of thinking only.

Lucas the ex-husband's phone number was burning a hole in her pocket.

Miranda walked up to her. "How's it going?"

Leslie gestured to her desk. "I'm on schedule and all caught up."

"I see." Her boss's face suggested she didn't like Leslie's attitude—maybe Leslie was reading too much into it, though. "How's your *article* coming?"

"I should be turning it in any day now." The words were out before she could stop it. What was she doing? It was like she was *trying* to get fired. Sure, she hated her job, but that was suicide. What if Sydney didn't like what she had?

"Isn't that good news? I'm sure you'll let me know if you're changing departments." And Miranda swept off without another word, shutting her office door with a little more force than was probably necessary.

Leslie had to get the article in. She knew that. Sydney had pretty much written her off, after her last attempt. She really needed to get it right.

You can't just interview people who have a vested interest in her success.

She picked up the phone and dialed.

"Lucas Sherman," a voice stated.

Leslie cleared her throat, took a deep breath, braced herself. "Hi, I'm Leslie Anderson. I'm with the *Bay Area Citizen*. I'm doing an article, and I was hoping I could interview you."

There was a pause of surprise, probably at the onslaught of

words she'd unleashed on him without taking a breath. "Um…okay. How can I help you? What's the article about?"

"It's about DJ PJ," she said, and when he didn't say anything, she clarified, "I believe she's your ex-wife. Persephone Jane Sherman."

She could hear the defenses snap in place. "I see. Well, as you pointed out, she's my ex-wife. I don't really have a lot to do with her life now."

This was going to suck. "I'm just looking for some background on her story."

"Did she suggest me?"

"Well…" Leslie wasn't sure which answer was going to get him to open up. "Not exactly."

"I just don't see how I can help you," he said. He sounded like he was trying to be pleasant, even reasonable, but he was just as closed off as the H.R. person at St. Genevieve. "It's nothing personal, it's just that my life is so different now. I'm getting remarried, my life's completely on track…it's just a complete one-eighty. I mean, I'd love to help, but…" He trailed off.

"That's okay," Leslie said, even though it was anything but. Then a lightbulb flashed in her head. "I just wanted to do a little fact checking, anyway. If you could just help me out there, that'd be great."

He seemed to sigh in relief. "Sure. I mean, if it's just fact checking."

"So, is it true that you left her?"

He paused. "Is that what she was saying? How did she put it?"

"I just wanted to check the fact, Mr. Sherman," she said…and waited.

He paused again, and then it was like the floodgates opening up. "I didn't abandon her, if that's what she's saying."

"But you did leave her?"

"What was I supposed to do?" His voice pitched higher, both in annoyance and with a plea for sympathy. "Here I am, thinking that everything's going fine, right? Next thing I know, she's coming home from work crying. Like every day. I ask her what's wrong, she says nothing. After a while, you get to the end of your rope."

Leslie scribbled notes, her mind racing. PJ had not mentioned much…but Leslie knew that PJ had nightmares, and that one time late at night, when PJ had called Sticky, she had mentioned an accident. It was worth a try. "So you're saying that the accident had nothing to do with it?"

This time, she could hear him let out an exhalation, as if her question had hit him in the stomach. She had hit more than a nerve with that one. She'd hit a live wire.

"Is that what's she saying? That I left her because of the 'accident,' if that's what she wants to call it?"

"It certainly seems that way," Leslie prompted, wondering what the hell he was talking about.

"I know it looks bad. But she'd been out of the hospital for two months when I asked her for the divorce. And she was practically begging me to leave her."

Now she was getting somewhere. "It does look bad," Leslie said, in what she hoped was a loaded tone. "Maybe…well, I want this article to be fair. Did you want to tell me your side of the story? So I can be sure the piece is balanced? I mean, it's going to be a cover story, after all…"

"Cover story?" He swallowed. "For God's sake, I'm going to get remarried in a few months. The last thing I need…"

She just let him stew for a second. "Mr. Sherman?"

She heard the sound of a door closing, and he started talking quickly, in a hushed voice. "She'd been depressed for some time," he said, with no preamble. "Personally, I'd blame her mother. That woman meddled in everything, wouldn't leave PJ alone ever. She thought PJ made a huge mistake, marrying me, but I think that she just hated losing the attention." He sniffed derisively.

"So you left her because she was depressed?" Leslie asked, forcing him back on topic.

"No! Jesus, no. I left her because she didn't want to deal with me anymore. She didn't want to deal with *anything* anymore. It wasn't my fault."

"Maybe you could clarify…"

"She hated her job, she said. God knows, she was working hard enough. I mean, I barely saw her. She was working eighty hours a week, easily."

A workaholic? PJ?

"She wasn't really interested…I mean, we were having some troubles as a couple."

"Were you something of a workaholic?"

A pause. "She didn't mention that I was unemployed?"

Oops. "She didn't bring it up in that context," she hastily improvised.

"I mean, I was going through a rough time, too. Her mother was giving me crap constantly, and I wasn't really seeing my wife, and I was depressed. But did I go into counseling? No, I didn't."

The guy was a bit of a whiner, Leslie noted in the margin. Still, he was the other side of the…

"Of course, I didn't wrap my car around the median divider of a freeway, either."

Leslie's train of thought derailed. "Excuse me?"

"I can't believe she's still calling it an accident," Lucas scoffed. "She drove into that thing intentionally. That's what the police said, anyway."

"She tried to kill herself?" Leslie squeaked in shock.

"I don't know about that," he hedged. "The shrinks seemed to feel it was more of a cry for help."

Oh, crap. "So that's why she was in the hospital."

"She wasn't really hurt. She didn't seem to be going that fast. But, of course, they put her in for observation," he pointed out. "I waited for the whole month that she was in the mental hospital. I would've been there more, but I'd finally gotten a job, and I thought that would make her happier…"

"So then what happened?" Leslie asked, at the edge of her seat. Then she realized—in theory, she already knew what happened. "From your point of view, I mean," she amended.

"She was in counseling for a while. She had a leave of absence from work. Then, a month after that, she just came home one day and said out of the blue that she'd quit." He sounded annoyed at this. "And she said she wasn't happy with her life. And she started making noises about wanting to be a DJ. Said she was miserable with everything, that she wanted to start over."

Leslie couldn't help it. With a pushy mother, an eighty-hour-a-week job, and a whiny husband, she couldn't really blame PJ for wanting to get away from it all.

"But she'd never even discussed it with me. And when I told her she was just being extreme, she blew me off. I got the feeling that I just wasn't *cool* enough for her new way of life, so I figured that the best thing to do was just end it."

"I see," Leslie said.

He seemed to take issue with her simple statement. "What was I supposed to do? She wasn't interested in working things out. She wasn't interested in looking at alternatives, you know? It was all or nothing, always. And from what I've seen, she's still the extreme PJ. Black or white, in or out, no middle ground."

"Um…"

"And you know something else?" Like he knew her. Like Leslie were somehow in his cheering section. "No matter what else PJ says, she's not happier with her life. She's just running away. And I hate to put it this way, but she's frankly not as cool as she thinks she is."

"Thank you, Mr. Sherman," Leslie said firmly, before he could turn this into a full-blown therapy session of his own. "I'll be sure to make sure your viewpoint is represented. I appreciate your time."

"I'm not saying she's a bad person," he replied. "I'm just saying she's…you know, troubled."

"That's very interesting," Leslie said. "Thanks very much for…"

"I mean, if she'd just…"

It took Leslie five more minutes to pry Lucas off the phone. When she finally hung up, she had pages of notes…and a whole new slant to her story.

"Looks like you're finally doing some real journalism, here."

She yelped, jumping with surprise, then forced her heartbeat to slow down when she realized it was just Sydney and not Miranda. "Just finishing up."

He grabbed the notes out of her hand. "Now we're getting somewhere," he said, with an almost lascivious grin. "Mental hospital? Car accident? And this line here..." He pointed to her hatchlike scribblings.

Leslie read the passage he pointed to. "The part about her running away?"

"No," he corrected. "The part where he says she's not as cool as she thinks she is."

Leslie shook her head slightly, not comprehending.

"There's your lynchpin," he said, with satisfaction. "Have it on my desk by the end of the day...and you might be on to something."

Samantha straightened the hem of her BCBG dress. She was trying really, really hard tonight. She had mentioned to her agent that she was going to be at Jonathan's house tonight, and her agent had just about drooled into the phone. The San Francisco hip set were going to be camped out at Jonathan's—he was having a dinner at the swank restaurant next to Technique, and then the A-list were going back to the party. Samantha hadn't mentioned that she wasn't going to the restaurant since it sounded as if everybody was. She was going to the private "after party." And she'd have her shot at Jonathan.

She was going to make sure she capitalized on every opportunity. Her agent was pretty much insisting on it.

She didn't look at it as mercenary. She had a genuine interest in Jonathan, that was no problem. If he could help her career, so be it.

She sort of wished that the other models knew.

She got out of the taxi, feeling a little tacky. The valet opened the door for her but still gave her this low-rent sort of appraisal. The valets had been scrambling up and down the street, and neighboring streets, trying to get parking for the cars they'd been put in charge of. The other guests were handing over the keys to Lexuses and Infinitis. They weren't that young, although many of them were good-looking, like nouveau riche Europeans in those chic clothes that Milanese people seem born in. She was wishing she'd kicked down and bought that vintage Ungaro.

Still, she was gratified to get at least a few looks at the door, from a guy in an amber silk shirt and matching amber sunglasses. His date looked to be about thirty-five, which probably meant a well-preserved fifty. It was a competitive thing, being trendy and popular. Fortunately, if you were rich, you knew how to stay in the game.

She wanted desperately to be in the game.

She steeled herself as she walked through the foyer. She didn't have too much of a problem walking into parties where she didn't know anyone…it wasn't the usual nervousness or anything, and as a model, she knew how to school her face to make it look as if she belonged there. Still, she searched the crowds for someone, anyone, she could connect with. Had Danielle actually come? Samantha was armed with the usual party stock phrases…how do you know the host, I love this house, blah blah blah. Nothing terribly sexy, but she was still gauging. There was an art here.

She saw a few businessmen standing in a knot around the bar, and walked over. They were laughing over something, and were doing that pause-for-a-breath-before-starting-up-conversation-again thing. Perfect timing.

"Hi," she said with a broad, bright smile. "I'm Samantha."

There was a casual round of "hi," "heys" and nods. And then silence.

"Having a good time?" She asked it with just the right tone—not too eager, just curious.

Again, the casual and subdued responses. Nothing she could really work with. And, unfortunately, the start of an edge of…awkwardness.

She excused herself. Not a live spot. The conversation started up slowly as she left, she noticed. She needed to find people to whom she was more attuned. She'd just picked the wrong group, that's all. She started scouting again, stopping at the bar to get a drink. She wasn't sure who it was that said if you're going to circulate at a party, get a drink in your hand. It made you look more…settled. Like you belonged there.

Not that she didn't belong there, she justified internally. Fiercely justified.

She saw a few women her age—models, possibly, from the look of it. They were standing in wallflower formation, standing facing the crowd, talking to each other. It was a little intimidating, actually, she thought as she decided at the last minute to make a pass. It wasn't wide enough, though, as she caught a snippet of conversation.

"Wonder how she got in?"

"I think she's one of Jonathan's groupies…you know how that is."

She lost the rest to the dull roar of the crowd. *Were they talking about me?*

She felt the slow but inexorable wash of party paranoia. She suddenly remembered why she hated parties. But she was a woman on a mission.

She heard the music and started gravitating toward that. A woman dancing always had a better chance, which was why she did so well at the club. She walked down a hallway and saw people crowding the doorway. She wiggled her way in, wincing when some people made a remark or two.

Nobody was dancing, she noticed immediately. Swaying a little, but for the most part they were just standing there, listening, trancelike looks of stupor on their faces.

There, on a sort of raised dais, was PJ. She was dressed respectably, at least…wearing the black skirt and Sleeping Beauty tank top she'd bought for her. Her hair was a little less successful, pulled back with a black band, but she was wearing those pink sunglasses. She was standing behind a table, hunched a bit over her laptop and iPod. She was focused on it as if the crowd wasn't even there.

She was playing stuff that was recognizable, at least, not just her own stuff. Samantha would've counseled her to choose that, but PJ wasn't exactly the type to listen.

"She's incredible," the guy next to her said to his female friend.

"Yeah. I mean, Jonathan's really doing the right thing. If he starts his label with someone like her—I imagine she could go mainstream in a heartbeat. But she's just edgy enough not to be a flash in the pan."

"You can see that she could make it," the guy agreed. "I mean, she'd have no problem getting packaged...and Jonathan's publicity machine? Second to none."

Samantha decided she might have a shot. "I'm her stylist."

They looked at her as if she was insane. "Um...that's nice," the woman said, obviously at a loss.

The guy had no such compunction. "Really? I'm the stylist for the Chemical Brothers and Fatboy Slim."

"Really?" To her knowledge, the Chemical Brothers and Fatboy Slim didn't have stylists. No offense, but they were basically, well, there was a certain geek-boy attractiveness to Fatboy, actually.

The guy sent her a shrewd smirk.

"Oh." He was kidding with her.

"When you mix like her, you don't really need to look like anything. Not unless you're going to be doing tours. She could go the same route as the Gorillaz and sell."

But Samantha already felt humiliated. She was striking out, a big huge goose egg. She worked her way through the crowd, ignoring their cheer as PJ put on some funked-up version of something, some mix of Parliament funkadelic and hip-hop. Even when the dancing started, she still felt as if she had to get out of there.

She bumped into someone. "Samantha?"

She turned, hoping it was a friendly face. But it wasn't, not technically. It was that reporter woman.

"Do you know when PJ's going to be finished spinning? I need to talk to her." Leslie was looking hugely stressed. When Samantha didn't respond, Leslie huffed. "Maybe I'll talk to Jonathan first."

"I doubt you'll be able to talk to him tonight," Samantha said flatly. "You're not important enough."

Leslie's mouth dropped open again. Admittedly this was over the top…even for Samantha. But tonight, PJ was riding the lightning, and Samantha herself was strinking out in every area. Samantha saw Jonathan, in the corner, staring at PJ, and she felt absolute venom course through her veins. A little sabotage might do her heart some good.

"Listen, I've known Jonathan for some time," she said. "He doesn't pay attention to anyone that's not A-list. He humors and smiles, but until you can prove you're A-list, he's going to treat you like a bug. You get my point? You see where I'm going here?"

"So, " Leslie said, her eyes going sharply green, "I suppose that's why you're here talking with me, and not somewhere sipping champagne with him, huh?"

Which got right to the heart of the matter.

"Take a hint. PJ isn't there yet…that's why she needs you. She can't stand you. She said so," Samantha said, feeling no compunction about being cruel. "She used me the same way. So I know. If you don't believe me, ask her yourself. If you can even get to her."

"Okay, this is getting very teen movie," Leslie said. "This isn't high school, you know. Although you're acting very, very cheerleader."

Samantha all but hissed. "Fine. Don't listen to me. But when you talk to her, find out why she agreed to do an article with you. See how far your career's going to go just by doing a favor for someone who will do absolutely nothing for you when you're trying to get ahead with your career. She's only thinking of herself. You're going to have to do the same."

Leslie blinked at her. "Okay…you're getting a little nuts here."

Samantha just huffed and walked off. Fine. Let the little kid be a schmuck. She'd understand.

Just like Samantha was understanding now.

If you're so A-list, what are you doing talking to me?

She was right. She was so…fucking…right.

She looked back in at the stage. The music was blasting. Jonathan was onstage. Standing next to PJ, who was obviously on autopilot. He was staring at her…God. Samantha had guys lust after her before, but she would give her right arm to have a man stare at her the way Jonathan was staring at PJ. It was almost…

Reverent.

"Hey, sexy," a voice whispered in her ear.

She looked over, startled. It was Aaron. "I…what are you doing here?"

"Are you kidding me? Anybody who's anybody's here!"

"Am I anybody, then?" It sounded downright whining…and that wasn't sexy. She tried for a smile.

It was enough. He stroked the back of her neck. "Are you kidding? I was hoping you'd be here tonight."

"Yeah, well, I've about had enough," she said, and she was bitter. She didn't care that she was, either. "I think I'm going to go home."

"Did you drive?"

She shook her head.

"Want me to take you? I'd be happy to."

"Shouldn't you be here…you know. Making connections? Getting ahead? Shit like that?"

He didn't turn away from her. "I'd much rather make a connection with you."

It was the world's cheesiest line. She thought back to the look Jonathan had given PJ. Aaron was staring at her as if he wanted to devour her.

It wasn't the same, she thought.

"Okay," she said. "Let's go."

It was close enough.

chapter 15

I've finished my set. I've never done a set in a living room as nice as Jonathan's, or in front of a crowd as influential. I haven't eaten since this morning, so I'm feeling a little light-headed, but I can't eat yet. Jonathan's motioning me over… I think he's got people he wants me to meet. No. I *know* he has people he wants me to meet. That's the point of this whole exercise, after all. True to his word, he's making my career grow at an exponential rate.

I feel naked without my duffel bag. I already sort of feel naked, thanks to the getup that Samantha had me buy. My haircut's held up, I've put on makeup. I'm wearing a black sleeveless shirt that emphasizes my shoulders (or, more to the point, deemphasizes my lack of a chest) and a long skirt that has a slit up both sides. I'm wearing heels. Hopefully, most people didn't notice that I played most of my set barefoot.

I walk to Jonathan, taking his hand for sheer moral support. I'm nervous as all hell. I'm also feeling sugar depleted. If I don't eat something soon, I think I may just pass out. And won't that make a good impression on the record labels?

I would give someone my right leg if they could make this whole experience over with.

"PJ…this is Dave Monroe. He works at Red Rover records. That's one of the dance imprints of…"

He says a name, but I swear to God, I blank it out. Warner? EMI? I don't know. "They're very influential," he says, as if I couldn't guess.

I shake the guy's hand. "Nice to meet you."

"DJ PJ," Dave says, pumping my hand like a used-car sales-man, and already I know…this isn't the guy, and this probably isn't the label. He looks at Jonathan, drops his voice. "We'll come up with a better name."

I see Jonathan's face remain completely impassive. I spend a few minutes talking to Dave about my style of music ("I think of it as tribal-progressive-hard house, with a breakbeat influ-ence" he says, and I wonder if he even knows what the hell he's talking about) and then a few minutes about my look ("Have you considered spandex?" Is this guy serious?). Luckily, after twenty minutes or so, Jonathan tells Dave I have to circulate, activating an avaricious gleam in Dave's eye. In the meantime, I breathe a small thank-you to Jonathan for saving me.

"Sorry about that," Jonathan muttered. "He's new to the di-vision. I think he used to work Top 40 and got demoted. Still, he was a good exercise. You're doing great."

You're doing great. He says that to me after every new person I meet…the Goth-looking Chinese woman from Trance-Scendant records, the tall, thin black guy from Dance Noir's label. I don't get completely comfortable, but I definitely get more used to speaking to people. It's like performing…a little warm-up goes a long way.

I glad-hand for about an hour and a half. I'm in the middle of speaking with a short guy with glasses, Bill somebody-or-other, about Final Scratch, when what I thought would hap-pen happens.

"Final Scratch gives you all the benefits of digital music, and all the physicality of—"

Yowl.

I stare down at my stomach. Surely that noise did not come out of my digestive system.

"I'm sorry," I say, horribly embarrassed, even as Bill laughs.

"I guess you're hungry," he says, chuckling. "I'm sure there's some food around here. Looks like the party's winding down, anyway."

I nod. I really should've eaten an hour ago.

"We'll definitely be calling you," he says, pressing his card into my hand. "Good luck with that food thing."

And that's when it occurs to me—it's over, it's all finally over. If I don't get a record deal after tonight, it won't be because I didn't try.

I find Jonathan, talking in serious tones with a couple of record people. He leans back, winks at me. I smile. When he says goodbye to them, he walks over to me.

I'm just about to ask him where some food is when, to my surprise, he sweeps me up off my feet, swirling me around. I'm already feeling light-headed, and the action makes me positively dizzy.

"You were *amazing.* Fucking *amazing.*"

I laugh, out of gratitude, out of an overwhelming sense of relief. "Can I just tell you how incredibly glad I am that this whole thing is over?"

He sets me down and holds me since I'm a little wobbly. "It's not over by a long shot," he says, and I start to feel a little nervous until he says, "It's just beginning. The record people *loved* you. Your set was unbelievable, and then you showed you were personable. You were spot-on note perfect, PJ!"

He hugs me then, and I just feel…I don't know how to describe it. Jonathan has always been there for me, since he finally agreed to be my manager. No matter what, it seems, he believes in me.

I'd walk over fire for Jonathan, I realize. Cliché as it sounds, I'd do anything for this guy.

My stomach makes another *yowl* in protest. Jonathan's eyes widen. "Oh, man. Why didn't you tell me you were hungry?"

"I forgot," I admit.

"Come on," he says, tugging me to another room. The guests have largely left…the security types that Jonathan hired are escorting the last of them out of the house. I pass the kitchen, where it looks as if a catering crew is working frantically to clean things up.

"Wait right here."

He leaves me in what looks like a spare bedroom. I see this is where my bag is stowed. Someone has kindly returned my laptop and records from Jonathan's sound system setup, as well. I feel better knowing where that is—my whole life is in that laptop.

I flop down on the bed, face first. I feel exhausted. Spiritually I'm flying, but physically, I feel as if I could just roll over and sleep for a year.

He returns with a plateful of food. I laugh. "I can't possibly eat all that!"

"It's good. The caterers were fantastic," he says, putting the plate down on the bed next to me and gingerly sitting on the opposite side of me. "Why didn't you eat before?"

"I never eat before a gig." I smile at him, feeling inexplicably shy. Then I fall onto the food like a starving woman, which, honestly, I am. He's right—it's fantastic, gourmet. There's Brie and hunks of fresh French bread, prosciutto wound around honeydew melon and cantaloupe, little teeny pizzas with Gouda and olives. Jonathan carries on a conversation, telling me about the prospective deals…development deals, vinyl-press numbers, the whole nine yards. I don't listen to a word. I'm too intent on food.

"So. What do you think?"

I push the empty plate away. Now I just feel the warm welcome of food coma. "Think about what?"

He takes the plate, puts it on a nearby desk. "You weren't really listening, huh?"

"I'm sorry. I was just starving."

He smiles, and then sits down on the bed next to me again, stroking my hair. "It's okay. The bottom line is, we'll be hearing about deals in the next week. I'll run all the details by you then, and we can figure out which one would be best for you."

"Okay."

I just feel so comfortable. Tonight, other than that whole nervous-panic thing, has been perfect.

It occurs to me that I have to check in and find a couch. I start to reach for my cell phone.

"What?" Jonathan's voice is low, soothing.

"I have to figure out where I'm sleeping tonight." Even the sentence feels like an effort.

He goes still for a moment, then stretches out on the bed. I feel a little zing of awareness.

"Why? It's three o'clock." He's propped up on one elbow, studying my face. He's smiling gently. "Why don't you just stay here?"

I tense minutely. "Um, here, specifically?"

His eyes darken.

When he leans forward, I'm expecting it. He kisses me gently, and I let him. After a minute, I lean into it. I mentioned I haven't been kissed in a long time. This is more than I've felt in a long time. It feels, well, incredibly good. But I'm also scared. Confused.

This man has supported me. I feel a lot for him—I owe him a lot.

If he left me now… If I did more than this…

I don't know if I could take it.

I'm the one who disengages, gently. "I can't do this," I whisper. "I mean, you know. More than this."

He sighs, leans his forehead against mine, and it just feels damn good. To have someone this close. Someone who seems to feel the right way about you.

"I understand," he says, and he really does seem to. It only makes me want him that much more, and that surprises me, as well. "Listen, this is my spare bedroom. If you wanted to move to the other one—to my room—I'd be out of my mind. But I'm your manager. I understand. This isn't the best situation."

"It's not that," I say. "It's just—"

"I really do know," he says. "When you trust me…well. We'll see."

He kisses me again, and I feel regret, sharp as a knife. He smiles before he closes the door behind him.

★ ★ ★

Samantha hadn't brought her car because she'd frankly planned on either having Jonathan take her home, or staying at Jonathan's house for the night. So here she was, in Aaron's car, a slightly messy compact something-or-other, getting a ride over the Bay Bridge back to Berkeley at one in the morning. She was in a foul mood. Still, it was her own stupid fault, she castigated herself. She had tried to push things, went too fast. She certainly hadn't meant for things to go this way.

"How're you doing, beautiful? Want the heater on? The air? Are you comfortable?"

She looked over. He was staring at her, eager to please. Puppylike in his adoration. Yes, it was a cliché, but she didn't know how else to describe the almost pleading look in his dark brown eyes, glowing green from the display of his dashboard.

"I'm fine, Aaron," she reassured him. "I just want to get home. I'm getting pretty tired."

That was meant to be the warning—the clue that said, as clearly as a headache, that this guy was not getting anything beyond maybe a kiss at the door when he dropped her off at home. No invite in. Certainly—and she almost laughed at the thought—no sex.

"I'll make sure you're feeling better."

She squirmed a little in her seat. That was a countermove, suggesting he got the message but wasn't really open to hearing it yet.

"Those parties really wipe me out," she said, laying further groundwork. "Especially Jonathan's parties. They're the best."

Read: I've been to Jonathan's house a bunch of times. I'm a regular. You don't have a chance.

"Yeah. Didn't see much of him tonight. Looks like he and PJ might be an item, huh?"

She blinked. His response, decoded: *You might be at his house a lot, but you're obviously not in his bed. Game's still on.*

Now she was feeling snarky at the reminder, that not only was she *not* in Jonathan's bed, but that a scruff like PJ might be beating her to the punch.

"He's just helping PJ with her career, that's all. You know how important his club is to him."

"Yeah, well, I've been a DJ at his club for the past year, and he's never had me spin at one of his private parties," he replied sourly.

She focused on him more intently now. "Seriously? I thought that he did that for all his DJs."

"Ha. All his *female* ones, maybe," Aaron responded. "Maybe a couple of guys, I don't know. All I know is, he's got special interest in PJ. I've never seen him go all out like this."

Samantha caught a glimpse of her own face scowling in the reflection in the passenger-side window. She carefully smoothed the expression out. "Yeah, well. We'll see if it lasts, I guess."

"Jealous, much?"

She laughed. It sounded a little forced, sure, but she was a model, not an actress.

"I want Jonathan," she said, deciding to just go for the kill. He was pulling off at her exit, anyway, and she could see that he was pretty determined. Better to see how determined she was. "The fact that he's wrapped up in PJ right now doesn't mean he will be forever. I mean, seriously. PJ has moments of cuteness, I suppose, but who would you rather sleep with?"

Ooh. Wrong tack, she realized immediately, when she saw his eyes widen with sexual avarice. "You. No question. I've wanted you since the minute I met you."

If she had a dollar for every time a club-skeeze used that pickup line on her…she shook her head. "I'm not in a great place right now. Turn left here," she instructed. Five more minutes. Only five more minutes, then she could wash the makeup off her face, have a sparkling water and climb into bed. Maybe pull out her vibrator and feel better.

He turned down the street, following her directions until he was in her driveway. Then, to her dismay, he shut off the car.

"You don't have to walk me to the door," she said, leaning over and kissing him on the cheek. "I'm right here. I'm perfectly safe."

But he was already getting out of the car. This was going to get very, very sticky.

Sticky. Now if *he* were here, she wouldn't be having this problem. He was a much better, well, friend, she guessed. As opposed to dogged admirer. She still thought of what he'd said to her at odd times.

I like you because you're a good girl. That's it.

That was *not* why Aaron was interested in her. That much, from the slight bulge at the front of his pants, was obvious.

"Why don't I come in for a nightcap? I'll rub your shoulders. Help you relax."

She winced. So, it was going to be a showdown. Well. She had no one to blame but herself for this one.

"In the first place, I don't have any alcohol in the house."

"You don't? Why not?" He stopped in front of her door, leaning on it. "Now that I think of it, I don't think I've ever seen you drink at a club, either. Some kind of moral thing?"

She gave him an indignant look. "Do you know how many calories are in alcohol?"

He grinned, and she realized she had a perfect out—say she was a hard-core Christian or something, use some excuse that would take sex out of the equation. Of course, with the way she'd behaved at the club, there would probably be some questions raised. At any rate, it was too late now.

"All right. Just the massage, then."

She shook her head, crossing her arms and shifting into full bitch mode. "I have a headache," she said bluntly.

His normally attractive expression turned ugly and derisive. "Sure you do. You couldn't come up with a better excuse than the old headache ploy?"

"And what about you?" She felt like kicking him. "Give me a *massage?* What, didn't want me to show you etchings or something?"

"Listen, you were getting the brush-off at that party. You were glad to see me. To have me pay attention to you, and I gave you a ride home. You didn't even have to ask," he blurted, and his voice was growing in both volume and indignation. "Frankly, I'm getting a little tired of being your door prize when some rich asshole doesn't decide to bone you."

"Fuck off," she said, trying to shove him away from her door…and to her surprise, he stood firm, nudging her away from the door.

For the first time tonight, she was starting to feel the real chill of fear. She had pepper spray in her purse, and for the first time she was thankful that her father made her carry it. She started fumbling with the latch, feeling in the darkness, her fingertips brushing against the cold aluminum tube. She felt for the safety latch, moved it off the nozzle.

"I'm not going to rape you, goddamn it," he hissed at her. "But you're going to listen to me. This may be the last time I fucking talk to you, so you're not going to ignore me like usual!"

She still held the pepper spray.

"And get your goddamn hand out of your purse. What have you got in there? Pepper spray?"

She winced. She wondered if she should pull her hand out, or if taking the spray out would make things worse. She did not want him more angry. She took her hand out, empty. She let it rest at her side even as she left her purse open.

"You've led me on," he said, his voice trembling with rage. "I thought if you made it up to me tonight, it'd be all right…"

"Made it up to you by having sex with you?" She felt a little teary, her throat constricting.

"Oh, don't go so feminist and Berkeley on me," he said sharply. "Don't cast yourself on the right of this one. You've made all sorts of promises—danced close, made all kind of innuendos. And then, before I got too close, you'd pull away. When somebody richer came up, somebody who might be able to help you, you pretended that I wasn't even there. That shit might work for saps like Sticky, but as of tonight, I'm telling you to fuck off."

"Fine," Samantha said, although it wasn't fine, it was far from fine. "Just get away from my door."

"You're just a tease. You're not even a real slut."

"Thanks very much," Samantha said as he moved away from the door. She picked up her keys out of her purse, her hand once again brushing against the pepper spray. She felt the urge to use it on him, more out of anger than fear now. But there was still fear boosting her system.

He got in his car and zoomed off, gravel kicking up from the squeal of his tires. One of her apartment neighbor's lights came on, and she saw the twitch of curtains from several others. She hurried inside, throwing both locks and the dead bolt.

She then sunk against the door, too dazed even to cry. Then she ran into the bathroom and threw up what little she had in her stomach.

I wake up in a bed, which is already a little alien. It's a really nice bed, too. I'm too ingrained to couch living...the half of the bed I didn't sleep on still looks pristine, the covers barely ruffled.

The room's dark because the curtains are so thick, but it's early. For me, at least, it's early: 10:00 a.m., from the blue glowing register of my cell phone.

I get up, avail myself of the bathroom that is attached to the room. Man. I haven't lived this swank since the last time I had to spring for a hotel room for myself, when Sticky was out of town and I was out of luck on the couch front. And this is a hell of a lot better than that roach trap.

"PJ?"

I'm toweling my hair dry when I hear Jonathan's voice through the door. I hastily tug on clothes, hating the sensation of damp from spots I missed in my quick drying session. I pull on sweats and a shirt, and socks.

When I open the door, Jonathan's pale eyes are practically glowing. He's pulled the curtain open, and the light is almost blinding in its brightness. It ought to make things look cheerful, but he's so intense, so dark, that the sunbeams are practically bending toward him.

Something's not right.

"Are you okay?"

He doesn't say anything. He just hands me a newspaper.

I'm wondering if something bad happened—terrorists finally got one of the bridges, or something. I'm not completely tuned out of world events. But the cover story on the newsweekly stops me cold, and suddenly the state of the nation is secondary to the state of my life.

REBEL WITHOUT A HOUSE

The byline says by Leslie Anderson. "It dropped today?" I don't even wait for him to answer, I start flipping to the story. I'm still kind of excited. It's not the best title in the world, but what did Jonathan expect, anyway? He knew Leslie wasn't going to just do a two page promotional spread, for God's sake, right?

I skim the introductory prose, a florid description of the club scene as told by someone who only has a passing acquaintance with it, and then jump right to the meat of the thing. "'PJ, real name unknown (or rather unstated), is a DJ who spins at some of the lower-echelon clubs in San Francisco,'" I read out loud, and snort. "'Her real claim to fame is the way that she manages to scrounge sleeping arrangements, and not the way you think— for the price of admission to whatever club she's spinning at next, you can have your very own pet DJ.'" I look at Jonathan, still trying to gauge what it is that's got his boxers in a knot. "Doesn't sound very flattering, does it? Still, it's not that bad."

"Keep reading," he says, in a tight voice.

Now I'm definitely nervous. I go into skim overdrive.

She's on the path to the big time, but her manager has to hire some-one to teach her how to dress…

She carries a huge blue duffel bag with all of her few possessions…

Eating éclairs in front of stick-thin models, she seems to have some-thing to prove…

I look up. He's still glaring at me. It's not the greatest article in the world, but what the hell crawled up his ass?

The problem is, it's all a front. Previously known as Persephone Jane Sherman, PJ isn't quite as cool as she'd like you to think she is. The self-proclaimed "Guerilla DJ" has a history she'd like to forget and a future she'd rather not plan for…

Suddenly, I do the mental equivalent of tripping, sprawled out headlong on two sentences:

After flaming out of the corporate world in the wake of a self-inflicted car crash, she reinvented herself. Or rather, invented a new self: DJ PJ.

She knew about me. The job, my accident, my divorce. All of it.

I'm reading faster now, ignoring any vibes from Jonathan. This isn't about the DJ business anymore. This is about my business, period.

Her ex-husband, Lucas Sherman, describes a woman possessed. Working eighty-hour weeks, she was the complete antithesis of the values she espouses now... "I'm not saying she's a bad person. She's just troubled..."

That prick. That absolute, utter prick. I am hyperventilating. I can feel bile gathering, my stomach starting to prep for stress-hurl mode.

"Why didn't you tell me?"

I remember Jonathan is in the room. "About which thing?" I am not being facetious...the bitch seems to have covered everything in my life. At least she didn't interview my mother.

I race through the rest of the article. Nope. Mom is not mentioned—and she would've given up enough dirt to fill up a page by herself.

"The mental institution," Jonathan says, in a low voice. "The car. Your husband. Getting fired from your job."

"I didn't get fired," I clarify, the whole thing feeling unreal. I haven't had to talk about this in two years. I didn't even know how to talk about it back then.

He steeples his fingers, pressing them to his lips. "You realize that it would have been great for you to mention all this earlier." His voice is cold fury. "It's not going to look good at all. I'm going to have a hell of a time working with this."

I lean my head to one side and stare at him. My very first impulse is to apologize, but I'm so spun and hurt by the article...and Jesus, don't I get a minute to deal with that?

"Well, shit," I drawl. "I sure hate that this is going to screw things up...you know, for *you.*"

"This is going to screw things up for you, PJ," he says, ignoring my sarcasm. "I'm supposed to be talking to Red Rover today, for God's sake. I told them you were going to be in the *Citizen*. And this reads like you're some kind of narcissistic nutcase."

He's right. It did read like that. But I just want a minute to process—I'm ill equipped to map out damage control right now.

"Maybe I am a nutcase, Jonathan," I mutter. "Did you think of that?"

Now he's staring at me. "You're not a nutcase," he says, but it's not as confident as every other statement I've ever heard him say. There's a silent, qualifying "…are you?" at the end of that sentence, and he's even now wondering what he's gotten himself into.

"I was in a mental hospital for a few weeks," I say, and I feel too damned tired to cry. "I got out. I quit my job. I got divorced shortly thereafter. Long story short, I started living the way I do—scoring couches, moving around. Guerilla DJ. End of story." I wince, as I recall, she called my "guerilla DJ" stance just that…a posture, a sham. I am über-poser.

"She makes you sound imbalanced," Jonathan says, raking a hand through his hair. "Damn it. I knew I should have…"

He stops.

"Should have what?" I prompt.

"Maybe we rushed into this, that's all," he mutters. "But it's not completely fucked. You can pull it out."

"How?"

He scowls at me at this point. "I don't know. Threaten to sue, make the paper print a retraction…no. That'll just be fueling the fire," he says, shaking his head. "Better idea—ditch the whole couch-living thing."

I'm about to ask how that's going to change things when he tacks on a muttered invective.

"If ever there was a time for you to grow the hell up, PJ, it'd be now."

I blink at him. "Excuse me?"

"Oh, come on," he says, and there is absolutely no patience in his voice. "Ever since I met you, heard about how you live…saw you in your goddamn underwear at a Laundromat, for God's sake, I knew that you were a little unbalanced. The article had one thing right, at least. You're just running away. I see that you probably had some kind of reason at the time. But that's over now. I need you to suck it up, and get through this."

"You need me to grow up and suck it up and fix this," I repeat, numb. "Can I ask one question. Why, exactly, do you care? You're a big named DJ, with a big house in Presidio, for God's sake. You don't need me. So why, exactly, do I have to do anything? If I fuck this up, it's my life. I've managed just fine on my very own!"

"Obviously," he snaps, and his eyes blaze. "I don't need this kind of hassle. If you're going to pull this kind of adolescent shit, maybe you're right. Maybe I *don't* need you."

I crumple the newspaper in my hand, my head spinning. Talk about déjà vu. How many times have I heard this chorus?

My boss didn't want to hear my complaints about being stressed, about feeling burned out. Crashing my car was a hassle that he did not want to deal with. I quit with only two weeks notice, instead of the six he tried to get me to negotiate for. He couldn't believe I was so insensitive.

My husband couldn't believe I'd quit without consulting him. He was also shocked that after supporting him for a year and a half, I'd be immature enough to think that "he somehow owed me" because he now was working and I wanted some time off. It was a hassle he didn't need…or so his note said, when he asked me to move out. The divorce papers only underlined his concerns.

The hassles I put my mother through were more legendary than I cared to relive.

I stare at Jonathan, who looks like he's carved out of marble. Really pissed off marble, I suppose, but still. He's got cold fury down to an art. It's shape up, or ship out.

I feel a quick, clawing moment of despair. Then I pick up my bag.

chapter 16

"Pham!" Samantha growled when she spotted her T.A. from across the quad between Moffitt and Doe Libraries on campus. He obviously heard her. Every student in a twenty-foot radius heard her. He slowed, and even from this distance, he looked hunched, hesitant.

In a word: guilty.

She had gotten almost no sleep the night before, after the disastrous episode at Jonathan's and the resulting scene with Aaron in front of her apartment. She still felt sick, and grumpier than a field-hockey team with coordinated PMS.

Getting the e-mail that she was flunking sociology on top of all of that was beyond unacceptable.

"What the *hell* is going on, Pham?" She did everything but poke him in the chest. Every syllable jabbed him, and he winced. "I turned in the homework!"

"You missed another quiz," Pham said. "And...you didn't ace the first one. The makeup quiz."

She had been in a rush, she mentally admitted. "I can make up the quiz I missed," she said sharply, reining in her temper. "And...I don't know. I mean, isn't there any extra credit for the other stuff? There has to be something else I can do. I can't be *failing.*"

To her surprise, Pham stood up straighter, staring her right in the eye. "You screwed up the last quiz, which I let you make up, then skipped the next quiz and blew off the last homework assignment," he pointed out. "Then you try to chew me out in front of half the student body—" and his voice raised in disbelief and anger, and it was her turn to wince "—*and* you expect me to give you extra credit? Are you kidding me with this shit?"

"All right. I'm sorry," she said, starting to feel truly nervous for the first time all semester. "I shouldn't have yelled at you. I'm just upset. This class…my grades mean a lot to me."

"Then maybe you should've thought of that before you stopped showing up to section, huh?"

Fury battled with desperation. Despair won. "I *have* to pull this grade out, Pham," she said, gripping his arm. "My scholarship depends on my GPA. If I let my average drop too far, I'll get kicked out of school!"

"I know how that is," Pham said, tugging away from her. "But I could lose my job, Samantha. Other students have already commented on my preferential treatment of you."

She sighed. "They're just jealous."

"They mentioned it to the *professor.*" And the pained look on his face suggested that the fallout from that bit of news was unpleasant. "There isn't anything else I can do for you now. You need to show up, just like everybody else. No makeups. And no extra credit."

She couldn't help it. She started tearing up, sniffling audibly.

Pham sighed again, more deeply, and for a brief second, she thought she had a chance.

"If you work hard," he said slowly, "you could still probably keep your grade at a C."

"Just a *C?*"

"I have to go," he said, reading her expression. Without another word, he fled.

She gritted her teeth as she crossed campus, her mind racing. Her modeling career was in the toilet. Her college career was quickly following suit. And the guy she'd fallen in love with was hot for an androgynous, tacky-dressing scrub who would *not* appreciate him the way Samantha would.

She sat down by the student union, watching the other students milling in front of Zellerbach Auditorium. She really did like college; the classes were a lot more interesting than the high-school ones, for the most part, and she just liked being independent. Going to college didn't have the same prestige as modeling did, of course. Over half of her graduating class went to a college of one sort or another. Even going to U.C. Berkeley didn't have the cachet it would have, since it was local for a lot of the students, and a slam dunk for anybody in her class that was a minority. Unlike modeling, where only the very best made it…and every girl recognized that fact.

She knew that most people—her parents, her agent, her friends—thought that, at some point, she'd probably have to make a choice between school and modeling. She'd never thought it would be necessary. She was focused, determined. She wanted both of them. And she got what she wanted.

At least, she did until now.

She decided to call Andrea, thinking absently that she really needed to find friends her own age.

"'Lo?"

"Andrea, it's Samantha."

"Samantha. I was just headed off to history class. What's up?" Andrea paused, squealed. "Don't tell me. You heard back from Danielle Ichiba? Did you get picked?"

Samantha frowned. "I haven't heard anything."

Samantha thought of the audition and cringed.

"Anyway, I think Jenna's still pretty pissed about not making it. She didn't even show up at school today. She said she was going to go see Stan herself, and that she's just not happy with the way he's handling her career…"

Samantha herself had considered that plan of attack, except at this point, it didn't matter. If she had a success to point to…if she had even one ace in the hole, it would be a different story. But she had absolutely nothing to bargain with.

She had that feeling of washed-up has-been again, and shifted back to listening to Andrea, letting her mind wander as Andrea chirped on about Jenna, modeling and life in general. In a weird way, her vapid voice was soothing, almost hypnotic. She stared off into space.

She'd read the headline on the *Bay Area Citizen* about eight times or so before it finally sunk in.

She sat up as if she'd been goosed. "Andrea? I have to call you back, okay?"

"Huh?" Andrea stopped, startled in midsentence. "Um…okay. Bye!"

"Bye." And Samantha hastily shut her phone, walking over to the newspaper holder. As if in slow motion, she picked one up, going over the headline.

REBEL WITHOUT A HOUSE

The true story of a DJ who proves that adolescence isn't an age…it's a state of mind

It was Leslie's article. And from the looks of it, it wasn't at all what PJ had meant it to be.

She read through the article, stunned. It started off ugly and only got harsher. Several opinions that Samantha had privately harbored about PJ—that she was a mooch, a loser and potentially a head case—were showcased. She herself was quoted as an anonymous source.

This changed everything, Samantha thought. Jonathan was probably re-evaluating his protégé and star client. So were the record execs that PJ was supposed to be impressing. And PJ herself—well, Samantha wasn't going to think about her.

Finally, *finally,* Samantha was getting a break.

Jonathan still owed her a favor, and right this second, she had absolutely nothing to lose. It was time to give him a call and see, with this new information, just what she could collect.

★ ★ ★

I hurt all over.

I take a taxi to Technique. It feels weird, but I know that Jonathan isn't going to be there, which was fine with me. I'm still angry at the whole thing. To make matters worse, every now and then I'd think about that kiss in his spare bedroom. It wasn't so much that I was attracted to him…although who was I kidding, right? But that wasn't the issue right now. I have to admit, the fact that I was still feeling weepy and sick over the whole thing showed that Jonathan and his response seemed to make everything worse.

Of course, that was just a figure of speech. Technically, it really couldn't get any worse.

I had obviously slit my own throat, from the sounds of it. I wasn't going to have a record label or make some big deal. In fact, it sounded like I was right back where I started. When I put it that way, it wasn't great, but it shouldn't have been that bad. I mean, I was making it reasonably okay on my own… wasn't I?

The bouncers were looking at me with both amusement and disgust by the time I got to the door. When I said hi to Josh, the guy who worked the line, he actually ignored me, turning his face away, staring at the kid whose ID he was checking as if his life depended on it. I felt angry, and shocked that he'd be so openly rude when I'd never been anything but nice to him. It hurt. I felt like somebody had worked me over with a base-ball bat ever since I'd stepped out of Jonathan's house.

I felt like shit. I needed to find Sticky.

When I saw him at the door, I half expected him to turn away, too. And he was looking at me differently, like he'd never felt so sorry for anyone in his life. I still had a bunch of anger running through my system, and now it was coupled with fear. If Sticky, the patron saint of the useless, cut me off now…I might as well just change my name and move to Iowa.

But Sticky opened his arms, and I dropped my bag and walked right into them, resting my face on his chest. He gave me a bear hug that practically asphyxiated me, and I've never in my life felt so grateful for it.

"I'm pretty screwed, Sticky."

Sticky put his hand on his headset. "Josh? Jason? I'm going on a break—ten minutes. Watch the line, and watch for those assholes with the black leather jackets. Yeah, the *Matrix* wannabes. I don't want to hear it from them later, got it? Okay. Ten minutes." He put his arm around me. "Bar's real crowded, so I'm going to take you to the office, where it's a little quieter. Okay? And I'll get us a couple of drinks."

I still feel queasy, from anger and from nerves but at the same time, I feel like a stiff drink is just what the doctor ordered. I followed Sticky, and he rushed me past the bar, asking Michele for something. She stares at me like I'd mimicked her and shaved my head. Then she mixes up the world's quickest Seven-down, plus a ginger ale, and Sticky grabs them, steering me upstairs, towards the office.

Madness. This whole thing is madness.

Sticky sits down in one of the office chairs, looking at a loss for words. Which, for Sticky, is saying something. "So what happened?"

I sit across from him and then down half of the drink in a few gulping swallows. Some of it goes down the wrong pipe, so I wind up gasping and coughing for a grand total of four minutes, eating up a good chunk of my ten-minute allotment.

"The article…you know Leslie. Did you know what she was going to write about?"

His eyes narrow. "Do you think I would have let her, or spoken to her, if I did know? Come on, now."

So I go through what happened…last night at the party, this morning with Jonathan. I gloss over a couple of things, but he gets the basic idea. I don't have a manager. My career's in reverse. I am sorely lacking friends. I'm back at square one.

"I really need a place to stay. Someplace a little longer term, if possible," I say, feeling humiliation even though I've asked things like this of Sticky forever. "I don't have any gigs lined up—that was Jonathan's thing, and now, I think, that's completely over. It's going to take me a few days to get things straightened out."

He sighs heavily. "As soon as I read the article, I figured you would."

I start to smile. I am too lucky to know Sticky. He's too good for me. Too good for everyone that I know of, actually.

"The thing is…everybody else read the article, too."

Oh, shit.

I wrack my brain. "How about the Strippas?"

He grimaces. He'd tried them, I realize. And they'd said no. When the Strippas abandoned you, then you really were persona non grata. I am more screwed than I thought.

"Sticky…I never ask this, but…" I take a deep breath. "Do you have a couch I could crash on? I mean, I hate to impose, and I wouldn't if I weren't really, really in trouble here…"

I know before he answers me. The crush of his shoulders, the defeated slump, all clues.

"You know I still live with my family. In-law unit, yeah, but still," he says apologetically. "I promised them that the people from this part of my life won't mix with them. They're my family, PJ. I take that seriously."

I know that. He loves his family. He doesn't talk about them much—usually only on off-hours, when he's drunk a bit too much, and purely only when he's with people he trusts. That he's offered me this much as way of explanation is good enough. Disappointing, true, but I can't blame him.

"PJ, I hate to bring this up," he says, and his voice sounds like he absolutely loathes having to bring it up. "But…maybe it's time you went home."

I blank out. "I don't follow."

"Your mom. She still lives in the East Bay, yeah? Maybe you should call her. See if she'll…"

"*No.*"

"PJ, come on." His voice is harsh, he's shifting into tough love, and I don't want to hate him for it. I just hate the fact that I feel like a teenager, like somebody's trying to ring in the runaway. That I'm being unreasonable. That I need to be reasoned *with*.

"You're running out of options. You kept saying this was

only going to be temporary, right? Well, now you're rock bottom. You're going to have to regroup. And the only way I can figure out how you'll be able to do this, is if you call your mom, and get back home."

"She doesn't understand. God, that sounds so juvenile," I say, half to him, half to myself. "The minute I walk into her house, I'll be telling her that I couldn't cut it with my music. She'll push me, press me. She'll lovingly encourage me into getting a 'real job' again. She's going to think that I just got derailed, probably because of all my lousy choices, but now, finally, I'm going to behave."

"Do you know how stupid that sounds?" Drill Instructor Sticky. "You're an adult, for Chrissake. She can't force you to do anything. I'm not feeling a whole lot of sympathy that your mom doesn't care about you."

I knew he wouldn't get this. From what I understand, his mother loves him dearly. His father, though separated, stays in touch from time to time. He's cared for, and he knows it. He's never felt what it's like to be told that everything that you're doing is wrong, even when you're doing exactly what's told. I doubt his mother ever said, "you're killing me" with the choices that he's made. If she did, I doubt he ever thought that she might really mean it.

I went through just enough therapy to know I'm still fucked up. Too bad I ran out of money before I figured out the solution to the emotional problem.

"I know it sounds stupid," I say. I dig in my heels. "I just…I'm afraid that if I go back into that life, I'll get all caught up, all over again. That I'll start with wanting to please. Then I start working hideous hours, trying to prove something. Next thing I know, I'm working from seven in the morning till nine at night, and I'm still not doing it right—and if I'm living with my mother, she'll be telling me about what she needs me to do in her life, and what I'm still screwing up. All with the best of intentions. And if I don't do it…" I shake my head. "I know. I should be over it, but I just…I can't go back to that."

He doesn't look convinced.

"So what are you going to do, huh? Sleep at a shelter to-night?" He's pulling out all the stops. "It's late, and most of them are going to be booked…and you don't want to be sleeping when you've got all that shit in your bag. You're going to wind up sleeping on the streets…maybe you should stake out a bench at Lafayette Park? So you can curl up around that laptop of yours? Be fucking serious. You're already becoming a joke at the club. Go without a shower, and see how far you're going to get on that one."

He's just being honest, I tell myself. Still, I stand up, grab my bag.

"I still love you, Sticky. You know that." And I know he does. "But I'm not going home. Not yet. Not until things truly turn the absolute worst."

He stands up and crosses his beefy arms. "Did it ever occur to you that if it gets worse, you may never make it home at all?"

I nod. "Despite current appearances, I'm not universally stupid."

"Okay." He doesn't sound happy—but he knows me. He knows this isn't something he can stop.

"Thanks," I repeat. Then I pick up my cell phone to make one more call—to a couch so low, I would have never considered it viable if I wasn't so desperate.

The line is noisy. Metallica is playing, and the guy who answers the phone yells at somebody to "turn it the fuck down!" He comes back to me with a mellow hello.

"Jason?" I'm guessing here.

"No. Jeremy."

They're interchangeable. "This is PJ."

"Oh?"

"The DJ." He's still not really getting it, I notice. I can tell from the way he's not saying anything. "Little brown-haired girl. Friend of Sticky's and Samantha's and Aaron's and…"

He's still working it out.

I give up. "Listen, I was wondering…you said, a long time ago that I could crash on your couch."

He laughs. "Sure. We've got some empty space. Coupla people already staying in the living room. But why not? More's a party, right?"

I nod. A party.

I haven't hit rock bottom, not yet. But I'm staying with the Weed kids…and honestly, that's pretty damn close.

Samantha decided to not even bother calling first, instead, she went directly to Jonathan's house. She didn't want to think too hard about what she was going to do.

She walked up to Jonathan's door, rang the bell. The intercom buzzed. "PJ?" Jonathan said quickly.

"No," she answered, frowning. But at least it told her that PJ wasn't here. "It's Samantha."

"Samantha?" He sounded odd…dazed. His tone was even more serious than it usually was. "What are you doing here?"

"Getting cold," she said with a small laugh to hide the irritation. "Could I please come in? I just wanted to talk to you."

A blatant lie. But she wasn't going to rush what looked like her last chance at Jonathan.

After a few minutes, he opened the door. "Um…hello." He looked confused to find her there on his doorstep.

She walked in, her body shivering more with nerves than with the brisk San Francisco weather. She felt as if she was at a call, at one of the most important auditions of her life.

She slipped off her coat, revealing the very skintight outfit she'd chosen. He stared, as he was meant to. She smiled, sat down. Crossed her legs slowly. Not a full Sharon Stone, or anything, but definitely suggestive.

He sighed, and instead of sitting down next to her, he sat opposite her. "What did you want to talk to me about?"

Why was he so stubborn? She felt her expression fall as desperation washed over her. Was it because he was older? Or because women threw themselves at him all the time?

When the hell am I going to be good enough?

"I read the PJ article," she said, plunging forward gamely. She watched with fascination as his face darkened. "I take it you didn't know about her past, or anything."

"No, I fucking well didn't." Confusion and anger.

If it wasn't for the slight slur in his curse, she never would've picked up on the fact that he had been drinking. She didn't necessarily like that in a guy, as a general rule. But Jonathan, who was ordinarily so controlled, was obviously drowning his sorrows. Which meant something had, indeed, gone wrong with PJ and him.

Which meant an opportunity, if she just had the guts to go for it. She steeled herself.

"Let me get you another drink," she purred, getting up and filling the glass in front of him with scotch from a crystal container on the wooden bar. She caught a glimpse of the Bay at night from his window—a clear night for a change, full of twinkling stars and dark waves in the distance.

Music, romantic music, would've made it all perfect. But she'd make use of what she had.

He took the drink from her hand and had a long swallow. "Did you know? About...the ex-husband? Everything?"

"PJ didn't say a word to me," Samantha said, skirting the truth. After all, she'd heard about all of this from Lucas, not PJ.

"I didn't mean to yell at her," he muttered, finishing the rest of the drink and putting the glass back down on the coffee table with a clink. "I just...I felt like we were getting closer. I thought she trusted me. Hell, maybe I was fooling myself, but I thought she was finally learning to care about me, you know?"

She had to get him to change the subject, and fast. Make-or-break time.

"I care about you," she said simply, and sat on the arm of the chair he was sitting in.

He focused on her face...or at least, he tried to. "You're very beautiful," he breathed, as if it surprised him.

She took that as her opportunity. Pressing forward, she moved onto his lap and kissed him with slow deliberation. He tasted like scotch, unfortunately, but that didn't stop her.

At first, he didn't react, just sat there as she kissed him with more and more urgency. She felt her heart plummet. She was screwing it up, he wouldn't care, he wouldn't...

Finally, he started kissing her back. She thought her heart would explode. After long minutes, she breathlessly took off her shirt. He didn't even open his eyes, just reached for her.

This was it. This was finally it. After this, he'd realize what he really wanted…and who he really deserved.

He mumbled something, and she felt a cold chill pierce her haze of passion. "What?"

"Nothing," he mumbled, pressing another frantic kiss against her throat.

She focused on the kiss, and everything that was about to come after it.

It was probably just her imagination, anyway. But for a second, she was afraid that he'd whispered PJ's name.

chapter 17

It would help me compose more if I could just shake off this contact high.

I've been staring at my laptop for over an hour, listening to old beats. I'm not that bad, but I really need to take it to the next level, and I can't do that if I keep futzing around with my laptop. Apparently, I've just been admiring the pretty swirl of colors that my CD-playing program puts up.

When the Weed Kids say they've got some prime shit, they are not kidding. The weirdos that are now my couch companions obviously can vouch for the quality. They've been smoking steadily, with giddy smiles on their faces, watching TV as if God were broadcasting live from Central Park. I catch myself giggling also and watching SpongeBob SquarePants with the kind of rapt attention that flower-distributing airport cultees usually devote. It's a little scary.

I also devoured an entire box of Ho Hos in under four minutes. Which I must say, Jeremy was not thrilled with. I had to go down to the corner store and replace it. I usually don't even touch the food at places where I know the people and I trust them. Yet here I am, in pajamas, hanging out with complete stoner dorks. I'm not actually smoking, mind you—I've tried, back in the day, years before, but I simply can't smoke. I'm borderline asthmatic, only happens maybe once or twice a year, and never really bad. However, the act of inhaling ash and smoke is something my lungs protest very, very strongly. The first time I smoked weed, I thought I was going to die. When I was in college, I had a friend who was a heavy user. She tried everything to help me out—water pipe, then ice in a bong, then floating the smoke through orange-juice-and-ice (I don't know why orange juice, it's apparently supposed to help). No go. The only real way for me to do it, if I'm going to do it at all, is brownies, and even if I wanted to (which I don't), the stoners here would look at me like some kind of tourist. So I don't partake, at least not intentionally. Still, there's a marijuana cloud permeating the living room…even the flip-out twin-size mattress I'm borrowing is saturated with the smell of Jamaican.

Perhaps I am sinking lower than rock bottom, if that's possible. All I know is, I haven't been back to the club, I haven't been back to San Francisco, and I haven't spoken with anybody from "that life" in seventy-two hours. Not even Sticky. Certainly not Jonathan. My only fear is running into Samantha, since she also lives in Berkeley, albeit in a better part of town than the Weed Kids in their pot-haven co-op. So I only leave the house at night, which isn't a hardship, when I leave the place at all.

I decide I'm not going to care. At least, I'll tell myself I'm not going to care, and keep repeating it until I believe it. Apathy through repetition.

Time to mix beats, I tell myself. Come on. This music isn't going to write itself, I try to goad myself, coax myself, shame myself.

Dr. Tejada, my old shrink, would probably have something to say about that.

Fuck Dr. Tejada.

Maybe watching TV would help, a little, evil part of me tries to persuade my mind. You could get a really good hook from a TV theme song, for example. *Dragnet* maybe. Something recognizable that you could turn into your own thing.

Oh, God, I am getting desperate. I should go out and eat something—I don't remember when the last time I fed myself was, except for the great HoHo fiasco. I wonder if they'd mind if I use their stove, mix up some ramen.

I look at my watch. It's like four in the morning. The clubs have long since shut down their bars. The DJs would be wrapping up, the hard-core clubbers trying to wind down with a mix of light trance and ambient. I've never worked that shift, but I would've loved to try it, just once. There's a challenge to it. Anyone can pump up a crowd. But there's a fine line between calming them down and boring them to death. Most people choose either up music or down. I like a mix. You've got to maintain even pacing, or else you're a one-note wonder…you'll have 'em falling asleep at the edge of their seats.

I really need to get some sleep. I've been up until sunrise or later for the past three days.

Two guys are on the couch, watching what looks like a sci-fi movie, bad fake blood and T&A victim running around, begging to get killed. I've got my pajamas on—missed laundry day today, must do that tomorrow. I've got my stuff on the coffee table, next to a set of metric weights. The guys are low-lidded but not sleeping. I pound my pillow for a second, startling them, and then settle down to try and drift.

I think I must have fallen asleep, because the pounding startles me, makes me wonder where I am. It's the sound of breaking glass that brings me all the way around. I sit up.

The guys are starting to run every which way. The guys upstairs, where the plants are, are yelling. A man's hand reaches in through the broken glass pane of the door.

I get to my feet, my heart beating a mile a minute. I pull on my shoes, hastily, sloppily, wondering for the first time if this place has a back door. If it does, I haven't seen it. I am in a two-story beat-up co-op, and I don't even think they have a fire escape.

Shit shit shit shit shit…

A man throws the door open.

He's got a gun.

I dive behind a couch and he throws the sofa, and my stuff, clear across the room. "Where's Jeremy?" It's a low yell. He's big, has no neck and a scruffy beard and oh, God, I don't want to remember details, I'm not going to be a witness.

There's one guy left on the couch, looking mildly distressed. He points upstairs.

The guy says, "Unless you want trouble, you'd better get the hell out of here. Now."

He heads up the stairs.

My bag. I need my bag. I think somebody moved it. I try to grab for my laptop.

There're sounds, crashing sounds. A body getting slammed against the wall.

"Put the gun away…"

I'm running. Before I know what I'm doing, I'm running. I don't have any of my stuff. I think I have my cell phone. I'm in pajamas, and running down the street.

It sounds as if they're tearing the place apart, and I'm sprinting now.

I finally stop, blocks away, closer to the university. I am breathing hard, holding the stitch in my side. A grown woman in pajamas, clutching a cell phone. I couldn't get my iPod. Nor my laptop. I am screwed. Jeremy, for all I know, is dead.

I don't know what the guy wanted. Sticky was right. I never, ever should've stayed there.

I don't have any money on me. I need to call…somebody. Need to get the hell out of here. Sunrise is in an hour and a half, I'm hoping. I feel conspicuous, like a transient. Now, this is what it really is to be homeless.

I turn on the cell phone—or try to. And that's when it hits me. It's not mine. It belongs to one of the couch dwellers I was bunking with. He had mentioned that he couldn't pay for it, and that he'd had the service disconnected.

I am screwed. Well and truly screwed.

I wonder who I can call. Sticky will have gone home. I try calling him collect.

There is no answer.

I wind up sitting on a curb, shaking slightly, rocking forward and backward. At least I am not muttering to myself. Then I realize I've whispered the statement out loud. Samantha lives nearby, I think. I can find her.

I get to her house by about six-thirty and knock on the door. No answer there, either.

She's probably at Jonathan's. I don't want to think about it. I'm not going to think about it.

It's seven o'clock, and the bustle of traffic starts as the city wakes up. Kids in navy blue sweatshirts with the word Cal or Berkeley embroidered on it in gold, backpacks slung over one shoulder. The ones that actually make eye contact with me quickly look away.

I have no money on me, and I'm desperately tired.

I'm sitting there wondering what to do, when a girl in a chestnut ponytail stops.

She gives me a dollar in change. "Get some coffee," she says with a smile. "And God bless. You might be able to find some-place to sleep—the church of…"

I try to smile back. It's too hard. I don't remember the name of the church she's pandering. She's got a fish button on and a Jesus Saves patch on her backpack. She seems like a sweetheart. I loathe myself. I feel like a pack animal.

I go back to the pay phone.

"Hello?"

I take a deep breath.

"Mom?"

There's a pause. "Persephone? Is that you?"

"Mom…I need your help."

Another pause. I know what she's thinking. *Hospital? Jail?* "Are you…"

"Can you please pick me up? I'm in Berkeley. On Shattuck. By—" I look around "—Mel's Diner."

"All right. I'll be there in about twenty minutes. Just…" She wonders what to tell me. "Be careful."

I agree. I hang up the phone.

★ ★ ★

"Can you believe the service tonight? I've never seen them this slow!"

Leslie watched as Rick fidgeted in his chair, craning his neck to see if he could get the waiter's attention. It was a busy night at Indigo, one of the newer and more chichi restaurants in Downtown. She was hoping to make a night of it. She knew Rick was expecting them to go out afterward, to a club.

She had other plans. She didn't have a ring, and it was sort of backward, but she was a woman who was through with waiting. She was going to propose tonight.

"Thanks for taking me out and celebrating my article, Rick," she said, reaching across the table and taking his hand. The gesture momentarily caught his attention, and he focused on her, smiling. "I mean, it was nice of your family to throw me a party, but this means more."

At the mention of his grandparents' party, he immediately scowled and looked away. She quickly tried to change the subject.

"I'm officially on features now, did I tell you?"

"No, you didn't. So…you'll be writing more exposés, stuff like that?"

Now it was her turn to frown. "He did mention that he liked that whole slant." Which hadn't exactly set her world on fire. "I guess it won't be that bad. I really love writing, I'm finding out. I even enjoy the research part…"

"Waiter!" Rick went so far as to snap his fingers. She'd never seen him this agitated.

"What's wrong?" she finally asked. She had hoped he'd be in a good mood for this.

He sighed. "Nothing. Rough day at work, that's all… Could you have taken longer?" he asked the waiter, and Leslie winced at his uncharacteristic rudeness. They both ordered, and she felt sure that the waiter was going to do something terrible to Rick's swordfish special. "You know, I'm thinking of quitting."

Leslie blinked at him. "Why? What happened?"

"Not one thing specifically. Just a bunch of little things."

He sighed, leaned back. "Maybe I'm just getting sick of San Francisco."

Alarms went off in Leslie's head. "But you love the city," she protested.

"I know. Maybe I could just do with less of my parents' expectations, my grandparents' pressures." He took a long sip from his Merlot. "You have to understand that. Your parents never let up. Haven't you ever thought about moving? Just chucking it all, starting someplace new?" He grinned, a winning smile. "Screening your calls?"

She laughed, and some of the warning went away as the new idea took hold. Moving out of the Bay Area. Someplace on the East Coast, possibly, where her parents would have a six-hour flight before they could tell her in person how much she was screwing up her life. Hell, even the long-distance phone bill would be a deterrent.

Not that they'd call much, maybe, she thought, then shook it off. "Where would you want to go?"

"I don't know. New York, maybe Boston… Hell, maybe even Miami."

"I always liked the idea of Boston," Leslie murmured.

He studied her face for a minute, then lit up. "Damn. You really do like the idea of moving, don't you?"

She grinned back. It was just a little private dream, nothing she dwelled on. But, if things were different, sure she'd consider moving.

And if he were considering moving—it might be the break they were both looking for. Away from his bar and club friends, away from her family. A whole new life in a whole new city.

A whole new life together.

They were served their entrées, and they stayed on small talk as Leslie processed this new information. By the time dessert and coffee came, Leslie steeled herself. "So…about moving."

He smiled, much more mellow now that he'd been fed. "I'm serious, Leslie. I think a change would be perfect."

"So do I." She took a deep breath. "So why don't we?"

He blinked at her, his demitasse of espresso halfway to his lips. "Why don't we what?"

"Why don't we move?" she clarified. "I don't even care which city. I mean, I can write anywhere, right?" She shrugged, getting into the excitement of the whole idea…the freedom. "It'd take a little time for me to establish my career, but I'd have to do that here. I'm not so far in the features career that starting somewhere else would be a step back."

He put the cup down. "Um, I was just talking, though."

"But you said so yourself. It would be the perfect chance to get away from our families," she said expansively. "So why not? What's stopping us?"

He turned the saucer in front of him slowly, studying the swirling dish as if he was trying to unlock a combination safe. "Leslie…what are you really asking me, here? You're saying let's go move to another city together. Are you saying you want to move in together?"

"I was saying that we should, yes," she said. "Rick, I'm saying we should get married."

He sighed. "Leslie, we've talked about this."

"I know what you said, about two people really needing to be sure of themselves before they try for marriage," she said, and she hated the way the words seemed coated with the film of desperation. "But I'm ready with that. The career is important to me, yes…but I think with writing, I've finally hit on something that I want to do for the rest of my life. You just can't understand how important it is to me. No matter where I go or what else I've got, I feel like I've finally got…I don't know. A cornerstone, or something."

"That's great, Leslie."

She waited. "But…?"

"I don't."

She stared at him. "I know you're not happy with your job."

"I've never been happy with my job, Leslie. I don't know what the hell I'm doing with my life."

She hadn't quite counted on this argument. "You'll figure it out."

"Yeah. Hopefully. Eventually." He pushed the coffee away. "But are you really willing to wait until I get my shit together? I can't get married, Leslie. Not with my life like this."

Oh, crap.

"But, Rick…" Her mind whirled. "You never mentioned this. Why did you always make it seem like it was *my* career? My problem, that was keeping us from…" She couldn't even bring herself to say it again.

"I didn't want to show what a screwup I was. Things seemed to be going so well. Even passed the one-year mark." He crumpled up his napkin, for lack of something else to throttle. "I feel like such a fuckup."

She wanted to comfort him. She wanted to strangle him. "So now what?"

"I don't know." And he really looked at a loss.

"Do you love me?"

He sighed heavily. "You know I do."

"So why can't you do this for me?" Her voice was a whisper. She could see her vision blurring with tears and wished, suddenly, that they weren't in this place. Wished that she weren't even in this city.

"I can't just marry you to make you happy. It would never work. You know that."

"Okay. Okay." She shifted into problem-solving mode. "So…maybe…maybe we just live together. To start, you know? See how it works out."

But he was already motioning for the check. "You know that wouldn't work, either, Leslie. You would want more. It wouldn't be enough."

"So what the hell options have I got, here, Rick?" She didn't care that the waiter was staring at her when she snarled out that statement. "We just stay like this indefinitely?"

"Why don't we wait until we get to the car?" His voice was low and annoyed.

"Just tell me."

He let out a deep, weary sigh. "I don't know what else to tell you, Leslie. This is the best I've got. I do love you. What else can I say to make you feel better?"

She blinked, hard enough for a tear to hit the linen tablecloth.

"I guess there isn't anything you can say," she finally admitted.

"I guess not."

"So…I guess that's it."

He stared at her in surprise. And then, just as she'd feared…he signed for the check and stood up without offering any fight, or counterargument. There was just his resignation.

"I guess it is," he said in a low voice.

She cried all the way to the car.

chapter 18

Samantha woke up in a bed that was like a cloud—pillow-top, she thinks, curling around what felt like a goose-feather pillow. The room was perfectly temperate, and blackout dark. She glanced over at a nightstand table.

It's ten o'clock. She was late for class, she realized with a pang, throwing the covers off and searching hastily for her clothes.

Then she heard the shower going on, and realized, with complete clarity, where she was—and what had just happened.

She'd just slept with Jonathan, who had treated her like a goddess and actually worshiped her body in a way she could not have imagined. She felt giddy-happy, more than she ever had with any temporal boyfriend, or puppy-eager suitor from college or from the club.

She had done it. She'd actually started something with the elusive Jonathan…and had a full night sleeping in his bed to show for it.

Naked, she walked toward the bathroom, then felt a little self-conscious. She saw his midnight-blue silk shirt, draped on the back of a chair, and she put it on, buttoning only two buttons. This gesture was classically sexy, and had that sort of

territory-marking aspect to it. You had to really mean something to someone to wear their clothes, she thought. She'd
never really done that before. A few crazy weeks with the first
guy she'd slept with, sure, but she was sixteen then, it didn't
even count.

The bathroom door was closed, and as much as she was
counting on this, she didn't feel comfortable enough to just
open it and walk right in. He might be…she winced. She
didn't want to think about what he might be doing in the bathroom, what she might be walking in on. The image wasn't really
conducive to romance.

She wondered why he was up so early. A lot of his meet-
ings were later. Maybe he was meeting with the record people,
she thought. He'd be down again…the last thing she wanted
was for him to start ruminating on PJ and getting depressed.
Maybe she'd suggest that they go out to lunch or something.
Maybe she could work on taking his mind off PJ again.

If it were anything like last night, she'd suggest sex as often
as possible…no matter what was on his mind.

She was still hovering in the little hallway, wondering what
she should do, when he opened the door. She blinked against
the bright light of the bathroom—it was still so dark in the bedroom. He seemed like a big dark silhouette, with no details.
When he shut off the light, she felt blinded. He moved past
her, turning on a small lamp that let off a more gentle, nonin-
vasive glow. He looked at her, taking in the shirt, her nudity.

"Good morning," she said, leaning against his dresser and
smiling. She wished she had a better look at herself in a mirror, she realized. He looked fresh, showered, shaved, his damp
hair slicked back. He wasn't wearing a shirt, but he had his
trousers on, and bare feet. His torso was Greek-godworthy,
something that he never really emphasized with his clothing
choices. He looked somber.

"Samantha," he said with a heavy sigh.

She blinked, and straightened. Immediately, she realized that
this wasn't a man besotted…and she got the feeling that she was
going to have to work quickly to regain footing. That was a

look of remorse. She felt a twinge of panic. Remorse did not help her at all.

"I had a fantastic time last night," she said a little hastily, but sexy sounding all the same. "In fact, I'm sorry you took a shower without me."

He shook his head. "Samantha, I can't apologize enough for last night."

She felt as if he'd thrown a glass of water in her face. "Don't be sorry. I enjoyed every minute of it." And she had. More than she even realized that she would. "Didn't you?"

He didn't say anything.

That was when she realized—maybe he didn't.

"I was upset…pissed off. Confused." He sighed again, this time full of regret. Remorse, regret. This was only getting worse. "I was mixed up. I don't know what I was thinking. You're what? Twenty-one or something, for God's sake."

She blinked. "Is this about my age? Because I'm too young?" That was a new one. Did he think it would reflect badly on him? As in, he was getting old enough to need a trophy girl-friend (or wife? she wondered) to make him feel better?

She had never thought of her age as a hindrance—in mod-eling, maybe she'd thought she was getting a little too old at nineteen, not getting enough of the prime shows, that perhaps she'd started too late. But she'd never considered herself too young for anything. Or anyone.

"Samantha, you're lovely." Now he did sound old, she thought. "But you're…I have always liked you."

Liked, she thought. Wonderful.

"The thing is, I haven't really…I don't usually sleep with someone like this."

"Like what?"

He paused, looked at her. "Casually."

She'd had no idea how much four syllables could hurt. She hadn't expected it to be marriage, but… "Casually?"

"Not to say that I didn't enjoy it," he said, and his voice was full of apology now, and she wanted to choke back the bile and the tears, wanted to tear his shirt from her body. "But I really…I usually only sleep with people I plan to have a relationship with. I'm sure that sounds really square, and pathetic, and strange for a guy…."

"I'd admire it," she said, her voice holding steady. "If it didn't mean I'd just had a one-night stand."

He let out a breath of relief. "I had hoped you wouldn't feel that way about it. I mean, it was just…it was a special situation. I know it was for me. Really…unprecedented."

She shrugged. At this point, she didn't give a shit.

"You're beautiful. I'm sure you'll find someone who treats you right. Somebody who's much better for you than me."

She shrugged again.

"Are you going to have trouble getting home?"

She blinked at him. And now he was kicking her out. Apology accepted—don't let the door hit you as you exit the building.

"I don't suppose," she said, taking off his shirt and letting him get a good look at what he was so remorsefully turning away, "that you could do me a favor."

"Anything," he said. But he looked away, damn him. He didn't…she wasn't going to think about it.

"I need you to put in a good word. You're friends with Danielle Ichiba," she said. "I want to be on the runway for her next show. It would give me a real boost."

He blinked, and now he did look at her—not at her breasts, or her nakedness, but at her eyes, and with an expression of shock. "You want me to pull some strings."

"Yes." She put her chin up.

I think I've fucking earned it, don't you?

He nodded slowly. "Sure. No problem. No problem at all."

He didn't seem regretful now, she realized. "Your clothes are over there," he said with a gesture. He went into his closet, pulled a fresh shirt off the hanger, rummaged in his drawers for socks. His closet was perfectly organized, dark colors, light colors, few colors in the palette in between.

She pulled on her own clothes, ignoring him, hating the way that old, day-dirty clothes felt against her skin. She wished she could take a shower, but suddenly the dark walls were closing in on her. She'd pulled off her transaction. She'd gotten what she wanted. In the long run, she probably wouldn't have wanted a relationship with Jonathan anyway, she told herself. She was better off on her own. And at last the modeling stuff was looking up. She was going to be better than before. She'd still need to solve the bad-grade problem, but she'd manage. She always managed.

They dressed in uncomfortable silence. When she had slipped on her heels, he was finishing up his tie, with a perfectly dimpled knot. The guys on *Queer Eye* would be proud of this little metrosexual, she thought unkindly.

He was looking at her as she stood up. "Samantha," he began.

She wondered—would he apologize? Suddenly, she wanted to. For making everything like a deal. Even, in a small way, for PJ. She didn't want it to be like this.

"I'll make sure Danielle gets that call."

She nodded. And that was that. So she left.

To her credit, my mother didn't really say much of anything when she picked me up as I was standing on Shattuck Avenue in only a T-shirt, ratty sweats and my socks. My hair was sticking out from my head as if it was trying to escape…or perhaps commit suicide. I probably smelled like two-day-old weed smoke and that naturally abhorrent scent of the Berkeley streets. Yet she restrained herself, saying nothing more than "are you all right?" until we got home. Even once we got there, there was nothing more stringent than "why don't you go take a shower" and "you must be tired." I followed her, numb until the heat of the shower hit me and all the emotions of the past seventy-two hours cleared from a marijuana haze, finally emerging, scrubbed off and raw. I cried, because the shower is the best place to cry. You're wet already, for one thing. Also, in my house, it's the only safe place my mother won't take the initiative and walk in on you. Odds are good she's going to catch me crying at some point soon, I can tell, but this first one is all me.

I feel…relief, at being home, knowing that I'll actually have a bed and a hot meal. Shame, knowing that not only did I fuck up my DJ gig with the Leslie Fiasco, as it would be known in infamy…I finally proved, conclusively and to the entire reading population of the SF area, that I am a loser, a complete asshole who couldn't hack it in the real world and consequently failed spectacularly in her fantasy life. Now, the only evidence of my utterly stupid plan, my laptop and iPod was probably being sold by the great weed-avenger for fifty bucks to some schmuck UC student on a street corner somewhere. Or thrown out in a Dumpster. Perhaps I'm bitter, but the violent, angry guy didn't strike me as computer literate.

So I was, at twenty-nine, clothesless, careerless, friendless, and crying my eyes out in my mom's shower. I was a walking, breathing Lifetime Channel special event.

I couldn't stay in the shower forever. My first day back home and I use up all the hot water? Not exactly the right foot, and at this point, I had no other option. I couldn't afford to fuck this up, too. I finally forced myself out of the comforting fog of warm water, toweled off and went back to my room.

I smelled bacon. Even—unless my nose deceived me—French toast. My stomach immediately caterwauled in protest of being denied what my nose was alerting it to. My mother would know I wouldn't want to talk. She also knew I'd be hungry.

Like a contract hit, she had this thing planned. Except she only had the best of intentions.

My stomach didn't care what her intentions were. It would kill me if I didn't go.

I didn't want to think about what would happen once I talked to her—which would be inevitable. My pride might have put up a fight now, if it had survived, but the one moment of sheer terror while fleeing from the Weed Kids' dive had pretty much nailed the coffin shut on my pride.

I rummaged around for long-neglected clothes. It wasn't like I was going to go eat breakfast naked in a state of abject pathos. I discover a worn pair of gray sweats with a hole in the knee and a sweater my grandmother had given me for Christmas, which I'd opened and then abandoned here…a pink monstrosity in chenille with an appliquéd poodle.

I briefly reconsider abject pathos.

It's chilly as it is, and we've established that I have no pride, so I pull the sweater over my grumbling stomach, tug on the sweats and head downstairs.

My mom looks up from the pan of sizzling bacon, expertly removing the last slice from the molten fat, placing it with its mates on a plate in the prewarmed oven. There's a pile of French toast already sitting companionably next to it, on its own heated plate, as well as a very cheesy-looking omelet on the range, nestling in its stickproof sauté pan. My mom's a thing of beauty when she's cooking, and her admittedly savory food is a potent weapon. It's made vulnerable much stronger individuals than myself.

Still, I find my appetite diminishes when she smiles at me— that maternal smile of complete and almost unconditional love. Almost. It's a thing I used to take for granted. It was a thing that began to make subtle and not-so-subtle demands…until I made some not-so-subtle choices of my own.

She and I have spoken often, but rarely talked.

This promises to be both delicious and painful.

I sit down and she goes into motion. She loads up a dinner plate full of all three food groups—bacon, French toast, omelet. "Eat," she says, both order and encouragement.

I'm feeling shame on several levels. "I could've gotten that, Mom," I protest. And yet, I sat down, making no movement toward the stove. I knew that she would provide. We both knew it.

She just continues smiling. "You look…" The pained pause. "Thin. Eat, while it's hot."

I dig in. The food's delicious, as always, and fattening. She doesn't eat like this as a rule—since she and Dad split up, she's taken good care of herself. She's trying for the comfort-food aspect, sure. The rest of it is that she took in what I saw stepping into the shower—my prominent collarbone, rib cage protruding a bit. My T-shirt hadn't hidden any of that to eyes as

sharp as hers. She stares at me as if I'm back from a con-
centration camp. She's just on the edge of tears, I notice, so I
try to focus on my food. Cheddar cheese. Crisp bacon. The way
she puts just a hint of orange zest in the French toast, to com-
plement the clove, cinnamon, allspice, vanilla. All this, in the
forty-five minutes I spent weeping under the spray of the sec-
ond-bathroom shower.

I reluctantly finish, my stomach distended, stretching the
shot elastic of my sweatpants. I'm more full than I can remember being in months. I wonder if I could just go and take
a nap. I can't remember ever being this tired.

She's got me right where she wants me. Helpless to dodge
or evade, muzzy from food and warmth and love. Not that she
wants to hurt me. At least, not deliberately.

"Persephone, honey…you know you always have a place
here."

I nod. Yes. I have always known that. It's probably my choos-
ing to sleep in the den of pot growers that makes this much more
painful to her. Am I crazed, or just stupid? Obviously both. She's
just fed me a feast fit for a queen, and she obviously hasn't drawn
out wire hangers to beat me. What the hell is my problem?

She takes a deep breath. My lush, giving mother, wondering
how her child could be so injurious to us both. If I had an answer, I would've shared it with her when I was seventeen. I'd
even do it now.

At the same time, if I hadn't loved her, I would never have
seen her again since then.

Yeah, I know. I don't get the dynamic, either.

"I'm sorry," I say as best I can against a throat that's starting
to clench up with tears. I don't say that because it's an easy way
out. It's not easy. It's painful because I mean it every single time.

"Tell me what happened," she says, all but bracing herself
against the table.

I don't know where to start, but know it must be told. So I
start with Leslie, and then introduce Jonathan…and before I
know it, words are tumbling out, tangling my tongue with
tears of fear and frustration.

She doesn't get a lot of what I'm saying, though she desperately wants to.

I get to the part where I'm staying at the Weed Kids', and I see the hurt crinkling the corners of her eyes—and I try to gloss over what happens next, but there's no quick and painless way to say, "Oh, and then this guy came in and I had to run so I left my cell phone and computer." It was ridiculously painful for both of us. I felt like one big, aching bruise, and tears leaked out of me because I didn't have any energy left to sob.

She sat with it for a long minute. I sat, too, waiting. I knew the love was there, like always. Knew how incredibly lucky I was to have it.

"So. What are you going to do now?"

I knew the price, too.

"I was…" I cleared my throat. Took a deep breath, considered my options. Ripped off the figurative Band-Aid. "I was hoping I could live at home. With you."

She smiles, just a ghost of one.

"For a while," I amend.

She sighs. "You know how much I love you, PJ."

I nod back.

"It hurt when you went off to…to live on the streets. To actually turn your back on me, on all of this, and put your life in danger…"

"It wasn't actually on the streets, Mom. Not really."

She gives me the pained look and I can't counter that. I shut up.

"You became a homeless person for this pursuit of music. Not even really music! Fooling around with your computer with those people…"

I try really hard not to say or do anything. It's not the time.

"We both know you were just running away, PJ. You were stressed, you couldn't handle the pressures of your old job. That's all."

But that wasn't…no, I need to shut up, I need to just ride this out.

"It's not too late," I hear her say, and it's all I can do to keep it together. "I know a woman, looking for an assistant…the pay's not spectacular, but the stress level will be considerably lower, and until you get on your feet…"

I listen to her detail, carefully, my plan of recovery and redemption. She's right on one thing: I have to change now. I'm pathetic, she loves me, and I have to change.

"Okay, PJ?"

The job. The house. Straighten up and fly right.

"Yes, Mom," I answer. To anything.

chapter 19

Samantha stood in the chaos that was behind the scenes at Danielle Ichiba's show. There were dressers running around in tennis shoes and all black clothing, pins stuck in cushions around their wrists. Danielle herself was barking like a small shih tzu.

"That hem looks like shit! Fix it!"

"Where's the duct tape? Her tits look like pancakes! Fix it!"

"Makeup! I don't want her to have any expression. And can you emphasize those lips?"

"Fix it! Fix it! *Fix it!*"

Samantha closed her eyes as the dresser stuck her with a long pin for the eighth time in the past ten minutes. She was wearing a pink crepe creation, an evening gown of sorts. It looked like she was frosted or something. She looked like a *quinciñera* cake.

"You're all set," the dresser said. "Wait in line for your cue."

Samantha did as she was told. She stood, trying to breathe as best she could in the constrictive dress.

She hadn't spoken to Jonathan since the disastrous morning after. True to his word, he'd contacted Danielle, and Samantha's agent had gotten a call shortly thereafter. She wanted Samantha there, for one outfit. As a favor. It was the break Samantha had been looking for—the break she desperately needed. Her agent had said as much. If she blew this, he doubted he'd be able to get her a commercial for dog food.

This was it. Make or break. That simple.

On the plus side, she thought, she'd worked out like a fiend. The resulting benefit was she'd finally lost those last few pounds. She was at a lean, fighting weight. Ready to take on anything.

Sure, she'd ditched class to focus on the show. And she'd dodged her parents increasingly worried phone calls.

"Samantha…honey, are you all right? We haven't talked to you in over a week. Please call me." That, from her mother.

"Samantha, the school sent us a letter. Your grades are dropping. What the hell is happening with you? They're saying your scholarship might be in jeopardy if you don't show some drastic improvement. Have you spoken to your guidance counselor?" Her father left that one, or a variant.

The next step would be a personal visit, she knew it. But it didn't matter. The only thing that mattered was this show. She could bring her grades up in her sleep. And the popular people, the powerful people, didn't give a shit if she was on the dean's list or not.

Her parents might exert a lot of pressure on her, but for the first time in her life their opinion didn't matter. The only thing that mattered was that ramp and how people reacted to her. She was beautiful. She was going to be powerful and popular. And show everyone, including Mr. Jonathan Hadeis, that she was not someone to be fucked with because she was nice and convenient.

"And now, a silk crepe confection of…"

"That's you," the dresser hissed. "Out! Now!"

Samantha took the stage.

The lights were brighter than she expected, and there was a sea of faces. She'd felt pressure before, but this was different. She froze for all of a second.

"Walk!" the dresser said in a low, furious voice.

She moved. One foot, then the other. A little tilt of the hip. Danielle wanted no expression, so she stopped herself from a sly, sexy smile at the last second. She stared forward, like an automaton.

There was a murmur of interest. She felt her adrenaline spike.

She made it to the base of the runway, turned. A flash of cameras distracted her.

I'm doing it. I'm making it.

She forced herself to slow, giving the rich faces in the crowd plenty of opportunity to stare, to envy, to covet. She *was* beautiful. They wanted to be her. They wanted her.

She took a few final steps. It was over far too quickly. Now her agent would return her calls. She'd finally stop going to cattle-call auditions. All talk of tacky TV commercials would stop. When she started making huge money, when famous people started to talk about her, her parents would finally get off her case about getting good grades. What did that matter, when how you looked counted for everything?

She stepped off the runway.

"What the hell were you thinking?"

Samantha blinked.

Danielle flew at her. "You were wearing the wrong shoes! And that…that *display* you put on. I took you on as a favor, and this is how I'm repaid?"

Samantha blinked. "What…what did I…"

"I will make sure that you never, *never* work on any runway ever again," Danielle promised, then looked at one of the cowering dressers beside her. "Get that off her. And make sure that she leaves the building."

Samantha felt tears spilling out of her eyes, ruining her makeup. She'd gotten her shot. And lost it.

She was looking at the faces of the other models, who were either staring at her with a combination of pity and horror, or those who were smiling because they'd been pissed that she was added at the last minute. There was no friendly face. Nobody gave a shit about her. Now she'd just have to work hard at the classes—the ones she was currently fucking up.

Her parents would be furious. She didn't have Jonathan. She

didn't have her modeling career, and she was even screwing up her scholastic career.

She didn't have anything. And no one cared.

That was the last thing she thought of before the floor came up to meet her. She gave herself over to the blackness, hoping for a split second that the sensation would last forever.

"Here's to the happy couple!"

Obligingly, Leslie lifted her glass of champagne. It was the fifth toast in the past hour. Mark's friends, it seemed, were a celebratory people. Either that, or they were as astonished as she was that Mark was marrying anyone (much less someone as fine as Aimee).

They were having their engagement party at the bar/restaurant in W., the trendy Westin hotel in the city, the one that looked like a gigantic Hugo Boss ad. Leslie had fortified her position in a booth farthest from the rest of the party. Other than her toast participation, she might as well have been a stranger.

She hadn't spoken to Rick since he dropped her off from Indigo a week ago. It was just too painful. And infuriating…although her temper was more directed at herself than at him.

Her mother kept invading her territory, sneaking back periodically while Leslie's father regaled the group with one of his old sales war stories. "Why are you being so antisocial?" her mother whispered. "If you're going to just sit here and not talk to anyone…"

"Mother, I don't know anyone," Leslie said with no heat in her voice, just a note of weariness. "These are Mark's friends and Aimee's friends, and friends of yours and Dad's."

"So? That's why it's called socializing, dear. You don't have to know them. You're just being social."

"I don't feel like being social." She sounded and felt like a depressed teenager. The oldest teenager in San Francisco.

Her mother picked up on the sulk in her voice. "All right, what happened, then?" She looked around as if just now noticing Leslie was the only inhabitant besides herself. "And why isn't Rick here?"

Leslie sent her mother a flat stare. *Wait for it. Put two and two together.*

Her mother's eyes widened. "He finally dumped you, then?"

"Nice, Mom." Leslie drained the last of her champagne, motioned to the waiter. "Just for the record, I left *him,* by the way. And under completely justified conditions."

Good God. She was beginning to sound like PJ's ex-husband. "Why did you leave him, for pity's sake?"

"Because he didn't want to marry me, Mom." Saying it out loud was like pouring raw lime on a blister. "And he had no idea when he was going to get his life together enough to even consider marriage in general, much less me in specific."

Her mother sat in silence absorbing what Leslie had just said. "Well. He *is* younger than you, Leslie. It takes men longer to settle down." She waited a second. "He did seem to genuinely care about you."

Which is why it had hurt so much, Leslie thought, wishing her champagne glass weren't empty. She wanted to keep drinking until she passed out, and she couldn't even *dream* about how shitty she was feeling. "It just wasn't going to work, Mom."

"Leslie, I don't want to say anything about your choices, or your lifestyle…"

Of course you do. Leslie braced herself.

"But I hate seeing you this unhappy," her mother front-loaded. "Is marriage really that big a deal?"

Leslie blinked at her. Was this her mother saying this? The one who had practically hired a skywriter when her brother had announced his wedding plans? The one who had made catty remarks about not getting another chance at planning a wedding? The one who had all but skewered Rick with pointed questions about his intentions toward her daughter?

What the hell happened?

"After all, Leslie," her mother said, covering Leslie's hand with her own, "since your last birthday, I've been thinking. I hate to bring it up, but, well, it's only going to get, you know, harder."

The champagne must be kicking in, Leslie thought, because that statement made no sense. "Harder?"

"Harder to conceive, dear," her mother clarified in a low voice.

"Jesus." Leslie looked at her mother, aghast.

"If you haven't had a child by the time you're thirty-five, it gets that much more difficult to have one after. And you don't want to try those fertility drugs." She wrinkled her nose. "They're so expensive, for one thing. And then there's that risk of anything from twins to septuplets, and God knows you don't want that."

"I can't believe I'm having this conversation," Leslie muttered.

Another comforting pat. "Just think about it for a while," her mother said. "That journalism career of yours seems to be finally taking off, and you wanted that so badly. I understand they offered you a permanent job on staff? Is that right?"

Leslie nodded. "Writing exposés," she said.

Her mother shrugged. "I'm sure you can parlay that into even more success, maybe even at a more reputable newspaper, hmm? And who's to say that Rick won't come around, given a little time?"

Leslie felt any drunken effects from the champagne vanish, like the sudden sobering of a teen who hears sirens while at a party. "Mom, if Rick doesn't know what he wants now, after we've been together for four years, what makes you think, when he does decide to settle down and have kids, that he's going to stay with a woman that you yourself say is going to have trouble providing them?"

Her mother's mouth opened, then closed as her eyes clouded with confusion. She paled. "Well. Maybe it *is* best that you broke up," she said, her voice much less confident than it was a few minutes before. "Why don't you look at it as a whole new start, then?"

Leslie sat for a second. That she'd wanted a whole new start for some time was the problem. She'd gone for the new job, the new lifestyle of being married. In a way, she was sick of new starts. She was tired of trying to be what her boyfriend wanted, what her parents expected.

Unbidden, PJ's words echoed in her mind.

If there wasn't anybody whose opinions you worried about…what would you do?

Slowly, she smiled.

"See, you're feeling better," her mother said with obvious relief.

There was clanging on a glass, and Mark stood up. "To my wonderful family, for being so supportive!" And all the partyers lifted their glasses yet again.

Her father walked over to stand by her and her mother, showcasing said supportive family. "And how are my girls?" he said, never pausing as he smiled and toasted the party crowd in return.

A waiter handed Leslie and her mother new champagne glasses. "We're much better," her mother said in a satisfied voice.

"We certainly are," Leslie said in a warm haze as the idea in her head started to take hold. "I broke up with Rick."

"Oh?" her father said with a nervous laugh, taking a sip of champagne.

"Oh, and I'm quitting my job," Leslie said dreamily. "And I'm moving!"

Her father choked on the champagne he'd just swallowed. Her mother's eyes bulged. *"What?"*

"Congratulations!" Leslie called to her brother from across the room, and grinned broadly. "To all of us!"

My mother said two things to me before I headed off to this interview. First, don't be nervous. Second, don't screw up. (Or, as she put it, "you need this too much to throw it away, so don't tell them anything bad and don't say anything that would jeopardize the job.") Naturally, she missed the irony.

So right now, I'm sitting in a spare cubicle, working on the Zen of not screwing up. The cubicle is empty, and the desk surface has the gummy film of dust that signifies it's a hotel cube that isn't used much. A surly looking administrative assistant has informed me that another applicant is currently interviewing with the director and the head of H.R., and so I should wait here. I do as I'm told. I even manage to say "thank you," which prompts her to offer me a small cup of water. I sip it, gingerly. It wouldn't do to have to excuse myself from the interview to pee. Gotta make a good impression, if it kills me.

I'm going to have to buy a car to get here, eventually. I'm going to need a place to live. That'll mean utilities. Insurance. These things don't pay for themselves, as my mother points out. Not that she's pressuring me. She just wants to see me on my feet.

I take another long sip of water. I'm not sleeping on the street. Sticky's right…I need to suck it up, shut up, stop whining. Not that he put it that way, but I understand. I had my shot at being a DJ, and I screwed it up. I'm lucky to have another shot at the corporate world.

I have to get this job.

"Persephone Sherman?"

I stand up, startled. "PJ," I correct her, and then smile, to take some of the sting off. "Please, call me PJ."

"Right." She looks middle-aged, not as well preserved as some of Jonathan's friends, but pretty good. She's got a cheerful face. "Would you follow me?"

She leads me to a beige conference room with a large rectangular table. There are two other people sitting down: a tall, lanky-looking guy who seems to sprawl in the conference chair he's plunked into, and a very sophisticated-looking woman, maybe in her early sixties but who could probably give some young forty-year-old hotties a run for their money. She's obviously the honcho, the one in charge. I make sure to smile at her, especially, as I shake hands all around and everyone introduces themselves. She's a vice president. He's a director of business systems. The cheerful, round-faced lady is H.R.

They settle in, and I take out a pad of paper, just to give me something to do. I try not to focus on the fact that the sweat on my palm makes the pen a little slippery.

The vice president looks down at my résumé. "So, Persephone…"

"PJ," I correct again, and they all look at me. I laugh nervously. "Persephone's sort of a mouthful for most people."

"I sort of like Persephone. It's got that whole mythic ring to it," she muses, and then looks down. "Anyway, PJ. We liked your credentials. You seem to have done a lot of systems work for hospitals. You don't see a lot of that."

They're one of the largest hospital chains in the country. I imagine they see plenty of that...just not outside their offices. I make a sort of encouraging noise anyway.

"I did notice that there's a rather large gap in your résumé, though," she said, and she looks at the H.R. woman, the one who had presumably recommended me. I think she's the friend of a friend of my mother's. "Could you explain what you've been doing for the past two years?"

"I've been pursuing a music career," I reply, just as mom coached me.

"Really?" I can't tell if she sounds intrigued or unimpressed. Or maybe she just doesn't believe me.

"What sort of instrument do you play?" This, from the director, the guy. He's got a sort of nervous energy—he'd been doodling on his copy of my résumé, but now he's sitting at attention, and the tip of his pencil is tapping frenetically on the surface of the tabletop.

"Not that kind of musician. I'm a DJ."

I catch the vice president's expression when I say this. We can definitely mark her down as unimpressed. "But I...it didn't work out. So I decided I'd go back to systems work," I say, in as clear a voice as I can manage. It's not exactly perky, but it's hard to sound chipper when you feel like you've got "LOSER" branded onto your forehead.

Jesus, Sticky would be so disappointed in me. I'm glad he can't see me this way.

"And from the looks of it, you certainly did a lot of impressive work over a number of languages," H.R. woman pipes up, trying to save face for herself, at least. "And you designed all these databases..."

"So, what prompted you to leave the field in the first place?" Ms. V.P. is not letting go of this.

I sigh. "I just thought it was a good window of time for me,"

I demur, deliberately vague, again as coached. "I was really intrigued with being a DJ. It's a fascinating…"

I see her shift some of her papers in a leather portfolio. And there it is. The article.

She knows exactly who the hell I am.

I stop talking.

H.R. woman is starting to look concerned. The tall, thin director-guy is still tapping the table incessantly, completely oblivious. I just stare at the vice president.

She smiles back at me, but there's no warmth. "So. How do we know you're not going to just abandon us and decide to pursue music again, say? I want to hire someone who's devoted to the company. It's a stressful position, no question, so we'd want someone dedicated. You left your last systems job, after only, what, a few years? Tell me something that indicates you're capable of handling the pressure of our expectations?"

"Well for one thing, I'm sitting here," I say, in a complete monotone. "As far as an indicator, if my car made it here in one piece, you've got a leg up on my last employer."

H.R. woman's eyes bug out. The director's pen hovers in midair and his jaw drops a little.

I blink.

Oh, high holy flaming *crap.*

The vice president pulls out the article all the way now, placing it in the center of the table. The H.R. woman is staring at it, puzzled.

The director does a quick double take at the copy of the *Citizen,* then stares at me. "That's *you?*"

I nod.

"You've been homeless for two years?" He sounds shocked. The H.R. woman looks beyond appalled. And the vice president is crossing her arms, all but sneering at me.

"Not exactly," I flub. "I just…I mean…"

The job. Now I'd messed that up, too. My mind was reeling, searching for some way to salvage the situation. To save myself.

"And you deliberately wrecked your car?" he added, in a tone of disbelief.

I shrug, barely paying attention, and blurt out the first innocuous phrase that comes to mind. "Well, you know what they say…"

And that's when it hits me. What Dylan told me, on my big night at Technique. With that painful scratch that I thought was going to end my big-time career. The night I thought I was ruined, before I knew what it meant to be ruined.

"Yes?" The vice president prompts me.

"Any accident you can walk away from," I whisper, beaming at them, "isn't that serious."

I stand up.

"Thank you for your time."

They're saying something I'm not even listening to as I walk out, down the hall, out the front door. I didn't fuck up. I mean, yeah, I *did* fuck up. But they were just that…. Mistakes. Accidents. I could focus on being a loser. I could be the woman who Leslie wrote about, the one who couldn't get past it, the one who stayed in the perpetual present so she wouldn't have to think about her past or her future.

Or, as Dylan would say, I could be memorable and fuck up big.

Samantha felt woozy—strange, disoriented. She opened her eyes to see a beige ceiling, one of those industrial-looking ones separated by a crisscross of iron strips.

She also had an IV in her arm. That should've been the first thing she noticed.

"You're awake?" Deep voice, whispering.

She looked over. Sticky was sitting in a small chair surveying her with worry. He actually looked like he was overpowering the chair, spilling over the sides.

She looked around frantically. There was an ugly flowered curtain hanging from the ceiling in the middle of the room, on one of those metal rails. There was a funny antiseptic smell to everything. She was draped in a flannel sheet and an ugly mauve blanket. There was a beeping sound from the other side of the curtain. There was a TV bolted to the ceiling.

Hospital, she thought. Idiot. What had happened?

"What…why am I here?"

"You passed out at that fashion show. They called 911. They also called your parents."

"They did?" She looked around, groggy. "Where are they?"

"Your parents are both getting a little food in the cafeteria. I'm sure they'll be right back."

Beeping increased. Her heart rate, she realized blankly.

He scooted the chair across the floor, pulling it next to her bedside with a squeaking scrape.

"How did you know to come here?"

He smiled gently. "I called, looking for you. Guess your cell phone was here, and your mom answered, and she explained. So…here I am."

She realized immediately that she couldn't be wearing makeup, or whatever was left was probably smeared. And she was wearing one of those awful hospital-gown things, one step up from wearing a paper bag. "Oh, God. Why?"

"Because I'm your friend," he said, simply.

She shrugged, squirming uncomfortably. "I don't even know why I'm here. It was probably—I don't know. Something I ate?" She winced. "Or the flu or something."

"Yeah. Right." He leaned back, sighed. "Samantha, I care a lot about you."

"I don't have time for a heart-to-heart, Sticky," she said, looking around frantically for her phone. Stan would probably tell the agency to drop her on the spot. She had to try to stop him. Maybe she could…

Sticky held her hand, firmly, and she was surprised enough to stare at him.

"That's why I'm going to peel your cap."

"What?" His words were making no sense.

"You're full of shit, Samantha."

She gasped.

"The flu? Something you ate? Come on." He let go of her hand, now that he had her attention, and glared at her. "You're anorexic. You're malnourished. Oh, don't give me the look…there's absolutely nobody who knows you who would be surprised by that, either. Including you."

She was too stunned to say anything for a second.

"That's why you're cold all the time," he continued, relentlessly. "That's why you passed out. For Christ's sake…I know, I know, it's probably mental, and maybe you don't realize it and all that. But you've got to admit to yourself that weighing about a hundred pounds at your height just isn't normal."

"Well, maybe not to someone *your* size," she snapped.

And could have slapped herself from the sudden look of hurt that crossed his face. It was just as quickly replaced by a look of pure anger, and she cowered against the bed.

"I know you're in a bad place," he said, his voice edged in frost. "I…oh, fuck it. I don't care what kind of place you're in. Do you know why I care about people like you and PJ?"

"No," she said. "I honestly have no idea."

"Because you need people to take care of you. You're damaged. I know something about being damaged," he said, and his voice was low, almost a whisper. "I was pretty fucked up when I was a kid. Got into a lot of trouble. Went to juvie, the whole nine yards. I'm not saying I'm all right or that I've got all my shit together now, either. But I'm a hell of a lot better off than you are. And at least I have a mom and sisters and brothers who love me no matter what I look like. Or what kind of grades I'm getting. Or any of that bullshit. They just love me because I'm me, and no matter what I do, I'm still going to be me."

It was as if he were speaking a different language. "Lots of people love me," she ventured, but the words felt alien.

"And you believe that enough and you still feel you've got to lose another five pounds," he spat out. "Please."

"Sticky," she said, feeling more miserable than she thought possible. "I didn't mean to…I'm sorry." She felt the tears welling up at the first statement, and by the last few words, they had spilled over, crawling down her face. She had one final weird pang—her makeup was definitely ruined now if it wasn't already—and then shut her eyes, letting his anger wash over her in a wave.

"First PJ, then you. You know what?" He got up and put his jacket on. "I'm sick of helping people who obviously don't give a shit. You want to kill yourself so some rich guy will think you're hot shit or all those cheerleaders will finally let you into their clique or your parents will finally say you're doing a good job—well, then. Go ahead. I'm sick of being a one-man fucking rescue squad."

Without another word, he strode out the door.

Well, obviously he didn't love her, she thought, and started to cry all over again.

I'm standing in my kitchen, waiting for my mother to come back from a hard day's work. When I left last time, I remember leaving her a note saying I'd e-mail her and let her know I was okay. In retrospect, it seems like a chickenshit thing to do. I couldn't even face her. I knew I'd get hit with guilt and recriminations. If I was going to leave anyway, why stay for a double helping of that, and one more for the road?

But this time is different. On all sorts of levels. Then, I'd felt like I was floating, numb, so scared of my thoughts that I practically shut them off completely. Then, I was scared, but almost jumpy with the sense of freedom.

Now, I feel almost on fire, in a good way. It's similar to the way I feel just before I go on the decks at a club—a bundle of energy and nerves shot through with excitement. And that's how I feel. She's not going to be happy.

For the first time in my life, I'm starting to realize that the fact that she's not going to be happy isn't the point. The point here is, *I'm* going to be happy.

At some point, that has to be enough.

I hear the garage door open, and my heart starts to pound a little. She opens the door, and goes through her usual ritual…hanging up her coat, kicking off her shoes. "Hi, baby. How was the interview?" she asks immediately, her voice chipper and light. Then she takes one look at my face. With the uncanny sixth sense of card-carrying mothers everywhere, her internal alarm starts going off. "What? What happened?"

How to approach this.

"The interview didn't go as well as it could have." I'm hedging. Sure, yeah, I've had this epiphany. But bravery's something a girl's gotta gear up to.

Okay, I'm *really* hedging. Sue me.

"What happened?" she repeats. "Was it the gap in your employment history?"

"It was a little worse than that," I correct. "They had a copy of the article. I didn't stand a chance."

Her face falls. "Damn it. Why did you have to go and do that interview, anyway?"

"I thought it was going to help my career, Mom," I point out.

She shakes her head. "Okay. We'll get around this. Don't worry, baby…it'll be fine. There are plenty of other jobs out there. And it wasn't that big an article. I'm sure plenty of reputable companies don't even read that trash."

I sigh. "Mom, I don't want to go on another interview. Not to be a systems analyst, anyway."

She tenses.

"I still love music, Mom. I'm not going to just abandon it because I made some mistakes."

As soon as I said "I still love music," I could see her having a one-second freak-out. Then she sits down on the kitchen chair across from me, and I watch as she arms her intellectual guns. She's been expecting backsliding, that much is obvious.

"Honey, now let's talk about this. You can't live that way. Literally. You were lucky you didn't get killed this time, you have to know that." She takes a deep breath, and her eyes are dark and sad. "You won't be so lucky next time. And it would kill me if anything happened to you. I can't even think of the nights I stayed up, worried, not knowing where you were or what was happening to you. You could have been on the streets for all I knew…"

There's a little catch in her voice. And she wipes at the corners of her eyes.

Her eyes, wet with tears, still stay trained on me alertly.

I know her, after twenty-nine years. And after all those years, I finally realize that not only was she expecting this, she was actively prepping for this eventuality. Gotta give her props for that.

"I'm not talking about couching it anymore, Mom. You're absolutely right there," I agree.

The dampness halts as her eyes narrow. "You mean…wait. What do you mean?"

"I'm talking about seriously pursuing a career as a DJ, and a music producer."

Now she's frowning. "But Persephone, those aren't really careers. How do you expect to support yourself? How do you expect to eat?"

"I think I can come up with something," I start to say, but she interrupts me.

"Of course you think that!" She's so agitated, she's literally trembling in the chair, like an overwrought Chihuahua. "You always think that! When you married that spineless little wimp Lucas, you had to support him while he 'figured out what he wanted,' you said you could handle that. When you…"

"Let's leave Lucas out of this," I say, more sharply than I mean to. The happy glow I started off with is fading, but the determination is still there.

She doesn't concede, just makes this half nod and then barrels forward. "You didn't say anything, no, but next thing you know I'm getting a call from the police and you're in a mental ward, and that didn't help, either, did it?"

"Maybe if I'd stayed in longer, or tried therapy," I offer.

Her eyes widen, as if I've insulted her. "You needed to come home! Your boss was working you too hard, but you were afraid to say anything! And now, here you are, a twenty-nine-year-old girl, still trying to run away from every damn thing that scares you."

"I used to do that," I admit. "I'm not anymore."

"Oh, really?" And her voice is tremulous. "Prove it."

"I am," I say. "I'm here, aren't I?"

She stares at me, not comprehending.

"Did you really think I was looking forward to this conversation? I knew you were going to hate this idea. But I'm not just flaking out now. Being a DJ *makes me happy.* Period. Just that easy."

She's not quite sure what to do with this information. Her counterarguments weren't set up for this.

"First off, the couch thing. Yeah, that wasn't very bright, but I'm not going to complain about it. I've made a ton of mistakes. Odds are, unfortunately good, that I'll make a ton more." I wince just thinking about it.

"You're making one now if you go back to that life," she says sharply.

"Why?" I huff, exasperated. "Mom, what's so incredibly wrong with it?"

She just gapes at me like a guppy for a second, then gets up, starts pulling out bowls and dishes like she's going to cook supper. She slams a pot down on the burner, with passive-aggressive force. "That life…" She's got that tremor back, but this time it's more genuine, with some raw edge to it. "I pick you up, and you look like a crack addict, you weigh next to nothing, you smell like *marijuana* for God's sake…you think I don't know what goes on in those clubs?" She whirls on me, brandishing a salad spoon. "You think I'm an idiot?"

"Mom, I don't do drugs. It's not like that. I'm just in it for the music."

"So you've got to live your whole life in places like that? With people like that?" She's on the verge of hysteria.

"With people like *me,* Mom. I'd be with people like me."

She just waves that away with a swatting hand gesture. "And you still haven't told me how you plan to live. With *your* people."

I need to learn not to have these kinds of conversations in the kitchen, or her home turf. As long as I'm here, I still feel like I'm seventeen.

But, for the first time, I know I'm right.

"I've been thinking about this since I left the interview. It's expensive to live in the city, but not impossible. I was thinking that I'd move to the East Bay, someplace close to a BART station, for starters. Someplace cheaper. Maybe just a little studio."

"Some place cheaper. You mean like Oakland, or Richmond? Someplace where you'll probably get killed, coming back from one of your late-night gigs? Some…"

"Mom," I say, in a calm voice that means business. "Let me just get through this once, okay?"

Her eyes widen. Her lip quivers a little, before she bites it so it'll stay still. She's pissed, but also surprised. I'm not yelling, I'm not crying.

I think at this point, she's also noticed that I'm not withdrawing, and I'm not leaving.

"Even if I just share a place in the city, or get a studio, or something, housing will be my first concern. I need to find someplace permanent to live." So far, so good. "Next, I need to make money a little more steadily and reliably than I've been making it. I need to think about health insurance and transportation. I've written out a list of all my costs. I need to get a new setup, probably an old fashioned turntable as well as a new Final Scratch record and a high-end laptop."

She's just staring at me now. I know that last bit probably made no sense at all to her.

"It's going to take time to save up enough for all of my equipment, and some time to save up for deposit and rent, as well as find a place," I say.

"And how, exactly, were you planning on saving up?" Her interjection is more subdued, but it's still accusatory.

"I applied for another job today."

Her eyes light up, a faint glimmer of hope that somehow I'll get back on plan.

"I applied for a job at Wall of Sound." I shrug off her instant disappointment. "It's retail, and the pay's not great. Hell, it'd probably be part-time to start. But it would be a way to get some money, and I can use their DJ equipment. I'll also be teaching DJ lessons. I'm putting an ad in some newsweeklies."

"Those cost money," she mentions dully.

"I factored that in."

My mother goes silent. "And I suppose you just expect to live here until you get enough money to try launching this plan of yours?"

"I was hoping," I said. Now it's my turn to be subdued. "But I'll understand if you'd rather I found someplace else to stay."

Now she looks sour, and the tears that have been hovering in her eyes spill over. "Don't. Don't make me the bitch just because I care enough about you not to want to see you ruin your life."

I sit down next to her, feeling achy and hollow. And sorry. "Mom, I was wrong to leave the way I did. I screwed up a lot. I should have left Lucas a long time before he left me, and I probably shouldn't have quit the job. I probably shouldn't have lived the way I did at all." I put an arm around her shoulders. "But it got me here. And I know that I can't be what you want me to be. And I'm sorry about that."

"I can't be happy about this," she says around a sob. "You can't expect me to be happy about this."

"Yeah," I answer. "I know."

She knuckles the tears away, stares at the stove for a long minute while she gets her composure back. "Why don't you just live here, then. It's not so far from the BART. I could cook for you. Take care of you. I wouldn't have to worry about how you're doing. And maybe you…"

"Mom," I interrupt slowly, in as gentle a voice as possible. "I lived here all through college, until I got married and lived with Lucas. Then I just lived…well, nowhere." I take a deep breath. "I need a place of my own."

"It wasn't like that. We took care of each other. That wasn't so bad, was it?" She takes in a quavery breath. "When your father left me…"

She breaks down again. The last card in the deck. It always winds up here.

"When your father left me, after everything I'd given him. We took care of each other, baby," she whispers. "I just want to make sure you're taken care of."

"I know, Mom," I answer, hugging her. "But you're just going to have to trust that I will be."

She looks at me, a little wild-eyed.

"You're going to have to trust that we *both* will be," I add. She hugs me tight, and just like that, it's done.

chapter 20

Samantha sat in her bedroom, the one she'd grown up in. She'd moved out of her apartment temporarily...her parents weren't thrilled with the idea of her being by herself. She had a leave of absence from school.

She wasn't going to be modeling anymore. Just thinking about it made her chest clench. Her agency would have done back flips for her if only she hadn't fucked up the Danielle Ichiba show. Now she doubted that they'd even bother trying to place her on TV commercials.

She was nineteen, and she was a has-been.

She sat on her bed, feeling a little claustrophobic by the pale lavender color of everything. She kicked a big purple panda off her bed, comforted when it landed nose first on the floor.

Her mother walked in nervously. "Are you okay, sweetie?"

She'd been asking that fifteen times a day since Samantha got out of the hospital. She'd also tried fixing all of Samantha's favorite foods, from her "chubby" junior high days. Macaroni and cheese. Twice-baked potatoes. The calorie and carb counts alone were enough to make Samantha feel nauseous. She had been eating more, and she hadn't done anything like throwing up yet. She had broken out a few packets of Metamucil, but decided to save them instead. She just felt like a failure. A big, fat failure.

The doorbell rang. "I'll get it," Samantha said, getting up. Anything to get away from her mother's probing stares. She bounded down the stairs and answered the door.

It was Sticky, wearing a nice shirt and slacks, holding a bouquet of roses. "Hey there," he said, handing her the flowers. "You look good."

"I look like shit," she said, surprised. "And I thought you hated me."

He shrugged. "It's complicated," he said, then smiled broadly as he saw her mother came down the stairs.

"Michael!" her mother called, heading straight for him.

He put his arms out wide. "Mom," he said warmly, giving her a bear hug.

Samantha goggled.

"Oh, it's so nice of you to come and visit," her mother cooed. "And don't you look nice."

"Just for you, Mom," he said easily. "Thought as long as I was saying hi, I'd check on Samantha, bring her some flowers."

"Ooh, they're beautiful! Here, Samantha, let me put them in some water."

And she took the flowers back to the kitchen.

Samantha was still stunned. "Okay, what just happened?"

"I know you don't believe it," Sticky sniffed, "because you just don't understand the true power of Sticky. Everyone loves me, my dear. It's a fact of nature."

Samantha couldn't help it. Her lips twitched into a grin. "That so?"

Her father turned the corner, frowned…and then broke into a wide smile. "Mike! How're you doing, man?"

He gave Sticky a hug and one of those tough-guy handshakes, the kind accompanied by a slap on the shoulder. "Mr. Regales," Sticky answered, warm but polite.

"What did I tell you in the hospital? Seriously. Call me Pedro."

Oh. My. God. Her wildly protective father, telling a guy who regularly made lecherous advances toward his precious daughter to "call me Pedro"? What, was there a new world order?

"Can I fix you something to eat?" her mother called from the kitchen. "We've got tri-tip, if you'd like to stay for dinner."

Samantha felt the bile build. Tri-tip. She looked at Sticky.

"I'd love to stay for dinner," he called back, his gaze never leaving hers.

"Well, why don't you two kids relax until then?" her father suggested. "I'm watching the game, if you're interested. Basketball."

"Maybe in a bit," Sticky said, still smiling, even though his eyes were serious. Her father retreated.

Samantha herded Sticky into the den, feeling awkward. "I'm sorry…"

"I know," he said. "How are…"

"Don't," she interrupted, sinking into an armchair. He sat across from her, on the couch. "Don't ask me how I'm feeling."

He let out a low, rumbling sigh. "It's going to take a while. You know that."

She crossed her arms, shrugging uncomfortably.

"I know what I'm talking about," he added.

She tried to laugh it off. "And you've got a degree in psychology now, as well as generating universal love from everyone but me."

He leaned back, looking at her reflectively. Even well dressed, he was chubby, to the point of heaviness. With a cherubic smile hidden by his scruffy goatee, he just stared at her for a minute.

"When was the last time somebody gave a damn about you, without it being about your body or how well you were fucking doing at school?"

She sucked in a surprised breath. He'd changed in a flash, from the friendly suitor he'd displayed to her parents to someone more dangerous. She hadn't seen him this pissed off since, well, the hospital. "Sticky…"

"I like you, Samantha. I think you're an amazing person, if you'd just wouldn't let this other bullshit get in the way." He moved closer and she noticed that he really did have some muscles going on there. He could probably snap her like a pencil. "Do you honestly think I keep coming on to you because you're beautiful?"

She didn't know him, not in this mood.

"I honestly, truly have no idea why you keep coming on to me," she admitted, in a small voice, and hugged her knees to her chest, looking away. She laughed a little, with no humor. "It sure isn't because I treat you well."

He didn't laugh. "No, you treat me like shit. And I let you get away with it because I know you're hurting and I think you're worth it."

"What, out of our entire past history together makes you think that?" she asked, baffled.

He shrugged. "Because you don't know why I'd ever care about you if it wasn't because of your body. Because you talk to me sometimes, and I see that you're not Ms. Perfect Student or Ms. Diva Bitch or Ms. Thang. Sometimes, you're just Samantha. Sometimes, you just like listening to music. You like reading sappy love stories that have nothing to do with your business classes and you like watching action movies. You're just you." He smiled. "And when you're just you…that's what I'm in it for."

She stared at him. She'd told him that stuff at various points, not even thinking about it, mostly in between conversations with people she was trying to impress. Occasionally, she'd simply ramble on, late at night, because he was a good listener. She didn't think he was actually paying attention, and she certainly never thought he'd remember.

She looked at the floor, and to her surprise, saw a teardrop hit the tile. She scuffed at it with her foot. "Maybe you shouldn't bother," she said, and her voice wobbled, embarrassing her.

"Come here," he said, patting the couch next to him.

She looked at him, skeptically, wiping her eyes.

He shot her an irritated look. "This isn't a come-on. In your parents' house? Please." He patted again. "You haven't lived until you've had a true, all-comfort, no-holds-barred Sticky hug."

She sat down, and true to his word, she was slowly pulled against his chest. He was squashy, she thought, and sort of immense. Then his arm closed around her, and she just felt warm. And comforted.

She probably shouldn't have started crying as hard as she did. His shirt had been pretty nice, probably dry-clean only. Saltwater tears were probably not what it needed.

When she was finished, she pulled back to see the big splotch she'd left on him. "Oh, God, I'm so—"

"Don't be sorry," he said, and he stroked her hair, smiling at her with a gentle look that made her stomach feel better. "You needed that. We're going to talk plenty, you and me."

"Oh?"

"I'm your friend now," he said. "Anytime you need anything, you call me."

She raised an eyebrow, feeling some of her old cockiness come back. "And there's absolutely nothing in it for you?" Her tone held just a hint of flirtatiousness.

He looked at the door, looked back at her. "If I said I didn't want to sleep with you, I would be lying my ass off. But that's a long way off, yet."

"Oh?" she repeated. She didn't want to think about that. She didn't want to think about sex, or men, or anything along those lines, especially after the Jonathan incident. That one still bruised her heart. Still, she looked at him curiously. "How do you know I'm going to say yes?"

"Universal love, baby," he said with a wink. "You'll come around."

She laughed.

"You can laugh now, but believe me, I'm persistent. And I have more confidence than the average guy."

"Maybe," Samantha said, with a deliberate note of humor and no trace of her former bitchiness, "you just have more stupidity than the average guy."

"That was usually PJ's stance," he rumbled, and she laughed.

"Of course, now she's come around, and seen the error of her ways. So who's stupid now?"

Samantha thought about Jonathan, and how much he cared for PJ. And how much she'd done to hurt PJ as a result. "How is PJ?"

Sticky looked surprised that she'd asked, and it simply underlined what kind of a person Samantha must have been. She swallowed, hard. "PJ went through a really rough patch," Sticky said. "She'd understand what you went through—put it that way. But she's much better now."

"Is she still spinning?"

"As a matter of fact, I helped her pull together a warehouse party tonight," he said, and he sounded proud. "I have to leave right after dinner."

Samantha thought about it.

"Can I come with you? I'd like to talk to her."

To her shame, Sticky looked thoughtful…and wary. "Okay," he agreed, finally. "Right after dinner."

She nodded, satisfied. "Well, dinner should be soon."

"Good," he announced. "I'm a little hungry."

She thought about it, and a surprised smile crossed her face. "That's funny," she whispered. "So am I."

"Thank you so much for letting me sublet," the girl, Amanda, said enthusiastically. "I had no idea it was going to be so difficult to get housing here! And this one…it's so great. I mean, *really* great."

"No problem," Leslie said easily. Amanda was a daughter of one of her father's friends. She was making a small profit on the sublet, and since the father was paying for it, she didn't feel a bit guilty. Besides, she needed all the money she could get her hands on.

"So, why are you leaving the city?"

"Just wanted an adventure," Leslie said.

Amanda stopped staring around the apartment long enough to send her an inquisitive glance. "Where are you going? Africa, or something?"

"Thought I'd try the U.S. first. Then I'm going to Europe...then, who knows?" Leslie mused. "I always wanted to see Hong Kong."

Amanda's eyes widened.

There was a knock at the door. "Excuse me," Leslie said, going to the door.

It was her mother. "Leslie..."

"Sorry, Mom. Could you wait a second?" She walked over to Amanda, handed her the keys. "I've faxed my signed copy of the sublease agreement to your father, and everything should be taken care of from there. You can move in Monday after next. All right?"

"Great. Thanks!" And Amanda gave her a hug, one of those squealing, sorority-sister deals. Leslie patted her on the back. Still, she was glad once Amanda and her perkiness were finally gone.

Leslie turned to her mother. "Just handling some last-minute business."

Her mother's mouth made her trademark little moue of disapproval. "Sit down, Leslie. I wanted to talk to you before all this business came up, but I guess I'm a little late."

She sighed. "I know that you're not wild about this, but my mind's made up."

"I know what you're going through," her mother said instead, sitting on the couch.

Leslie tilted her head. Of all the things she'd expected her mother to say, this wasn't on the list. "Um...okay," she said, sitting on the armchair to her mother's right.

"It's a midlife crisis," her mother said as definitively as if she were reading it off Leslie's medical chart. "Nothing to be ashamed of. We all go through it, or something similar."

Leslie had difficulty picturing her mother going through a midlife crisis, but then, she'd never pictured her mother as anything *but* midlife. Now she looked at her carefully. She had been twenty-four when she had Leslie, twenty-six when she'd had Mark. Now, at sixty, she supposed her mother was past middle-aged.

Still, Leslie hadn't realized that she, herself, had reached it—psychologically speaking.

"So. What did you do when you hit your 'crisis,' Mom?"

"Don't be snotty," her mother said, folding her hands primly in her lap. "I had an affair."

Leslie choked. *"What?"*

"Actually, I just took some classes in Chinese cooking," her mother said, and a twinkle of humor that Leslie hadn't seen in her mom in years actually shone through. "But 'I had an affair' sounds much more exciting, don't you think?"

"Jesus, Mom," Leslie breathed.

"It's sort of flattering to know that you'd believe me if I said I did," her mother continued. "But the fact is, I do love your father. We see eye-to-eye on a lot of things, still do after all these years. And when I was about your age or so, I did feel a bit restless." She sighed. "I imagine it would be different if I weren't married. If I didn't have kids, or didn't think I'd be able to."

Leslie felt like someone had put a lead jacket on her shoulders. She felt herself hunch protectively, forced herself to sit up straight. "I could still have kids," she said. "I'm just…at this point, I'm not sure I want kids. At least, I don't think I'll want to be a single mother. I'm just not sure what I want."

"And you feel like time's running out," her mother said sagely. "Well, the bottom line is, you've got a choice. You can either bear what's going to happen anyway, or you can go crazy and do something wild and, ultimately, self-destructive. I don't want to see you go through this, dear," she said in a voice more gentle than she'd used in years. "You're my daughter and I love you. I don't think any man is worth ruining your life over."

Leslie felt a flurry of emotions. Anger, at her mother's presumption, and hurt that her affection was coming out this way, of all ways. She forced herself to calm down, before lashing out the way she had at the last family gathering.

"Mom," she said. "What makes you think traveling is somehow going to ruin my life?"

Her mother sat up, eyes bright. "Leslie, you're already unmarried, with no hope of children. Why would you ruin what chances you have at a career while you're at it? What are you going to wind up with when you get older?"

Leslie felt those words like punches. "Do you really see me that way? As a complete failure?"

Her mother sniffed and looked out the window. "I didn't say complete failure. I just think that, well, you're only thirty-six. And there was that cover story. Maybe you could go to journalism school. Get somewhere. Print publishing won't really care if you're older, I would think, it's not like you're on camera. You could still make a name for yourself."

Leslie stared at her mother. "What if I never do, Mom? What if I never get married, never have kids, never have a career that anybody thinks is impressive? Then what?"

Her mother stood up. "I just don't know how to talk to you when you're like this!"

She stood up, too. "Why can't you just love me for who I am?"

"Oh, for God's sake, Leslie. Why do you have to be so dramatic about everything?"

Leslie shook her head. "Mom, I'm doing this for me. So when I die, poor, unmarried, alone and ignominious…at least I'll be able to say I did something interesting with my life, okay?"

"Leslie—" her mother's eyes blazed "—your brother has never, *ever* been able to infuriate me the way you do."

"Yeah, well, he's got a few years till midlife," Leslie said, walking to the door. "Just give him a little time. I have high hopes for him."

"Fine. Fine." Her mother walked toward the door, huffing like a teakettle. "You just go off and live like a wastrel. Live like that little couch person you wrote your article about. You yourself wrote that she was a loser, a…a *slacker.*" Her mother's smile was cruel, triumphant. "And then what will that make you? I wonder."

"Free," Leslie said promptly, opening the door. "I'll call you from Anchorage."

I'm at a warehouse party. Sticky, my best friend in the world, helped me set this up.

There is a huge banner out front that says **SAVE PJ** in

huge, black block letters, just like "Save Ferris" in *Ferris Bueller's Day Off*. The other DJs, people I've traded demos with or worked with, and a lot of new DJs are playing tonight. All the proceeds of the party are going toward my new Final Scratch records and laptop fund. I don't think I'll get all the money I need tonight, but I'm still going to be miles ahead of where I am now. I've already worked three full weeks at Wall of Sound, and I have two guys and a girl who are taking turntable lessons. As soon as I get a laptop again, I'll start digitizing other people's vinyl. I've gotten a bunch of requests already…about ten of them.

That's been the unexpected beauty of losing my laptop. My model had been years old, heavy as hell. Now I'll be able to get a newer, lighter, faster one. I feel like the bionic DJ.

"Hey, PJ."

It's Dylan. He's been spinning for the past hour and a half, and people have been going nuts. "Hey, you." I give him a hug. "Thanks for doing this tonight."

"Are you kidding? This is music lovers' paradise," he says effusively. "I hear you're going to even have some out-of-town talent."

"Not to my knowledge. Just locals on the slate."

"Are you going into promoting now?"

I laugh. "No way in hell. But you might want to talk to Sticky. He pulled most of this together."

"You should make that Sticky of yours your manager," he says with a wink. "That guy could charm anything out of anybody."

"Almost anybody," I respond…and then I see him. With Samantha, of all people. "Holy shit."

Dylan looks over his shoulder and bursts into laughter when he sees what I'm staring at. "Absolutely anybody," he corrects me. "I want to get the demo of the next guy up. Be back later, and hang in there. And let me know when your housewarming is."

I make some sort of noises of assent, but I'm too floored by Samantha coming in on Sticky's arm to really pay attention.

"Sticky?" I say, looking at Samantha, then at his broad grin, then at her again. "Um…glad…you could make it."

Samantha steps up and gives me a hug. I'm wondering if she's still medicated.

"I wanted to talk to you," she says, pulling me off to one side while Sticky motions that he's going to check out the DJs. I look at his disappearing figure with some concern. What exactly is going on here? "I asked Sticky if I could come. I hope that's okay?"

"Sure," I say, shrugging. "Why wouldn't it be?"

She took a deep breath. "I sort of…got together with Jonathan. After the article dropped."

It takes me a minute to figure out what she means. Then it hits me. I didn't expect it. I certainly don't expect it to hurt the way it does. "He's a free agent," I say, realizing just how true that statement is. "And hell, he's not even my manager anymore." If he wanted to do whatever, with whomever, it was his prerogative. If I was going to be stupid enough to feel hurt, it would be my own damn fault, right?

Then I realize what she's just said as I'm looking at Sticky.

Before I can even stop to think, I grab her stick-thin wrist. "If you're fucking around with Sticky, I will break you in half, you little…"

"Whoa, *whoa!*" She tugs away, rubbing at her wrist. "It wasn't like that. It was just one night."

I glare at her.

"I was always jealous of you." She's staring at me, dark eyes and voluptuous good looks. "Did you know that?"

I don't have any response to that.

"Well, I was. Jonathan cared about you so much, because of your music…because of a lot of things. I wanted him. For a lot of different reasons," she says, and she looks pained. "So I tried to screw you over."

I take a deep breath. "A lot of shit has happened," I say, since she's looking as if she's about to burst into tears and I just don't think I can handle that right now. "Trust me. Dressing me like a hooker wasn't really all that bad."

"I gave Leslie your ex-husband's phone number."

"Oh." I feel myself go numb. "Really."

"I just wanted to hurt you. I didn't know...the article wasn't..." She shakes her head. "I don't know that I would've cared if I did know."

Sticky told me she'd collapsed, that she'd gone to the hospital. She's beautiful, more beautiful than I could ever hope to be in my entire life. And I get the feeling that she's probably one of the most fucked-up people I've ever met in my entire life.

I sigh. "You made a mistake." I think about Jonathan, ignore the weird ache that the thought brings, push it aside. "Okay. A couple of mistakes. That's all."

"You don't hate me?"

"We're not going to be painting each other's toenails," I say dryly. "But...no. I don't hate you.

She smiles tentatively. It's sort of sweet, actually.

"Mess with Sticky," I add quietly, "and that changes."

The smile falls, and she nods slowly. "Thanks, PJ."

"Don't mention it."

She walks away, looking for Sticky. I'm too busy thinking about her to notice who's sidling up to me.

"That was pretty generous of you," Leslie says.

I jump, my heart thumping with surprise. "Jesus," I mutter. "What, did you two split a cab or something?"

She winces. "I just wanted to tell you how sorry I am. About the article. I was just about to leave town when my old city editor mentioned that you were having a rave."

I have no idea what to say to her. I'm still spun by the whole conversation with Samantha. "Um. Well."

"How are you doing?" She looks around. "Looks like a great turnout."

"Sticky pulled it together," I repeat, trying to shake off the dazed and confused feeling. Sticky, who appears to be courting Samantha, who apparently slept with my ex-manager.

I may need a drink.

"Are you still, you know, couching it?"

I shake my head. "I'm renting an absolutely tiny studio, in a low-rent district, in a really awful neighborhood that they're slowly trying to renovate."

"Congratulations!" She grinned. "If I'd known you were looking, I could've sublet my apartment to you."

If it were not for this woman, I would probably have a rocking career, I think. I'd be signed with a record, possibly. Jonathan would still be my manager. And that whole Samantha episode I just went through would be utterly erased.

"So you're moving, huh?" I only ask to buy a little time. I could probably just as easily walk away from her. Or get Sticky to kick her out. I bet he'd really enjoy that.

She shrugs. "I quit my job."

"What happened to that whole 'I need a promotion' thing?" I clear my throat, cross my arms in front of me. Buy some time. "I figured that after the article, you'd get that reporter job you wanted so badly."

"I wanted a lot of stuff badly," she says, and I get the feeling she's making one of those deeper-than-you'd-think statements. "I really didn't need any of it."

"That's very, er, Zen of you," I state. "What does your boyfriend feel…oh." I can tell from her face. "Quit him, too, huh?"

She nods. "It was time," she says, and leaves it there. "Anyway, after seeing what you've done after two years—how you turned out—I figured, what the hell do I have to lose, right?"

She puts a hesitant hand on my shoulder. The music is sick, pounding. The whole scene is surreal.

"Forgive me?" she asks quietly.

I think about it. Think about telling her to fuck off. Think about just how much she screwed me over. It burst like a blowtorch in my chest, for a quick minute.

Damn. Is this really what I want to carry around?

Then, impulsively, I grit my teeth, and I awkwardly hug her. She hugs back with a gratitude that's overwhelming.

I feel better almost immediately.

The two years on other people's couches weren't easy, but I don't tell her that. Not out of revenge, or anything…but because there's no way to tell her.

"Thank you," she whispers to me, and I pull away, nodding. "Great party."

"Stay away from the bar," I caution her, and she laughs.

I lean back, listening to the swaying trance with a bass line that would revive a dead person if they had any funk in their soul, at all. I feel weird. Free. Sort of restless, really.

I look around, and realize I'm scoping out every tall man in the whole rave. I'm waiting for Jonathan. I'm looking to make it three for three.

It's eleven already and I realize that he's not going to be here. He's not going to show up.

I hunt down Sticky, who is talking to a bunch of DJs, with Samantha looking on, a growing expression of amusement on her face. "Sticky," I interrupt, putting a hand on his shoulder.

"We are kicking ass," he bellows with a big grin. "You'll have a laptop, your record, *and* rent money at this rate. I'm pretty good at this, if I say so myself."

"I've got to bounce for a little bit."

His eyes widen. "But this is your party," he points out.

"I know. I just…gotta do this thing, okay?"

He sighs and nods. I run out, catch a cab, and sit in silence as the taxi moves at a breakneck speed toward Jonathan's house. I get out, pay the cabbie, and head up to Jonathan's door with all the resolution of a fanatic. I ring the doorbell.

It's not until I hear his footsteps that I realize this may not be the sterling idea it seemed like it was in the warehouse, riding on the high of group forgiveness and new-life epiphanies.

He opens the door. I swallow hard.

"Hi," I croak.

He stares at me for a second. "Hi."

"Got a minute?"

"Several," he says, and opens the door wide for me to walk in. "What's up?"

"I have an apartment," I say without preamble, and turn, just standing in his foyer as he closes the door behind me. "And I talked with Samantha."

He stiffens, his expression turning regretful. "Listen, it was a mistake. I didn't...she's a nice kid and I was in a bad..."

I shake my head rapidly, motioning him to be quiet. "You were right you know. I needed to grow up, a bit. Just took me a little while. And I'm sorry for acting the way I did. I can't change it. I just thought maybe the two of us ought to start over."

He's quiet. Reflective. Then he nods. "Okay." A pause. "I'd like that."

So here we are. Beginning again. Brand-new.

He smiles at me and I smile back.

I can live with that.

epilogue

Six months later…

I wake up completely disoriented. My neck is killing me. It's dark. Three a.m. dark. I'm on a short, piece-of-shit couch that feels very Salvation Army.

I have no idea where the hell I am.

Out of the darkness, I hear a deep, masculine laugh.

"You did it again."

Suddenly I'm flooded with relief. "Damn it." I lean over, close the laptop that I've got propped up on the floor. "I was working, I think."

"You're two steps from the bed, dummy."

I stand up. It's more like one and a half steps, really. My studio is just that—small.

Jonathan is standing there in the SpongeBob boxers I got him for his birthday. He looks good in the dim light from my window. He scoops me up and drops me on the bed.

"Get some sleep," he says against my neck, curling an arm around me, the only way we both fit on my bed.

I smirk.
Oh, yeah. That's right.
I'm home.

New from Ariella Papa, author of
On the Verge and *Up & Out*

Q: What are the two most dreaded words that a single
girl can hear from her married best friend's mouth?

A: We're trying.

And that's just what Voula's best friend, Jamie, tells her,
quickly ending their regular drinks-after-work tradition.
So with Jamie distracted by organic food, yoga and
generally turning her body into a safe haven for her
impending bundle of joy, Voula sets out in search of a
bundle of joy to call her own—an apartment. In the
New York real estate game, though, she's more likely
to stumble upon an immaculate conception than an
affordable one-bedroom....

**Available wherever
trade paperbacks
are sold.**

RED DRESS INK
™